The first romance stories ... e set against the backdrop of ... inue to exert a special attraction ... e dry world of professional science, Stephanie started writing Regency romances, and she is now a *New York Times, USA Today* and *Publishers Weekly* bestselling author.

Visit Stephanie Laurens online:

www.stephanielaurens.com
www.facebook.com/AuthorStephanieLaurens

Praise for Stephanie Laurens:

'This sensual tale of lust and seduction in nineteenth-century England will leave you weak at the knees'
Now

'Stephanie Laurens' heroines are marvellous tributes to Georgette Heyer: feisty and strong' Cathy Kelly

'Sinfully sexy and deliciously irresistible'
Booklist

The
Elusive Bride

The Black Cobra Quartet

Stephanie
LAURENS

piatkus

PIATKUS

First published in the US in 2010 by Avon Books,
An imprint of HarperCollins Publishers, New York
First published in Great Britain as a paperback original in 2010 by Piatkus
By arrangement with Avon
Reprinted 2010, 2011, 2013, 2014

A CIP catalogue record for this book
is available from the British Library.

ISBN 978-0-349-40003-7

Printed and bound in Great Britain by
Clays Ltd, St Ives plc

Papers used by Piatkus are from well-managed forests
and other responsible sources.

MIX
Paper from
responsible sources
FSC
www.fsc.org FSC® C104740

Piatkus
An imprint of
Little, Brown Book Group
100 Victoria Embankment
London EC4Y 0DY

An Hachette UK Company
www.hachette.co.uk

www.piatkus.co.uk

Dear Diary,

I have waited for so long and will admit that I had fallen into the habit of imagining it would never happen, that now that it might have, I find myself rather cautious. Is this what my sisters meant when they said I would simply know? Certainly, my stomach and my nerves proved to be singularly sensitive to Major Hamilton's nearness, but how reliable is that indicator?

Until I know more about Major Hamilton, I cannot know if he is "the one"—my "one," the gentleman for me—so my most urgent need is to learn more about him, but from whom?

And I need to spend more time with him, too—but how?

I must devote myself to finding ways—I have only a few days left.

. waiting for him

Prologue

September 2, 1822
Road from Poona to Bombay

"*Ul-ul-ul-ul-ul!*"

The battle cries of their pursuers faded momentarily as Emily Ensworth and her escort thundered around the next bend. Gaze locked on the beaten surface of the dirt road, she concentrated on urging her mare even faster—on fleeing down the mountain road as if her life depended on it.

She suspected it did.

They were halfway down the hill road from Poona, the monsoon capital for the upper echelons of the British governing Bombay. Bombay itself was still hours of hard riding

beauty of the hills,

grisly tales, and had no wish to
installment.

1

She and her escort, led by young Captain MacFarlane, had fled at a flat gallop, yet somehow the cultists had closed the distance. She'd initially felt confident she and the troop could outrun them; she was no longer so sure.

Captain MacFarlane rode alongside her. Her eyes locked on the sharply descending road, she sensed him glance back, then, a moment later, he glanced at her. She was about to snap that she was an accomplished rider, as he should by now have noticed, when he looked ahead and pointed.

"There!" MacFarlane waved at his lieutenant. "Those two rocks on the next stretch. With two others I can hold them back long enough for Miss Ensworth and the rest of you to reach safety."

"I'll stay with you!" the lieutenant shouted across Emily's head. "Binta and the others can carry on with the memsahib."

The memsahib—Emily—stared at the rocks in question. Two tall, massive boulders, they framed the road, with the sheer cliff face on one side, and an equally sheer drop on the other. She was no general, but while three men might delay their pursuers, they'd never hold them back.

"No!" She glanced at MacFarlane while they continued to thunder on. "We all of us stay, or we all of us go on."

Blue eyes narrowed on her face. His jaw set. "Miss Ensworth, I've no time to argue. You will go on with the bulk of the troop."

Of course she argued, but he wouldn't listen.

So complete was his ignoring of her words that she suddenly realized he *knew* he wouldn't survive. That he'd die—here on this road—and it wouldn't be a pretty death.

He'd accepted that.

His bravery stunned her, rendered her silent as, reaching the rocks, they pulled up, milling as MacFarlane snapped out orders.

Then he reached over, grabbed her bridle, and drew her on down the road.

"Here." Drawing a folded parchment packet from inside his coat, he thrust it into her hand. "Take this—get it to Colonel Derek Delborough. He's at the fort in Bombay." Blue eyes met hers. "It's vital you place that in his hands—his and no others. Do you understand?"

Numb, she nodded. "Colonel Delborough, at the fort."

"Right. Now ride!" He slapped her mare's rump.

The horse leapt forward. Emily shoved the packet into the front of her riding jacket and tightened her grip on the reins. Behind her, the troop came pounding up, forming around her as they again fled on.

She glanced back as they rounded the next curve. Two of the troop were taking up positions on either side of the rocks. MacFarlane was freeing their horses, shooing them on.

Then they swept around the curve and he was lost to her sight.

She had to ride on. He'd given her no choice. If she didn't reach Bombay and deliver his packet, his death—his sacrifice—would be for naught.

That couldn't be. She couldn't let that happen.

But he'd been so young.

Tears stung her eyes. Viciously she blinked them back.

She had to concentrate on the godforsaken road and ride.

Later that day
East India Company Fort, Bombay

Emily fixed the sepoy guarding the fort gates with a steady direct gaze. "Captain MacFarlane?"

visiting her uncle for

Delborough. Where may

* * *

The answer had been the officers' bar, the enclosed front verandah of the officers' mess. Emily wasn't sure it was acceptable for her—a female—to go inside, but that wasn't going to stop her.

Idi, the Indian maid she'd borrowed from her uncle's household, trailing behind her, she mounted the shallow steps. Moving into the dim shadows of the verandah, she halted to let her eyes adjust.

Once they had, she swept the verandah left to right, registering the familiar click of billiard balls coming from an alcove off one end, several officers in groups of twos and threes gathered about round tables, and one larger group haunting the far right corner.

Of course they'd all noticed her the instant she'd walked in. A serving boy quickly came forward. "Miss?"

Transferring her gaze from the group to the boy's face, she stated, "I'm looking for Colonel Delborough. I was informed he was here."

The boy bobbed. "Yes, miss." He swung and pointed to the group in the corner. "He is there with his men."

Had MacFarlane been one of Delborough's men? Emily thanked the boy and headed for the corner table.

There were four very large officers seated at the table. All four slowly rose as she approached. Remembering Idi dutifully dogging her heels, Emily paused and waved the maid to a chair by the verandah's side. "Wait there."

Holding the edge of her sari half over her face, Idi nodded and sat.

Drawing breath, head rising, Emily walked on.

As she neared, she scanned, not the men's faces—even without looking she knew their expressions were bleak; they'd learned of MacFarlane's death, almost certainly knew the manner of it, something she was sure she didn't need to know—but instead she searched each pair of broad shoulders for a colonel's epaulettes.

Distantly she registered that, in common female parlance, these men would be termed "impressive," with their broad chests, their height and their air of rugged physical strength. She was surprised she hadn't seen them in any of the drawing rooms she'd visited with her aunt over recent months.

Another captain—blonder than MacFarlane—and two majors, one with light brown hair . . . she had to tug her gaze on to the other major, the one with rakish dark hair, then she finally found the colonel among them—presumably Delborough. He had dark hair, too.

She halted before him, lifted her gaze to his face, set her teeth against the emotions surging about the table; she couldn't let them draw her in. Down. Make her cry. She'd cried enough when she'd reached her uncle's house, and she hadn't known MacFarlane as, from the intensity of their feelings, these four had. "Colonel Delborough?"

The colonel inclined his head, dark eyes searching her face. "Ma'am?"

"I'm Emily Ensworth, the governor's niece. I . . ." Recalling MacFarlane's instructions—Delborough's hands and no others—she glanced at the other three. "If I could trouble you for a word in private, Colonel?"

Delborough hesitated, then said, "Every man about this table is an old friend and colleague of James MacFarlane. We were all working together. If your business with me has anything to do with James, I would ask that you speak before us all."

His eyes were weary, and so sad. One glance at the others, at their rigid expressions—so contained—and she nodded. "Very well."

the two majors. The

She glanced at Delborough. I g
lar, but if I could have a small glass of that . . . ?"

5

He met her eyes. "It's arrack."

"I know."

He signaled to the barboy to bring another glass. While they waited, beneath the table's edge she opened her reticule and drew out MacFarlane's packet.

The boy delivered the glass, and Delborough poured a half measure.

With a smile that went awry, she accepted it and took a small sip. The sharp taste made her nose wrinkle, but her uncle had allowed her to partake of the liquor in an experimental fashion; she knew of its fortifying properties. She took a larger sip, then lowered the glass. Quashing the impulse to look at the brown-haired major, she fixed her gaze on Delborough. "I asked at the gate and they told me. I'm very sorry that Captain MacFarlane didn't make it back."

Delborough's expression couldn't get any stonier, but he inclined his head. "If you could tell us what happened from the beginning, it would help us understand."

They'd been MacFarlane's friends; they needed to know. "Yes, of course." She cleared her throat. "We started very early from Poona."

She told the story simply, without embellishment.

When she reached the point where she'd parted from the gallant captain, she paused and drained her glass. "I tried to argue, but he would have none of it. He drew me aside—ahead—and gave me this." She lifted the packet. Laying it on the table, she pushed it toward Delborough. "Captain MacFarlane asked me to bring this to you."

She finished her tale in the minimum of words, ending with, "He turned back with a few men, and the rest came with me."

When she fell silent, the distracting major on her left shifted. Spoke gently. "And you sent them back when you came within sight of safety." When she glanced his way, met his hazel eyes, he added, "You did the best you could."

The instant she'd sighted Bombay, she'd insisted all but two of the troop return to help their comrades; unfortunately, they'd been too late.

Setting a hand on the packet, Delborough drew it to him. "And you did the right thing."

She blinked several times, then lifted her chin, her gaze on the packet. "I don't know what's in that—I didn't look. But whatever it is . . . I hope it's worth it, worth the sacrifice he made." She raised her gaze to Delborough's. "I'll leave it in your hands, Colonel, as I promised Captain MacFarlane I would." She pushed back from the table.

They all rose. The brown-haired major drew back her chair. "Allow me to organize an escort for you back to the governor's house."

She inclined her head graciously. "Thank you, Major." Who was he? Her nerves were fluttering again. He was standing closer than before; she didn't think her lightheadedness was due to the arrack.

Forcing her attention to Delborough and the other two, she nodded. "Good evening, Colonel. Gentlemen."

"Miss Ensworth." They all bowed.

Turning, she strolled back down the verandah, the major pacing slowly alongside. She waved to Idi, who fell into step behind her.

She glanced at the major's carefully blank expression, then cleared her throat. "You all knew him well, I take it?"

He glanced at her. "He'd served with us, alongside us, for over eight years. He was a comrade, and a close friend."

She'd noticed their uniforms, but now it struck her. She looked at the major. "You're not regulars."

her, watched as the major raised a hand,
tion of a sepoy sergeant drilling his troop on the maidan.

The sergeant quickly presented himself. With a few words, the major organized a group of sepoys to escort her back to the governor's residence deeper in the town.

His innate yet understated air of command, and the attentiveness and willingness—even eagerness—of the sergeant to obey, were as impressive as his physical presence.

As the sepoys hurried to form up before the steps, Emily turned to the soldier beside her and held out her hand. "Thank you, Major . . . ?"

He took her hand in a warm, strong clasp, met her eyes briefly, then half bowed. "Major Gareth Hamilton, Miss Ensworth." Releasing her, he looked at the well-ordered sepoys, nodded his approval, then turned again to her.

Again met her eyes. "Please. Be careful."

She blinked. "Yes, of course." Her heart was thumping unusually quickly. She could still feel the pressure of his fingers around hers. Drawing in a much-needed breath, she inclined her head and stepped down to the dusty ground. "Good evening, Major."

"Good evening, Miss Ensworth."

Gareth stood on the steps and watched Emily Ensworth walk away across the sunburned ground toward the massive fort gates. With her porcelain complexion, rose-tinted and pure, her delicate features and soft brown hair, she looked so quintessentially English, so much the epitomization of lovely English maids he'd carried with him through all his years of service.

That had to be the reason he felt as if he'd just met his future.

But it couldn't be her, couldn't be now.

Now, duty called.

Duty, and the memory of James MacFarlane.

Turning, he climbed the steps and went back inside.

3rd September, 1822
My room in the Governor's Residence, Bombay

Dear Diary,

I have waited for so long, and will admit that I had fallen into the habit of imagining it would never happen, that now it might have, I find myself rather cautious. Is this what my sisters meant when they said I would simply know? Certainly, my stomach and my nerves proved to be singularly sensitive to Major Hamilton's nearness—as Ester, Meggie, and Hilary foretold—but how reliable is that indicator?

On the other hand, this does sound like fate playing her usual tricks. Here am I, virtually at the end of my stay in India—a sojourn expressly undertaken to broaden my horizons vis à vis marriageable gentlemen, exposing me to more specimens of varying character so that my well-known "pickiness" might become better informed—and I finally stumble on one who affects me, and after an entire day, I have barely learned his name and station.

It is no help that Aunt Selma remains in Poona, too far away to provide advice, and so all my information needs must come from my uncle, although Uncle Ralph does answer without thinking of the motives behind my questions, which is all to the good.

Until I know more about Major Hamilton, I cannot know if as I am starting to fervently hope, he is "the

appear, ana coming an that way

sailing away and leaving my "one" behind just doesn't bear thinking about.

E.

September 10, 1822
The Governor's Residence, Bombay

Emily frowned at the Indian houseboy standing in the patch of sunlight slanting across the silk rug in her aunt's parlor. "He's leaving?"

The boy, Chandra, nodded. "Yes, miss. It is said he and his other friends have all resigned their commissions because they are so cast down by the death of their friend the captain."

She resisted the urge to drop her head in her hands and tug at her braids. What the devil was Hamilton about? How could he be her "one" if he was so cowardly as to run home to England? What about honor and avenging a friend—a comrade and fellow officer killed in the most ghastly and gruesome manner?

A vision of the four men as they'd stood around the table in the officers' bar swam across her mind. Her frown deepened. "All of them—all four—have resigned?"

When Chandra nodded, she specified, "And they're all heading back to England?"

"That's what everyone says. I have spoken with some who know their servants—they are all excited about seeing England."

Emily sat back in the chair behind her aunt's desk, thought again of those four men, of all she'd sensed of them, remembered the packet she'd placed in Delborough's hands, and inwardly shook her head. Any one of those four turning tail was hard enough to swallow, but all four of them? She wouldn't lose faith in Hamilton just yet.

They were up to something.

She wondered what.

She was due to board ship on the eighteenth of the month, sailing via the Cape to Southampton. She needed to learn more about Hamilton, a lot more, before she left. Once she was convinced he was not as cowardly as his present actions painted him, as he was going home, she could—somehow would—arrange to meet him again there.

But first . . .

She refocused on Chandra. "I want you to concentrate on Major Hamilton. See what you can learn of his plans—not just from his household but from the barracks and anywhere else he goes. But whatever you do, don't get caught."

Chandra grinned, his big smile startlingly white in his mahogany face. "You can count on Chandra, miss."

She smiled. "Yes, I know I can." She'd caught him gaming, which was forbidden for those on the governor's payroll, but on learning his need for rupees to pay for medicine for his mother, had arranged for him to have money advanced from his pay, and for his mother, who also worked in the governor's mansion, to receive better care. Ever since, Chandra had been her willing slave. And as he was quick, observant, and all but invisible in Bombay's busy streets, he'd proved extremely useful in following Hamilton and the other three.

"One thing—Hamilton has no other Anglo friends, just those three officers?"

"Yes, miss. They all came from Calcutta some months

"He's *left*?" Emily stared at Chandra. ...

"This morning, miss. He took the sloop to Aden."

"He and his servants?"

"So I heard tell, miss—they were already gone when I got there."

Mind racing, she asked, "The other three—have they gone, too?"

"I have only had the chance to check on the colonel, miss. Apparently he left on the company ship this morning. Everyone was surprised. No one knew they were leaving so soon."

The company ship was a mammoth East Indiaman which went via the Cape to Southampton. She was due to board a sister ship in a few days.

"See what you can learn about the other two—the other major and the captain." If all four had precipitously departed Bombay . . .

Chandra bowed and left.

Emily felt a headache coming on.

Gareth Hamilton—he who might be her "one"—had left Bombay via the diplomatic route. Why?

Regardless of his motives, his sudden departure left her with a very big unanswered question—and an even bigger decision to make. Was he her "one," or not? She needed more time with him to tell. If she wanted to get that time, following him might—just—be possible. If she acted now.

Should she follow him, or let him go?

Closing her eyes, she revisited those moments in the officers' bar, the only moments on which she could judge him. Surprisingly vividly, she recalled the sensation of his fingers closing around hers, felt again that odd leap of her pulse, the frisson that had set her nerves jangling.

Felt, remembered, relived.

On a sigh, she opened her eyes. One point was inescapable.

Of all the men she'd ever met, only Gareth Hamilton had affected her in the slightest.

Only he had set her heart racing.

September 16, 1822
The Governor's Residence, Bombay

"Good evening, Uncle." Emily swept into the dining room and took her seat on her uncle's right. They were the only two at dinner. Her aunt was still in Poona—which was a very good thing. Flicking out her napkin, she smiled at the butler, waited for him to serve her and step back before she said, "I have an announcement of sorts to make."

"Oh?" Her uncle Ralph rolled a wary eye her way.

She smiled. She and Ralph had always got on well. "Don't worry—it's only a minor change in my plans. As you know, I was scheduled to depart on the company ship two days hence, but after speaking with others I've decided that, as I came by that route, I should instead go home by the direct and more scenic way." She waved her fork. "See Egypt and the pyramids—and as it is the diplomatic route, there's unlikely to be any serious danger, and plenty of embassies and consulates to call on for help if luck says otherwise."

Ralph chewed, frowned. "Your father won't like the idea, but then he won't know—not until you're standing in front of him again."

Emily grinned. "I knew I could trust you to see the salient point. There's really no reason I shouldn't go home that way."

"Assuming you can find passage at short notice. Your parents are expecting you back in four months—going via Cairo you'll be able to surprise them, if you can find a berth—"

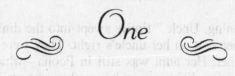

One

17th September, 1822
My cabin aboard the sloop Mary Alice

Dear Diary,

As usual, I will endeavor to record my thoughts at 5 o'clock every afternoon, before I dress for dinner. This morning I departed Bombay, and I understand we are making good time as the Mary Alice *slices its way through the waves to Aden.*

And yes, I acknowledge that it's undeniably bold to be pursuing a gentleman as I'm pursuing Major Hamilton, but as we all know, fortune favors the bold. Indeed, even my parents should accept the necessity—they sent me to Bombay because I dragged my heels over choosing any of the young men who offered, opting instead to wait for my "one," as all my sisters—and I suspect my sisters-in-law, too—did. I have always maintained that it was simply a matter of waiting for the right man to appear, and if Major Hamilton proves to be my right man, then at the ripe old age of twenty and four, I doubt anyone would argue against my pursuing him.

Of course, I have yet to determine if he truly is my "one," but I can only decide that after meeting him again.

Speaking of which . . . he and his party are two days ahead of me.

I wonder how fast a sloop can go?

E.

1st October, 1822
My cabin aboard the Mary Alice

Dear Diary,

The answer to my last question is: quite amazingly fast when all sail is risked. My being extra charming to the captain and challenging him to demonstrate how fast his ship can go has paid a handsome dividend. We passed the Egret, the sloop carrying the major and his household, sometime last night. With luck and continuing fair winds, I will disembark in Aden before him, and he will have no reason to suspect I set out on this journey to follow him.

E.

wharf alongside.
They'd followed another of the company sloops into the

harbor, and had had to wait for that vessel, the *Mary Alice*, to be unloaded first.

His bags, along with the minimal luggage carried by his small but efficient household—his batman, Bister, his house-man, Mooktu, an ex-sepoy, and Mooktu's wife, Arnia—were being stacked that very minute on the wooden wharf, but that wasn't the cause of the consternation—to put it mildly—that had seized him.

He'd noticed the parasol bobbing down the gangway of the *Mary Alice*, tied up almost at the end of the long wharf. He'd watched the bearer, a lady in matching pale pink skirts, tack and weave through the crowd. She and the contingent of staff following at her heels, with one heavily muscled man clearing a path through the noisy, jostling throng ahead of her, had to pass along the wharf beside the *Egret* in order to enter the town.

Until a moment ago, he hadn't been able to see the parasol holder's face. But passing the *Egret*, she'd tipped the para-sol aside and glanced up—and he'd glimpsed . . . a face he hadn't expected to see again.

A face that, for the last few weeks, had haunted his dreams.

Yet all but immediately, the damn parasol had come up and re-obscured his view.

"*Damn!*" One part of his mind was telling him, calmly, that it couldn't possibly be she, that he was seeing things he wanted to see . . . Some other part, a more visceral part, was already sure.

He hesitated, waiting to see again—to know for sure.

Movement in the crowd behind the parasol caught his eye. Cultists.

His blood literally ran cold. He'd known they'd be waiting for him—he and his people were expecting a welcome.

But Emily Ensworth and her people weren't.

He'd vaulted the railing on the thought. He landed on the wharf, his gaze locked on her.

He came up from his crouch with considerable momentum, cleaving his way bodily through the crowd. He came up with her just in time to grab her and haul her away from the blade a cultist thrust at her.

Her gasp was drowned beneath a cacophony of sound—exclamations, shrieks, shouts. Others had seen the menacing sword, but even as the crowd turned and garrulously searched, the cultists melted away. Taller than most, Gareth saw them pull back. Over the heads, one cultist—an older, black-bearded man—met his eye. Even across the distance, Gareth felt the malevolence in the man's gaze. Then the man turned and was swallowed by the crowd.

Mooktu appeared by Gareth's shoulder. "Should we follow?"

Bister was already further afield, scouting.

Gareth's instincts screamed *follow*, to pursue and deal appropriately with any cultist he could find. But . . . he glanced down at the woman he still held, his hands locked about her upper arms.

With her parasol now askew, he looked down into wide, moss-hazel eyes. Into a face that was as perfect as he recalled, but pale. She was stunned.

At least she wasn't screaming.

"No." He glanced at Mooktu. "We have to get away from here—off the docks—quickly."

Mooktu nodded. "I'll get the others."

He was gone on the word, leaving Gareth to set Miss Ensworth back on her feet.

plastered to the side of his body. His thick was sively warm—not to say hot—body.

17

She didn't think she'd ever be the same.

"Ah . . ." Where was a fan when one needed one? She glanced around, and noise suddenly assaulted her ears. Everyone was talking, in several different languages.

Hamilton hadn't moved. He stood like a rock amid the sea of surging humanity. She wasn't too proud to shelter in his lee.

She finally located Mullins—her grizzly ex-soldier guard—as he came stumping back through the crowd. Just before the attack, a wave of bodies had pushed him ahead and separated them—then her attacker had stepped between her and Watson, her courier-guide, who'd been following on her heels.

Her people were armed, but having lost her assailant in the melee, they gradually returned. Mullins recognized Hamilton as a solider even though he wasn't in uniform, and raised a hand in an abbreviated salute. "Thanking you, sir—don't know what we'd've done without you."

Emily noted the way Hamilton's lips tightened. She was grateful he didn't state the obvious—if not for his intervention, she'd be dead.

The rest of her party gathered. Without prompting, she quickly put names and roles to their worried faces—Mullins, Watson, Jimmy, Watson's young nephew, and Dorcas, her very English maid.

Hamilton acknowledged the information with a nod, then looked from her to Watson. "Where were you planning to stay?"

Hamilton and his people—a batman in his mid-twenties but with experience etched in his face, a fierce Pashtun warrior, and his equally fierce wife—escorted her party off the docks, then, with their combined luggage in a wooden cart, continued through the streets of Aden to the edge of the diplomatic quarter, and the quietly fashionable hotel her uncle had recommended.

Hamilton halted in the street outside, studied the building, then simply said, "No." He glanced at her, then past her to Mullins. "You can't stay there. There're too many entrances."

Stunned anew—and she still hadn't managed to marshal her senses enough to think through the implications of the cultists' attack—she looked at Mullins to discover him nodding his grizzled head.

"You're right," Mullins allowed. "Death trap, that is." He glanced at her and added, "In the circumstances."

Before she could argue, Hamilton smoothly continued, "For the moment, at least, I'm afraid our parties will need to stay together."

She looked at him.

He caught her eye. "We need to find somewhere a lot less . . . obvious."

There was nothing the least obvious about the house in the Arab quarter Emily later found herself gracing. Not far from the docks, and in the opposite direction to the area inhabited by Europeans, she had to admit the private guesthouse was quite the last place anyone would think to look for her—the Governor of Bombay's niece.

Nestled behind a high stone wall off a minor side street, the modest house was arranged around a central courtyard. The owners, an Arab family, lived in one wing, leaving the main living quarters and two other wings of bedchambers for guests.

could be.

She'd been just a little distracted at the time as the impli-

19

cations of the attack on the docks had finally impinged. Realizing she'd come within an inch of death had sobered and shaken her, but had also raised questions—ones she couldn't answer.

She was fairly sure Hamilton could. As soon as she'd seen her people settled, and had washed off the dust of the streets, she made her way to the salon that served as drawing room-cum-parlor.

Hamilton was there, alone, seated on one of the long cushion-covered divans. He looked up, saw her, and came to his feet.

With an easy smile, she went forward, and sat on the divan to his left. Opposite, wide doors stood open to the courtyard, with its small central pool and shading tree.

He resumed his seat. "I . . . er, hope you have everything you need."

"The accommodations are adequate, thank you." They were not what she was accustomed to, but they were clean and comfortable enough—they would do. "However"—she fixed her gaze on his face—"I have a number of questions, Major, that I hope you'll be able to answer. I only caught the briefest glimpse of my attacker, but I saw enough to know he was a Black Cobra cultist. What I don't understand is why he would attack me, or why a cultist should be here, in Aden, at all."

When he didn't leap into reassuring speech, she went on, "The only contact I've had with the Black Cobra cult is through the incident with poor Captain MacFarlane and the packet I delivered for him to your friend, Colonel Delborough. I presume the attack today was connected with that?"

Gareth studied her face—her determined expression, the directness of her gaze—and regretfully jettisoned his preferred option of revealing nothing at all. If she'd been a typical miss with not a great deal of wit . . . but there was intelligence, willfulness, and a definite—potentially dangerous—curiosity lurking behind her lovely eyes . . . "I suspect the cultists are here to intercept me, and yes, that's linked to the packet you brought to Bombay. The only reasons they would have for attacking you is if they recognized you, and either thought you might still have the packet, or simply wanted to punish you for your part in the packet's loss."

"What's in the packet the Black Cobra wants so desperately?"

As he'd thought—far too quick-witted. He'd hoped to gloss over his mission, conceal the major aspects, but . . . her moss-hazel gaze was too acute, too intent. And many—she, certainly—would argue she had a right to know, now more than ever given the cult had just demonstrated that it wasn't inclined to overlook her part in the affair. He inwardly sighed. "I assume you'd prefer I start at the beginning?"

"Indeed."

"Five of us—Delborough, me, Major Logan Monteith, Captains Rafe Carstairs and James MacFarlane—were sent to Bombay by Governor-General Hastings with specific orders to do whatever was needed to bring the Black Cobra to justice." He sank back against the cushions, his gaze fixing, unseeing, on the wall opposite. "That was in March. Within a few months, we'd identified the Black Cobra, but the evidence was circumstantial, and given our suspect, our case needed to be beyond question."

"Who is the Black Cobra?"

He turned his head and regarded her. If he told her . . . but

at Poona fetching you, he stumbled on a letter from the Cobra to one of the princelings. We'd found similar missives, but this one was different. It was signed by the Black Cobra, but sealed with Ferrar's personal seal—the ring seal he wears on his little finger and can't take off. Once you'd brought that letter to us, we had what we needed, and we'd already consulted others back in England, so we knew what we had to do."

He saw her shut her lips on an eager prompt, but she'd guessed at least part of it. "We have to get that letter—the original—to the Duke of Wolverstone in England. Ferrar, of course, will do everything in his considerable power to stop us. Our instructions from Wolverstone—he's the key planner in this—were to make four copies, and each bring one home, all traveling by widely different routes."

"To make it harder for the Cobra to stop you."

He nodded. "With James gone, there are four of us, now all on our way back to England. Only one of us has the original, but the Cobra doesn't know which one, so he has to try to intercept each of us."

Head tilting, she studied him. "Are you . . ." She paused, eyes on his, then went on, "I suspect you're carrying one of the copies—a decoy, as it were."

He was glad there was no one else in the room. He frowned. "How . . . ?"

Her lips curved briefly. "On the wharf, you and your men wanted to chase the cultists—if you'd been carrying the original, you wouldn't have risked engaging directly. You would defend, not attack—you'd do all you could not to draw attention to your party."

He humphed. "Yes, well, from here on, we'll be running. My orders are explicit—I'm to do all I can to distract the cultists between here and the Channel, do all I can to make them chase me, to make the Cobra throw as many of his forces in Europe into dealing with me."

"*Without* making it obvious you're carrying a copy and not the original." She nodded, then looked frowningly at him. "You're not carrying the letter on you, are you?"

"No." He couldn't see any reason not to tell her. "It's in

one of those wooden scroll holders the Indians use to ferry documents."

"Ah—I see." She studied him a moment more. "Arnia's carrying it."

He stared at her. "It can't be that obvious."

She lifted one shoulder. "That's who I'd leave it with—she's from a warrior tribe and quite dangerous, I imagine, yet to the cultists she'll be all but invisible. They'll never think of her."

He grunted, partly mollified. "Watson mentioned you'd decided to return home by the overland route—that you hoped to see the pyramids and other sights along the way."

She shrugged again. "It seemed sensible to see more of the world while I can, and as I was already in Bombay . . ."

"Be that as it may, now that the cult have sighted you, and clearly would be happy to do you harm, it would be wiser, for safety's sake, to combine our parties, at least until we reach Alexandria." He paused, then went on, "I don't believe Ferrar knew of our endeavor before we left Bombay, but he must have learned soon after, and has moved quickly to get cultists ahead of us—I believe they were waiting, watching the docks. They were already here."

"Which means they might be ahead of us, potentially all the way home?"

He nodded. "If I were Ferrar, in the position he's now in, that's what I'd do, and he has men to spare. Which, of course, is the principal aim of my mission—reducing his forces."

shoulders, yet he'd just taken on all responsibility for her safety. For her life. With the cultists at large, that wasn't putting it too highly.

She continued to smile at him. "Besides, I became involved in this through helping poor Captain MacFarlane, and in light of his sacrifice I feel compelled to do whatever little I may to ensure his mission succeeds."

The mention of James reminded him that, in some respects, he now stood in James's shoes, taking on a responsibility that originally had been James's—seeing Miss Ensworth safely home.

For a moment, he felt as if James's ghost hovered in the room beside them—he could almost see his insouciant smile. James had died a hero. He'd been dashing and handsome, a few years older than Miss Ensworth—hardly surprising if, in the circumstances, she harbored some romantic feelings for his dead friend.

He wondered if that was what he saw in her eyes.

Somewhat abruptly, he stood. "I must check with the others about setting a watch—we can't be too careful. I'll see you at dinner."

She inclined her head. "We'll need to decide how best to journey on."

"I'll check what our options are tomorrow. I'll tell you once I know." He headed for the door.

"Excellent—we can discuss it in the morning."

In the doorway, he looked back, then nodded. "In the morning."

He strode down the corridor, a sense of relief returning. She'd agreed to travel on together. He'd be able to keep her safe. That was the critical point. The instant he'd seen the cultist making for her on the dock, he'd known he'd have to keep her with him, almost certainly all the way back to England, until he could leave her somewhere the cult couldn't reach her.

The responsibility wasn't one he could possibly shirk. Quite aside from all else, honor wouldn't allow it. She'd become a target for the Black Cobra through helping with their mission, and he and his comrades, James included, owed her a huge debt. If she hadn't played her part and brought the letter to Del, they would still be chasing cultists through the Indian countryside, and the Black Cobra would be continuing his reign of terror and destruction unabated.

Instead, thanks in large part to Emily Ensworth, the Black Cobra was now chasing them.

All they had to do was keep one step ahead of the fiend's minions all the way back to England, and all would be well.

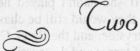

Two

3rd October, 1822
Morning
A private guesthouse in Aden's Arab quarter

Dear Diary,

I was too distracted to write last night. I suspect that while traveling, the time of my entries may vary due to whatever exigencies might arise. But to my news! First and most importantly, I've learned that Major Hamilton is innocent of any degree of cowardice in returning home—indeed, he is on a mission to vanquish the Black Cobra, and by extension avenge his friend, MacFarlane. I had felt that the major could not be cowardly—how could he be my "one" and be so?—but I freely admit I had no idea of the level of noble enterprise on which he and his friends have embarked. It is truly humbling, and I am delighted to report that, by a twist of fate, it appears I, too, will be able to play a part. Thus the second half of my news—we are to combine our parties and travel on together!

26

While I must admit I am not at all keen to meet any further cultists—they are fanatics and quite mad—I do feel moved to do whatever I may to avenge poor MacFarlane given he was, after all, there to be killed because he was escorting me. However, my primary consideration in agreeing to Hamilton's request to join forces is more prosaic—what if I declined, and something happened to him? Something I might have, had I been with him, prevented?

No. Now that I know he is no coward—in fact, quite the opposite—and the opportunity to aid him has come my way, if, as I ever more strongly suspect given the sensory turmoil he continues to evoke in me, he is my "one," then it is clearly incumbent upon me to continue by his side.

That said, I am writing this this morning as I discover I have time on my hands. I rose fresh and rested, and emerged from my chamber ready to discuss our onward journey, as I believed we'd arranged, only to discover he had already quit the house. Apparently his definition of "morning" means before 8 o'clock—which as a start to our joint journey does not bode well.

E.

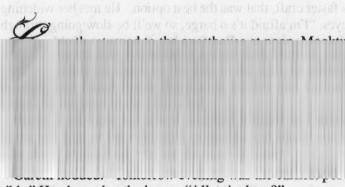

sible." He glanced at the house. "All quiet here?"

"Seems to be." Bister went back to his whetstone. "But the lady's in the parlor—I think she's waiting for you. Been pacing something fierce."

Gareth was unsurprised to learn that Miss Ensworth was keen to learn of his arrangements. "I'll speak with her now, tell her the news. You can spread the word to the others— we'll be leaving tomorrow on the evening tide."

Bister nodded.

Rather than use the main door, Gareth crossed to the open doors of the salon. As he paused on the threshold, the sun threw his shadow across the room—making Miss Ensworth, who was indeed pacing, whirl to face him.

"Oh! It's you!"

"Yes." He inwardly frowned at her tone, unsure of the emotion beneath it. "I have guards on the gate and in the courtyard—there's no need to fear the cultists getting in."

She looked at him. "That hadn't entered my head."

Not fear, then. Before he could think of his next leading comment, she stated, "I've been waiting to discuss our onward journey."

"Indeed." Maybe she was just impatient? There was a crispness in her tone that made him think of folded arms and tapping toes. As she was still standing, he remained standing, too. "We'll be leaving on the evening tide tomorrow. While I would have preferred an earlier departure and a faster craft, that was the best option." He met her widening eyes. "I'm afraid it's a barge, so we'll be slow going through the straits into the Red Sea, but once we reach Mocha, we should be able to hire a schooner to take us on to Suez."

He wasn't sure, but he thought her jaw had dropped.

"You've made the arrangements."

A statement of the obvious, but in an oddly distant voice.

He nodded, increasingly wary, unsure of her thoughts. Unsure of her. "We have to leave as soon as possible, so—"

"I thought we were going to discuss our options."

He thought back, replayed their conversation of the previous afternoon. "I said I'd assess our options, and tell you once I knew. The barge is our best option for evading the cultists."

Her chin went up. "What about riding? People ride to Mocha—it's the usual route for couriers. And surely, being mobile is better than being stuck on a—as I understand it—slow-moving vessel?"

True, but . . . were they having an argument? "The road to Mocha goes through desert and rocky hills, both inhabited by bandits with whom governments make arrangements to let their couriers through. And that's the route the cultists will expect us to take—they'll be on our heels the instant we leave town, or worse, waiting for us up in the passes. You may be an excellent rider, and all my people are, but what about your maid, and Mullins and Watson? Will they be able to keep up in a flat-out chase?"

Her eyes held his, then slowly narrowed. Her lips had compressed to a thin line.

The moment stretched. He wasn't accustomed to consulting others; he was used to being in command. And if he and she were to journey on together, she was going to have to accept that there could be only one leader.

He was inwardly steeling himself for her challenge when, to his surprise, her expression changed—exactly how he couldn't have said—and she nodded. Once. "Very well. The barge it is."

In the distance a bell tinkled, summoning them to luncheon.

To his even greater surprise, and his unease, not to men-

head.

Humored.

He snorted, rolled over and pulled the sheet up over his shoulder. He wasn't worried—she would learn.

> *4th October, 1822*
> *Still in Aden, at the guesthouse*
>
> *Dear Diary,*
>
> > *In just a few hours, we will depart on the first leg of our shared journey home—and once we're away, he—Gareth, Major Hamilton—won't be able to send me back. I was on the brink of explaining that I wasn't one of his men, and he should not therefore assume that I will simply fall in with any decision he makes, but just in time I recalled that in Aden we are within reach of the company ships. Should he take it into his head that my accompanying him is too difficult—or as he would put it, too dangerous—then it might well be within his scope to commandeer a sloop and pack me and my party off, either back to Bombay or on to the Cape, thereafter to travel on a ship of the line home.*
> >
> > *I abruptly changed my tune. Given my need to learn more of him, the opportunity to share the journey home, in daily contact and close proximity, is simply too good to let slip through my fingers.*
> >
> > *True, his habit of command is sadly entrenched, but I can make my opinion on that issue clear later.*
> >
> > *On reflection, I really couldn't have planned things better. How ironic that I owe this chance to confirm, and hopefully, in the fullness of time, secure my "one"—the one and only gentleman for me—to that horrible fiend of a Black Cobra.*
> >
> > *E.*

They returned to the docks with the sun a glowing fireball hanging over the sea. The low angle of light glancing off the waves made recognizing people difficult. Gareth hoped the cultists clung to their black silk head scarves, their only readily identifiable feature.

He glanced at Emily, walking briskly alongside him. At his suggestion, she'd worn a dun-colored gown, and her parasol was safely stowed in the luggage. At this hour, everyone on the docks was striding purposefully, all the vessels keen to make the evening tide, so their rapid and determined progress was in no way remarkable.

What might have alerted a shrewd observer was the way he, and the other men in their small group, constantly scanned the crowds, but that couldn't be helped. The cultists were sure to be hanging about the docks.

He'd managed not to think too much about Emily, not in a personal sense. He kept trying to make his mind conform and label her *Miss Ensworth*, preferably with the words *the Governor's niece* tacked on for good measure, but his mind had other ideas. Striding along the dock where just days before he'd saved her from an assassin's blade, he couldn't ignore his awareness of her—of her body, slender, warm and femininely curved, moving gracefully beside him.

He wanted her much closer—at least his mind and body did. Both could recall—could re-create—the sensations of the moments when he'd held her tucked protectively against him.

She nodded crisply, and made a beeline for the appropriate gangplank.

Grasping her arm, he halted her at its foot. "Wait." He signaled to Bister, who with a nod went racing up the gang-plank, Jimmy, Watson's seventeen-year-old nephew, at his heels.

Two minutes later, Bister reappeared. "All clear."

Getting the women, their luggage, and then their men aboard took ten minutes. The captain nodded benignly; the crew all smiled.

Shouts ran the length of the barge, ropes were cast off, and at last they were away.

The barge moved slowly, ponderously turning on the in-creasingly fast-rushing tide. One of many so engaged, the throng of vessels gave them extra cover. To Gareth's relief, all three females—Emily, her maid Dorcas, and Arnia—had retreated without prompting into the cabins built along the length of the barge. Watson had gone inside, too, taking Jimmy with him, leaving Gareth, Mooktu, Bister, and Mul-lins to keep watch.

They found what cover they could, but the barge was car-rying little freight beyond its passengers.

Gareth had hoped that by timing their departure to the very last usable minute of the tide, then even if the cultists spotted them—as he felt sure they would—their pursuers wouldn't be able to sail after them for at least another twelve hours, if not more.

At this point, a day's head start was all he could hope for.

They got away, swinging out of the harbor and onto the ocean swell, then turning along the coast for the straits with-out challenge. But as they rounded the last headland, Jimmy caught the reflection off a spyglass directed their way.

Bister drew the younger lad with him to report to Gareth. "I saw it, too, once he pointed it out. Sure as eggs, someone was watching us."

Gareth grimaced. "No prizes for guessing who. But at least we've got away, and with the straits ahead, I doubt they'll catch us up, not before Mocha."

Later that evening
Elsewhere in Aden

"Uncle—we have news!"

The tall bearded man known throughout the Black Cobra cult simply as Uncle slowly lifted his gaze from the pomegranate he was peeling. "Yes, my son?"

The younger man he'd sent to supervise the watch on the harbor drew himself up, head high. "We saw the Major Hamilton leave on a barge, but the barge was on the ocean, heading for the straits, before we could get a clear sighting."

"I see." Uncle paused to eat a piece of pomegranate, then asked, "Did he have a woman—the Englishwoman he saved from our blades on the docks—with him?"

The young man turned to his colleagues, who had followed him into the courtyard. A whispered conference ensued, then the young man turned back. "She was seen briefly on the docks, but we didn't sight her on the barge—howsoever there were cabins."

"Ah." Unhurriedly Uncle finished the pomegranate, then carefully wiped his hands. Then he nodded and looked to his second-in-command. His only true son. "In that case, I believe my work here is done."

His son nodded. "We will catch them in Mocha—there are men already there."

"Indeed." Uncle slowly stood, stretching to his full, impressive height. "Our illustrious leader has truly foreseen come this way. But I and mine"—he glanced at his son and smiled—"we ride to Mocha."

His gaze passed on to the older, more hardened men—assassins all—lined up behind his son. His anticipatory smile deepened. "Find horses. The overland route is shorter."

October 5, 1822
The mouth of the Red Sea

Dawn broke in a pearly golden wash spreading like gilt across the waves. Stepping out of the narrow corridor running the length of the cabins, Gareth drew the salty air deep, slowly exhaled. The barge was angling northwest, following others into the narrowing mouth of the Red Sea, still some way ahead.

Seeing Watson leaning on the railing, eyes on the distant shore, Gareth ambled over. Watson glanced at him, then straightened.

Gareth smiled. "Go in and get some sleep—I'll take over until Mooktu appears."

Stifling a yawn, Watson nodded. "Thank you, sir. It's been quiet all night." He looked over the water. "Lovely morning, but I'm going to find my bed. I'll leave you to it."

With a half salute, Gareth settled, still smiling, against the rails. He heard Watson stump off into the cabins. The slap of waves against the hull was soothing, the faint mumble of voices from the stern—the crew chatting—punctuated by the call of a wheeling gull.

Over the last days, while avoiding their mistress, he'd made an effort to get to know her people. If they were to travel on together, he needed to know what manner of troops he had under his command.

Both Watson and Mullins were unreservedly grateful for his rescue of their charge. Mullins had been an infantryman until after Waterloo. He'd returned to his home village in Northamptonshire, looking for employment, and had run into Watson, who, with Bonaparte defeated and the Continent safe again, had been setting up as a travel guide to take young gentlemen on the modern equivalent of the old Grand Tour. Watson was the courier-guide, Mullins the guard. Jimmy, Watson's sister's son, had been brought on this trip to learn the ropes.

Over the years, Watson and Mullins had worked frequently for the Ensworth family, who they consequently knew well. The family was large; they'd conducted three male Ensworths around the Continent, as well as escorting the elder Ensworths on various trips. The family were valued and well-liked clients; just the thought of losing Emily—one of the younger of the brood—was enough to make both Watson and Mullins, experienced though they were, literally blanch.

They also liked Emily herself; seen through their eyes, she was a sensible, calm, and even-tempered young lady they had no qualms over conducting halfway around the world.

Both Watson and Mullins were in their middle years, and shared a tendency to corpulence. Although still hale, able, and active, as Gareth had earlier intimated to Emily, neither rode well, and it sounded as if Jimmy's equestrian abilities owed more to enthusiasm than skill. It was a point he would have to bear in mind in arranging their transport onward.

Mullins took his duties seriously; in Aden he'd asked Mooktu to help sharpen his sword skills. Meanwhile Bister had, unasked, taken Jimmy under his wing; Gareth had seen the pair practicing knife throwing, Bister's specialty.

tall, bustling and competent female somewhere in her late thirties, had required the application of a certain amount of self-effacing charm, but she'd eventually thawed enough to admit that she rode very poorly, and that she'd been with Emily and her family for most of Emily's life.

Dorcas, too, was grateful for his rescue and subsequent protection of her mistress, yet she continued to view him with an underlying suspicion she did nothing to hide. As he'd been careful to suppress, and if not that then conceal all evidence of his unhelpful attraction to her charge, he wasn't sure what lay behind Dorcas's watchful, ready-to-be-censorious eye.

He heard a footfall—*her* footfall. He was turning to search for Emily even before she rounded the cabins in a gown of lilac cotton that fluttered in the breeze.

Seeing him, she smiled and strolled his way.

He struggled to keep his answering—too revealing—smile from his face, managed to replace it with a frown. "What are you doing up at this hour?" He glanced around. "You shouldn't be on deck—it could be dangerous."

She tilted her head, studied him for a moment, then, smile still flirting about the corners of her rosy lips, she looked out across the waves. "It's so peaceful and quiet, you'd hear any other vessel approaching, surely?"

She looked back at him, met his eyes.

The best he could do was humph, and lean back on the railing. "Couldn't you sleep?"

He was being deliberately off-putting. Just having her near . . . but the more he replayed their earlier conversation, the more he dwelled on the soft light he'd glimpsed in her eyes, the more he was certain she was carrying a torch for MacFarlane, and he had no intention of trying to compete with that. With his friend's ghost.

"I seem to have been sleeping too much, if truth be told. And it's such a lovely morning."

She settled against the railing beside him.

The warm softness of her body called to his, a siren song weakening his defenses. He told himself he should push back and move away—seize the excuse of being on guard to do a circuit of the barge.

Instead, he stayed exactly where he was, from the corner of his eyes watching the breeze playing with her hair, teasing out tendrils to lie alongside her porcelain cheeks.

After a moment, he forced his attention back to the waves. "I . . . gather you come from a large family."

Emily laughed. "That's an understatement. I have three sisters and four brothers. I'm the second youngest—only Rufus is younger than me."

"So you're the baby of the girls?"

"Yes, but that's something of an advantage. We're all very close, although of course the other three are all married and have their own households. Nevertheless, we still see each other often." She was perfectly willing to discuss her family, as it allowed her to turn his way and ask, "What about you? Do you have brothers and sisters?"

He stiffened, straightened. "No." He glanced down at her, then softened the single syllable with, "I was an only child."

She noted the past tense. "Your parents . . . have they passed on?"

Eyes back on the waves, he nodded. "There's no one waiting for me in England." He shot another swift glance her way. Half smiled. "Not like you."

"Ah, yes—there'll be a fattened calf and all manner of celebrations when I get back." And if matters unfolded as she hoped, he'd be there to share them. Her delighted smile as she looked out across the waves was entirely genuine.

tive was his middle name, at least as far as women were concerned. However, she'd yet to see any clear indication that with respect to her, that protectiveness had moved beyond the general to the specific.

But they had plenty of journey ahead of them, plenty of time for her to watch and see.

She was still at the stage of mentally ticking items off the list of characteristics her "one" should possess. Her ideal was fairly clear in her mind, but matching the reality to her list was proving more challenging than she'd expected. There were all sorts of issues one had to take into account.

But at this moment, she was content. She fully intended to work on him, on encouraging him to allow his attitude to her to grow less stilted. A moment's consideration had her stating, "I believe I'll take an amble about the deck."

That brought an instant frown—as she'd expected.

"It would be safer to go back inside the main cabin." He stepped back from the railing, frowning down at her.

She smiled sunnily back. "If you're on watch, perhaps you should walk with me—you can view the rest of the barge as we go." She didn't give him a chance to refuse, but turned and started to stroll down the walkway between the cabins and the barge's rail.

Then she turned and smiled at him over her shoulder. "Come on."

Gareth couldn't resist. Feeling inwardly grim, he found himself following in her wake—responding all too definitely to that alluring smile.

To his inner self she was far too attractive, and with every passing day, with each new fact he learned about her, grew only more so. She was distraction, and fixation, and potential obsession, and he knew he should back away, but . . . unlike the men under his command, she was elusive and difficult to manage, and—as she was demonstrating—their journey was going to make keeping his distance close to impossible.

He joined her as, holding back her waving hair, she excitedly pointed to a cormorant diving in the waves. And he wondered why, instead of feeling weighed down, his heart felt light—lighter than it had in a long, long time.

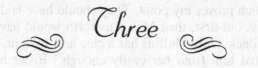

    5th October, 1822
    Before dinner
    My cabin on our barge heading for the Red Sea

    Dear Diary,

        Matters are progressing as I'd hoped. It's said that
    one learns the truth about people by observing them
    under stressful conditions. Our journey looks set to pro-
    vide such conditions, and I have great hopes of learning
    all I need to know of Gareth—enough to be absolutely
    certain that he is the one and only gentleman for me.
        My hopes are high.

His battalion looked up, nodded, and continued to sort.
"No sign of any of those idiot fiends."

Gareth lounged on the railing nearby. "Why idiot? They nearly did for Miss Ensworth in Aden."

"Which proves my point. They should have laid low and taken us out first, then Miss Ensworth would have been a sitting duck. Only Mullins has a clue how to fight, and they separated him from her easily enough." Bister held up a knife, examined its edge.

"Not everyone has had the experiences we've had, but it would be unwise to treat the cultists too lightly."

Bister nodded sagely. "Never underestimate the enemy."

"Indeed." Gareth looked away to hide his twitching lips. Bister was barely five and twenty. He'd joined Gareth when he'd been all of seventeen—just as gullible and inexperienced as Jimmy.

"Meant to mention."

Gareth turned back, brows rising.

Bister kept his gaze locked on his blade, kept rubbing. "Miss Ensworth. Jimmy said as she was supposed to go home via the usual route—booked on a ship of the line to Southampton via the Cape. But a day or so before, she up and changed her mind, and decided she should go via Aden."

Gareth let a few seconds go by. "Did she give any reason for the change in route?"

"Nope—just that she'd taken it into her head to go this way, rather than the other."

"When, exactly, did she change her mind? Did Jimmy know?"

Bister nodded, still absorbed with his blade. "His uncle heard first, as you might imagine. Jimmy said it was a bare two days before they set out—they left on the seventeenth."

Gareth and his household had departed on the fifteenth— the day Emily Ensworth had decided to change her plans.

The facts lined up, but . . .

Coincidence. It had to be. Aside from all else, she couldn't have known about his leaving . . . could she?

Even if she had known, why would she bother changing her plans to follow him? It made no sense.

A niggle of a suggestion tapped his mental shoulder, but that was self-important arrogance if ever he'd heard it.

"Let me know if you learn anything more." Pushing away from the railing, he continued on his rounds.

> *7th October, 1822*
> *Morning*
> *Still in my cabin aboard the barge*
>
> *Dear Diary,*
>
> *I have missed several entries for the simple reason that I have nothing to report. I suppose, in lieu of anything more interesting, I should remark on what I have seen.*
>
> *Water. And interminable sandy shores. Barren sandy shores. With the occasional rocky headland. This is not a picturesque part of the world. The sun glints off the water constantly, which is pretty the first time one sees it, but my eyes now ache from squinting so much.*
>
> *As intimated, I have endeavored to learn more about Gareth, but he is proving annoying adept at eluding me, even in such a restricted space. When I do manage to run him to earth, he remains stiff, literally, and tries to keep even a conversational distance. It is really most irritating. I have concluded, given he is so determinedly*

Their barge drew into the Mocha docks in the early afternoon.

41

With Watson's help, Gareth had their party formed up and ready to disembark the instant the ropes were cinched tight. Within minutes they were moving swiftly along the wharf and into the town, Emily, Dorcas and Arnia walking quickly before the luggage, with the men positioned around them, all on high alert.

As Gareth passed Emily, she reached out and clutched his sleeve. Tugged him close.

Looked up and met his eyes. Hers were narrowed. "What haven't you told me?"

He considered, but it couldn't hurt for her to know. "The cultists might have come on by the inland route. We have to assume they're here, and we don't want to meet them unnecessarily."

She held his gaze for an instant, searching his eyes, then nodded and released his sleeve.

He watched her for several moments, but far from exhibiting any degree of fear, she merely scanned the crowds, watchful and now alert. He hadn't made any conscious decision not to spell out the situation for her as he had for the men. The men had to be on guard. Her . . . he simply hadn't thought of it.

"Where are we heading?" She asked the question without looking at him.

He, too, kept his gaze on the noisy crowds. "Somewhere you and the others will be safe while I find a schooner to take us to Suez."

Bister, scouting ahead as usual, returned at that moment with directions to a small family-run tavern down a narrow side street only a few blocks from the docks.

When they reached it, Gareth approved. The front was mostly wall, with only one door and a small glassless window covered by a leather flap, presently lowered against the day's heat.

They went in. Given the hour, the front room was empty.

Gareth directed Emily and Dorcas to the front corner furthest from the door. Arnia followed. To his relief, although

Arnia was usually exceedingly reserved, she seemed to have made some pact with Dorcas, and the pair had reached a working accord—which would certainly make his life easier.

Mooktu, with Mullins, had gone to chat with the proprietor, a middle-aged Arab who smiled and nodded. They returned bearing a tray with a pitcher and mugs. Without words, they pulled together tables, arranged benches, and sat down to refresh themselves.

And plan.

Gareth looked at Watson. "You, Mooktu, and I need to go back to the docks and look for a schooner to hire, preferably one that will take us and only us, no other cargo, and so sail to Suez in the shortest possible time."

Watson grimaced. "That'll cost a pretty penny."

"Money we have," Gareth returned. "Our safety is my primary concern."

Watson nodded. "Whenever you're ready."

"We need supplies." Emily waited until Gareth looked her way. Raising her hand, she ticked off on her fingers, "We need flour, lentils, rice, tea, sugar, and all the other things we didn't have on the barge."

They'd learned that although their households could happily share the same foods, Indian or English, a steady diet of fish and only fish suited none of them.

Beside Emily, both Arnia and Dorcas were nodding, as were Bister and Jimmy.

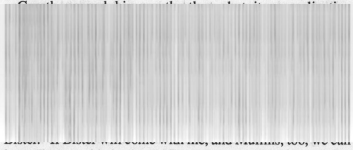

leave Jimmy with Arnia and Dorcas to guard the luggage."

It was a reasonable division of labor and guards. Her gaze steady on his face, she waited to see if he would accept. If he had it in him to be reasonable.

His lips thinned, but slowly he nodded—forced himself to nod. "All right." He looked at Bister and Mullins. "But take all care. So far we've managed to avoid the cultists. If at all possible, we don't want to be seen."

The souk was a bustling hive of humanity, located within a quarter of narrow winding streets. Both traders and customers hailed from many different nations, and all were talking loudly in many different tongues. Luckily, with the expansion of French and British influence, most traders spoke a smattering of pidgin English at least, and some spoke passable French, enough for Emily to get by.

She was firmly determined not to feel cowed by having to deal with such *foreign* foreigners. And, indeed, she discovered that if she approached with confidence, the traders treated her with deference and politeness, and after her months in Bombay, bargaining was second nature.

They got through their list of required purchases with commendable speed. She was completing the last transaction—for chickpeas—when Gareth and Mooktu joined them.

She smiled and handed Gareth the peas. "Here—you may as well make yourself useful . . ." Looking into his face, she saw his expression, saw the way his eyes scanned the crowd. "What?"

Without glancing down at her, he quietly said, "As we suspected, there are cultists in town. We saw them, but thus far I don't think they've seen us. If at all possible, I'd like to keep it that way."

Emily glanced swiftly around. She made no protest when Gareth's hard fingers closed about her elbow, and with a terse nod to the stall owner, he turned her away, back toward the tavern.

They had to backtrack across the souk to reach the tavern.

As they walked, keeping their pace no different to those around them, she murmured, "Did you find a schooner?"

"Yes. We were lucky—we'll be able to leave this evening." Eyes constantly surveying the crowd, ready to take evasive action if he spotted any cultist, Gareth registered her nod, but again didn't glance her way.

He was feeling exceedingly exposed, and not a little vulnerable. Mooktu, in his tribal robes, merged easily into the crowd, but there were few Europeans about, and he, Emily, Bister, and Mullins stood out.

Without warning, Emily halted.

Already frowning, his grip on her elbow tightening, he turned to urge her on. And saw she was staring down an alley of stalls.

She looked up at him, eyes bright. "Disguises."

He looked again, and saw that the stalls were selling robes and other items of local clothing.

"We can't merge with the crowds as we are, but if we buy some Arab robes, we'll be able to waltz right past the cultists."

"We don't need to get that close, but . . ." He looked down and met her eyes, brimming with enthusiasm. Nodded. "Let's take a look."

Collecting Mooktu, Bister and Mullins with a glance, he followed Emily into the narrow, winding alley.

It didn't take her long to discover a shop selling all manner of outer robes. She tried on a burka—a long robe that com-

In a flurry of material, she pushed up the front of the robe and fixed the shopkeeper with a direct glance. "I'll take this one, and" —she pointed to another in brown— "that one. How much for both?"

Leaving her haggling, spurred on by just how well disguised she'd been, Gareth applied himself to finding robes for himself, and urged Bister and Mullins to do the same.

Initially reticent, they were soon caught up in the transformation. Gareth was pleased with the end result. With any luck, they might—just might—escape the eyes of the cultists. If they could, it would be well worth this small effort.

Leaving the shopkeeper with instructions that there would shortly be some others of their party calling, and that he was to show them similar garments, they left the shop, all now in Arab guise.

No one so much as looked their way.

From beneath her burka, Emily studied the other Arab women, watched how they behaved. She quickly adjusted her position in their party so she was walking a pace behind Gareth. Given Mooktu and Mullins were walking behind her, Gareth made no demur; he, too, must have noticed the local practice.

When he paused at the corner of the souk and glanced back, checking that they were all behind him, she blinked, then smiled delightedly behind the concealing veil of her burka. In his flowing white robes over loose trousers, with a long, loose scarf wound about his head and another dark band cinched about his waist, he looked every inch the desert sheik—a man of mystery, dangerous power, and untold sensuality.

The others .... simply looked dangerous.

As he started forward again, she meekly fell into step behind him, still smiling happily to herself.

Once back at the tavern, they sent Mooktu back to the shop with Watson, Jimmy, Dorcas, and Arnia for the others to buy suitable disguises.

While they were gone, Emily, with Mullins's, Bister's, and Gareth's help, reoganized the luggage, packing their recent purchases into two large hemp bags they bought from the tavern owner.

"Arnia said she would cook for us, and Dorcas offered to help." Emily stepped back from the bag as Gareth and Mullins worked to lash it closed. "I can cook, but I'm afraid I've had little experience with these sorts of ingredients."

Gareth glanced up at her. "I doubt we'll need to call on your culinary skills." He suspected he could cook better than she, and he wasn't any great chef. "Both Mooktu and Bister are passable over a campfire."

Mullins snorted as he straightened from the now secure bag. "Just as well. If Watson or I had to help . . . well, you'd probably rather not eat."

The others returned in good time. They all stood in the, thankfully, still empty tavern and admired their ingenuity. Dorcas, too, was taken with the burka, although for Arnia, who normally wore a scarf wound about her head with a long end she often pulled across her face, the change wasn't all that remarkable.

"No one saw us," Mooktu reported. "I saw two of the cultists through the crowd, but that was after we'd left the shop. They didn't give us a second glance."

"Good." Gareth surveyed his small band, now very local-looking. He caught the glint of Emily's eyes through the lace panel of her black burka, and had to fight to suppress a smile. He inclined his head to her. "Y

them how the locals used pieces of flat bread in place of

spoons. While they ate, other patrons drifted in. By the time they'd finished the food and tried small quantities of the local drink, a species of thick coffee, the tavern was full and it was dusk.

Gareth paid the tavern owner and he *salaamed* them out of the door.

They formed up in the street, in the order they'd spent some time over the meal discussing, then started for the docks. Gareth and Watson strode in the lead, confident and assured—two well-dressed, wealthy Arabs heading for their ship. A pace or two behind, Emily, Dorcas and Arnia followed, hands clutching the front of their burkas to keep them in place so they could see through the lace panels, heads down so they could watch where they were placing their feet. The true reason Arab women always appeared so meek as they followed their husbands was now amply clear.

Behind the women, Bister and Jimmy pushed the wooden cart they'd piled with their luggage; they would leave the cart on the dock, as most people did. Behind them came Mooktu and Mullins, in their true roles of guards.

Their procession wended its way down to the docks unhurriedly, as if they belonged. As if their only care was to reach their ship in time to sail.

They passed two cultists on the main street.

Passed another two close by the docks.

All of the cultists saw them. Not one suspected who they were.

They reached the schooner, tied up at one of the further berths.

The captain grinned and hailed Gareth. "Major Hamilton!"

Gareth swore beneath his breath and took the gangplank in three long strides. Reaching the captain, he engaged him with questions about their accommodation, distracting his attention from those who followed in his wake.

When he glanced around and saw everyone—he did a quick head count—gathered in a knot further down the deck, the sudden tension that had gripped him eased. But not by much.

Striding down the deck, he swung open the slatted door of the companionway, and brusquely gestured the women down.

Emily glanced at him but went. Even through the mask of the burka, he felt her disapproving gaze.

But eventually, of their party there was only him, Mooktu, and Bister left on deck, with the captain calling orders to cast off.

The lift and roll of the Red Sea under the deck was comforting. Reassuring. From the stern, Gareth watched Mocha recede.

Saw the cultists gather on the dock, saw them point—at the schooner.

They'd got away without the battle he'd feared. No one placed that many watchers in such a small town without some definite intent, some plan of engagement.

They'd slipped away, but someone had been clever enough to put two and two together—to add up the respective members of their parties. Six men, three women. Given the cultists standing on the dock and pointing, he felt reasonably sure their schooner had been the only one to put out that day with such a complement of passengers.

They'd escaped before they'd been challenged, but they'd been noted.

The Black Cobra's minions knew where they were.

the tension—which was positively palpable during

49

those moments on the dock and while we waited for the schooner to sail—has not abated. I do not know why, but it is clear Gareth—and the others, too—fear the Cobra will locate us, that we are not yet free.

I have to admit that in following Gareth, I did not foresee this degree of danger and the consequent abiding tension. It is very distracting. True, I am being given the chance to observe his character under pressure, which will undoubtedly be more revealing than if we were meeting in conventional and unthreatening surrounds, but that pressure has other effects, and affects me, too.

I have discovered that I do not appreciate living under dire threat of imminent and awful death, but in the circumstances, I am determined to make the most of it.

E.

Once again she joined him as dawn lit the sky.

The deck of the schooner was empty of all others except for the night watchman yawning by the helm. Coming to stand beside him at the railing in the bow, she shook back the tendrils of hair that had come loose and, eyes closed, lifted her face to the morning breeze.

Gareth seized the moment to study her face. Not intentionally. He simply couldn't help it. Couldn't tear his gaze from the gentle curves, the delicate features.

He sensed the morning zephyr flow across her fine skin—nature's kiss, one he longed to mimic. The thought of his lips cruising the rose-tinted curves, dipping into the shadowed hollows . . .

Silently clearing his throat, he straightened, refixed his gaze on the waves ahead. Closed one hand about the upper railing and gripped hard. He wished she'd worn her burka . . . but then he wouldn't have been able to see her face. Still . . .

"There's a surprising number of ships around—I didn't think there would be so many."

He glanced at her. "There's a lot of trade done up and down the Red Sea. Goods brought from lower Africa and India—even China—destined for the markets of Cairo and beyond."

She wrinkled her nose, eyes on a junk tacking on a parallel course some hundred yards away. "I suppose, in that case, we should wear our burkas, even on deck." She looked at him inquiringly.

"I was about to suggest it," he admitted. "However, I imagine it must get quite warm under them. At least these"— he gestured to his new robes— "are cooler than our ordinary clothes."

She nodded. "That's the problem—the burkas go on top of everything else." She paused, then went on, "Perhaps if instead we restrict our walks to either after dark or when we can see there are no other ships close enough to make us out, it will serve as well."

He nodded. "Most likely. By any reasonable estimation, it will take the cultists a day or two to catch us up." He met her gaze. "They spotted us as we pulled out of Mocha."

She grimaced. "They will come after us, won't they?"

"I fear so."

Silence of a sort enveloped them, punctuated by the slap of waves, the creak of the sails, and the lonely cry of a gull. It should have felt awkward, but instead was companionable—

and the other three—you're doing this in memory of Captain MacFarlane, aren't you?"

The question caught him off guard. "Yes." The sudden surge of emotion, the memory of James, shook him. He drew in a breath, shifted . . . but then tightened his grip on the rail and went on, "It's our mission, and so of course we're determined to see it through—we would have done the same if James had lived, and with equal resolve. But . . ." For the first time he truly looked, and saw. "You're right—each of us is doing this in part to avenge him."

He felt her gaze on his face, sensed her approval before she looked away. "I'm glad. Given Captain MacFarlane died while escorting me, I feel I have an interest in avenging him, too."

That came as no surprise. Gareth could still so easily bring James's youthful engaging smile to mind. His sunny vitality had often made Gareth—and the others, too—feel like world-weary old men. James had always been popular with young ladies. Gareth slanted a glance at Emily. It wasn't hard to imagine what romantical notions having such a dashing young man die in your defense would evoke.

Her comment, however, again raised the niggling question of whether—strange though it seemed—she'd changed her plans to follow him. But why him, and not Del, or one of the other two?

The question made him uncomfortable, and how on earth could he phrase it without sounding entirely too full of himself?

"So." She turned to face him, leaning back against the rail. "What do you plan to do once this is all over and you're back in England?"

He stared down at her. "I haven't really thought." He hadn't, not at all. His mental slate should have been blank, but to his considerable surprise his mind was thinking now, supplying all manner of desirable images . . . all of which involved her. He blinked, turned aside. "I should check the decks. I'm supposed to be on picket duty."

A frown showed more in her eyes than her expression. "But you would hear any other vessel draw close."

"They might swim. I wouldn't put it past them."

"Very well—I'll walk with you."

"No!" That was the last thing he needed. It wasn't just his mind that was reacting to her nearness. He scrambled to find a cause for his vehemence. "The light's strengthening, and you're not in disguise. And" —he pointed to the group of slower ships they were steadily coming up on— "we'll soon be close to those ships. No telling how far ahead of us the cultists have reached."

She stared—all but glared—at the ships ahead. Then her lips firmed, one step away from a petulant pout.

His errant mind suggested he kiss the expression from her lips . . .

"Oh, very well."

Thank God.

She turned to the companionway, but bent a sharp glance his way. "I'll catch up with you later."

He inclined his head noncommittally. The instant her feet hit the companionway stairs, he set off to stride down the deck, grateful for the camouflage his new robes afforded him. One issue he didn't need to worry quite so much about.

But he could see further problems looming.

They were on a journey that would be strewn with dangerous situations, most likely becoming increasingly fraught the closer they got to England, yet he'd had no choice but to bring her along, and now had no option but to keep her with him. Quite aside f

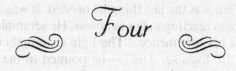

Four

8th October, 1822
Afternoon
The deck of our schooner on the Red Sea

Dear Diary,

> *I am starting to question how much one can learn of another while constantly on edge. On guard. With one's head forever twisted to look over one's shoulder. I swear I now have a permanent crick. Unfortunately we know the cultists are out there. Bister and, later, Mullins sighted their telltale black scarves.*
>
> *Beyond the constant fear of an attack, we go on relatively comfortably. Dorcas thought of draping some of the ubiquitous mosquito netting over a section of the stern, giving me, her, and Arnia some cover beneath which we can sit free of the weight of our burkas. I am seated in our tent of sorts now, watching the passing ships. We are making good time, or so I have been told. The scenery hasn't notably improved, but the weather is not quite so enervating, at least on the water . . .*

once again I find my eyes trepidatiously scanning the vessel our sleek schooner is passing.

The men of our party take turns on watch, which is distracting and makes engaging Gareth in revelatory conversation somewhat difficult, for he, of them all, is most constantly on duty, ready to respond to any alert.

I would almost rather an attack was made so that we might relieve this unending pressure.

E.

ate that evening, a light shawl in her hands, Emily stepped out of the companionway onto the stern deck. Straightening, she paused to flick the silk out and over her shoulders. After a glance around the immediate area—empty of all life—she set off to indulge in a late stroll.

And if by chance she ran into Gareth Hamilton, she fully intended to encourage him to take advantage of the cover of night and, so to speak, her. At least to take her hand, kiss her fingers—kiss her lips if he would. She'd done with observations and cogitations, considered as far as she could, and had yet to discover any trait or behavior incompatible with his being her "one."

Physical attraction and interaction seemed the obvious next step. Courtship of a sort, although as yet unstated. How could she assess if they were down onto the deck; Emily walked confidently toward the prow.

She'd just drawn level with the middle-mast when a shift in the air behind her had her turning.

A dark, dripping head, a mahogany face with wild, staring eyes, a long lanky body, bare but for a sodden loincloth, materialized out of the darkness. Teeth flashed in a wicked grin. One hand rose, a wicked blade gleaming in the moonlight.

She screamed, loud and long as she whirled and fled.

The man lunged and seized. His fingers caught her shawl.

She let it fall and fled on.

Only to see more cultists step out from the shadows by the railings ahead. She skidded to a halt. They smiled, and hefting knives in anticipation, came on.

"Here—take my hand!"

She looked up. Saw a crouched shadow silhouetted against the sky—but she knew his voice, knew him. She reached with both hands, gripped the hand he was stretching down to her.

He rose and pulled her straight up, swinging her onto the rear of the roof of the forward cabin beside him.

The cultists howled, and flung themselves after her.

Gareth released her the instant her feet touched the roof.

As she whirled to face the threat, his saber flashed—a wild swing that had the cultists ducking.

But they immediately popped up again, and, blades waving, scrambled to gain the higher ground.

With thrust and slash, Gareth beat them back.

Then someone leapt onto the roof behind them. She whirled, but it was Mooktu, coming to his master's aid.

She stepped back a little to give them both room, but kept a hand locked in the back of Gareth's robes—enough to keep her anchored, not enough to impede him.

The cultists surged forward and up, more appearing, crowding the deck below Gareth and Mooktu, trying to tempt them forward, arms reaching, hands grasping to pull them down.

Twin *bangs* rent the night—both companionway doors slamming open. Feet pounded the deck as sailors poured from the fore and aft stairways. Emily glimpsed Mullins and Bister leading the charge from the stern.

The majority of the cultists didn't spare the newcomers a glance. Eyes fixed on Gareth, they desperately tried to reach him . . . and her.

Through the wildly shifting shadows, she saw one darker apparition separate from the mass, slipping around the grappling, wrestling men. His gaze fixed on Gareth's back, the cultist wove silently nearer.

A quick glance showed Gareth was fully occupied with the enemies before him. The cultist ignored her, his attention locked on the more dangerous opponent as he slipped into the shadows beneath the edge of the cabin's roof.

He'd be up in a second.

Her heart in her throat, Emily glanced about—and saw a metal pail hooked to the jib arm. With her free hand she grabbed it, realized from the weight that it was half full of sand.

Just as a dark hand, followed by a dark arm and shoulder, came over the edge of the cabin roof.

She didn't stop to think, just swung the pail the opposite way, then, as the cultist's head cleared the roof's edge, swung the pail back with all her might.

The solid *thunk* of the pail sent th

give up.

In the end, they were all slain and their bodies tipped overboard.

Gareth didn't stand down until the last body splashed into the water. Even then, he waited until Bister checked, with Mullins doing one last circuit of the deck before signaling that all was clear.

He straightened, easing the fingers cramped about the hilt of his saber. His and Mooktu's new robes were liberally bloodied. A quick check confirmed none of it was theirs.

Only then, with the grip of battle fading, did he look at Emily.

She was still standing on the roof alongside him, watching the activity on the deck below. Her arms were tightly folded, hands gripping her elbows as if she were cold. Shock, yes, but not hysterics, for which small mercy he was grateful.

For the much greater mercy that she was still alive, he metaphorically went down on his knees and gave thanks.

He'd known she was up on deck. He'd heard her footsteps. He'd started circling, on the opposite side as she, avoiding her as he had whenever possible over the last days.

Her scream had put paid to that.

It had ripped through the night, and ripped through him. His heart had stopped, then started pounding so hard he'd been sure the cultists would hear and see him as he climbed up and over the roof.

But she was still alive; she didn't appear to have taken any wound.

And she'd very effectively covered his back, which was the last thing he'd expected.

He was sincerely grateful for that, too.

The deck below was clearing. Mooktu grunted, then dropped down off the roof and strode away to reassure Arnia, who had appeared at the stern.

With his free hand, Gareth touched Emily's slender back. "Come. I'll lift you down."

He dropped down to the less bloodied side of the deck,

then, setting aside his saber, turned to her, reached up, set his hands about her waist and gripped.

And swung her down.

Felt his heart pound just a little harder as he set her on her feet before him. As he looked into the face that haunted his dreams. Chest swelling, he had to force his hands to ease their grip and let go.

Bister unwittingly helped, coming up to take his saber to clean it.

He'd just handed it over when Captain Ayabad turned from giving orders to have the decks sluiced and swabbed.

Gareth spoke before the captain could. "I'll have four of my men help scour the decks tomorrow."

Ayabad inclined his head. "And while they are doing that, I think, Major, that you and I will have a talk. There are things I don't know that it appears I need to know."

Gareth nodded curtly. "In the morning, we'll talk."

"*Bon.*" Ayabad, tall, dark, of similar age to Gareth, again inclined his head, then his teeth flashed as he turned to Emily. "I must thank you, mam'zelle, for an entertaining evening."

Emily regarded him rather frostily. "I'm glad you enjoyed the excitement, Captain."

Ayabad, an Arab but his mother had been French, which was in part why Gareth had chosen his vessel—flashed his smile again, half bowed, and departed.

By then Bister, Mooktu, and the other men of their party

her toes, and, tugging him down a few inches, pressed her lips to his.

His instincts surged, purred, reached—

Ruthlessly he slapped them down.

It was a thank-you kiss. He knew it, yet . . .

Every particle of his awareness locked on the gentle touch, on the warmth of her body mere inches from his own, on the feel of the petal-soft, resilient, yet giving curves pressing so innocently against his lips.

His hungry, starving lips.

He fought to deny the greedy passion that swelled, to hold back the compulsion to sweep her into his arms, crush her against him, and kiss her back.

To taste, then claim, then devour.

Fought to hold steady, to not move, not an inch, to let her kiss him for how ever long she would . . .

Her lips lingered.

Then, on a sigh, she drew back.

As her heels touched the deck, he straightened—reluctantly. Disappointedly.

Those lovely lips curved. His gaze still locked on them, he saw her words form.

"Thank you, Major."

He forced his gaze up to her eyes.

They were smiling, too, then she inclined her head. "Good night."

He couldn't reply, said not a word as she turned and headed for the companionway. It was all he could do to keep his feet planted and not follow her. To keep the tip of his tongue from skating over his lips and tasting her.

He didn't need the torment. Her kiss had been a thank-you, fueled by gratitude, not desire.

It had been nothing personal, meant nothing of great moment.

Not to her.

He swore beneath his breath, then forced his feet in the

opposite direction. There was nothing between them—he'd be a fool to think there was.

This—whatever it was—was all in his mind.

10th October, 1822
Very early morning
In my cabin in the schooner, bobbing on the Red Sea

Dear Diary,

I am in two minds about having my last wish granted. The attack was truly frightening, and brought home to me—as if that were necessary— the true violence of the cultists' natures. They are fanatics and think nothing of fighting to the death. If it hadn't been for my gallant major . . . but that, of course, was what I gained from the experience, ter- rifying though it was. Gareth was nothing less than superb in whisking me from the imminent clutches of the fiends, and then protecting me against the rabble. He accounted for numerous of their number. The others, too, and the crew, did their part, I'm sure, but understandably I had eyes only for my rescuer, a fact that enabled me to account for one cultist of my

*sition to report that Major Gareth Hamilton is no
frog. Even though the kiss was all on my part—he
very properly did not respond—I could sense, and
feel . . . suffice it to say that the aftermath of the
experience disturbed my slumber for the remainder
of the night.*

*Naturally, given its success, that kiss can only be
my first step. It has opened the door, so to speak, and
now I must learn what lies beyond.*

I have to admit I am insatiably curious.

E.

The next morning, as he'd promised, Gareth went to speak
with the captain.

In order to give himself every advantage in the negotiations that were sure to ensue, he took Emily with him.

He tapped on the captain's cabin door, and when Ayabad
bade them enter, opened the door and ushered Emily, fetch-
ingly dressed in a flimsy spring green gown, over the threshold.

Ayabad came to his feet in a rush, then hurried to hold a
chair for Emily, who returned his greeting coolly and sat.

Drawing up a second chair, Gareth sat alongside her.

She'd been as pleased as punch when he'd asked her to ac-
company him; he was growing adept at reading her expressions. Of course, she didn't comprehend exactly why he'd
requested her presence, but he saw no harm in allowing her
to imagine he needed her counsel, and distracting Ayabad
was, he judged, a strategically wise move.

"Now, Major." Ayabad resumed his seat behind the small
desk. "Perhaps you will be so good as to explain the inter-
ests of those who attacked this ship last night, and whether
it is likely we will encounter more of their ilk on this
voyage."

Having already decided what to reveal, Gareth smoothly
explained the basis of the Black Cobra cult, and the cultists'

62

interest in Emily as the one who had bravely brought critical evidence to the authorities.

Ayabad was suitably impressed and intrigued. He exclaimed at the tale of Emily's ride from Poona and asked various questions, which Emily answered with just the right degree of feminine self-effacement.

By the simple expedient of not mentioning the copy of the letter he was carrying, Gareth's tale, supported by Emily, left Ayabad with the impression that Gareth was acting as Emily's escort on her journey home to England, because the Black Cobra was expected to seek revenge through attacks such as the one the previous night.

After that, it took little to convince Ayabad that he should support them by continuing to ferry them north to Suez, beating off any cult attacks along the way. Gareth was a shrewd judge of men like the captain; Ayabad and his sailors were only too ready to enliven their lives by joining in a good fight. There was, of course, a fee to be paid. He and Ayabad haggled over the additional sum.

A glance at Emily showed she was horrified—whether by the amount or simply the fact of the extra sum, he couldn't tell—but to his relief she remained silent, although he, certainly, felt her disapproval.

Emily was indeed incensed, but as Gareth seemed to think nothing of either the captain's demand, or of the—to her quite horrendous—sums being bandied about, she felt she had to hold her tongue.

His wealth therefore would not derive from his army stipend alone.

His affluence or otherwise made little difference to her—if he proved to be her "one," she would marry him regardless—but his relative wealth would certainly help in securing her parents' approval of the match.

She brought her attention back to the captain's cabin to discover he and Gareth were shaking hands.

Both were smiling identical smiles.

They both looked like pirates.

She rose as Gareth did, and they took their leave of the captain, who bowed very prettily over her hand. She made a mental note to be sure to do nothing to encourage Ayabad. She judged him a womanizer, undoubtedly with a woman in every port on the Red Sea.

When the door had closed behind them, Gareth smiled at her. "Excellent." He waved her to the companionway.

She preceded him up the stairs. He fell in beside her as they strolled down the deck.

"That went well." Gareth glanced at her face. "I wanted to avoid mentioning my mission, and you were a great help in that." He looked ahead, matching her step for step as they neared the stern. "You behaved in just the right way to evoke Ayabad's chivalrous streak. I felt sure he had one. He's an honorable man, which is why I hired him in Mocha."

She halted by the stern railings, gripping them and staring out over their wake.

Halting beside her, he glanced back along the length of the schooner. The decks had been scoured first thing that morning; there was no sign remaining of the night's battle. His lips twisted. "I should upbraid you for strolling the deck alone last night, but everyone in our party is feeling rather better for having weathered the attack we all knew would come. We took a few cuts and bruises, but no one sustained any serious injury."

He paused, recalling—vividly—that moment when, looking down from the roof, he'd seen the cultists closing in on her, seen her helplessness, understood her peril . . . but he'd been there, and had rescued her, for which she'd been duly appreciative.

And in the midst of the melee, she'd rescued him. He glanced at her, but she was still looking out over the waves. "I haven't yet thanked you for your assistance last night. Indeed, to commend you on your quick thinking and levelheadedness. If it hadn't been for you, I might have been seriously wounded."

Or killed, Emily thought, as she swung to face him.

She caught his gaze. Expectantly waited. If he wanted to thank her, she'd shown him the way.

Her jaw had dropped, mentally if not physically, when he'd revealed his reasons for requesting her presence that morning. Every word he'd uttered since had only succeeded in prodding her temper to greater heights, but if he was going to redeem himself by thanking her appropriately, she was willing to overlook his arrogance.

So she waited.

His gaze traveled her face, returned to her eyes. "I . . . have to admit that when I suggested we join forces, I imagined myself taking responsibility for you much as a nursemaid with her charge, but you've already contributed in a positive way—many positive ways—to our joint party's well-being, and deserve our, certainly my, thanks and gratitude."

She waited. Waited.

He seemed to sense her expectation, but all he did was shift uneasily, then say, "I'm sure the others—"

felt again the hardness, the sculpted lines of his cheeks and the bones above them, traced the latter lightly with the tips of her fingers even while she registered, absorbed, and explored again the fascinating hardness of his lips with hers.

Again he didn't return the kiss, but he did respond—she could sense it. She could all but feel the battle he waged to hold back, to keep the inch of separation between their bodies, to keep his arms from her, to keep his lips from seeking hers.

It was a battle he won—damn him!

Head starting to spin from lack of air, she was forced to draw back.

Gareth hauled in a breath the instant her lips left his, shackled his instincts in iron, nearly swayed with the effort it took.

He frowned down at her as her eyes searched his. "What was that for?"

Her eyes narrowed, golden flints sparking in the mossy green. "That was to shut you up. And to thank me for last night!"

With that, she spun on her heel and, skirts swishing angrily, stalked to the companionway.

Gareth watched her disappear down the steep stair.

Leaving him with the taste of her on his lips.

And thoroughly confused over what was going on.

11th October, 1822
Morning
My cabin on Captain Ayabad's schooner

Dear Diary,

> *I fear that in the matter of Gareth Hamilton, I am in danger of becoming quite wanton. I kissed him again, in the middle of the day, on the stern deck, in full view of anyone who might have been watching. I'm not sure anyone was, but I was in such a temper that I strode off before checking.*

My temper, of course, was all his fault. He admitted he commenced our journey thinking of me as a charge—a burden to be borne. No doubt out of honor. Huh! I refuse to be cast in such a light—to have him view me in such a patronizing way—but after recent events, he is, it seems, adjusting his perspective. Just as well. Him being my "one" necessitates his seeing me as the lady with whom he wishes to spend the rest of his life.

Which was in large part the reason I kissed him again—to assist in rescripting his view. And for that I cannot be sorry. My next step, clearly, is to get him to kiss me back. I did hope, for a moment, but he patently needs further encouragement to step over that line.

I am now adamant about pursuing him further. No one would expect me to desist given he is shaping up so well. With every day that passes, I grow more convinced—everything I see in him is laudable and attractive . . . well, except for his tendency to assume absolute command. And his continuing reticence over allowing himself to respond to me. I know he is not immune to the attraction that flares between us.

Sadly, no further opportunity to advance my cause presented itself yesterday. After stealing that second kiss, I did not feel I could initiate another, not without risking his seeing me as fast. Today is unlikely to offer

The next morning saw the schooner sliding over calm waters into the bay in which Suakin Island sat. Connected to the mainland by a causeway, the island itself remained the center of the bustling township. Indeed, as far as Emily could see, buildings covered the entire island, all the way to the waterline.

Their vessel circled to come into the docks. They passed craft of every conceivable type and style, but other than the heavy barges, off to one side, none were larger than the schooners.

Captain Ayabad joined her, Gareth, Dorcas, and Watson in the bow. "We must take on water and supplies, which will occupy most of the day, but I am keen to put out in mid-afternoon, to use the tide to carry us down the channel and back into the Red Sea. So if you are planning to go ashore, you must be back by then."

Gareth nodded. He looked at Emily. "The market?"

"Yes. We need supplies, too."

"The souk is roughly in the center of the island." Ayabad pointed. "That is the Hanafi Mosque—if you go past it a little way, you will find the stalls."

Gareth thanked him. By the time the schooner was made fast and the gangplank rolled out, their party was ready to depart. After some discussion, Gareth had agreed that Arnia and Dorcas had to see what was available in the souk for themselves. He'd attempted to suggest that Emily might stay on board—the implication was "safe"—but after being cooped up on the schooner for days, she wasn't about to pass up the chance of stretching her legs.

Or of being present if the cultists attacked again.

In the end, their entire party, bar only Watson—who agreed to remain aboard and keep an eye on their possessions— went ashore. Walking through the narrow streets, which only got narrower beyond the mosque, Emily was very conscious of trying to look everywhere at once.

The others were the same. The last contact with the cultists was days past; none of them imagined they'd given up and gone home.

Once in the souk, the tension only grew. While Emily, Dorcas, and Arnia haggled over flour and dried meat, Gareth and Mooktu loomed beside them, their hard faces and menacing stances making it clear they were guards. Bister, Jimmy, and Mullins lurked nearby. Bister seemed to be educating Jimmy in how to merge with crowds, and how to find the best vantage point from which to keep watch.

Emily was glad when she could turn to Gareth and inform him that they'd completed their purchases.

He humphed, and signaled the others to form up for their journey back to the ship. No one suggested ambling around to take in the sights.

Gareth heaved an inward sigh of relief when the last of their party passed him on their way up the gangplank. He turned and followed. What they'd all hoped would be a few hours of relaxation had instead been filled with burgeoning tension.

It was now almost palpable, that expectation of attack.

Stepping onto the schooner's deck, he paused to look back at the town. They hadn't sighted a single cultist. That didn't mean they hadn't been there.

What troubled him more was that his instincts were pricking—not just a little, a lot.

The same instincts had kept him alive through a long career of often unpredictable fighting; he wasn't about to discount them now. But according to Ayabad, their next stop would be Suez. Once they were away from here, they would

down the channel linking the bay to the Red Sea proper.

With the mouth of the channel in sight, and the wider waters of the Red Sea stretching beyond, she quit the railings and went below.

In the tiny cabin she had to herself, she sat on the edge of the bed built out from the curving outer wall, and pulled her leather-covered diary from her bag. Opening the clasp, she caught the small pencil before it could roll away. She spent a moment reading her last entry, then turned the page and smoothed it down. Pencil clutched in her fingers, she stared across the room, marshaling her thoughts, her impressions of the day.

With a sigh, she looked down and set pencil to paper.

"Hola!"

She looked up at the cry from somewhere on deck.

For one second all was still, then shouts and curses broke out—a rapidly escalating racket punctuated by the pounding of many feet.

Her diary went flying as she dashed to the door. As she hauled it open, the noise she dreaded hearing—the metallic clang and clashing slide of blades—joined the din.

Looking down the corridor, she saw Mullins disappearing up the stair, Watson behind him. Arnia and Dorcas stood at the bottom of the stairway, looking up. As Emily joined them, Arnia muttered something, then thrust a cooking knife into Dorcas's hand. "Stupid to stay trapped down here when us being up there might tip the balance."

With another, wicked-looking cook's knife in her hand, Arnia climbed quickly up.

Dorcas glanced at Emily. "You'd better stay here." With that, Dorcas went up the ladder.

An instant later, Emily stood looking up the steep stairway at blue sky—intermittently broken by a passing body.

She couldn't tell anything from the shouts, grunts, and the thudding of feet. Couldn't tell how many they were battling, or who was winning.

Dorcas was right—she had no weapon, so she couldn't help. But . . .

She crept up the stairs. Standing one rung down, she peered out. All she could see was a shifting mass of bodies filling the stern. Taking the last step, clearing the companionway housing, she looked back along the schooner—everywhere she looked was the same.

Then she saw the ship that had slipped in close alongside. There were cultists on board. Every time the swell pushed the vessels close more jumped across onto the schooner's deck.

Snapping her gaze back to the action around her, she realized Arnia was right—they would need every hand fighting to win this time.

Her assessment had taken less than a minute. Expecting to be noticed by some cultist at any second, she frantically looked around for something to use . . . and saw the trusty pail she'd wielded before. Avoiding a wrestling pair, she inched around, stretched out, and snagged the pail—just as a cultist focused on her.

Thin lips stretched in a vicious grin. Uttering a horrible yell, he flung himself through the melee at her.

She just had time to draw the pail back, then swing it forward—upward this time. It caught the cultist under the chin and lifted him off his feet, throwing him onto the backs of two other cultists. The three collapsed in a writhing heap. The sailors who'd been fighting the other two leapt on top.

Emily left them to it as she swung the other way—swung the pail again.

She knocked out another cultist, but . . . "Oh, no!"

a wicked-looking brass hook on one end.

She rose with the pole held between her hands, as she'd

seen her brothers do when they fought with staffs. The hook was heavy and weighed down that end. She juggled, found the balance—just as a cultist stepped away from a knot of shifting bodies and, grinning, came at her.

She stood her ground and flicked the hook end up. It caught the cultist in the throat and he halted, gurgling, then went down.

She felled two more, but of course they didn't stay down, but then Bister popped up out of the melee and used his short sword to ensure they did.

Emily seized the moment to take in what was happening around them. The sailors were holding the rest of the ship, while their party were fighting mostly in the stern. Bodies—all cultists as far as she saw—were piling up. The throng was thinning, but four cultists still had Gareth and Mooktu backed against the stern railing. Jaw setting, she hefted her pole.

"No—wait!" Bister frantically signaled her to give him one end. "Like this."

He crouched, held the pole low, waved with his other hand.

Emily saw what he meant. Holding her end, she crouched, too, and she and Bister swept in behind the four cultists.

The pole took them across the backs of their knees. With yells and flailing arms, they tumbled back—and Gareth and Mooktu sprang forward and finished them.

Emily was now behind Gareth, pressed up against the rails, with Bister in a similar position on the other side. Mooktu had seized the moment to leap forward and, sword slashing, win through to Arnia and Dorcas, who'd been fighting with Watson, Mullins, and Jimmy off to the side.

And still the cultists came on, hurling themselves forward, but the ranks behind were lessening. Further down the schooner, Emily glimpsed Captain Ayabad, sword swinging, a feral grin on his face, his massive Nubian first mate wielding a scimitar beside him.

The clang of swords at close quarters snapped her attention back to Gareth and Bister, who were furiously defending against another three cultists. Hauling her pole back up, she angled behind Gareth, picked her moment—and jabbed the nearest cultist in the throat.

He recoiled, and Gareth stepped forward to deal with him, allowing Emily to slip past behind him and engage one of the two cultists Bister now faced.

Her intervention allowed Bister to gain the upper hand, then Gareth joined in . . . and suddenly they were free.

But there were still writhing knots of men covering most of the deck.

Emily drew in a huge breath, looked to the side—then grabbed Gareth's sleeve. "Look!"

She pointed to the cultists' ship. It had drifted sufficiently so the gap between the vessels was just too great for men to leap across. On the other ship's deck, a few dozen cultists yelled and shook their swords in their impatience to get aboard the schooner and fight, their attention locked on a number of their fellows, who were attempting to fling grappling hooks over the schooner's rails.

Gareth swore, jammed his sword into his waistband, and grabbed Emily's pole. "Come on."

He leapt over bodies to the side railings. Leaving Bister, who had followed, to cut the ropes to the grapples that had successfully lodged over the schooner's rails, Gareth half straddled the rails, set the end of the pole below the deck line of the cultists' smaller vessel, and pushed.

Using all his weight, he managed to keep the smaller ship

her hands in his robes, leaning back, she anchored him in place.

73

The cultists were all screaming, trying to find poles to knock theirs aside and pull the ships closer.

Gareth snapped a look over his shoulder. "Mullins! Jimmy!"

The pair had just fought free of their assailants.

"Get more sail on—quickly!"

Jimmy leapt up onto the stern housing. Mullins clambered up behind him. Together they managed to unfurl a small midship sail, then they hauled and tugged—and the topsail unfurled.

For one instant, the sails billowed, then they filled, grew taut.

The schooner leaned, then leapt forward.

The cultists on the smaller ship screamed in fury, then raced to let their own sails down. But the schooner was bigger and carried much more sail. As the smaller ship fell behind, Gareth turned his attention to the cultists left on board.

But seeing they were now on their own and couldn't win, this time the cultists remaining dived overboard. Within minutes, all the fighting was over.

Captain Ayabad gave orders for more sail to be set. They'd come out of the narrow channel from Suakin on only the jib, which was how the other craft had been able to slide so close so easily.

Eventually Ayabad made his way to the stern, where Gareth and the others were all slumped, catching their breaths after disposing of all the bodies overboard.

Ayabad nodded to Gareth, bowed to Emily. "My apologies. I should have been more aware, but I did not think these vermin would attempt to board like that."

Gareth grimaced. "Neither did I." He glanced at the exhausted members of their group. "A few cuts, some bruises and knocks, but we took no lasting damage." He looked at Ayabad. "Your men?"

"Some injuries, but none life-threatening. These cultists—they are not well trained."

"Most aren't," Gareth replied. "Those used as guards and

74

assassins are, but the majority are farmers with knives in their hands."

Ayabad nodded. "It shows. However, after this, if you have no objection, I am inclined to make for Suez by the fastest possible tack."

Gareth nodded his agreement. "We've been lucky so far—no sense in inviting another attack."

By evening the schooner's decks were clean once more, with everything shipshape and as it should be as they cleaved through the shallow waves under full sail, running before an increasingly stiff breeze.

After tending the injuries of their own small company—a number of slashes and two deep cuts—Emily had gone with Arnia and Dorcas to offer their potions and salves to Captain Ayabad and his crew. The sailors were happy enough to have more gentle hands patching their hurts, but Emily gathered from their comments that, much like their captain, they'd enjoyed the battle.

After dinner, once the sun had set and night had wrapped the waters in velvet darkness, she went up to the stern deck. Given their speed, she doubted there was any lingering danger. Leaning on the stern railings, she stared out into the night.

As she'd hoped, Gareth joined her.

She heard his footsteps before she sensed his large body beside her.

time, our injuries were minor, so I suppose the triumph is ours to enjoy."

"Do you think, after today, that we'll reach Suez without further incident?"

He glanced back and up at the sails. "Given our speed, with luck, we might. Those we left behind will have to report back to someone. The general cultists operate under the orders of more senior members, and I doubt there were any of those more senior men on that ship. So I don't think we need to worry about being chased. However . . ." After a moment, he went on, "We have to assume there'll be cultists keeping a watch in Suez—not specifically for us but for any of the four of us who might pass through there. It's one of the major staging points on various routes back to England."

She nodded. "So once we reach Suez, we'll need to be on guard again." She glanced at him. "How do you plan to travel on from there?"

He shook his head. "I don't know."

Gareth saw no reason to explain that, until he'd had to take her and her party under his wing, his mission had had a somewhat different tone. Then, he'd intended to act as an open decoy and draw as many cultists after him as he could. With Mooktu, Bister, and Arnia all capable of looking after themselves, he wouldn't have had to worry unduly about the danger.

Having her with him changed all that.

He straightened from the railing. "I'll have to call in a few favors, and work out the best route and manner of transport to ensure we evade the cultists' notice. Suez will also be the last city in which we can be sure of getting suitable supplies this side of Marseilles, so we'll need to attend to that, too."

"All without being seen by the cult?"

"Indeed. And speaking of the cult . . ." He met her eyes, then grimaced. "While I should disapprove mightily of your coming up on deck in the middle of a fight, I can't be such a hypocrite."

She held his gaze for a moment, then her lips curved. She looked out over the water again. "Arnia said something about how foolish it was for women to cower and hope their men won, if the women's presence in the fight might tip the scales and ensure it. I've decided I agree with her. Her philosophy might not apply to battlefields and army engagements, but with the sort of skirmishes we're having to face, she has a valid point."

No matter how much he recoiled from the notion, not addressing the issue might be worse. She'd managed today, and in the earlier fight, but finding impromptu weapons was relying on sheer luck—which next time might fail.

Quelling his instinctive reaction, he asked, "You don't know much about weapons, do you?"

Her smile broadened; she cast him a quick glance. "I know a sword has a pointy end, and usually only one sharp edge."

He snorted. After a moment's consideration, he said, "Bister is very good with knives, and so is Arnia. I'll ask them to give you lessons, and find you a knife or two of your own. As you say, given what we have to face, it's better that you shouldn't be defenseless."

She'd swung to face him as he spoke. Now she straightened from the railings. Even in the faint moonlight, he could see her expression; it held something more than gracious delight.

"Thank you." Her lips were lusciously curved. Her eyes seemed to softly glow.

Her movement had brought her close. She stood less than a foot away.

For a moment, they stood locked in each other's eyes. He could have sworn the moon, the earth, and the heavens stood still. That there was no other reality beyond the pair of them

brushing the fragile bones of her jaw as he tipped her face up to his.

77

He bent his head. "Thank you for today—for saving me."

She lifted her lips, and they brushed his. But this time it was he who kissed her, who pressed his lips to hers—gently, slowly, achingly carefully.

She didn't back away. He felt her hand rise and cup the back of one of his, anchoring her, him—them.

Accepting.

Urging.

He angled his head, and pressed just a little harder, persuaded—when her lips parted, he teased them further, then, still riding his instincts hard, reining them in, he entered, slowly, deliberately, but definitely.

When she made no demur, he pressed deeper, and laid claim.

And something flared.

She moved into him, sending a shocking wash of heat cascading through him. Her lips moved beneath his, drawing him deeper, returning the caress.

And desire was suddenly there, unfurling within him—and her.

Familiar, yet not. More specific, more aware.

He couldn't mistake it, not in him, or in her.

Unexpected, yet beguiling, appealing, enticing. For long moments he did nothing more than savor the taste, the heady drug of having a willing woman in his arms.

What with one thing and another, this mission, the Black Cobra, it had been some time since he'd last sipped from desire's cup, but not even that pleasure, and the promise of more, could dim his mind to the reality of *which* woman he was holding.

Yet the warmth remained, the promise remained—undimmed.

He wasn't sure what this was—where they were heading. There could be no easy roll in some hammock—not for him, not with her.

This, whatever it was, was different. That much he knew, but what next . . . that was shrouded in mystery.

He drew back—he had to, for he didn't know what came next. Not here and now, not with her.

He didn't even know if she knew what he did—if she recognized the tug of burgeoning desire and understood where it would lead. If they went on, if they blindly followed the road their feet were now treading.

So he eased back from the kiss, reluctantly—so reluctantly—drew his lips from hers.

Looked down into her face as her lashes fluttered, then rose. Looked into her eyes, and saw . . .

Nothing beyond soft delight.

Her lips, sheening from the kiss, lightly curved.

Her hand fell from his. He released her face and she stepped back.

Still smiling that soft, elusive smile.

"Good night, Gareth."

He heard, but said nothing.

Could do nothing but watch—trusted himself to do nothing more than watch—as she turned and unhurriedly walked to the companionway, then went down.

He heard her footsteps travel the lower corridor, heard her door open, then close.

Only then did he fill his lungs, breathing deeply and long. Then he turned and leaned on the railings again, and stared out at the moonlit water rippling in their wake.

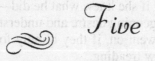

Five

12th October, 1822
Very late night
My cabin in Ayabad's schooner

Dear Diary,

*He kissed me! I am, at last, making headway, and
flatter myself that I have, at the very least, engaged his
interest. And the kiss was wonderful—so much better
in every way than any kiss I have experienced before.
He was masterful, yet in no way overwhelming. It
was the sort of kiss I have every intention of experiencing frequently—preferably with greater fervency, but
that I am sure will come.*

*Equally promising was his unprompted recognition of my part in the day's action—and who would
have thought that he, an army major, could be so progressive and clear thinking as to accept the need for me
to be better able to defend myself—and him, although
I doubt the latter occurred to him.*

*Nevertheless, I have to report that all is progressing
most favorably. Given his estimation that we will be*

safe from further attack until we reach Suez, I have
great hopes of what the next few days will bring.

I lay my head down to sleep in excited anticipation.

E.

16th October, 1822
Afternoon
My cabin on the schooner

Dear Diary,

I have written nothing for several days, as, to
my irritation, I have nothing of note to report. I had
great hopes that Gareth, having broken the ice and
kissed me—and we both know it had little to do with
gratitude—and having realized the nature of our
bond, as I am quite sure he did, would accordingly
seek to kiss me again.

Sadly, he has shown no evidence of such sensitivity—
indeed, his reaction to the event appears to be to try to keep
me at arm's length! Not that he is denying the attraction
that flared between us—I can see knowledge of it in his

E.

19th October, 1822
Very early morning
Cabin on blasted schooner

Dear Diary,

I am penning this in a hurry as we are packing and preparing to quit this restricting vessel. Suez has materialized out of the mists ahead, and we expect to be docking in a few short hours. This section of our journey is at an end, and if its revelations have been significant—I now know Gareth Hamilton bears all the hallmarks of my "one"—and subsequent developments—that kiss!—encouraging, indeed promising, I must report that I have yet to further engage with Gareth.

He has proved to be annoyingly elusive.

Exactly what the next stage of our journey will encompass neither I nor he knows, but I am hopeful it will afford me greater scope to pursue him—or, more accurately, to encourage him to pursue me.

I go forward in hope.

E.

They quit the docks as the sun rose above the eastern quarter of Suez, painting pale walls a glowing amber-pink. Gareth squinted at the buildings silhouetted against the morning sky, minarets and the domes of mosques underscoring that they walked in a foreign land.

Luckily, since the defeat of Bonaparte, this foreign land was increasingly falling under British sway.

Garbed in his Arab robes, he strode confidently forward, as if he belonged, as if he knew where he was going—which he did. He'd stopped in Suez on his way out to India. Walking into the square beyond the docks, he glanced back at the small procession trailing him—Mooktu by his shoulder, Emily, Dorcas, and Arnia in their burkas a respectful pace behind, then Bister and Jimmy with the luggage, with Watson and Mullins bringing up the rear.

Facing forward, he led the way across the crowded square to the opening of a street that led, not to the diplomatic quarter, but into a quiet residential area. Halting beneath the awning of a shop that had yet to open, he waited until the three women, Bister, Jimmy, Watson, and Mullins drew near and halted, close enough to hear.

He hadn't told them where he was taking them. He didn't want any questions or protests along the way, nothing that might mar the image they were projecting. *Don't look around openly as if you're searching,* he'd told them before they'd walked down the gangplank. The cultists would definitely be in Suez; they needed to avoid waving any flags.

Quietly, he said, "We can't risk going to the consulate." He glanced at Emily. "Ferrar has connections in diplomatic circles—he might have asked staff there to alert him or his creatures if any of us pass this way."

"So where are we going?" Emily peered at him through the lace panel of her burka.

He met her eyes. "To call on an old friend."

With that, he led them on, into the quieter residential streets.

He knew Cathcart would render whatever aid he could. What Gareth didn't know was if his old friend's abilities ran to organizing the sort of transport they needed. But Cathcart

the green-painted door he remembered. Raising a fist, he thumped.

A minute passed, then the panel shielding a narrow rectangle of ironwork slid aside, and dark eyes looked out.

Gareth met them. "Does Roger Cathcart still live here?"

The middle-aged Arab on the other side of the door nodded. "This is Mr. Cathcart's residence."

"Excellent. Please inform Mr. Cathcart that Gar is here, and wishes to consult him on a matter of grave importance."

The man blinked. After a moment, the panel slid shut.

Less than two minutes later, Gareth heard swift bootsteps approaching the gate from the other side.

He was smiling when the gate was hauled open and Roger Cathcart stood staring at him, pleased surprise and rampant curiosity warring in his face.

"Hamilton? What the devil are you doing here, man?"

Before he could explain, there were the introductions and billeting to be dealt with. Cathcart's house was large enough to accommodate them all, and his small staff were highly discreet—something Cathcart, understanding the need for secrecy after one glance at their clothes, was careful to give orders to ensure.

After serving as first secretary to the British Consul for more than eight years, Cathcart knew all the ins and outs of Suez, the political and social vicissitudes, and, Gareth was hoping, various ways and means of traveling on to the Mediterranean and beyond.

Cathcart was delighted and intrigued to meet Emily, especially after learning of her connection to the Governor of Bombay, but he reined in his curiosity until Emily, Gareth, and he were seated on soft cushions around a low table, addressing the food displayed on beaten copper and brass platters.

Cathcart waved at the fare. "Consider it a late breakfast, or an early lunch." He glanced at Emily, busy looking over the offerings, then he blushed lightly. "I say—I must apolo-

84

gize. All these are local dishes—I didn't think to order more English fare—"

"No, no." Emily smiled as she helped herself to small grain cakes. "After six months in India, I've grown accustomed to spicy food."

"Oh. Good. Six months? That's a good long visit."

"A comfortable visit catching up with my aunt and uncle." Emily concluded her selections and set down her plate. "Have you been here long?"

While he piled his plate with the freshly cooked delicacies, Gareth listened as Roger answered with a glibly charming, condensed version of his years abroad.

Emily seemed quite cheery and encouraging.

She and Roger kept up a light conversation until, with his plate filled and the pair of them eating, Roger caught Gareth's eye. "So what 'matter of grave importance' brings you to my doorstep?"

When Gareth glanced at the door, Roger added, "They've all returned to the kitchens. There's no one about to hear."

Gareth nodded, and between mouthfuls of unusually spiced but delicious sustenance, he told Roger the whole tale, from Hastings's directive to their need for the robes they had arrived on his doorstep in.

Roger was one of the few men in the world in whom he had sufficient confidence to entrust with the unvarnished truth. He'd known Roger since they were both pupils at Winchester Grammar School; neither had ever let the other down. While

and as far as possible avoid the area around the consulate.

He met Gareth's eyes, then glanced at Emily. "I've seen a few turbans with unusual black silk bindings recently."

"Cult members." Emily's eyes widened.

Gareth nodded. "I feared they'd be here, ahead of us, keeping watch."

"That's what they're doing, all right. The only place I've seen them is in the streets around the consulate."

"We've no reason to go into that area, but"—Gareth trapped Roger's eyes—"you'll need to be careful, too. Someone at the consulate might remember our connection from when I was here six years ago."

Roger pulled a face. "Possible, but unlikely, but I will take care to ensure I'm not followed, not back here, and not to where I suspect I'll have to go to arrange your transport onward."

"Speaking of which." Gareth picked up the last of the flat bread and dipped it into the sauce on his plate. "I don't think we should go via Cairo."

"I wasn't about to suggest it. I imagine if we have some of these cultists here, then Cairo will be swarming with them. Far better if you leave that wasps' nest alone, and head straight to Alexandria."

"Is it possible to do that?" When he'd come the other way, he'd traveled from Alexandria up the Nile to Cairo, then part by river, part overland, to Suez.

Roger nodded. "It's straightforward enough, and"—he glanced at Emily—"given your entourage, it has the added benefit of being the last option anyone would expect you to take."

Gareth wasn't sure he liked the sound of that.

"Why not?" Emily asked.

Roger opened his mouth, then paused, as if, faced with Emily's wide eyes, he, too, was having second thoughts about the preferred option. But when Emily merely waited, expectant and determined, he threw Gareth an apologetic look, and explained, "I think you'll be safest if you travel with one of the Berber caravans across the desert direct to Alexandria."

Gareth frowned. "Aren't they—the Berbers—unreliable?" Warlike. Devious. Not to be trusted.

Roger heard what he left unsaid, and smiled reassuringly. "Some are, but I know a few of the sheiks, and . . . for want of a better description, they're honorable. You'll be safe with one of their tribes, but I'll need to learn if any of them—those I'd trust—are here at the moment, and when they'll be leaving for Alexandria."

"How frequently do they make the trip?" Gareth asked.

"They're on the move most of the time. The only halts between here and Alexandria are desert oases. But the tribes spend a week or two in camps outside town every time they reach here." Roger glanced at Emily; it was to her he spoke. "If you think you can manage the privations, it would almost certainly be the safest way."

Gareth expected her to question what the "privations" were likely to entail, but instead, her neatly rounded chin firmed. She shot him a quick glance, then looked back at Roger. "Is the caravan option the one most likely to result in us reaching Alexandria without encountering the cult?"

Roger hesitated, then nodded. Decisively. He looked at Gareth. "Any other way, and you're almost certain to find yourself walking into their arms—and given the numbers I've seen around here, they're likely to be a significant force."

"In that case, we'll take the caravan option, if you can ar-

in camp, and find out who's leaving in the next day or two.

19th October, 1822
Before bed
In my room in Cathcart's house in Suez

Dear Diary,

Well, at last I can report that I have indeed seen some development in Gareth's attitude to me, although one can hardly describe it as decisive in any way. Over dinner he turned into a veritable bear, growling and grumpy, and all because his friend Cathcart paid me due attention. Not undue attention, but merely the customary appreciation any sociable and sophisticated gentleman might pay to a lady supping at his table and of a mind to be engaging. At no point did Cathcart step over the line. Gareth, on the other hand, turned positively surly. Not that he made any open fuss, but as he is normally even tempered, his disaffection was apparent to me—and I largely suspect, old friend as he is, to Cathcart as well.

I wonder what he made of it.

Regardless, although he didn't find those he was seeking today, Cathcart is doing his best for us, and therefore entitled to my smiles.

If Gareth sees no reason to engage my attention, and invite my smiles himself, then he shouldn't complain if I bestow them—smiles only, mind you—elsewhere.

I am not of a mind to indulge him in his present mood. He can hardly view Cathcart as a rival. It is Gareth I've kissed—three times! If he doesn't act, and commence pursuing me soon, I will have to take more drastic action.

E.

The following afternoon, Gareth found himself wandering the corridors of Cathcart's house with nothing to do, nothing requiring urgent—or even nonurgent—attention. It had been so long since he'd been at loose ends that he literally felt at a loss.

Earlier he'd gone with Emily and the others to the souk to replenish their supplies. On returning to the house, Roger had joined them for a light luncheon before setting off to scout through the Berber tribes currently encamped outside the city walls.

Once Roger had left, Emily had gone out to the front courtyard with Arnia and Bister, who was taking his new role as Emily's weapons master very seriously. After watching through a window, seeing Bister reaching around Emily and holding her hand while he demonstrated various thrusts and feints, Gareth had, briefly, regretted not volunteering to teach her himself.

But he wanted her proficient, at least to have some defensive skills, and if he'd been her teacher, he—and maybe even she—would have ended distracted.

His Arab robes swirling about him, he'd wandered off to the other, more contemplative, courtyard, but hadn't found any subject able to hold his interest, contemplative or otherwise. Dwelling on what his three brothers-in-arms were currently doing wasn't likely to calm his mind.

Thinking about the Black Cobra's minions was even less help.

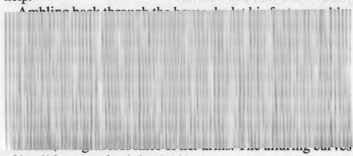

of her lithe, very feminine body.

He shifted, and she looked up, met his eyes.

"What are you thinking of?" The words were out of his mouth before he'd thought.

She raised one shoulder in a slight shrug. "Just this and that."

The faint color in her cheeks gave her away.

He should have asked *who* she was thinking of.

Him? Cathcart?

Or MacFarlane's ghost?

It was suddenly imperative he know. Ever since he'd been unwise enough to kiss her on the schooner, he'd been plagued by questions—of what she thought, what she wanted, what was going through her mind. Of what was right, honorable, what was acceptable in the circumstances. Of just how much those circumstances were to blame for her apparent interest in engaging with him. Moving into the room, he stepped around the numerous floor cushions and low tables to the divan. "May I join you?"

"Of course." She straightened amid the cushions, drawing her skirts in, in a clear invitation for him to sit there, close beside her.

He did. But divans weren't designed for sitting formally. Emily wriggled her hips, curled her legs beneath her green skirts, shifting around to face him. He lounged among the cushions, arms spread across the colorful silks, one bent knee on the divan so he was angled toward her. "How have you enjoyed your trip thus far?"

She waved in a gesture that encompassed many things. "It's been . . . enlightening, illuminating, and undeniably exciting."

"I fear we won't make it to the pyramids or the sphinx."

"As that route would take us through Cairo, I don't feel overly exercised by that. I would rather arrive in Alexandria alive, and not in the hands of the Black Cobra's men."

"Indeed." He let a moment go by, then asked, "It must have been a shock to learn James had met his death at their hands."

She frowned for a moment, then her face cleared. "Mac-Farlane?" She considered, then grimaced and met his eyes. "To be perfectly honest, when he insisted on remaining behind like that, given the numbers, I would have been more surprised had he survived."

"It was an immensely brave act."

She inclined her head. "It was an act of great self-sacrifice—I acknowledge that. Had our roles been reversed, I doubt I could have done the same."

Emily watched Gareth's face, and wondered why he'd introduced the topic. "Your MacFarlane died a hero, but he is still dead, and those remaining alive have to go on living." She tilted her head, feeling her way, her eyes locked on his. "Given my chances of continuing to live were significantly improved by his sacrifice, then the best way I can honor him, I feel, is to continue with my life—more, to live life to the full."

With you.

Her heart was beating just a touch faster. They were alone. Although the others were in the house, no one was near. And he'd made the first move by coming to sit with her—surely a clear declaration of intent.

Expectation welled; she struggled not to jig, not to lean toward him and precipitate—initiate—matters herself.

His gaze lowered to her lips as if he could hear her thoughts, but then he snapped it back to her eyes. "Cathcart. You . . . he . . ."

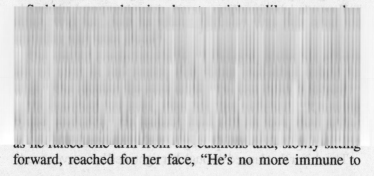

as he raised one arm from the cushions and, slowly sitting forward, reached for her face, "He's no more immune to being appreciated by a lovely lady . . ." His hand curved about her jaw and he drew her closer; fascinated, mesmerized by the temptation in his eyes, she leaned forward, closer still . . . until her lids fell, her gaze lowering to his lips in time to see the end of his sentence fall from them. ". . . than the rest of us."

Her mind took in the implication. Her lips curved as they met his.

The contact set her heart leaping.

She parted her lips, surrendered her mouth gladly, welcomed him in, and quelled a telltale shudder. His lips were firm, resilient, dominatingly male; his tongue stroked, sensation burgeoned and spread.

She leaned in, sank in, to the kiss.

Felt him shift closer, felt his hand slide from her face. He reached around her, drew her to him, his arm banding her waist as she joyfully obliged.

Inching closer yet, she placed her hands on the white fabric covering his upper chest. Felt the hardness of the rock-solid muscles beneath her palms and rejoiced. Greatly daring, her lips locked with his, her tongue tentatively tangling with his, she leaned further, reached further, slid her hands up, over his shoulders, then on, until she could clasp his nape, until her fingers tangled in the soft locks of his hair.

She sighed through the kiss, exhilaration and expectation melding. He gathered her closer, then tipped slowly back, sinking deeper into the cushions, taking her with him.

He ended half reclining, with her above and alongside him. She felt his lips curve beneath hers, sensed his satisfaction as, holding her locked within one muscled arm, he raised his free hand, and caressed.

From the swell of one hip to her waist.

His hand lingered, anticipation building, the heat of his palm sinking through her gown to her flesh.

Than his hand moved again, from her waist upward to, with the lightest of whispering touches, stroke her breast.

The shiver that lanced through her tightened her nerves, made something within her clench . . . then release as his hand, hard palm and long, knowing fingers settled, cupped. Claimed.

Her fingers firmed, tightening on his skull as he played, as with his tongue and lips he distracted her, only to draw back and let the heat, the warmth, the enticing pleasure of his caresses fill her mind.

She was lost in sensation.

And so was he. Gareth was submerged in the subtle pleasure, his mind awash with tactile delight. It had been too long since he'd held a woman in his arms and so unhurriedly pleased her and himself. And even sunk in the moment, he—all of him— knew this wasn't just any woman. She was who she was— Emily—and that made the moment even more special.

Even more addictive.

Ever more enticing.

The minutes spun on. Delight swelled, grew.

She sank closer, pressing more definitely against him.

Hauling in a breath, he gave in to the building compulsion, closed his hand about the firm mound of her breast—felt his chest tighten as she gasped through the kiss. Her spine bowed slightly as he traced the firm curves, found her nipple, circled it, then closed his fingers about the turgid peak.

She arched into the caress, the movement pressing her flesh more firmly to his palm. He closed his hand again, kneaded, and felt her melt.

Heard her softly moan.

Heat and desire shafted through him, straight to his groin.

He broke from the kiss—just as she did, gasping.

93

One look into her dazed eyes told him she was, suddenly, as uncertain as he.

That she had realized, too, just how far they had gone.

That she, like he, needed to think before they went further.

They stared at each other, gazes locked, searching. For what, he wasn't sure either of them truly knew.

Their positions, the physical closeness, gradually impinged on their minds as they slowly returned to the here and now.

Muscles tensed—hers and his—and they started to sit up and move apart.

"I think they're in the salon."

Watson, heading toward them, with others in his wake.

When her courier-guide appeared in the archway, Emily was sitting primly upright on the divan, with Gareth standing before the nearby window, apparently looking out.

He turned as Watson halted, and arched a brow.

"Thought you'd like to know," Watson said, "that Mullins and Jimmy spotted a band of cultists patrolling the streets not far from here."

The bearded cultist known to all as Uncle sat by the pool in a small courtyard. "We know they are here, somewhere in this small city. So where are they?"

The quietly uttered words were loaded with silent menace.

The three cultists kneeling before the pool trembled. One gathered his courage and spoke to Uncle's feet. "The watchers at the consulate have seen nothing. We are combing the streets, but with the high walls all these houses have . . ."

Uncle studied the speaker, a faint frown in his eyes. The silence stretched, then he nodded. "The major is proving a worthy opponent. You are right, Saleeb, there is little point wasting our effort searching the warren of these streets. Instead, we must surround the town with eyes and ears and wait for them to show themselves. They must head either north or west. Go out, my sons, and befriend the herdsmen, the nomads, and those others who gather outside the town walls. Recruit them to watch and listen for us—we have coins aplenty, thanks to the bountifulness of our esteemed leader." Uncle held up a hand, palm up, at shoulder height. His own son quickly fetched a purse and placed it on the waiting hand.

Uncle hefted the pouch, then presented it to the kneeling man who had spoken. "Here—take this, and with it buy the information we need. Then when the major and his party try to leave, we will know." He sat back. "Go."

The three men rose and went, bowing from his presence as fast as they dared.

Leaving Uncle to mull over the vicissitudes of fate.

He'd ordered a night attack on the major's boat, hoping to kill the woman at least, but she'd shrieked, and despite there being a goodly number of his cultists on the deck, the major and his party had prevailed.

But then a ship carrying a large number of cultists had reached him, sent on from Aden as he'd ordered. He'd sent them and their ship to attack the major's ship as it had, necessarily slowly, eased out of the Suakin Channel. He'd been certain of success, had already started planning what means he would employ to break the major, only to see his men repulsed again, and their ship left wallowing in the faster schooner's wake. He'd watched his failure unfold from the deck of another ship not far away—and cursed.

Who would have thought the captain and crew of the schooner would take up arms against his men?

In India, the cultists were not opposed by others. Others

will, my son.

Failure was not an option.

Six

20th October, 1822
Before dinner
My room in Cathcart's house

Dear Diary,

*I am rushing to write this before dinner. Although
I sat down with plenty of time, I stared into space
for so many minutes that now I must hurry to get
my thoughts down. I have further developments to
report, having spent a sizable portion of the afternoon
in Gareth's arms while we explored the depth and
potential of our mutual attraction. The result is as
yet undecided, for when we called a halt, by mutual
accord, I for one needed to think and cogitate—not
having indulged in either activity throughout the time
his lips were on mine.*

*The truth is we have reached a point beyond which
I cannot wisely go, not until and unless I am absolutely
certain that Gareth Hamilton is my "one"—that one
and only gentleman for whom I have waited for so long.*

What will make me certain, I do not know—just

as I do not know what, on this dangerous journey of ours, tomorrow will bring. Our way forward is as yet unclear. Regardless, we must forge on to England, eluding cultists and all dangers the fiend throws in our path. In similar fashion I will grasp every opportunity to convince myself that Gareth is my "one," but whether I will be able to do so this side of Dover remains to be seen.

I am, however, determined to press on.

E.

*L*ate the following morning, Emily was sitting in the salon repairing the hem of her green gown, when a stir in the courtyard had her looking out to see Gareth greeting a smiling Cathcart.

Cathcart had gone to speak with a Berber sheik about their joining the man's caravan. From Cathcart's expression, he was the bearer of good tidings.

Both men turned and came striding toward the house. Emily put aside her mending, and looked up expectantly as Cathcart led Gareth into the room.

Cathcart swept her a bow. "Your carriage has been arranged, mademoiselle. You will be leaving at dawn tomorrow." Straightening, Cathcart grimaced. "Sadly, there is no carriage as such, and, equally sadly, I fear that when Ali-Jehan says dawn, he truly does mean the instant when the

Gareth humphed. He didn't, to Emily's eyes, look entirely pleased.

97

"Well," she put in brightly, "that's excellent news!" When both men looked at her, she continued, "We have to forge on, and journeying with a caravan will certainly be an adventure." She caught Gareth's eye. "One quite the equal of seeing the pyramids."

He humphed, and prowled forward to sit on the other end of the divan she'd favored.

Turning back to Catchart, she smiled. "We must thank you, sir, for your help and hospitality. You've provided a much-needed respite." She raised her brows in query. "Is there any message we can carry for you back to England? To family, perhaps?"

Cathcart thanked Emily for her kind thought but declined. Gareth watched as his friend continued to bask in the glow of Emily's readily bestowed approbation. He tried not to growl or grind his teeth. She had no real interest in Cathcart—it had been he she'd permitted to kiss her—but Gareth wasn't entirely sure Cathcart, happily accepting her feminine accolades, had no interest in her.

She glanced at him at that moment, a conspiratorial, inclusive expression in her eyes, then she turned back to Cathcart and continued to charm him . . .

Gareth realized he was scowling, and banished the expression. At least outwardly. Inwardly, he scowled even more. *She knew.* That's what that brief glance was all about. She knew her charming of Cathcart was provoking him.

Of all the developments in the last hour, that pleased him least of all.

21st October, 1822
Before dinner
My room in Cathcart's house

Dear Diary,

After Cathcart's confirmation that we are to leave

98

tomorrow, our party paid another necessary visit to the souk. *The tension was palpable throughout, but despite keeping our eyes peeled, we saw no cultists at all—which, instead of making us feel less tense, only escalated the uncertainty. None of us believes the fiend has given up. His calling off his hounds only raises the question of what else he's planning—how else he intends to corner us.*

But as for our journey's next stage, while I raised no open demur, I am not entirely sanguine about traveling with a caravan. However, as there appear to be no viable alternatives, then I will, of course, hold my head high and soldier on.

On the personal front, I have noted a certain dog-in-the-manger tendency on Gareth's part. A degree of possessiveness in his attitude to me, and on that count I am uncertain how to respond. While I am not thrilled by this development, and can see definite problems looming, I suspect that with certain types of males, possessiveness is ingrained, and not easily eradicated.

My sisters, I am sure, could advise me, but sadly, they are out of reach, and there are no others I might question on such a subject. In this, I truly miss them, and Mama, too.

I am reasonably sure that when it comes to Gareth

with the others of their party, likewise disguised and gathered about their baggage piled on a cart, while Gareth and Ali-Jehan—who proved to be a handsome devil of similar age to Gareth and Cathcart—conducted a low-voiced discussion, with Cathcart looking on. Peering through her burka's little window, Emily used the minutes to see what she could of this unknown world.

There were numerous encampments dotted about the area. All appeared peopled by nomadic tribes, but not all were the rather haughty and handsome—and thus readily distinguishable—Berbers. From where she stood, Emily could see three other Berber camps, presumably three other tribes. From the other sites, men were observing their group, watching the discussion among the three men.

Turning back to see what was transpiring, Emily caught both Gareth and Ali-Jehan looking her way—specifically looking at her. Then Ali-Jehan asked Gareth a question. He nodded, and they went back to their negotiations.

Eventually Ali-Jehan flashed a white smile. When Gareth offered his hand, Ali-Jehan clasped it in his. With a nod, he released Gareth, then beckoned their group forward as he turned and shouted orders to the various men and women engaged in breaking up their camp.

Cathcart and Gareth turned to meet them as they trudged up.

"Everyone in this tribe speaks English, French, or both," Cathcart told them. "You'll be able to make yourselves understood, and with them, you should be safe." Smiling, he glanced at Gareth. "As safe as it's possible to be."

Emily couldn't interpret the look Gareth and Cathcart exchanged, but then Gareth looked at her. "Dorcas and Arnia will travel with the older women. Mooktu, Bister, and I will ride with the men guarding the caravan. Mullins, Watson, and Jimmy will assist with the carts carrying our luggage."

Beneath her burka, she frowned. "And me?"

Gareth looked up, over her head. "You have a steed of your own."

She turned—and saw Ali-Jehan returning with another

man, who was leading a huge camel by a rope rein.

There were other camels linked in a long train, kicking and braying and shuffling about, each loaded with baggage of all sorts, but this camel was different. Instead of baggage, it carried a cushioned contraption lashed behind its hump.

As the camel approached, he opened his mouth and bared his teeth in a bray Emily took to be a camel protest.

"Oh, no." She tried to step back.

Gareth's hand pressed against her back. "Sadly, yes. In the circumstances, on this beast's back is the safest place for you—the safest way for you to travel across the desert."

"According to whom?" Emily's eyes widened as, with a great show of teeth—both from the attendant and the camel—the beast was brought around and made to kneel, his side to her.

Ali-Jehan rounded the beast, drew down a rope stirrup-cum-ladder, then bowed, black eyes alight. "Your steed, dear lady."

He spoke perfect English, but there was nothing civilized about the way his eyes tried to penetrate her burka.

Ignoring that, knowing full well that he couldn't see through it—and regardless, she was fully clothed beneath—Emily eyed the camel's shaggy head. Tentatively she stepped forward. The huge head swung her way, lips curling back.

Gareth pulled her to the side, to the saddle. "Be careful—they spit."

Emily turned to stare at him. "*Spit?*"

Gareth's hands grasped her hips and pushed her up. "No—you can't ride one of their horses."

"Why not?" She tried to twist enough to glare at him.

He kept hold of her hips and held her where she was. "For a start, in English terms they're only half broken."

"I could manage—"

"Perhaps." Clipped accents were infusing his speech. "But the other reason you're riding this animal is that it's Ali-Jehan's personal pet."

Growing tired of her ungainly position, and distracted by having his hands gripping her hips, she gave up, swung around, and plopped down into the surprisingly comfortable saddle. She frowned at Gareth, but he was looking down, adjusting the twin rope stirrups. Glancing around, she saw the Berber chieftain striding through his people, yelling orders and gesticulating. "What does that have to do with anything?"

When she looked back, Gareth met her eyes. "It won't leave him."

She frowned harder. "So?"

"So" —with a last tug, he stepped back— "if raiders attack the caravan and try to steal you away, they'll have the devil of a time shifting him. Nothing is more stubborn than a camel."

He looked at her for an instant, then nodded to the attendant, still standing holding the camel's head.

The attendant said one word.

Emily bit back a scream as the beast—in a series of ungainly lurches—got back to its feet.

Once it had, she stared down at Gareth. "This is—"

"What will keep you safe." Hands on hips, he looked up at her. Then he glanced at the attendant. "This is Haneef. He'll teach you how to guide Doha."

"Doha?"

Haneef smiled toothily up at her. "He is really a very good beast."

Uncle eased down to the cushions set before a low table holding an assortment of dishes he neither recognized nor particularly cared for. But in the service of his chosen master he would endure any privation necessary for success.

Before he could reach for the first dish, a stir arose in the courtyard beyond the archway. With a wave, Uncle dispatched his son to see who had arrived. An instant later, Muhlal returned with one of the lowlier cult members in tow.

The man bowed low. "Great one—we have just had word that the major and his party were seen in the grounds beyond the town."

"And?"

Without lifting his head, the man continued, "They left with a Berber caravan. Those we paid said the caravan goes west."

Uncle nodded. "Excellent. You may go."

Surprised, the man looked up. He met Uncle's eyes and quickly lowered his. "Yes, great one." The man backed from the room, still bowing.

Once he was gone, Uncle looked up at his son. "You heard?"

Muhlal nodded.

Uncle smiled. "No doubt but that the major will make for the embassy in Cairo." Uncle waved Muhlal to sit beside him. When he did, Uncle set one hand on his shoulder, leaned closer and lowered his voice. "This is your chance, my son, to shine in the service of the Black Cobra. Our leader is magnanimous to those who serve well. It has been

Smiling, Uncle nodded. He clapped Muhlal's shoulder. "Let us eat, and then I will see you on your way. A caravan

is slow. They will not escape you." When Muhlal eagerly reached for a plate, Uncle's gaze softened. "And I will be waiting in Cairo to celebrate with you."

As the sun sank, coloring the wide expanse of the desert sky with oranges, reds, and purples, Emily eased her way out of the high saddle and carefully climbed to the ground.

Doha flicked her a scowl, then ignored her.

Emily inwardly humphed, then shook out her skirts and the enveloping burka, and, leaving Doha to Haneef's care, turned to find the others. It had taken a while to grow accustomed to the camel's strange gait. Once she had, and was no longer in danger of tipping off, Haneef had shown her how to use the reins to exert some control—minimal control in Emily's estimation—over the ungainly beast.

Contrary to her expectations, her first day's travel had passed without disaster. When the caravan had halted for a light meal and refreshments a little before midday, she had asked Haneef the obvious question—if Ali-Jehan went careening off on his horse through the desert dunes, chasing attackers, for instance, wouldn't Doha follow him?

Haneef had shaken his dark head. "Oh, no, miss. Doha is a clever beast—he knows this" —with a wave Haneef had encompassed the caravan— "is his master's place. He will stay here and wait for Ali-Jehan to return. There is no need for him to chase after him if he knows he will come back."

That the camel was lazy to boot hadn't been any great surprise to Emily. "Are you sure it's not you whom Doha is attached to?"

Haneef had smiled. "Well, I am always here—I have a bad leg and cannot ride well enough to chase raiders."

Sighting the others across the campsite, Emily picked up her skirts and trudged their way, eyes on her feet so she didn't trip in the sand. She couldn't say she was enamored of her camel—he stank remarkably, much worse than horses— but riding him had been a luxury. For the most part, the others had walked.

There were carts with barrel wheels, but some were handcarts pulled by the men who, like Haneef, weren't the mounted guard. Other carts were drawn by donkeys, and the older women and older men took turns riding in those, but in the main most of the tribe, and most of their party, had trudged steadily through the sand throughout the day.

Finding Dorcas and Arnia amid the bustle of the tribe setting up camp, she gripped her maid's arm. "Are you all right?"

Dorcas smiled wearily. "Perfectly well."

Understanding her question, Arnia nodded. "It wasn't as hard as it looked. They keep a steady and reasonable pace."

Dorcas nodded in agreement. "It's like a long, easy stroll. Not so difficult once you get the hang of it."

Somewhat reassured, Emily turned her attention to the camp taking shape around them. Tents were being erected around a central area, in which others were constructing a large fire pit. Bister, Jimmy, Watson, and Mullins were helping men erect one of the large Berber tents. "We didn't bring tents."

A snort came from behind Emily. Clawlike fingers gripped her elbow. "You will not need tents—you will share ours, lady."

Turning her head, Emily met a pair of bright dark eyes in a deeply tanned, heavily wrinkled face. The old woman smiled, showing surprisingly white teeth with a gap in the center. She tapped Emily's burka in the vicinity of her nose.

The old woman studied Emily's gown, thus revealed. Reaching out, she fingered the fabric. "So fine." She shook her head. "It will never last." She looked at Dorcas and Arnia's clothes, and clucked her tongue. "Come." Beckoning, she started for the carts that had been lined up behind the ring of tents. "I am Ali-Jehan's mother. You call me Anya. You will join me and the other older women in my tent and we will find more suitable clothes for you."

"Thank you." Emily inclined her head respectfully.

Anya shot her a shrewdly assessing glance. "And afterward, you will repay us by telling us what is going on, yes?"

Hiding a smile, Emily nodded. "Yes, if you like." Older ladies were the same the world over, it seemed.

"Good." Anya waved to the carts. "First, we need to take our things inside."

They all helped ferry rolled rugs, wool blankets, silk hangings and cotton sheets, cushions and pillows and sets of beaten plates and mugs, all the paraphenalia of nomadic comfort, into the dark tent. They were joined by four other older women, whom Anya introduced as Marila, Katun, Bersheba, and Girla. As they organized the tent, curiosity abounded on all sides.

When they finally settled cross-legged on fine rugs around the small brazier set in the center of the tent, and shared small glasses of rose-hip tea, Anya told them, "The younger women will cook on the big fire." She pointed out of the open tent flap to the fire pit in the center of the camp. "You may assist if you wish—they are always glad of hands."

Both Dorcas and Arnia nodded.

"The rules of our camp," Anya went on, "are that all unmarried women must sleep in the tents of their families. As you have no families here, you must sleep in this tent, and for the most part, stay close by. It is not permitted for unmarried women to wander among the men unchaperoned."

Emily glanced at Arnia. "Arnia is married."

Anya inclined her head. "I have observed this. But your husband does not have a tent of his own but is sharing the tent of my son and his guards. Therefore, you" —she looked at Arnia— "will do best to remain with us here, but you may walk and talk with your husband freely."

Arnia bent her head in graceful acceptance.

Emily shifted, and set down her empty tea glass. "I will need to speak with Major Hamilton often while in camp."

Anya narrowed her eyes, looking rather severe. "That is only permissable if he approaches you, and only in the central space in full view."

"But—"

"This is not negotiable." Anya's dark eyes held Emily's. "You are guests among us, and will, of course, respect and follow our ways."

Put like that, Emily could do nothing but incline her head. "As you say."

She had no doubt Watson, Mullins, Jimmy—even Bister and Mooktu—would come to find her if they had any issue to discuss. But Gareth? She was fairly certain he would use the Berbers' ways as an excuse to avoid discussing anything with her.

"Good." Anya patted her hand, and set down her empty glass. "Now, let us see what we can find for you to wear."

Emily, along with Dorcas and Arnia, spent the next hour trying on a selection of clothes the older women found for them. The women who shared Anya's tent had all been married once, and their daughters and daughters-in-law were among the married women in the camp. As the three newcomers' requirements were defined, the older women—the

The Berber style of dress was much better suited to crossing the desert. A lighter, loose robe worn over a simple sheath of a chemise was ideal for wearing beneath the burka. Once the burka was doffed in favor of a *chador*, a head scarf with veil, the skirts and vests were donned over the robes, giving warmth, weight, and color.

The three of them were finally deemed suitably garbed to pass as Berber. Anya approved with a brisk nod. "Good. Now let us join the others outside."

Across the camp, Gareth was lounging on cushions before the brazier in Ali-Jehan's tent while learning the ins and outs of Berber life from his host. The sheik concluded with a philosophical shrug. "I rule the tribe and the caravan, but my mother rules the camp. This is the way of things. So you will not be able to meet with your women privately while with us."

Gareth nodded and drained his glass of refreshing tea. "I foresee no difficulties adhering to your ways." He omitted to mention that none of the three women of his party were "his." If Ali-Jehan and his unmarried men—many of whom had found cause to pause alongside Emily's camel through-out the day, ostensibly inquring after her comfort—had leapt to the conclusion that Emily was, in their terms, "his," he saw no reason to correct their mistake. Safer for her—safer for him, too. She was, after all, in his care.

"Now, come." Ali-Jehan clapped his shoulder and rose. "We should join the others—it's nearly time for the evening meal."

Gareth followed him from the tent. The central area was abuzz, people clustering here and there, chatting and watching the food cooking over the fire pit. Women bustled back and forth, no longer concealed beneath their robes, but most with *chadors* wound about their heads and draped over their faces.

It was a colorful sight, familiar in some ways, yet the pres-ence of the women lent the camp a different air.

"We sit here." Ali-Jehan gestured to an area about one end of the rectangular fire pit. "All the men sit at this end."

Gareth joined him on the colorful rug flung over the sand,

drawing his legs up to sit as the others were, cross-legged. He saw Bister and Mooktu, and Watson and Jimmy, and finally located Mullins scattered among the grouped men. Each was talking animatedly to one or more of their hosts.

"This black snake leader." Ali-Jehan broke off as a woman approached, bearing a tray of flat bread and spiced meat. After helping himself, Ali-Jehan waited for Gareth to do the same, then went on, "You have told me a little of this person." He caught Gareth's gaze. "Tell me more."

As they ate, Gareth obliged. Others of the caravan's guards, the warriors of the tribe, edged closer to listen. Gareth saw no reason not to give them the full tale, from when he and his colleagues had received their orders from the Governor-General, to their last clash with the cultists on the Red Sea.

From the comments and exclamations his story provoked, the Berbers' reaction to the atrocities of the Black Cobra was similar to his, their favored solution—beheading—eerily echoing that of his colleague Rafe Carstairs.

By the time he reached the present, the fire had died down and the wind had risen, sending heavy shadows flickering over the tents. The women had retired earlier, leaving the men to their talk.

When a comfortable silence finally fell, Ali-Jehan slowly nodded. "It is an honorable thing you do—your journey to stop this fiend's reign of terror." He eyed Gareth measuringly, continuing to nod. "We will assist you in this—it is

to pray to Allah that this fiend shows his face, so we can exact the vengeance of the righteous upon him."

The guards rose along with Gareth and his men, entirely at one with that idea.

22nd October, 1822
Very late
In Anya's tent, somewhere in the desert on our way
to Alexandria

Dear Diary,

I am scribbling this by the light of an oil lamp, which I will have to turn down very soon so the ladies and I can sleep. It's strange to lie rolled in sheet and blanket on a rug placed on sand, with the tent sides moving just a little in the wind, but there's been so much of the unusal today that it seems all of a piece.

I have to ride a camel—who stinks!—and while I would rather be on one of their wonderful Arabian horses, I can't complain, as most of the other women and some of the men have no mounts at all and must trudge through the sand. And, as I have discovered to my dismay, sand in the desert gets into everything. And everywhere. Everywhere including places sand was never meant to be. And again that is something I can do very little about—just another something I must endure.

But undoubtedly the most exercising aspect of traveling with our nomads is the absolute separation of men and women. How can I pursue Gareth—how can he pursue me—how can we further explore our mutual attraction—if the only times we can so much as exchange words is in full view of everyone else?

Clearly nomadic courtship follows different rules.

I suspect I will have to learn those rules, if only to work out how to bend them.

E.

Gareth settled to sleep on a rug in Ali-Jehan's tent. As shuffles and snuffles faded, and snores swelled, a gentle symphony played against the whine of the wind, instead of drifting straight to sleep, his mind insisted on wandering . . . over the day, and how matters had played out, and how things looked set to go tomorrow, and in the days to follow.

His mind snagged on a mental image of his last glimpse of Emily, as she'd followed Ali-Jehan's mother into the women's tent, pausing at the flap to cast one last, frustrated glance his way before she'd followed the other women inside and the tent flap had fallen closed behind her.

The separation, enforced as it would be through this leg of the journey, would, he lectured himself, be helpful. Useful. It would give him time to think. To work through things and understand.

As that kiss in Cathcart's salon had proved, he'd somehow fallen under Emily's spell. What he didn't know was why. Why he wanted her. Was it just lust—a more virulent form—that made him feel so drawn to her, so compelled to make her his? Yet given who she was, if he gave in and surrendered, there could only be one outcome. Marriage.

Was that what he wanted—Emily as his wife?

take shape and substance in his mind.

Only to discover that, beyond her, he could see very little of it, his putative future.

He shifted, growing more uneasy as reality impinged. It didn't matter what he thought, what he wanted, if she didn't think and want the same.

Was he the man she wanted as her husband?

Even if he was the husband she wanted now, how genuine and deeply rooted was that want? What drove it? What had given it life?

Had she turned to him in lieu of MacFarlane? His friend had surely been a more romantic figure. Was he in effect standing in a dead man's shoes?

Or was her wanting him more the outcome of being involved in dangerous and violent action? That wouldn't be surprising. He was the only one suitable to whom she could cling. But reaction born of fear and the need it evoked was no proper basis for marriage.

He inwardly scoffed. What did he know of marriage?

The answer whispered across his mind as sleep dragged him down.

He knew no more about marriage than he knew about his future, yet he knew beyond question that unless Emily wanted him for the right reason, he wouldn't have either, couldn't have either—not with her.

The cultists attacked mid-morning the next day.

The caravan was wending its slow and ponderous way along the top of a dune when horsemen rose up in a dark wave from a sand valley just ahead, and came pounding over the dunes, shrieking and yelling, swords cleaving the air.

The nomads reacted with well-trained precision. While the guards wheeled their mounts, then streamed forward to meet the threat head-on, all those with the carts and the camel train grouped and clumped together, both animals and baggage providing protection for those on foot.

From her elevated perch almost at the center of the huddle, Emily had an excellent view of the clash. Squinting into the sun, she saw cultists amid the attacking horsemen, their black scarves streaming as they flew across the sand.

What surprised her were the others—other Berbers. She looked at their defenders—their guards with Gareth and Ali-Jehan in the lead, Mooktu and Bister close behind, all flashing swords and scimitars as they charged—then glanced down and located Anya, sitting with the older women, calmly waiting.

"There are other Berbers with the cultists!"

Anya looked up at her. Thought, then with unimpaired calm, nodded. "The El-Jiri. They are always ready for a fight."

Emily glanced back just as the opposing groups of horsemen met—like two waves crashing and smashing together. She winced at the scream of steel sheering off steel, the crash and pounding of blows, audible even at a distance.

Her heart climbing steadily up her throat, she watched, waited, strained her eyes to see . . .

Gareth broke through, followed closely by Mooktu and Ali-Jehan. All three wheeled, swords swinging, then fell on the attackers' rear.

It was over so fast that Emily, still catching her breath, was left wondering if all battles were so quickly won. She doubted it, but suddenly the body of attackers fractured, splintered and scattered, Berbers in their darker robes breaking off in twos and threes to ride down the dune and head back the way they'd come.

The guards chased them, but only so far. Once the attack-

transparent delight illuminating every male face.

"They were successful, yes?"

Emily looked down at Anya. All the women, surrounded as they were, couldn't see the action. "They're riding back, grinning like small boys."

Anya smiled widely. "They have won, and they are happy. There will be much rejoicing in our camp tonight."

As Anya had foretold, the mood in camp that evening was distinctly festive. While the women prepared the evening meal, the men gathered in a large clump outside Ali-Jehan's tent.

With great cries to his health, they toasted Gareth, then settled to some deep discussion, which he seemed to be leading. As far as Emily could tell from the other side of the camp, he was drawing diagrams in the sand, pointing to this and that, holding his audience in the palm of his hand.

Bister came to check her knives.

She handed them over, then drew him aside and pointed to the male huddle. "What's that all about?"

Bister settled on the edge of a cart to hone the edges of one knife on a whetstone. "None of that lot have seen a real cavalry charge before."

"So?"

"There's differences, see, in how a cavalryman sits, how he holds his sword. They just wade in, shoulders wide, all but asking to be cut down. We go in low, blade extended—makes both offensive and defensive work easier." Bister nodded toward the knot of men. "That's what he's explaining."

Emily looked across the fire pit. "Is that why the fight ended so quickly?"

"Partly." Bister looked up, handed her back her knife, and grinned. "He also told us to go for the cultists—that if we accounted for them, the others would flee. He was right, but Ali-Jehan and the others are a trifle miffed they didn't get more of a fight."

Emily humphed. After a moment, she said, "But there'll be more attacks, and more cultists, won't there?" She met Bister's eyes as he stood. "There were only five with that lot today—there have to be more chasing us."

Bister nodded. "So the major thinks." He tipped his head to the men across the camp. "That's why he's laying it all out for them—how best to attack and what to watch for from the cultists. We haven't seen the last of them, for sure."

The celebrations continued over the meal and on into the night. Emily considered them a trifle overdone. There was, however, no carousing. Cathcart had mentioned there'd be no spirits, beer, or wine carried with the caravan, which, in light of the men's revelry, Emily could only view as to the good. If there had been ale, they would have been drunk, and there were still cultists out there.

Sitting with the older women outside their tent, she eyed the male gathering with a jaundiced eye. She battled not to scowl, or worse, pout.

If there was celebrating to do, she wanted to join in.

That wasn't, however, the nomads' way.

Then Gareth stood. She saw Ali-Jehan say something, to which Gareth replied. When the Berber sheik started to get to his feet, Gareth dropped a hand on his shoulder, clearly telling him to not disturb himself—he, Gareth, would see to it, whatever it was.

Emily tracked Gareth as he beckoned Mullins and Watson, and two of the guards, then led the way out of the circle of tents.

Pickets? Emily hoped so. The notion of more cultists lurking among the dunes wasn't going to make sleeping easy.

Anya arched her brows, but then nodded. "It is permitted, but do not dally, or we will have to send others to find you."

Emily waited for no more, but quickly got to her feet. When Dorcas looked at her inquiringly, she shook her head. "I won't be long."

Wrapping her *chador* over her head and shoulders, as she'd seen other women do around the camp, she walked down the avenue between two tents and stepped into the moonlight beyond.

The night would have been pitch-black if it hadn't been for the large moon, hanging low on the horizon. Emily duly gave thanks as she skirted the tents, hoping . . .

"Where are you off to?"

Gareth stepped out from the gap between two tents as Emily whirled to face him.

"Oh! There you are." She smiled.

He frowned. "You shouldn't be out here—it's not safe."

He'd been in the dark space striding back to the camp's center when he'd sensed . . . something. Movement, perhaps. He'd glanced back, and seen her pass by. The moonlight had played on her pale hair, her fair skin.

She'd drawn him like a beacon; turning on his heel, he'd backtracked.

He halted just beyond the rear of the tent as she backtracked, too, drawing near.

Her eyes searched his face. "I thought you were setting pickets."

"I was."

"Then it's safe enough, surely?"

He felt his lips thin. "Possibly."

She smiled, as if she understood the contradictory impulses clashing within him. *Keep her safe. Ravish her.*

He reminded himself that the honorable tack was to keep her safe from him, too.

She stepped close—close enough that he could sense her alluring warmth. Close enough to lay a small hand on his chest.

He stepped back, back into the shadows between the tents.

She followed, her hand never losing contact. He felt the touch almost as acutely as if it were skin to skin.

"I watched the fight from atop Doha. It was . . ." Eyes darkening, she broke off with an evocative shiver. "Frightening."

"Frightening?" That shiver made him long to sweep her into his arms. He clenched his fists against the impulse.

She nodded. "Swords, scimitars, unarmored bodies. Not a good combination." She lifted her chin, eyes locking on his. "Not when the bodies are people I care about."

He stilled. He told himself not to ask, not to expose his vulnerability. "You care about me?"

She held his gaze steadily. "Yes."

His heart leapt, swelled.

He reached for her as she pressed closer, lifting her face to his.

Effortlessly tempting him to bend his head and cover her lips with his.

In the instant before he did, she brought him back to earth. "Of course."

Of course? Because he was the one standing between her and frightening cultists? Because . . . ?

He decided he didn't need to know. He could think about it later. She was here, with him, and she wanted him to kiss her—wanted to kiss him.

Before he could act, she closed the distance, pressed her soft lips to his. The pressure, light, beguiling, called to him,

Sensation flashed, streaked through him. Passion erupted, powerful, explicit, focused.

She broke from the kiss. Gasped, "I wanted to celebrate with you, but I was trapped on the other side. With the women. I wanted—"

He kissed her again, more ravenously. More rapaciously.

She answered in kind.

And rocked him back on his mental heels.

Desire flared, hot and arcing, achingly potent, burning and sweet.

In Cathcart's salon they'd both stepped back, but this . . . this was fire and life, and everything he wanted.

Everything he needed.

And she wanted it, too.

She couldn't have made her wishes clearer, and with his own need pounding a tattoo in his blood, he couldn't deny what he felt. Didn't want to.

No longer had the power to.

He couldn't step away.

The kiss deepened, not gently, not slowly, but in spiraling leaps. His hands found her breasts, closed, kneaded. Her fingers slid into his hair and she clung, evocatively gripped.

Held him to her, to the kiss. Anchored him within the whirlpool of passion they'd unleashed.

His hands slid over her, learning, needing to know, wanting to possess.

That she was with him was never in doubt. Her lips were as hungry as his, her mouth as demanding. She pressed herself to him, flagrantly imprinting her flesh on his, the giving tautness of her belly impressing itself against his aching erection.

No invitation had ever been so explicit.

Then she made it more so.

She reached between them, and touched, stroked.

He shuddered—and couldn't recall ever shuddering in quite that way at any woman's touch before.

Her touch . . . he craved it. Craved her in a way that shocked even him.

Filling both hands with the lush promise of her bottom, he

lifted her against him, shifted his hips evocatively, provocatively, and sensed her aroused gasp.

Holding her there in one arm, locked helplessly against him, he sank his free hand into her hair, palmed her skull, and kissed her—voraciously.

He tensed to turn, to press her back against something solid . . .

There wasn't anything solid around.

"The night air is fresh and cool, don't you think?"

The words, uttered in Anya's calm voice, hauled them both from the kiss.

Lifting their heads, they stared, first at each other, then out along the gap between the tents, toward the voice.

But there was no one there.

"Perhaps the miss is still walking around the tents—she might be on the the other side."

"Katun," Emily whispered. Licking her lips, swollen she was sure, she looked into Gareth's face. "I have to go."

He nodded.

He set her down, but the reluctance with which his hands released her told its own story—one that gladdened her heart.

She shook out her skirt, resettled her makeshift shawl. Looked up at him, then stretched up and brushed her lips across his. "Until next time."

With that, she stepped out from between the tents, looked, and saw the two older women strolling slowly, their backs to

carefully folding her skirts and blouse before snugging into her blankets.

Marila snorted. "He is courageous—that is more important. You heard the sheik—the major is a great warrior."

Emily could feel Dorcas's and Arnia's gazes, equally intrigued, join the older women's, all trained on her face.

"But men are men, great warriors or not," Katun stated. "They need to have their . . . egos stroked. Frequently."

"It wouldn't surprise me," Anya said, "if after the battle today, in which he and my Ali-Jehan led our men to victory, the major was in need of a degree of stroking. Men, after all, are very predictable in their ways. They crave having their bravery acknowledged."

"Especially by those they seek to protect," Girla put in.

"Especially if those are also ones they seek to impress," Katun stated. After a heartbeat, she added, "With their prowess."

Emily wriggled into her blankets. "I daresay you're right. Good night."

She laid her head down, tugged the blankets over her shoulder, and prayed the dark had hidden her flaming cheeks. Older women, it seemed, were incorrigible the world over. What was rather more interesting was that male behavior seemed equally universal.

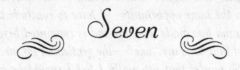

Seven

26th October, 1822
Early afternoon
Anya's tent in our camp at a desert oasis

Dear Diary,

We arrived at the oasis just after noon. There's a clear lake, somewhat larger than I expected. It must be spring fed, and is surrounded by palms and various plants that form a ribbon of greenery around its shore. There are two other caravans, both smaller than ours, also camping here, but there is more than enough lakeshore for all. I gather it is customary to spend a

Berbers easier than I'd thought.
Likewise, it has, apparently, been easier than I'd

expected to make up my mind about Gareth. Given my behavior last night—and I would behave the same given the same opportunity—I have to conclude that my mind has made itself up and is convinced beyond doubt that he is my "one"—the gentleman for me.

No matter that rationally I feel I should be cautious, with respect to him there is nothing of caution in me. After our interlude in Cathcart's salon I felt sure I would need time to consider before taking the next step—that step which, once taken, cannot be undone—but no. As was made transparently clear to me—and to Gareth—last evening between the tents, I am ready and willing to lie with him.

Not that that is something that can occur while we travel with the caravan, but I had thought it would take more than watching him fight in my defense to convince me.

Apparently heart is not necessarily dependent on mind in this matter.

E.

When she emerged from Anya's tent, Emily discovered that most of the men of their party had decamped, leaving only a small number on guard.

She paused beside Arnia and Dorcas, where they sat on rugs helping some of the other women prepare the evening meal. "Where are they?"

She didn't need to specify who "they" were.

Arnia snorted, an eloquent sound. She didn't look up as she replied, "The major sent scouts out. They returned to report there was another band of Berbers, of the same tribe that attacked us yesterday, camped a little way ahead, and they have more cultists with them."

"Naturally," Dorcas said, slicing a cleaned yam into a pottery bowl, "our men were all keen to turn the tables and

122

attack the others before they can attack us." She looked up at Emily. "That's where they've gone."

Emily frowned. "It's almost like a game to them. A chess game, perhaps, but a game nonetheless."

"Our men, their men." Arnia shrugged. "All are warriors. They live to fight."

"That is truth." One of the Berber women nodded sagely. "Any fight is welcome to them, but they are happiest when they fight to defend us." She, too, shrugged philosophically. "What would you? It is their role, so they are pleased to be useful." With a gesture, she encompassed the circle of women happily preparing the meal. "As are we. We are not so different in that."

Emily hadn't thought of the matter in that light. After a moment, she nodded in acknowledgment, and moved on, strolling along the lake's edge to where Anya and the older women— the dowagers—sat on rugs in the shade of a palm grove.

Anya waved her to join them. She sank down onto a rug next to Girla, whose fingers were busy knotting a fringe. Emily sat with her arms around her drawn-up knees. Resting her chin on them, she gazed out over the lake, gently rippling in the faint breeze, and let her mind wander.

After a time, Anya said, both voice and face serene, "If, as we must hope, our men return victorious, there will be celebrations again tonight."

The other women nodded. Katun said, "They will expect it—it is their due, after all."

that they somehow, in some unspecified way, own you.

Her heart may have made up her mind regarding Gareth,

but she hadn't forgotten his dog-in-the-manger behavior over Cathcart, something she'd been reminded of only a few hours before, when they'd arrived at the oasis and Gareth had once again transformed into a bear, dispersing the young Berber men who had gathered around eager to help her from Doha's saddle.

She didn't like being treated in such a patently possessive way.

Katun heaved a huge sigh. "It is the bane all women must bear."

Anya's lips lightly curved. "All women whose men are warriors, at least." The others nodded. Anya's old eyes met Emily's. "It is the price one pays to have a warrior as your mate. He will protect and keep you safe, but in return . . ." Her smile widened. "They are, in truth, such oddly vulnerable creatures, at least where their women are concerned."

"Their woman becomes their one true vulnerability," Girla offered, "so as warriors to the core, of course they guard her most fiercely."

"From anything and everything—real or imagined."

The others laughed and nodded at Katun's bald statement.

"It is truly said," Anya concluded, "that the true value a warrior places on his woman is revealed by the depth of his . . . what is the word?"

"Possessiveness?" Emily suggested.

Anya pulled a face. "I was thinking of protection, but possession? That is true as well, I suppose. It is the other side of the coin, no?"

Emily thought, then nodded. "Yes, you're right. Where one ends and the other begins . . . with warriors, the line is blurred."

On top of a dune some miles from the oasis, Gareth, Ali-Jehan, and Mooktu passed Gareth's spyglass among them as, on their bellies in the sand, they assessed the strength of the band of Berbers and cultists gathered in the dip below.

"There are many more of your cultists than I had expected to see." Frowning, Ali-Jehan lowered the spyglass. "If they had such numbers, why did they not make a better show against us yesterday?"

Gareth had been wondering the same thing. There were significantly more cultists than tribesmen below. He took back the spyglass, again assessed the numbers. "In light of what we're seeing, I suspect yesterday was a feint—a battle they never expected to win, but one to make us feel they pose no real threat. That's why the other Berbers left so abruptly—they were committed only while the cultists were there to see. Once the cultists fell, they didn't need to remain."

"So it was by way of a charade, in the hope we would . . . what is the phrase, let down our guard?"

Gareth nodded.

"There's too many of them," Mooktu murmured. "And those cultists down there—most have the look of assassins."

Gareth had noted the same worrying facts.

Ali-Jehan frowned. "We might be able to take them, yet . . ." He waggled one hand. "With my mother and the other women in the camp" —he looked at Gareth— "and your women as well, I would prefer not to engage this group. I know my cousins the El-Jiri, and they are fierce warriors. If you say those others are also very able, then . . ."

When Ali-Jehan unexpectedly fell silent, Gareth glanced at him. "Can we avoid them?"

Gareth judged, not all that dissimilar in character. With that last in mind, he ventured, "Is there any way we can contact your cousins down there—some way that won't alert the cultists?"

Ali-Jehan looked at him, then looked down at the camp, surveying the outer edges, the horse and camel lines. "Perhaps." He turned back to Gareth. "Why?"

Gareth explained his thinking, his putative strategy. A smile slowly spread across Ali-Jehan's face. At the end, he nodded. "This we will do."

They scrambled back down the dune, then Ali-Jehan picked two men, two of his extended family, and carefully explained what he wanted them to do.

Gareth and Ali-Jehan resumed thir position on the dune, and watched, patient and still, while the two tribesmen successfully carried out their mission.

It was another hour before the leader of the El-Jiri Berbers walked into their midst. He and Ali-Jehan exchanged elaborate greetings at some length, then set formality aside and got down to business.

Gareth was introduced and joined them.

Half an hour later, the El-Jiri leader smiled—a gesture that foretold death for someone. He nodded to Ali-Jehan. "It is good. We will do as you say. I must return to my men and pass the word. You will see when we are ready."

Ali-Jehan smiled a similarly chilling smile. "And then we will rid our lands of these minions of the snake."

Gareth watched the two Berber sheiks take leave of each other, watched the El-Jiri leader stride off through the dunes.

The unrolling of his strategy had gone more smoothly than he'd thought. With luck, the execution would be equally successful.

Emily was standing chatting about the cook-pots when the men, who had been absent for most of the day, rode back into camp—victorious.

There was no need to wonder at the outcome of their day's adventures—the whoops, the prancing horses, the face-splitting grins were declaration enough.

Other Berbers arrived with them, including a leader who Ali-Jehan took to introduce to Anya. Relegated as usual to the company of the women, Emily heard only that the newcomer was the sheik of the El-Jiri.

Puzzled, she exchanged a glance with Arnia, beside her. "Weren't the El-Jiri the Berber tribe who attacked us yesterday?"

Arnia nodded. "It seems they turned against the cultists."

This time, however, there were wounded. Emily went to help tend them. From those she helped care for she gained a better description of what had happened.

Assassins. The word made her blood run cold. She'd heard too many tales of the viciousness of the cult's most hardened followers. As she understood it, there had been more cultists, mostly assassins, than all the Berbers combined, but with Gareth commanding a joint attack—quite how he'd managed to get the two normally bickering Berber tribes to work together she didn't hear—but all together and well directed, they'd triumphed.

Half the cultists had died, and the other half . . . they were the El-Jiri's reward.

When she clearly didn't understand what that meant, the woman whose husband she was helping bandage leaned close and whispered, "The El-Jiri sometimes deal in slaves. A group of men trained to fight? They would be happy to have them to trade."

Emily paused, mentally questioning how she felt about

way they waited upon their men. Their defenders and protectors. She'd heard enough to realize that, the way matters had stood before this afternoon, their caravan had been in grave danger of being attacked and overwhelmed when they attempted to move on.

The action of the afternoon had eradicated that threat. The men had indeed defended and protected them.

She saw Gareth across the fire and was conscious of a flaring desire to go to him, to congratulate him, to smile and fill his cup and offer him the sweetmeats being passed around.

But she and he weren't married.

She wasn't his—so he wasn't hers.

She didn't have the right to share his triumphs, to laud and celebrate, and make much of him, as the other women whose husbands had fought were doing with their men. Even Arnia, she noted, smiled and waited on Mooktu, sitting just behind him, leaning against the back of one broad shoulder as she ate from her own plate.

Emily slowly circled the fire. Her eyes returned to Gareth—and his found her as she paused by Anya's side. He smiled, and she smiled back—honestly, joyously—feeling within her the same emotion that colored the married women's eyes—but then Ali-Jehan asked him something and he turned to answer.

Emily sank to the rug beside and a little behind Anya.

A second later, the older woman reached out and, without turning her head, patted her hand. "They are difficult, our men, but they are worth it in the end."

Her gaze fixed across the fire pit, Emily discovered she agreed.

Three days later, a single cultist, disheveled, dusty, bearing wounds that, untended, had festered, groveled on the flagstones of a small courtyard in a quiet section of old Cairo.

Uncle looked down on the bedraggled head of the man who had just reported the complete and utter defeat of the men he had sent to capture the major. One question burned in his brain. "What of my son?"

The man, forehead to the stones, visibly shook with

fear. "Gone," he managed to gabble. "They're all gone. All fallen."

Uncle knew a moment of sheer madness, of keening devastation, but by sheer force of will he held it all within. "The Arabs we hired turned against us." He still couldn't take that in. In India, no one—*no one*—would dare betray the Black Cobra.

According to all precepts, he should ensure the offending Arabs were suitably dealt with—their children slaughtered, their women debauched and killed, a long slow death for the men. His vengeful soul cried out for that succor—he craved vengeance for his only son—but here, now, he didn't have the time.

And he was running low on men. He had few of the elite he'd left India with left.

Swallowing his fury, his grief, his rage, wasn't easy, but if he didn't satisfy his master, all would be in vain.

He forced himself to swing away from the groveling man, to glare at his acting lieutenant, the one who would now take Muhlal's place at his side. "Make sure—*sure*—that the major and his people are captured the instant the caravan comes in. Put men—"

"No. Uncle . . ."

Uncle swung back to see the man on the flagstones raise his hand in placation. "*What?*"

"The caravan is not headed here. I heard the Arabs talking before we were attacked—the major's caravan heads to

31st October, 1822
Before dinner
Anya's tent in the Berber camp

Dear Diary,

    Tonight will be our last with the Berbers. Tomorrow we will reach Alexandria, and go our separate ways. Entirely contrary to my original expectations, our time with them has not simply been a matter of traversing distance, of moving from one place to another, but a journey laced with interest and discovery.

    I have learned much—from Anya and the dowagers, from observing the Berbers going about their straightforward, more open and less complicated lives. Through that, my appreciation of Gareth has moved onto a new plane. I feel I am now viewing him through better-educated eyes.

    I have also learned more about the important things in life—or rather, what things are important to me. That has led me to reevaluate what I am willing to give ground on in return for what marriage to Gareth will bring. Such a decision is not a simple matter, yet I am looking forward to returning to civilization to see how those traits I have grown more adept at discerning in him in less civilized surrounds will then appear.

    Strangely, and this almost beggars belief, I suspect I will miss my stinky camel. I have grown used to his rolling yet steady gait.

E.

They arrived on the outskirts of Alexandria just before noon the next day. The El-Jiri had taken their captives to some desert meeting place to the south. Gareth hadn't asked too much about their plans.

He had suggested his party separate from the caravan some little distance from the town walls, but Ali-Jehan would have none of it. The caravan halted at their usual grounds, then Ali-Jehan, his mother, and a detachment of the guards, walked with them to the town gate.

There they parted, with much slapping of backs and shaking of hands—and, Gareth noted, embraces among the women. If asked two months before whether the Governor of Bombay's niece could find her feet in a Berber tribe, he would have said no, but he hadn't then met Emily. He was beginning to think very little could seriously discompose her for long; she seemed to possess the happy knack of coping, regardless.

Emily blinked rapidly and as they strode off down the street, looked back one last time to wave to Anya. She was even sorry to see the last of Ali-Jehan. He'd been an excellent companion for Gareth. Then again . . . she glanced at the man striding forcefully a pace ahead of her, his Arab robes swishing about his calves. After their days in the desert, he looked every inch an Arab sheik, and they his retinue, trailing after him.

Consorting with Ali-Jehan had uncovered a more primitive streak, or at least made it more readily detectable. She wondered how long it would take for the patina of civilization to gloss over it again.

ing being caught. If the cultists knew for certain that they'd arrived, they would be systematically hunted—and given that they had no transport onward yet organized, being sighted at all raised the prospect of being cornered before they could get away.

By the time they left the central part of the town behind, Emily's nerves had tightened, stretching taut in a manner she'd forgotten over recent days.

Eyes flicking watchfully from side to side beneath the veil of her *chador*, she discovered something else to miss about traveling with the Berbers. Security. Safety. She'd forgotten what not having them was like.

Accustomed to command, to managing men, Gareth was aware of the rising tension in the group at his heels.

He shared it.

Alexandria was an ancient town. The narrow, twisting streets, with house walls built right to their edges, formed warrens tailor-made for assassins. If assassins were trailing them, by the time any of them saw the danger, it would be too late.

The last days had seen them cross out of the desert into the wide, flat fields of the Nile delta. Low lying, with numerous minor rivers cutting through the landscape carrying the waters of the mighty Nile to the Mediterranean Sea, the delta region was not only easier to traverse but also provided much better cover in which to conceal a caravan. Ali-Jehan had planned to take his people across the main channel of the Nile today, so that they would be well away from the usual places where caravans to Alexandria camped.

Gareth had enjoyed his time with the Berbers, and hoped they would be safe, that no harm would befall them through helping him and his small company.

He glanced briefly to the side, from the corner of his eye confirming that Emily was walking no more than a step behind him. While they'd been with the Berbers, he'd known she was safe. Safe with their women—as safe as she could be. Now . . .

He was once again gripped by a familiar tension, felt responsibility for her safety once again weigh heavily on his shoulders. He didn't resent the burden; not for one minute would he have handed it to another.

What he did resent was that, courtesy of his mission—no, courtesy of the Black Cobra—she, her life and her future, were once again in real danger.

Under real threat.

He wasn't at all happy to be back in civilization.

They found the guesthouse, and were made welcome by Ali-Jehan's cousin and his wife. To Gareth's relief, the guesthouse had no other patrons staying that night. He immediately negotiated to close the house to all others, something Jemal—Ali-Jehan's cousin—was happy to do when Gareth dropped triple his expected takings into his palm.

They were accustomed by now to settling into new accommodation. Mooktu, Bister, and Mullins walked the perimeter and assessed the defenses, while the others efficiently stowed their belongings in the guestrooms they chose, then gathered in the main salon, where, it then being early afternoon, their hosts served them a meal of flat bread, fish, and mussels.

When Jemal placed a large platter of prepared fruit on the table, then bowed himself out, Gareth looked around the table, and decided everyone seated about it deserved to hear all he had to say. All of them, having selected various fruits, seemed to sense his intention, and looked expectantly up the

until we're ready to quit this town, it's vitally important they don't know we're here."

He looked at Mooktu, Bister, and Mullins. "What are our defenses like?"

The other two looked to Mullins.

"Better than we'd hoped. The other houses are built right up to this one at the back and both sides, and the wall at the front is nice and high." Mullins pointed upward. "Best of all, this house is the tallest in the immediate area. From the roof, we can keep watch over all approaches while staying largely out of sight ourselves."

Gareth put a few more questions, but Ali-Jehan had steered them well. The house was a highly defendable abode. "Good. We'll keep a guard on the roof at all times. Aside from all else, it's the most obvious way for them to try to gain access to the house. To us."

Jimmy volunteered to take first watch.

Gareth nodded. "You can go up when we finish here." He glanced around the table. "Our most urgent need is to find transport onward. We need to reach Marseilles, preferably as quickly and as easily as we can."

"Is there anyone here you can approach for help?" Emily asked.

Gareth shook his head. "Not safely. Theoretically the consulate would assist us, but with Ferrar's political clout, it's too risky, and I have no old friends here, no one I can absolutely trust."

No one he would trust with his life, let alone hers.

"As I said," he went on, "we need to be cautious. If that means all the rest of you stay here, indoors and out of sight while Watson, Mooktu, and I spend a few days finding the right ship, then that's the way it will have to be."

He expected arguments, protests at the very least. Instead, after a moment of regarding him, Emily surprised him by nodding. "Very well."

There was little else to say, not until they'd assessed their chances of finding a ship to carry them to Marseilles. He, Watson, and Mooktu resettled their robes, then left the house for the docks.

Emily watched them go, then followed Jimmy up onto the flat roof, but couldn't spot them amid the teeming hordes in the streets.

Anxiety—a feeling that was sufficiently unfamilar it impinged on her awareness—blossomed, spread through her. And gripped.

After a moment of staring across the roofs of Alexandria, she turned away and went downstairs. Finding Dorcas and Arnia, calling Bister and Mullins to join them, she sat at the table and briskly said, "We need to make lists. One, of the items we need for the next few days, and another, of the supplies we should have to see us through to Marseilles." Determined to keep busy, she looked at the others. "Do we have two pieces of paper?"

Gareth, Watson, and Mooktu returned to the guesthouse as evening was closing in.

Emily was waiting in the large front room. She searched their faces. "No luck?"

Gareth shook his head. "Although there are a large number of ships putting out each day for Marseilles, most are booked for months ahead." He sat at the table as she sank into the chair at the other end.

Watson and Mooktu sat as Mullins came to join them. "So what are our options?" Mullins asked.

Dorcas wandered in as Watson replied, "Today we were inquiring about the most direct route, but there are other routes we could take."

Gareth nodded. "My route specifically directs us through Marseilles."

135

Watson grimaced. "That reduces our options, but still—we could go via numerous routes around or over the Mediterranean."

"But, for example, a route north along the coast and then east via Turkey, Greece, and Italy to France would surely take much longer." Emily glanced at Gareth. "Do we have the time to amble?"

He met her gaze, shook his head. "It's taken us longer to get here than Wolverstone anticipated. He wants me—us—in England by mid-December."

Emily blinked. "Today's the first of November."

"Exactly. So allowing for the necessary days to cross France . . . we need to reach Marseilles as soon as possible."

"In that case," Watson said, "we'll have to travel by ship all the way." He glanced at the others. "Travel by sea is significantly faster than travel by land. On one of the more direct routes, a fast ship could make the run to Marseilles in anything from nine to fifteen days."

"But we can't find passage on one of those," Mooktu rumbled. He looked at Gareth. "And we don't have time to wait here until berths become available."

Gareth humphed. "Sitting here just waiting for the cultists to stumble over us is not an option in any case."

"So we take our next best option." Emily turned to Watson. "Whatever that is."

Watson frowned. "I would say . . . either via Italy, then Corsica, to Marseilles, or, possibly, west to Tunis, and then north to Marseilles." He looked at Gareth. "I know the distances, but sailing times are harder to guess. We'll need to ask around, then see what ships might be heading that way with space enough to take us."

Gareth nodded. "Tomorrow. We'll go down to the docks at first light. It's less crowded then."

"I have been thinking," Mooktu said, "that if the cultists sent to watch us here have not yet been warned that we are going in disguise, then they are less likely to spot us."

"True. So we'll need to remember to always go disguised."

Gareth glanced around the table. "It would be preferable to stay in our Arab clothes even in here."

Emily was perfectly happy to do so; her Arab clothes were less confining and in this climate certainly more comfortable than gown and petticoats. She'd tried to hand back the garments the Berber women had loaned her, but they'd waved their hands and told her to keep them and use them while she was in Arab lands.

She caught Gareth's gaze. "We'll need to go to the souk tomorrow. We'll do that while you're at the docks. We'll take Mullins and Bister, and be extra careful, but it won't hurt to take a look around."

He didn't like it—she could see that in his eyes—but eventually he inclined his head. "No, it won't."

Eight

2nd November, 1822
Early morning
My room in the guesthouse at Alexandria

Dear Diary,

Something has altered between me and Gareth, al-though I cannot put my finger on exactly what. There is a greater sense of shared endeavor, as if he now ac-cepts that I can contribute in real ways to our survival. The timing suggests that our sojourn with the Berbers is responsible for his altered attitude, but why spending time, largely separated, in a less-civilized society that only exacerbated his protective and possessive streaks should result in a more inclusive attitude is a mystery. However, we are once again under such threat of being discovered by cultists sent to await our arrival and cut off our heads that it is difficult to find time, or space in my mind, to dwell on such personal questions.

Today I must lead an expedition to the souk to replenish necessary supplies, while Gareth searches for

*passage onward. The tension is palpable. He hasn't
yet stated it, but I can see he is concerned for us all—
and perhaps most especially for me . . .*

*Despite the exigencies of our situation, there are
moments such as this when I realize in which direction the changes between us are steering us.*

More anon.

E.

he souk in Alexandria was set well back from the
harbor, tucked inside the old city wall. There was a
central covered marketplace, with alley after alley
of stalls, most selling fresh produce or clothing. Narrow,
cramped, and winding streets gave off the marketplace,
tentacles leading deeper into a labyrinth of tiny shops and
clustered workshops. There was a goldsmiths' alley, and
a basketweavers' alley, and lanes for clothing, metalware,
glassware and every conceivable commodity.

Feeling entirely comfortable in her Berber clothes beneath her enveloping burka, Emily led their party through
the marketplace, finding the items they required, then haggling in French—something at which she'd grown increasingly proficient through the journey.

It didn't take long to gather all they required for the next
few days. Buying supplies for their journey onward would
have to wait until they knew when they would be leaving,

shoppers thronging the narrow space.

Emily's heart leapt, then thumped. Hard. Instinctively she halted. Luckily an Arab man crossed in front of her, temporarily blocking her and the rest of their party behind her from the cultists' view—giving her time to realize that stopping and staring would be very unwise.

When the Arab shifted, then turned and moved away, Emily dragged breath into her suddenly tight lungs and, head high beneath her burka, continued on, idly strolling onward as if she had not a care in the world—praying the others followed her cue and did the same.

The cultists saw them—they couldn't very well miss them—but their gazes passed over them without a flicker of interest, much less recognition.

Greatly daring, Emily continued on and passed by both cultists. Stepping into the marketplace proper, she walked on until the crowds between her and the alley grew thick enough to risk halting and, while pretending to look at some fabric, cast a sideways glance back.

Dorcas and Arnia had followed at her heels. Bister and Mullins were nowhere to be seen.

Dorcas leaned close to whisper, "Bister and Mullins slipped into a shop. Their faces . . ."

Emily nodded. Although all their men's faces were now deeply tanned, their features were still too European to flaunt.

Arnia pressed close on Emily's other side. "If we stay here, they'll catch us up."

Watching the cultists still hovering in the mouth of the alley but now surveying the marketplace, Emily nodded again.

A moment later, the cultists moved on. Unhurriedly. Still looking and searching.

Emily breathed easier. She, Dorcas, and Arnia wandered back up the aisle toward the basketweavers' alley. As they neared, Bister and Mullins emerged from the crowded alley and fell in with them again.

"Let's get back to the guesthouse," Mullins growled.

Emily nodded. "Yes. We'll go now."

They made it back to the guesthouse without further incident. Once there, once she could throw off the burka and think and pace, Emily's imagination came unhelpfully alive.

The cultists hadn't recognized her, but why would they? Covered by the burka, there was nothing of her to see. But Gareth . . . he was taller than most Arabs. Tall, and broad-shouldered. Even in England, in a crowd he would stand out. And while he'd adopted the Berber style of head-dress, covering his neatly cut hair, if the cultists got a look at his eyes, at his cheekbones above his lean, sculpted cheeks, let alone his chin, they couldn't fail to recognize him as an Englishman.

Arms crossed, she was pacing back and forth in the front room, telling herself she shouldn't panic until dark fell and they were still not back, when the rattle of the gate latch stopped her in her tracks.

The gate swung inward—and Gareth stepped through, followed by Watson and Mooktu.

She had never been so relieved to see anyone in her life.

She was halfway across the courtyard to meet him before she realized.

The almost relaxed expression—the smile that had been in his eyes—slid away as he searched her face. "What happened?"

The words were rapped out, and then he was there. Fingers closing about her elbow, he turned her and urged her

He blinked, shook his head to clear the visions. She was here, with him, and patently unharmed.

141

Watson and Mooktu slipped past them, heading deeper into the room. Mooktu continued on, no doubt to find Arnia.

Emily looked into Gareth's face. "I was so worried they'd see you—you're much more recognizable than we are." Turning, she walked into the room.

Releasing her, he followed more slowly.

"We were in our burkas, and Mullins and Bister were behind us, so had time to hide before the cultists could get a good look at them." She turned to face him. The worry and utter relief he'd seen blazoned in her face earlier had faded. She seemed happy, quite cheery, now.

She studied his face, then tilted her head. "But you're back early. Does that mean—"

She broke off. They both turned to the gate as it opened again. This time it was Bister, even more heavily disguised than usual with scarves swathing his head and face, who strolled in.

He closed the gate, then, all nonchalance falling away, came striding quickly to them.

He nodded to Emily, then reported to Gareth. "After we got the ladies back here, I thought I'd take a quick gander to see if I could follow those damned cultists back to their nest. I didn't find those two again, but two others, also wandering the streets, keeping an eye out, true enough, but not searching like they knew who they were searching for."

"Did you find their base?" Gareth asked.

"Yes, and you're not going to like it. They're in a house opposite the consulate, strolling in and out as calm as you please. Bad enough, but while I was watching, a party rode in. A group of assassins, but in the lead was an older, bearded man. Point is, I think I saw him on the docks at Aden."

Gareth's face felt like stone. "Tall, slightly stooped, black beard, definitely older?"

Grimly, Bister nodded. "That's him."

Damn! They had one of the cult's upper echelon on their heels.

Emily was looking from his face to Bister's. From her increasingly sober expression, she understood the implications. "I was going to ask," she said, "whether your returning early meant you'd found a ship to take us to Marseilles?"

"Not quite." He met her eyes. "Watson asked around. Seems our best chance of avoiding the cultists and reaching Marseilles in reasonable time is to go west along the coast. We found a merchant with a xebec and space for us all heading that way, but he isn't ready to leave yet."

He glanced at Bister, then at all the others who had come into the room to hear the news. "One of the cult members who was in Aden when we arrived there has just arrived here. From now on, we need to assume the cultists are specifically searching for us, that they know the composition of our party—how many men, how many women, approximate ages, and so on." He paused, then walked to the table and halted at its end. He looked around at the faces, all familiar now. "Alexandria" —with a wave he indicated the area around them— "this quarter in particular—is not a good place to get caught in. Trapped in. Although this house is defendable, if the cult learns we're here, they'll be able to hem us in and keep us here."

Until they wear us down.

Until they pick off enough of us to overrun the house.

And then . . .

three days from today."

3rd November, 1822
Early morning
Tucked away in my room in the guesthouse
in Alexandria

Dear Diary,

I am starting to suspect Gareth has a natural tendency to gravitate to persons who appreciate a good fight. He mentioned last night that the captain of the xebec on which we will sail to Tunis expressed disappointment that the cultists—Gareth having felt it necessary to mention their possible interference—were unlikely to engage with us on this leg of our journey.

Huh! For myself, I will be inexpressibly grateful for a respite from the cult's persistent hounding. Gareth and Watson feel certain that they—the cult—will be expecting us to take the customary diplomatic route through Athens and then overland, and that by the time they realize we've gone west along the coast of Africa, and then reorganize to follow, we'll be too far ahead for them to catch. A xebec, Gareth tells me, is a fast ship, and once on it and clear of Alexandria, we are unlikely to be caught.

All of this, of course, is contingent on the cult not locating us in our bolt-hole here. They will, presumably, now know that we are going about disguised, but there are rather a lot of people in Arab clothing in Alexandria.

We shall see, but the number of times I have written the word "unlikely" above does not, to my mind, bode well.

E.

144

The next day, Emily, Dorcas, and Arnia, guarded by Mullins, Bister, and Mooktu, went to the souk for the supplies they would need on their journey to Tunis. Given they'd seen the cultists in the souk the day before, they felt it was better—potentially safer—to go that day rather than the next.

They accomplished their mission without sighting any cultists, and returned through the crowds thronging the midday streets.

They were just yards from the guesthouse when Dorcas, stepping around a hole in the road, collided with an Arab man going in the opposite direction.

"Oh! I'm sorry." Luckily both kept their feet. Regaining her balance, bobbing her burka-covered head apologetically at the man, Dorcas hurried to catch up with Emily.

Who, alerted by the words, halted and turned.

In time to see the man whirl, stare, then snarl and lunge for Dorcas.

Emily grabbed Dorcas and yanked her away from the man—a cultist! She could see the black head scarf beneath the hood of the Arab-style cloak he wore.

She also saw the knife in his hand, saw the blood—Dorcas's blood—staining it. Saw him change his grip and draw back his arm. "Mooktu!"

The big Pashtun was already there. He closed with the man—just as two more robe-draped cultists materialized out of the crowd.

Arnia appeared by Emily's shoulder. "Go! Take her inside.

They were almost at the gate when it was wrenched open. Gareth raced out, followed by Jimmy and Watson.

Gareth saw her, paused to grasp her arm.

"We're all right." Emily tipped her head at the knot of wrestling bodies. "Three cultists, at least."

Gareth nodded and went, the other two at his back.

Emily bundled Dorcas into the house, then sat her at the table in the front room.

And saw Gareth's sword lying on the tabletop.

"Stay there," she ordered Dorcas. "I'll be back."

Swiping up the sword, feeling the weight drag but determined to use it if need be, she hurried back to the gate.

Before she reached it, Arnia opened it and came quickly in, followed by Watson and Jimmy, carrying, amazingly, the supplies the other men had dropped.

Bister followed a moment later with the last bag.

He saw Emily, saw the sword in her hand. "Here—you take this and give me that." When she opened her mouth to argue, he added, "He won't want you out there, not now."

She could see the sense in that. She took the bag and handed him the sword. "What's happening?"

Bister met her eyes, hesitated, then said, "The three of them are dead. We have to do a cleanup, quick, before any of their friends come looking for them." He hefted the sword. "I'll take this just in case." With a nod, he turned and went, closing the gate after him.

Emily stared at the gate for a moment, then turned and briskly waved the others on. "Let's get inside, and get things sorted."

That's all she could do—keep on keeping on, and get the things done that needed to be done.

Gareth returned half an hour later to find Emily ministering to a very shaken, almost hysterical Dorcas.

The maid, her complexion pasty white, was seated at the table, with Emily crouched beside her, carefully dressing a long gash on the back of Dorcas's forearm.

Entering quietly, Gareth heard Emily soothingly murmur, "Truly—you'll see. It'll be perfectly all right. It was just a piece of sheer bad luck that the man who bumped into you was one of the cultists—if he hadn't been, your slip of the tongue wouldn't have meant anything. It's hardly your fault he wasn't paying attention and ran into you."

They heard his footsteps. Both turned. Emily stared up at him. "Is it all right?"

She might have been doing her best to soothe her maid, but her eyes were wide, with a species of shock in the mossy depths.

Gareth let himself down into the chair at the head of the table. "They're dead—they won't be reporting to anyone that we're here." Looking at her, knowing how close they'd come to disaster, the best he could do by way of reassurance was to explain, "We found a covered channel not far away. We hid the bodies there. Mooktu, Bister, and Mullins are scouting around, keeping an eye on things. They'll be in as soon as it gets dark."

Emily gazed at him for a moment, then, smile brightening, she turned back to Dorcas and briskly patted her arm. "See? It's all taken care of."

4th November, 1822
Before dinner
My room in the guesthouse

Dear Diary,

.... the tension that rides

signs of cultists ....
has been no alarm, but they have seen far too many

147

cultists slipping through the crowds to allow any of us to relax.

In such a fraught atmosphere, further exploring the evolving connection between Gareth and myself has been impossible. I haven't asked, but I hope a xebec is a reasonable-sized craft, one that will afford us a modicum of privacy in which to further our as yet un-declared courtship.

Until we are free of Alexandria, there is nothing I can do but wait.

E.

They left the guesthouse at dawn, and quietly made their way through silent streets to the docks. Mullins had had the bright idea to exchange their trunks—solid English trunks—for simple wooden ones, also solid but clearly Arabian, that Jemal had lying in his storeroom. They'd all seen the value in that, and had subsequently worked diligently to eradicate any hint of the English, even of the European, from their collective appearance. The party that arrived that morning at the docks, already bustling with ships preparing to leave on the morning tide, was utterly indistinguishable from the many others waiting to board.

Gareth, head swathed in the typical head scarf, which, happily, largely obscured his features, led them down the docks with a long-legged, unhurried stride. His attitude conveyed the impression that he owned a small Arab kingdom somewhere.

The rest of them followed in their customary order. When Gareth paused at the foot of a gangplank, looked up at the ship, then hailed the captain by name, Emily turned her head quickly, took in the vessel—and only just managed to stifle her groan.

A xebec was smaller than a schooner.

And piled with goods.

Where the devil were they all going to fit?

The question continued to resound in her head as the captain formally welcomed Gareth aboard, then beckoned the rest of them up onto the deck.

There, Emily's frustrated suppositions were confirmed. The three burka-enveloped women were quickly conducted belowdecks—to a single cabin in the stern, with three hammocks strung in the small space.

Their luggage followed them in short order. Once that was set on the floor, leaving them just room enough to walk from door to hammock to small porthole, and the door had shut, Emily fought her way free of her burka, and, with unrestricted vision, looked around again. But . . . "There's not even anywhere to sit!"

Men! The word, loaded with fulminating frustration, echoed in her head. Dorcas frowned, Arnia muttered. Emily didn't even have room enough to pace.

The ship rocked. Emily caught hold of the door frame, then, realizing the vessel was definitely putting out, used the hammocks for balance to cross to the porthole. Peering out, she saw the docks receding—quickly. "At least this thing seems to go quite fast."

She, Dorcas and Arnia were under strict orders to remain belowdecks to reduce the chance of their party being recognized by the cultists certain to be watching from the twin headlands of the large harbor.

. . . . gained clearer water further out in the bay,

. . . . itively leapt

view of . . . . .
free of the harbor's mouth.

She had an excellent view of the cultists on each point.

A perfectly clear view of the spyglass one was holding, trained on the xebec's deck.

She saw that cultist turn and say something to another. Saw the second cultist grab the spyglass and look through, then nod excitedly. After one more look, both turned and ran . . . she couldn't see where.

But she'd swear they'd been smiling.

Once the headlands faded into the early-morning sea mist, she quit the cabin and made her way onto the deck.

She found Gareth leaning on the railing to one side. She leaned beside him. "Did you see them on the headland?"

He nodded, glanced at her, met her eyes. "It wasn't possible for us all to get below. With the added weight, some of us needed to help the sailors."

She looked out across the waves, toward where, a long way ahead, she imagined Europe lay. "I can't be sure, but I think they saw us."

After a moment, he lifted a hand, placed it over hers on the rail. Gently squeezed. "They did—I think we must assume that. But they didn't see which direction we took. The captain stayed on an uninformative course until we were out of sight."

Emily stayed where she was, digesting that information and its implications. Absorbing the warmth of his large hand covering hers. "So they'll know we left, and that we're on some xebec, but, with any luck, they'll search for us—"

"In every direction but the one in which we're going."

She nodded, reassured, but stayed where she was, content enough in that moment.

In the house opposite the British consulate, Uncle paced incessantly. "This is unacceptable! We are hunting these people—how is it then that three more of your number have disappeared?" His tone demanded an answer, an answer the cowed men abased before him could not give. "Have they deserted our cause? No! How could that be when they know the vengeance the Black Cobra will take? How our revered leader will strike, and maim, and torture until they scream—"

He broke off as his new lieutenant, Akbar, came striding in.

Akbar made obeisance, then straightened and reported, "They were seen—the major and his party—on a fast vessel leaving the harbor an hour ago."

Uncle was silent. Silent for so long those abased before him started trembling even more than when he'd been berating them. The silence stretched as Uncle hauled his formidable temper back under control. Finally he drew breath, and, fighting not to grind his teeth, quietly asked, "And where is this vessel sailing to?"

Akbar's lashes flickered. "The men do not know. It wasn't possible to tell which heading they took before the sea mist swallowed them."

Uncle drew in an even longer, tighter breath. Slowly exhaling, he said, "I suggest you set inquiries in train. There are only so many ships that can have left this morning. Ask until you learn where that one was heading."

Akbar bowed low, then turned and left.

Uncle looked down at the trembling men at his feet. "Get out."

They tripped over themselves obeying.

Alone in the room, Uncle slowly wandered. Akbar was

He would do whatever was needed to extract the

." Uncle mut-

Nine

6th November, 1822
Before dinner
The cramped shared stern cabin on the xebec,
somewhere in the Mediterranean, heading for Tunis

Dear Diary,

Contrary to my hopes, a xebec is a ship designed for trade, not for passengers. There is no privacy anywhere. Indeed, we women are lucky to have a cabin to ourselves. The men of our party are sharing with the crew.

It is impossible to have a private conversation anywhere, let alone indulge in non-verbal communication. Add to that that there is nothing to see and less to do, and it is no wonder Dorcas, Arnia, and I are already bored beyond bearing. The men, on the other hand, appear to be merging with the crew—I even saw Watson getting sailing lessons. Gareth and the captain get on well. Exceptionally well. With Gareth striding about in a combination of robes and cavalry breeches and boots, his sword at his side, he, like the captain, looks like a buccaneer.

Watching him striding about the deck is one of the few distractions available to me.

E.

10th November, 1822
Before dinner
On the xebec, in the tiny cabin

Dear Diary,

I have nothing to report. We have been sailing along at a rapid clip for the last five days without incident of any kind. Gareth's ploy to lose the cultists in our escape from Alexandria appears to have succeeded—we have remained unmolested, even at night. There seems little reason to fear further attack, at least not on this leg of our journey. Gareth still posts pickets, and Bister and Jimmy spend a good portion of each day up on the main mast, but we have all largely relaxed our vigilance. The absence of the tension to which we've grown accustomed is now every bit as noticeable as the tension itself was.

This should be a perfect opportunity for Gareth and myself to further explore the potential connection between

credit that we have not had a chance to

Nowhere to go, nothing to do.

E.

153

11th November, 1822
Before dinner
Still on the blasted xebec

Dear Diary,

The captain must have heard my griping. Either that, or Gareth mentioned my threat to leap overboard if we are served fish for one more night. He—the captain—has in the last few minutes very cordially informed me that we are to make landfall—a halt for a whole day!—in Malta tomorrow. The ship must take on drinking water, and he hopes to trade some of the salt he is carrying. My spontaneous and heartfelt response was "Thank Heaven!" at which Captain Laboule grinned. Although he is a mussulman, it appears my words are nevertheless acceptable gratitude for divine intervention.

But to have a whole day ashore! I am both relieved and filled with anticipation. Surely, Gareth and I will be able to find a suitable place, and sufficient time, to advance our mutual understanding.

It strikes me that in exploring and mapping out our way forward together, we are undertaking another journey, one running parallel and superimposed upon our more physical journey to England.

I look forward to tomorrow in hope and expectation.

E.

Although founded by the Knights of Malta centuries before, Valletta was currently under British rule, a fact Gareth hadn't forgotten and took pains to impress on the other members of his party.

Standing by the railing as the xebec slid smoothly through

the waters of the Grand Harbor, the early morning sun glinting off ripples as the craft approached the quays lining the waterfront beneath the lowest bastions of the spectacularly fortified city, he glanced at the others flanking him. As per his orders, they were all in Arab dress. "We should avoid the area around the Governor's Palace. We'll almost certainly see plenty of soldiers in the streets, but they pose little threat—Ferrar's influence is diplomatic, not military."

"But we'll need to keep our eyes peeled for cultists," Mullins said.

Gareth nodded. "There will without doubt be cultists here, keeping watch, but it's unlikely they'll have yet been warned to look specifically for us—for a party of our size and composition—or that we might be disguised. As long as we do nothing to attract their attention, we should be able to slide beneath their notice."

Dorcas resettled her burka. "At least here we won't need to worry that speaking English might alert them."

"Perhaps not," Emily replied, "but it will probably be wise to wherever possible pretend to be Arab."

Gareth was grateful she'd made the point. Then the xebec bumped against the stone quay, and they turned to where the gangplank would be pushed out.

The instant it was, they went down to the stone wharf, then in a group walked along beside the bastion wall to the street Captain Laboule had pointed out as the most direct route to ~~~~~~~~~ district. As they climbed the paved street, ~~~~~~~~~~~~~ of churches and

He was somewhat surprised by how ~~~~ that conclusion evoked.

For once, they didn't need to gather supplies but could indulge themselves as they wished. When they passed a cross street reeking of spices and lined with intriguing shops, Arnia declared she wanted to see what manner of herbs and condiments was available. With a nod to Gareth, Mooktu and Mullins went with her. They'd agreed to meet back at the xebec by three o'clock, in good time to make the late-afternoon tide.

"I want to see the cathedral first." Emily glanced at Gareth as she walked alongside him. "Laboule said there are many fine buildings we can view, and a number of museums."

Gareth nodded in ready acquiescence. Much of the history of Valletta lay in the historic palaces the Knights of Malta had left behind, and from childhood he'd been intrigued by the soldier-crusader order.

Dorcas and Watson ambled at their heels. Bister, in need of more active amusement, took Jimmy under his wing and set off to find it.

They spent the day in churches and palaces. The latter were sufficiently magnificent to hold even Gareth's attention. Architecture, design, embellishment, and furnishings were so fabulously splendid they were every bit as awe-inspiring as the fortifications.

Despite her firm intention to make good use of the day, Emily was diverted, distracted by the sumptuous beauty of so much they found, as, eyes wide, they wandered the town.

They stopped at a quiet tavern for lunch. In order to eat, Emily and Dorcas would have to remove their burkas. As they'd detected no cultists, they all agreed the disguises were perhaps unnecessary.

"Valletta is merely a staging post—a stopover on the way to somewhere else," Gareth said. "Ferrar would know there's no point leaving any great force here—at the most we would spend only a day. Better simply to leave a man or two on watch, and have them report any sighting of us or the others, perhaps by diplomatic courier."

Emily looked at him through the panel of her burka. "If

you were going to leave someone to watch this place, where would you station them?"

"One of the forts. Most command excellent views of the harbor and the quays, but there are enough of them to make our locating and removing said watchers virtually impossible."

Emily nodded. She and Dorcas removed the heavy burkas, folding them into shawls, revealing their English gowns beneath, thus instantly becoming one with the many Englishwomen in the town.

They spent the rest of their lunchtime comparing sights and exclaiming over all they'd seen. It was only when they were leaving the tavern, she and Gareth in the lead, Dorcas and Watson chatting behind them, that Emily remembered her aim for the day.

She had a bare two hours left to accomplish it.

The next palace they entered was much like those before. Leaving Dorcas and Watson studying a coat of arms over a fireplace, she walked out into the corridor, then turned into the next salon, trusting to Gareth's protective instincts to ensure he followed her.

He did, but hung back, keeping distance between them. Halting before the windows, she looked back—mentally tapped her toe.

Hands clasped behind his back, he ambled slowly down the room, studying a long row of ceremonial swords dis-
_____ __ _he wall. Determined, increasingly aware of the

down the long room and into a small gallery _ _ _
she glanced back, waiting and willing Gareth to join her.

157

He walked, slowly, in her wake, making a show of studying the plate and crystal. Impatient, she waited. Gareth reached the threshold of the gallery, looked at her waiting, then turned and considered Dorcas and Watson, still only halfway up the huge room.

When he didn't turn back, didn't seize the moment to join her, Emily frowned. "Gareth." She pitched her voice just above a whisper. "There are . . . matters we need to address."

He turned his head. Across the gallery, he met her eyes. "This is not a suitable time or place."

She pressed her lips together, but couldn't disagree. "So when and where *will be* suitable for our particular discussion?"

"I don't know." His voice was even but, like hers, pitched low. After a moment, he said, "That subject might have to wait until England to be properly addressed."

"*England?*" She stared at him, swiftly estimated. "It might be another month before we reach there."

He nodded, but turned before she could respond. Stepping back, he let Dorcas precede him into the gallery.

Forcing Emily to spin on her heel and, with feigned brightness, lead the way on.

Another month?

Another month with no advance, no firmer definition, no further exploration of what lay between them?

"No," she muttered beneath her breath. "No, and no." On that score, he would need to think again.

Of course, now that he knew her aim, he would take evasive action. Nothing she could do—no place she could find in this palace—would be useful in cornering him, not with Dorcas and Watson dogging their steps, providing him with the perfect excuse to avoid any *tête à tête*.

Allowing him to believe she'd accepted defeat, accepted his decree, she calmly led the way out of the palace. On the pavement, she looked down toward the harbor—and spied the green of trees and lawns clumped on a level between their present height and the quays above the waterline.

Scanning the buildings ahead, she located what she needed. Another palace of another group of knights. Perfect.

She glanced at Dorcas. "Look—gardens." She pointed to the massed greenery below. The other three looked. Knowing Dorcas's weakness was for strolling and viewing scenery rather than buildings and museums, Emily smiled at her maid. "Why don't you and Watson head down there? I want to look through just one more palace." Halting beside the sign for the next "auberge," she met Gareth's eyes. "This one will do."

Watson and Dorcas were happy to go ahead.

"We'll wait for you there." With a nod to them both, Watson set off, Dorcas beside him, one arm looped in his, her other hand clutching her burka-shawl about her shoulders.

Once they were out of earshot, Emily glanced at Gareth. "Come along." Turning, she marched up the palace steps.

Gareth watched her go, hips swaying beneath her English skirts, inwardly sighed, then followed.

He knew what she wanted to "address," but that was one topic he wanted to avoid—a subject he'd spent far too many recent hours obsessing over. But his conclusion—the real and unpalatable, but inescapable conclusion—wasn't one he, or any man alive, would willingly discuss. Just the thought of putting his thoughts into words made him inwardly shudder.

Which meant that, for both their sakes, he had to let her

but he had to win—had to ensure she won no

He knew what he knew. There was no future in becoming aroused over her.

Emily set her lips, set her chin—and inwardly swore she wouldn't be denied. She didn't know why he was so intent on avoiding snatching a moment now—out of sight of the rest of their party and of any cultists—but she wasn't about to let him win. This, she inwardly declared, was a matter of principle.

A matter of need and want and desire.

And not just hers.

Leading the way back down to the ground floor, she swung into another wing of reception rooms. The first salon showed little promise, so she quickly walked back into the corridor and on to the next.

There, she struck gold.

A door on one side wall was placed close to the junction with the outer wall. Opening the door, she went through— and found herself in a narrow corridor connecting with the next room along. The door at the other end of the corridor was shut. Smiling to herself, she went forward, then halted and stood looking out of the lead-paned windows to the harbor far below.

Gareth hesitated in the doorway.

Without looking his way, she pointed out and down. "There's our ship."

After an instant's pause in which she could almost hear his resigned sigh, he stepped over the threshold, closed the door, then came to join her.

"See?" she said, as he paused beside her. Once she was sure he was following her gaze to the line of ships below, she went on, "That's the tiny vessel we'll be returning to in less than an hour, to spend the next several days cooped up with a score of others, unable to exchange so much as a private word."

Turning to him, she studied his profile, all she could see of his face. "Given what we've already exchanged, what has already passed between us, any other gentleman would be gladly seizing the opportunity" —just so he didn't miss the point, she flung out her arms— "*this* opportunity, to at the very least kiss me again."

He glanced sideways at her, then half turned so she could see more of his face.

She narrowed her eyes on his. "So why aren't you? *Why* are you suddenly avoiding me?"

Saying the words made them real. She'd known that's what he was doing, but hadn't—until that moment—allowed those words to form in her mind. They were too damning— and no young lady with any claim to modesty would ever voice such words aloud . . . . she wasn't a great believer in self-sacrificing modesty.

So she glared, folded her arms—refused to acknowledge the prick of the words, the sharp yet hollowing hurt—and waited.

Waited.

"I'm giving you time to come to your senses."

She blinked. "What?"

"You need to realize what this—our attraction—is about. What it springs from. What drives it."

She frowned. "I know what—"

"No. You don't."

She studied him through narrowing eyes, registering his rigid conviction. Slowly she raised her brows. "Indeed? So why don't you enlighten me?"

He'd walked into that one. Gareth gritted his teeth, kept locked with hers . . . . as the seconds ticked by and

"Regardless of what you imagine what's happe

us means, that, in reality, is all it means. It's an outcome of having survived a brush with death."

Her frown had evaporated into an expression of stunned blankness. Her gaze distant, her voice, too, seemed to come from far away. "That's not—"

"What you think, but *that* is what it is."

She stared at him wide-eyed, her face devoid of expression, her jaw a trifle slack, then she said, "You have no idea what I think. No idea why I feel what I do."

"What you *think* you feel has nothing to do with it. I *know* what this is—know why you want me to kiss you again—and therefore I know, unquestionably, that honor dictates that as a gentleman, as the one more experienced, I should refuse and keep a proper distance."

Enough of explanations. He swung into the attack. "You should be thanking me for not accepting your invitation to further dalliance." He made his tone resolute, even dictatorial. "Most men in my position would take advantage, but you deserve better."

Her eyes narrowed again, her gaze focusing more intently on him. "So . . . you're saying I'm suffering from . . . what? Some form of danger-induced delusional desire from which you need to save me?"

He hestitated, then nodded. "Yes. That's all this is."

"You need to save me from myself." Emily dragged in a shaky breath. "And you know this because . . . ?"

"Because I'm a great deal more experienced than you."

"I se-ee." Her temper erupted and made her voice quaver. Her eyes as narrow as they could get, she pinned him. Rage of a kind she'd never before felt pouring hotly through her veins, she opened her mouth—and discovered she couldn't get a word out.

She drew breath, held it, tried again to speak, but fury clogged her throat.

You have not the faintest idea what you're talking about!

"*Arrgh!*" Flinging up her hands, she swung around,

stalked to the door at the end of the corridor, hauled it open, and swept out.

So much for finding a suitable place. So much for arranging a suitable time.

So much for developing a relationship with him—he didn't even believe she genuinely wanted one!

Aggravated phrases, irritated declarations—all the things she'd love to say, to heap on his head if only she could speak, if only she could trust herself to berate him without furious tears strangling her voice—rang in her head as without pause she stalked straight out of the palace and on down the street.

Her expression must have been all suppressed fury; after one glance, everyone moved out of her way. She didn't look back to see if Gareth was following, but she heard footfalls behind her, and knew it was him.

She reached the gate in the railing enclosing the park. Pausing, she glanced back, at his face, scorched him with a look full of fulminating fury, then she swung around, summoned a relaxed expression and plastered it on her face, settled her burka-shawl about her shoulders and, head rising, walked forward to find Dorcas and Watson and return to the xebec.

12th November, 1822
Late

thinks—I am reduced to quivering rage. Hou

*What the devil does he mean by telling me what I feel
and why? Bad enough—but how dare he be so wrong!!*

*I am literally beside myself—I never knew what
that phrase meant before today. His temerity clearly
knows no bounds!*

*Mind you, there were a few sentences he uttered
that I suspect I should pay more attention to.*

Doubtless I will—once I've calmed down.

E.

Their xebec put into Tunis harbor three days later, in the afternoon. They had sighted not one cultist since Alexandria, which was just as well given the sea approach to Tunis lay via a narrow entrance into a so-called lake. The xebec had had to furl its sails and beat in under oars. Outrunning any pursuit would have been impossible.

After farewelling Captain Laboule and his crew, thanking them for their hospitality and commiserating hypocritically over the lack of fighting, Gareth led his party off the deck, onto the docks. All once again in Arab guise, confidently following Laboule's directions, they hired a small donkey-drawn cart from the many waiting to ferry passengers, luggage, and goods over the short distance from lakeshore to city gate. With the three women perched on their luggage in the cart, Gareth trudged along the sandy road, with the other men flanking the cart.

He kept his gaze from Emily. Since their "discussion" in Valletta, she had made no further advances, offered no further invitations to kiss her.

Just as well. If she had, he wasn't at all sure he'd have had the strength or willpower to resist.

But he'd done the right thing. Not what he wanted—he wanted her—but honor had dictated that he couldn't take advantage of her, that he'd had to give her the chance to back away.

And she had.

She'd drawn back, thought of what he'd said, and had seen the truth in his words, his assertion. She'd accepted the opening he'd given her to step back from any further interaction—which, given what had already occurred between them, would have only ended in one place, one activity.

He'd been right, and she'd finally seen that.

Over the days since Valletta, he'd been conscious of her watching him, broodingly, as if she were studying him.

Perhaps wondering at the passionate madness that had infected her, glad he'd explained and she'd seen it for what it was.

He trudged on, and tried not to think of her.

Tried to focus on his mission, on evaluating the possible threat from cultists in this out-of-the-way city. Concentrating on Laboule's helpful directions, he led the way through the city gate and on toward the medina.

A souk by another name, they could hear a rising cacophony of voices, smell the pungent pervasive scents of spices, long before they saw the narrowing streets and covered alleys ahead.

Just before they reached the medina itself, Gareth turned left, and found the guesthouse Laboule had recommended a hundred yards further on. A quick survey from the street was encouraging. Leaving the others in the street with the luggage, he knocked on the gate in the wall, and was admitted.

The guesthouse was well-suited to their needs, clean, large enough, but not too sprawling, with sufficient rooms

enough to stretch both arms out without her fingers touching anything.

The physical relief was wonderful.

"I would be quite happy never to set foot on a xebec again," she informed Dorcas, busy shaking out her traveling gowns and hanging them up in the armoire.

Dorcas snorted. "From what I overheard, seems likely we'll be on another of the things for our next leg to Marseilles."

Emily grimaced. "I heard the same thing." Laboule had given Gareth the name of another xebec captain who he'd thought would be agreeable to taking them to Marseilles. "But it does seem as if we'll have at least a few days here, on dry land."

"We'll need to go to the souk for supplies." Dorcas's voice was muffled as she spoke from inside the armoire.

"Tomorrow, I imagine." Emily laid aside her brush. "At least it's close."

She prayed that, as they all hoped, there were no cultists in Tunis.

If so, if all remained quiet, then their time there might afford her the opportunity to . . . redirect Gareth. To re-educate him as to the reality of her wishes.

And the real and very definite force driving her desire.

Turning, she caught Dorcas's gaze. "Come on. Let's go downstairs and see if we can organize a pot of tea."

She was an Englishwoman far from home—there were some things she really hated going without.

The lone, low-ranking cultist sent to Tunis to watch and report should any of the four soldier-sahibs pass through that town had known that his mission was a sop, that the chances of any of the officers the Black Cobra was chasing coming through the town was so remote as to be negligible.

But of course he hadn't argued, hadn't questioned.

He'd dutifully come to Tunis, and every day had walked out to the docks on the lakeshore, and watched.

Today, this afternoon, he had barely been able to believe his eyes.

Indeed, at first, his senses had deceived him. The group had passed under his nose and it hadn't even twitched. But then he'd caught a comment passed between the two men walking at the rear of the little procession.

The word *cultists* had fixed his attention.

He'd slipped from his perch on a stack of fishing pots and followed.

A short time later, crouched in the shadow of the donkey cart behind the one the sahib had approached, wrapped in a long robe and without his black silk head scarf, he'd listened rather than looked. What he'd heard—the accents, the commanding manner—had convinced him.

One of the sahibs had come to Tunis.

Why he was traveling with women—three of them—was beyond the watcher's ability to guess, but that didn't matter.

He'd trailed the small party at a distance, had bided his time and waited at the corner of the street down which they'd turned, and had been rewarded. He now knew where the sahib was staying.

Not that he could attack—not on his own. But he had plenty of coin, and knew his orders by heart.

He hurried off to the tavern in which he was staying, begged paper and pencil, and settled to write a message, a report. He knew to whom in the French embassy he should give it. And once he had, he would devote himself to carrying out his august master's orders with the utmost diligence.

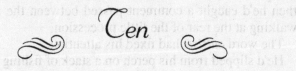

Ten

15th November, 1822
Late
My room in the guesthouse in Tunis

Dear Diary,

Since reboarding the xebec in Valletta, the restrictions of the voyage prevented me from re-engaging with Gareth—which, in retrospect, was a good thing. Not only did the enforced disengagement give me time to calm down and regain the ability to think clearly, it also gave me time to fully reevaluate my position in light of Gareth's views.

Quite aside from confirming just how completely unattuned to the female imperatives the male brain— even a superior specimen—is, a point on which my sisters have frequently remarked, our largely one-sided discussion in Valletta, once I was able to consider it in a calmer frame of mind, was distinctly revealing.

Far from dissuading me that he is my "one," Gareth's arrogant but nobly motivated stance under-

scored the fact—as if I didn't know it—that with him
I am utterly and completely safe. Even from him.

Of course, this leaves me in the position of having
to open my misguided major's eyes as to my own true
motivations and feelings, but I am confident, dear
Diary, that that is well within my powers.

I have my fingers crossed that our time here in
Tunis will yield the opportunity I need.

E.

The next morning, Emily, Dorcas, and Arnia, closely escorted by Gareth, Mooktu, Bister, and Mullins, all in their Arab disguises, left the guesthouse and walked down the street toward the scents and sounds of the medina.

No directions were necessary.

They hadn't gone fifty yards when three colorfully uniformed guards approached at a trot.

The one in the lead halted before Gareth. In clear and precise French, he delivered what was clearly a formal summons for Gareth to present himself at the bey's palace.

Ignoring the tension in the group at his back, Gareth smiled and, in fluent colloquial French, inquired what the problem was.

"It is a requirement, sir, that all foreigners report and make their bow to the bey. It is something all newcomers must do."

as you'd planned, but stay together."

There were careful nods all around, then Gareth turned to the waiting guards. "Gentlemen—lead on."

The leader inclined his head, turned and did so, striding back up the street; his two subordinates fell in behind Gareth and Mooktu as they followed.

Emily watched the little party until they turned the corner and disappeared from her sight.

Lips set, she glanced at the others, saw them staring in the same direction. She inwardly shook herself. Actively doing something—organizing, shopping—was better than standing around wringing her hands. "Right, then! We have supplies to gather. We should make an effort to find everything we need today—just in case."

Just in case something happened, and they had to leave Tunis in a rush.

It was late afternoon before Gareth and Mooktu turned into the street in which their guesthouse stood. Eager to get back and reassure the others, who by now were surely wondering whether something bad had befallen them, Gareth quickened his pace.

Their audience with the bey had been totally unremarkable. A few words in reply to the obvious questions: Were they here for trade? No, they were simply tourists passing through. Were they planning on staying long? A few days, perhaps more. What business was he engaged in? He was a retired soldier seeing the world.

That a few minutes' conversation had taken so long was merely an outcome of the usual diplomatic lack of urgency. Nothing of any consequence had occurred before or after. One thing Gareth had noted with some relief was the absence of any sign of an English diplomatic presence close to the bey. As far as he could tell, there'd been no other Englishman in the room, no Frenchman, either. An Italian and a Spaniard, but that had been all.

Gareth hoped the others had suffered a similarly unexciting day.

He and Mooktu were a few steps from the guesthouse gate when sudden footsteps rushing up behind had them both turning, instinctively putting their backs to the wall, their hands going to their sword hilts.

Just in time to yank the blades free and meet the onslaught of five men with long knives.

Gareth beat back three of the attackers, clearing an arc before him with a vicious swing of his cavalry sword. A long sword beat long knives every time. But three at once?

He had his work cut out for him. One glance showed Mooktu holding his own against their other two assailants. After reassuring himself of that, Gareth concentrated on disabling or disarming the three who, yes, were trying to kill him. Not wound or capture, but kill.

These were locals, not cultists, yet Gareth doubted they'd simply taken it into their heads to attack him and Mooktu. The two of them weren't carrying anything valuable, and no one with a grain of sense would miss that he was experienced military, and just the way Mooktu walked declared him even more lethal.

So their attackers had been sent, but by whom? The Black Cobra, or someone else? The bey? Someone in the palace?

Regardless, given they were locals, killing any would be unwise.

A knife flashed and nicked Gareth's arm. Jaw clenching against the sting, he shook aside all distractions and refocused his energies on defeating the men.

Just as the gate alongside Mooktu opened, and Bister, Mullins, and Jimmy rushed out, swords in hands.

And then the fight was truly on.

It was messy. It was confused.

Then one pair of opponents bumped into some onlookers, sending a woman sprawling, and that started a fight among some of the onlookers—and then it was impossible to tell what was going on.

Women joined the fray on the edges, thumping men over the head with basins, bundles, and baskets.

To Gareth's horror, Emily, Dorcas, and Arnia emerged from the gate. Armed with ladles, they started laying about them.

For one godforsaken instant chaos reigned, then shouts came from the rear of the crowd. Large, muscled bodies started forging their way in.

The bey's guards.

Gareth looked at Emily, trying to catch her eye to direct her back into the guesthouse—to no avail. Giving up, he fought his way to her side, arriving there just as the captain of the guard reached her.

It was the same man who had led the detachment to fetch them earlier in the day.

His dark eyes met Gareth's. After a moment, he said, "You must, if you please, all come with me."

It took another ten minutes to restore calm, but the captain evenhandedly gathered all those involved—those of Gareth's party as well as all the locals, including the women. The captain had brought a full troop with him. The miscreants were formed two-by-two into a long line and, flanked by the guards, marched to the palace.

Walking with Mooktu at the head of the procession, Gareth looked back, confirming that the five locals who had initially attacked them, plus the three who had later joined in, had had their hands tied. All the rest had been left unrestrained. The captain had spoken in Arabic to those locals who had hung back and abstained from involvement, and had clearly got the basic story straight. Gareth took that as a good sign.

Glancing at Emily and Arnia, walking directly behind

him and Mooktu, he murmured, "When we get to the palace, leave the talking to me."

Emily looked up at him through the lace panel of her burka. "I seriously doubt the bey will deign to speak with me. With us." With her eyes, she included Arnia, then looked away, head tilting as if beneath the burka she'd put her nose in the air. "Men always think men know everything."

Gareth thought he heard a small "humph." He also had the feeling she wasn't talking solely about the bey.

Facing forward, he tried to remember if there was a British consulate anywhere in Tunisia, or even in neighboring Algeria, currently Tunisia's overlord.

When they reached the palace, they were all ushered into a large hall, then left waiting there with the guards, armed, keeping watch over them. Unlike his earlier visit, this time they did not have to wait long. A bare ten minues had passed when a door at the end of the hall opened, and the bey, an average-sized man of middle years, tending slightly portly, with a silk turban wound about his head and a wide silk sash going over one shoulder and around his waist, came striding through, his personal guards at his back.

The captain bowed low.

The bey waved him up, and demanded an explanation for the crowd in his hall.

The captain's story was brief and to the point—and accurate, much to Gareth's relief.

The bey ran his eye down the line of those gathered. Then

five first, then when they called for support, those all joined in."

173

"Very good." The bey marched down the line until he stood directly in front of the five. "Why did you attack these people, who I had only just welcomed to our fair city?"

The five fell to their knees, then further, prostrating themselves. After uttering various obeisances, one hurriedly said, "We were hired, Excellency, by another foreigner."

The bey frowned, and glanced back at Gareth. "Who?"

"He wore a turban like the tall one" —the attacker pointed at Mooktu— "but his had a black band."

Gareth shared a glance with Mooktu and Mullins beyond him.

The bey noticed, and came striding back to halt before Gareth. "You know of this black-turbaned man."

A statement, not a question. Gareth met the bey's dark eyes. "Sadly, yes, Your Excellency. It appears we've been followed— or perhaps this person reached here before us—but they are acting on behalf of an Indian cult leader who wishes revenge against a lady, the Governor of Bombay's niece, who was instrumental in gathering vital evidence against the cult leader. The cult threatens the government and the people of India."

As Gareth had suspected, as a ruler himself the bey had no time for anyone who threatened any government.

"This cult," the bey declared to the room at large, "is to be given no help by my people." He paused, then returned to the five still kneeling men. "You have been foolish beyond belief in attacking one I had welcomed at the behest of a foreigner. Captain!"

The captain approached. "Yes, Excellency?"

"Take these five, and the other three as well, and have them sweep the streets about the palace and clean the palace stables for the next three months. Then perhaps they will think again before they take coin from a foreigner to attack one of this city's guests."

The eight men all prostrated themselves. It was a lenient sentence, but, Gareth felt, a wise one. He and his party would soon be gone, but the bey would remain and continue to rule these people.

The bey briefly interrogated, then dismissed the other onlookers who had joined the fight. As they all filed out, relieved to have been spared any punishment, the bey strode back up the hall to where Gareth and his party remained.

The bey's gaze raked the three women, all incognito behind their burkas, then lifted to Gareth's face. "This lady, the governor's niece—she travels with you?"

Gareth nodded. "It is my duty to keep her safe from the cult on our journey back to England."

"Good." The bey clapped a hand to Gareth's shoulder. "Come—walk a little way with me." He glanced back at the women. "And if it is not against your rules, as I believe it is not, perhaps your lady might join us?"

Without a second's hesitation, Emily lifted her burka, putting it back from her face, then stepped forward and curtsied. "Your Excellency."

The bey appeared pleased by the graceful obeisance. He bowed in return. "I am delighted to make your acquaintance." Gallantly he offered his arm. "This is how it is done, is it not?"

Emily smiled and placed her hand on his arm. "Just so, Your Excellency."

"Good." Looking to Gareth, the bey waved him on. "Come—walk with me in the cloisters."

Gareth glanced pointedly at the others of their party, standing quietly waiting.

Following his glance, the bey raised a hand. "My apolo-

They strolled, the bey pointing out various mosaics and sculptures, which they dutifully—and quite sincerely—

admired. Once they had completed a circuit of the court-yard, the Bey ushered them into a small parlor overlooking the courtyard pool, and waved them to fat cushions. Once they'd all sat, he got down to buisness.

"I have a small favor to ask—a minor indulgence if you can see your way to granting it." He looked from Gareth to Emily and back again. "It is my great hope to visit vari-ous European courts next year, and as it is expected and the European way, I will take my wife—my principal wife, the begum—with me. Also my closest courtiers. However, other than myself, and then only as a young man many years ago, we have little experience of European manners. No recent experience at all." He paused, then fixed his gaze on Gareth. "I was hoping I might prevail upon you and your lady to attend a dinner here tomorrow night, and give us—myself, the begum, and those who will travel with me—instruction in how to conduct ourselves at a European table."

Gareth blinked, then looked at Emily—read her surprise, and her curiosity, in her eyes. He looked back at the bey, formally inclined his head. "We will be delighted to oblige, Your Excellency."

17th November, 1822
Evening
My room in the guesthouse at Tunis

Dear Diary,

I am scribbling this in between rushing about madly getting ready for what surely will be the strang-est dinner of my life. The bey wishes Gareth and me to tutor his retinue in European ways. Given the bey is the absolute ruler of this city, it was impossible to refuse the invitation.

This afternoon, after spending the morning look-ing for the captain Laboule recommended as the most

176

*likely to get us to Marseilles safely, with as yet no luck,
Gareth spent some time discussing with me what particular manners it would be wise to address. Somewhat diffidently, he suggested that the bey most likely
assumes we are man and wife, as in this culture it
would be highly unusual for an unmarried woman of
good birth to travel with males not of her family. The
long and short of our subsequent considerations is that
I will wear my grandmother's ring on the ring finger of
my left hand tonight.*

*In the circumstances, pretending to be man and
wife seemed the safest course, protecting me and also
pandering to Gareth's protective streak, although naturally he did not put matters in those terms.*

*So now I am bubbling with eager curiosity, not just
over what dealing with the bey, the begum and their
retinue will be like, but even more over how it will feel
for Gareth and me to behave as one day we will be.*

Practice should never be sneezed at.

                                                    E.

The bey was taking no chances. He sent the captain with three
others to escort them through the narrow streets to the palace.
Given that both Emily and Gareth had dressed for dinner—
she in a pale green silk gown Dorcas had unearthed from her

the intricate carving, the jewel-hued mosaics, the
Arabic beauty everywhere she looked.

Halting at one especially ornate archway, the captain formally handed them into the care of a garishly dressed individual who appeared to fill a position equivalent to butler-cum-major domo. He spoke passable English, and after bowing low, welcoming them and taking their cloaks, he preceded them down a succession of long corridors, past uncountable doors and galleries, to a large, airy colonnaded room one side of which stood open to a treed courtyard.

The room itself was stylishly magnificent, but as they paused in the doorway, it was the people Emily focused on. They were rather magnificent, too, although to her eyes rather less stylish. Indeed, their liking for gold and jewels and ostentatious ornamentation verged on the garish.

The butler caught the bey's eye, then in stentorian tones proclaimed, "Major Hamilton and the Majoress Hamilton."

All heads turned their way. Emily kept her smile easy and relaxed. Clearly, they did think she and Gareth were married. Just as well they'd come prepared.

Smiling expansively, the bey came forward to greet them. He offered his hand to Gareth, and shook hands heartily. Then smiling delightedly, he turned to Emily, and paused.

Sensing he was at a loss as to the acceptable manner in which to greet her, still smiling, she held out her hand. "Take my fingers in your right hand, and nod," she murmured.

The bey's smile deepened as he smoothly complied, and she sank into a curtsy. As she rose, he patted her hand. "Thank you." He released her. "It has been a long time and I wasn't sure."

He turned and waved to the room at large. "Now come and let me introduce you to the others. All here will be accompanying me on my travels." He glanced at the women gathered in a group at one end of the room. "Well, all the men. Of the women, only the begum will be with us."

As the bey led them across the marble floor, her hand tucked in Gareth's arm, Emily tried to imagine what it would be like to be a woman alone in a different culture . . . then realized that for all intents and purposes she was exactly that at that moment.

The bey slowed and, frowning slightly, glanced at her. "I do not recall—is it customary to introduce a wife to other male guests?"

Gareth nodded. Emily stated definitively, "Yes, it is." The group before them was all male. She glanced at the women. "In fact, it's usually the case that men and women intermingle and converse from now—the pre-dinner gathering in the drawing room—and through the dinner itself. At the end of the meal, the ladies leave the men at the table to drink port or spirits, and talk among themselves, but only for so long. Then the gentlemen rejoin the ladies in the drawing room, and all remain together until the end of the evening."

Still frowning, the bey nodded decisively. "We must practice all this."

Thus it was that Emily found herself cast as social directress for the evening. Under her guidance and instruction, backed by the bey's authority and example, the men—at first rather stiffly—mingled with their wives. Luckily, the women were more amenable to indulging in broader conversation.

Getting the party to go in to dinner in the correct order of precedence was both an education and a challenge. The begum in particular, a sultry, black-haired, sloe-eyed beauty of lush and bounteous curves, many of which were barely decently screened by the gauzy draperies the bey's female court favored, proved difficult. She seemed to have taken it into her head that as the senior lady, it was her place to choose who sat beside her, namely Gareth. Emily had to be

easy to ignore the woman's pouts.

Although at first stilted, around the table conversation

gradually bloomed, then blossomed as the men found that the women they normally ignored were, if given the chance, engaging interlocutors.

The reverse, Emily strongly suspected, was also true. These women had barely exchanged two words with most of the men in their respective husband's circles.

She felt reasonably proud of her achievement. And indeed, from his position at the head of the table, the bey was beaming in contented delight.

Directly opposite her, Gareth caught her eye, and with a slight inclination of his head, raised his glass to her.

She smiled and inclined her head back, happiness and that sense of achievement welling and melding.

A little later, when the last dishes were being removed, she caught the begum's disgruntled eye, and using hand signals, instructed her hostess in how to call the ladies to order and lead them back to the drawing room. The begum bestirred herself enough to be interested, and under her husband's benevolent gaze, performed the task with aplomb.

Following her from the room, Emily decided that, strange though it was, with any luck at all, they would weather the evening well.

At the end of the evening, the bey insisted the captain see them back to the guesthouse. When they reached the gate in the wall, Gareth turned to find the captain bowing respectfully.

"The bey is pleased." Straightening, the captain pointed to two figures lounging in the shadows, one at each end of the street. "Throughout the rest of your stay, we will keep watch."

Gareth met his eyes, nodded. "Thank you—and our thanks to His Excellency."

The captain almost smiled.

Opening the gate, Gareth followed Emily in, then turned. The captain saluted and walked off. Closing the gate, Gareth heard his footsteps march up the silent street.

Following Emily across the shadow-strewn courtyard,

Gareth searched, and found Mullins keeping watch in one corner. Given the late hour, everyone else would long be asleep. The old soldier snapped off a salute. Raising a hand in reply, Gareth continued on into the house.

He would see Emily safely upstairs, and then, as he didn't feel the least sleepy, perhaps spell Mullins. But first . . .

Halting in the gloom, he focused on Emily. "You did very well this evening."

Of necessity he'd been forced to let her take point. He hadn't liked it, hadn't liked sitting back and watching her walk such a potentially dangerous diplomatic line, but she'd kept her balance, her poise, throughout.

When she turned and, wide-eyed, looked at him through the pervasive dark, he added, "You gave the bey exactly what he wanted without revealing anything he didn't need to know."

He saw her lips curve, caught the flash of white teeth as she smiled. "I enjoyed the challenge." Slowly, she came toward him. "It helped that they all thought we were man and wife."

True, but it hadn't helped him, not when he'd had to listen to the other men comment appreciatively, and then compliment him on having secured such a prize.

She was a prize on many levels—just not his.

The recollection had distracted him. He refocused, to find her much closer—too close. His blood beat just a little harder through his veins; his attention locked on her, captured, cap-

lifted her gaze to his eyes. "Did it occur to you that you might be wrong?"

Wrong? It took a moment for his mind, distracted by other things, to make sense of what she was suggesting. Trying to see where she was heading, and why, he started to frown.

Emily mentally threw her hands in the air and gave up trying to find the words—the right words to explain just how inaccurate his reading of her motives had been. Was. She'd always believed actions spoke much louder than words. Sliding her hand from his chest over his shoulder to his nape, she stretched up as she drew his head down, and kissed him.

Pressed her lips to his, not in persuasion but in confident expectation. They'd just spent the evening playing husband and wife—effortlessly, seamlessly, convincingly. Surely, he must now see there was only one way that could be, only one reason she had performed the charade so consummately.

She kissed him, moved her lips on his, and let all she knew, all she believed, all she felt well and pour through her. To lead her, free her, and free him.

Lure him.

She parted her lips and welcomed him in, thrilled when he came, when his hands tightened about her waist and he took—took over the kiss, sank into her mouth, and gave her all she asked for. All she wanted.

Him.

In the unfettered dark, in the silence of the night.

The kiss spun out, deepening, broadening, their senses reaching, spreading, searching.

Wanting.

She tipped her head back on a gasp. Her cloak slid from her shoulders as she wound her arms about his neck. As his hands closed about her breasts. Possessively. Passionately.

He kneaded and she moaned, then struggled to mute the sounds he drew from her as he bent his head and set his lips to her throat as his hands worked their magic and she melted.

He shifted, moved, steered her back, guided her until her back met the wall beside the door. He pinned her there and let his hands roam, and she grew hotter, needier, more wanton.

She reveled in the sensations, then he murmured something dark, tugged her suddenly loosened bodice down, exposing one breast, then he bent his head and set his mouth to her flesh and she cried out.

Breathlessly.

Achingly desperately.

The evocative sound shivered through the night. It sank like so many daggers into his psyche, each tipped with need and longing.

Gareth longed. Through all the heat, the welling urgency, above all else he longed to have her. But that have was no longer a simple verb. A possessive one, yes, but it encompassed so much more.

There was so much more he wanted of her. With her.

For her, and for him.

With her supple body in his arms, her soft skin beneath his lips, the taste of her wreathing through his mind, he could think of nothing more, knew nothing beyond that want, that need, that longing.

The soft mounds of her breasts, firm and swollen under his hands, the aureolas tight and puckered, drew him. He bent his head and feasted. Devoured.

She clung, the soft sounds that fell from her lips urging him on, stirring him deeply, ever more provocatively, on a primal level only she had ever breached.

His mouth on her breast, he reached down, caught one of her knees and raised her leg, crooked it around his thigh.

upon him, until it filled him as it did her.

Releasing her bottom, he reached around and back, and

found her ankle. Slid his hand upward from there, skating beneath her skirts and petticoats, skimming her stockinged calf, slipping higher still to pause and trace the frilly lace garter circling her thigh above her knee, then he reached higher.

Found and traced the outer planes of her thigh, gripped her bottom again, but this time skin to skin. Felt her tighten her arms about his neck, rise in his hold, then settle more firmly in his hand. Tipping her hips toward him, wordlessly offering.

He inwardly swore, but it was far too late to rein in his raging need.

His questing fingers slid over the locked muscle of her thigh, and slid inward. Exploring, seeking. Searching.

Finding.

Her slick swollen flesh slid like silk against his fingertips. He stroked, caressed, circled her tight entrance. Pressed lightly in.

She kissed him ferociously, then arched in his arms, helplessly begging.

He slid one finger in, slowly, reached deep, then stroked, equally slowly, equally deeply.

And she burned.

She turned all but incandescent in his arms, her body surrendered, his to pleasure as he would—

Metal clanked.

He jerked back from the kiss. Turned his head and looked.

Sensed her do the same.

The noise had come from deeper in the house. The kitchen courtyard perhaps. Stationed as he was, Mullins wouldn't have heard it.

Gareth all but swayed as he looked back at Emily. His breathing sounded ragged and rough in his ears. She was openly panting. His heart pounded under the influence of multiple imperatives. As he met her eyes, he saw that other tension that had relinquished its hold on them both over the last minutes return.

Infusing them both.

She blinked, then mouthed, "Who?"

He shook his head. Carefully, he withdrew his hand from between her thighs, from beneath her skirts. Grasping her knee, he eased her leg down, held her until she nodded that she could stand on her own.

He leaned closer. "Stay here. Don't move."

Drawing back, he reinforced the order with a glare.

She glared back, her expression grim. But her lips remained set in a thin line, and she stayed where she was as he slowly turned, then, soft footed, crept into the corridor leading further into the house.

Of course, she was behind him when he paused by the closed kitchen door.

Rustlings, bumps, the scrape of wood on tile, and the occasional clank came from beyond the ill-fitting door.

Then he heard the snuffling.

Tension draining, he reached out and pushed the door inward.

It swung wide, revealing the intruder.

The goat looked up, and baaed.

It took them half an hour to get the goat retethered and put the kichen to rights. And by then their heated moment had definitely cooled.

Emily was only too ready to light the flame again, but after trailing her back into the front salon, rather than follow

take—as her sisters had described it, he was like any

in that.

But did he really *want* her in the same way she wanted him?

What if he didn't?

The thought left her feeling suddenly exposed. Suddenly vulnerable in a way she'd never been before.

And as the silence lengthened, as he made no move to walk forward and join her, but just looked at her through the dark . . . she had to wonder if she'd got it all horribly wrong.

At last he shifted. Nodded. "Good night. I'll see you in the morning."

Her heart was lodged somewhere in her throat. "Aren't you coming up?" *With me?*

Gareth forced himself to shake his head. "I'll relieve Mullins. We still need to keep watch."

She hesitated for an instant longer, then inclined her head, turned, and slowly climbed the stairs.

He watched until she passed out of sight. Then he relaxed his hands from the fists they'd curled into and stared at the door, but made no move to open it.

After a long moment, he shook his head. He still felt as if someone had hit it. Hard.

Someone had. *She* had.

She'd scrambled his thoughts and connected with his lustful inner self—that self that wanted nothing more desperately than to have her beneath him, naked or not. She'd lured that more passionate primitive self out and set it—him—free.

But . . .

He'd been saved by that damned goat.

Even now he wasn't sure if he wanted to bless the animal or wring its neck.

In the deepening dark, the questions that now haunted him stood stark and clear in his undistracted mind. Did she truly want him, or had she been swept away by passion? By a need he still believed owed more to reaction than any true, unmanipulated emotion.

186

He wanted her—desperately, almost beyond thought—but he wanted her to want him for the same reason.

Simply because.

Because he was the man she truly wanted. Wanted at some fundamental, visceral level that wouldn't be denied.

He wanted her to want him.

Him. For himself.

Not *him* because he was the one there and she needed to lie with a man, needed to come alive in a man's arms to balance her brushes with death.

Not *him* in place of a fallen comrade.

And definitely not *him* just to fill the void, to be a husband to whom she could play wife.

None of those alternatives would do. Not for him.

Not for her.

They both deserved better.

His problem was, if it wasn't with her, he couldn't imagine his better would ever come to be.

Staring at the dark door was getting him nowhere. Heaving a sigh, he straightened his shoulders, opened the door, and went out to relieve Mullins, and to seek what solace he could in the quiet stillness of the night.

Eleven

18th November, 1822
Morning
Lurking in my room in the guesthouse in Tunis

Dear Diary,

I tried. Last night I tried to open his eyes, to make him see what I feel for him, that he is my "one" and how much his I am, and truly I thought—hoped and believed—I was succeeding, but then that damned goat interrupted us and the moment was gone.

Gone.

But that was not the worst. At the end, when he elected to go on watch rather than climb the stairs with me, I was struck by the most deadening thought. What if he doesn't—in his heart doesn't—want me?

I know my sisters would scoff, but they are biased.

On reflection, my continuing problem is that I cannot tell to what extent his high-minded ideas of what is best for me—as distinct from what I patently want—drive him. That what I discerned as lack of real interest was,

188

once again, him nobly stepping back to protect me from committing what he believes is a folly.

The sound I just made cannot be translated into words.

But what now?

After due consideration, I believe I should continue to view his insistence on distance as nobly driven. He is—and I know this beyond a shadow of doubt—so honest and true that if he were not attracted to me as a woman, and had no inclination to a deeper connection, I do not believe incidents such as last night would occur no matter how much I pressed my case. He is, after all, significantly physically stronger than I, and on no plane could he be described as a weak man. Nevertheless, after having my unvoiced invitation declined last night, it is only natural that I should seek some sign in confirmation of what I believe is the underlying nature of his regard for me. If he truly is my "one," that shouldn't be impossible, as by all rights I should then be his. His "one."

But once I have seen that sign, that confirmation, and gained the confidence it will bring, I swear that nothing will prevent me from forging the relationship I desire with him.

I remain unsweringly determined.

mended, and securing passage on his ????? to ?????.
They would leave the next day on the mid-morning tide.

189

They'd just drunk a toast in orange juice to the next leg of their journey, when a rap sounded on the courtyard gate.

A distinctly official-sounding rap.

Gareth rose, Mooktu beside him, as the gate opened to reveal the familiar figure of the captain of the guard. They'd learned he was the captain for this district, one that rarely saw dignitaries or palace-worthy residents. He was, he had assured them, grateful for the imposition of their presence—and its ramifications.

He smiled as he spotted Gareth in the open doorway of the salon.

Stepping into the courtyard, Gareth returned the smile, but his instincts were pricking.

"Major Hamilton." The captain bowed. "I bring another invitation to you and your lady to dine at the palace this evening."

"Thank you." Gareth glanced around and saw that Emily had followed him to the doorway.

The captain had spoken loud enough for her to hear. Stepping out into the sunshine, she came to join them. As she neared, he read the question in her eyes, saw the slight shrug as she realized he could give only one answer.

Returning his attention to the captain, Gareth inclined his head. "We are honored."

The captain beamed. "I will come for you as before, at the same time."

"Thank you, Captain." Emily smiled graciously. "We'll be waiting."

The captain bowed low and retreated. Once the gate had closed behind him, Gareth took Emily's arm and turned her back to the house. "Any ideas?"

She grimaced. "All I can imagine is that the bey wants to take advantage of our presence to rehearse his courtiers and the begum in their European roles some more."

Passing into the salon, she looked at Dorcas. "We're to dine at the palace again—we'll need to delve into my trunks for another gown."

The captain led them to a different entrance again. Smaller, less grand, the doorway was tucked away down one side of the palace, and was reached through a heavily screened courtyard. The man waiting to receive them was larger, oddly flabby, his robes much less gaudy and gilded than the bey's butler.

The man didn't speak, merely bowed low and, after taking Emily's cloak and handing it to an underling, gestured for them to follow him. As they were led down a series of corridors, Gareth noted that the décor was less ornate, less grand. Perhaps they were to dine with the bey *en famille*?

That notion strengthened when their guide halted and waved them into a relatively small but richly appointed salon giving onto a private courtyard. Following Emily in, Gareth saw the begum reclining amid the cushions set about a traditional low table, one just big enough for four.

Seeing them, the begum smiled. She inclined her head in response to Emily's curtsy, but her eyes skated over his companion to fix on him. "Major and Majoress Hamilton, I am very glad you honor me with your presence."

The purring tone, combined with the way the begum's gaze rested so heavily, almost hungrily, on him, raised the hairs on Gareth's nape.

Emily boldly walked forward, cutting off the begum's view of Gareth. "I take it the bey will be joining us?"

She'd already noted that the table was set for three.

ions. She suspected the begum wasn't interested in learning more about table manners. When Gareth's hand touched her back, a subtle prompt, she stepped forward and sank down to the begum's left.

Perching on the cushions in any manner that combined modesty and grace wasn't easy. It took a few moments to rearrange her legs and skirts. She glanced at the begum to see if there was any trick to it, and very nearly gawped.

The bey's wife had wriggled straighter, lithely sitting cross-legged amid the silk cushions, and had let the old gold silk shawl that had been draped over her shoulders fall, leaving her clad primarily in shimmering, translucent amber-bronze gauze.

Shocked, Emily looked—and detected a few inches of impenetrable bronze silk in strategic places. But really! The woman was all but bare!

The begum hadn't noticed her reaction. She was smiling widely at Gareth, her gaze, her whole attention locked on him.

Emily half expected her to lick her lips.

She looked at Gareth. Once again in his uniform, he'd taken the third place at the table, on the begum's right, settling cross-legged on the cushions. He was wearing one of his blandest expressions, but after all they'd been through, she'd grown adept at reading him. Tension sang in the line of his shoulders; every muscle was taut, ready to react. He was watching the begum much as he might a potentially dangerous animal he had to sit beside.

He was watching the begum's eyes, apparently neither attracted nor interested in all else that was on show.

Emily felt a *soupçon* of relief. The begum was very beautiful, albeit in a sultry, rather predatory way.

Sensing her gaze, Gareth glanced fleetingly at Emily. Through the brief contact she sensed his unease. He was uncomfortable and wanted to be anywhere but there.

Recalling the purpose for which they'd ostensibly been invited, she cleared her throat, smiled somewhat condescendingly when the begum glanced her way, then leaned closer and confided, "I feel I should warn you, my dear begum, that the attire in which you are honoring us tonight would not do at any European court."

The begum frowned, and glanced down at her translucent blouse. "These garments are considered entirely appropriate for a lady to wear to dine with guests in her husband's house."

"I daresy they are—*here*. But in Europe, appearing anywhere in such attire would cause a scandal, I do assure you. And, you will pardon me if I have this incorrect, but I assumed the bey's reason for asking us to coach you and the others in European ways was to avoid any unnecessary incidents."

The begum's attention was now all Emily's, but after a moment of frowning thought, the bey's wife turned and appealed to Gareth. "Is it as your majoress says? That if I go clad like this" —she spread her diaphanously draped arms— "I will create a bad impression?"

Tight lipped, his eyes commendably locked on the begum's face, Gareth nodded. "It would not be well received by society. People would disapprove, and the *grandes dames* would most likely" —he paused, then amended— "would absolutely *not* invite you to their select soirees."

"Oh." Arms lowering, the begum deflated. She looked back at Emily. "So." Her eyes scanned Emily's evening gown. "I must cover up like you?"

Emily glanced down at her pale amber silk gown with its scooped neckline and raised waist, both lightly trimmed

"I see." The begum looked not so much thoughtful as calculating, but then the large butlerlike man appeared in the doorway. She glanced at him, then turned to smile at Gareth. "Our meal is now ready, so we will eat." She looked back at the butler and issued a command in Arabic. With a deep bow, he withdrew.

A smile played about the begum's lips. She turned to Gareth. "And then you may instruct me in what I most wish to know."

Gareth exchanged a glance with Emily, and fervently prayed that gowns, bonnets, and social manners were all that was on the begum's mind, and that the impression he was receiving from the woman's glances and smiles was being scrambled in translation.

Unfortunately, he didn't think that was the case, but while the begum continued to believe he and Emily—his majoress—were married, he—they—should be safe.

The meal placed before them on intricately carved brass dishes owed nothing to European sensibilities. Luckily, he and Emily had been eating Arab fare for some time. They partook of the various dishes and numerous side dishes without hesitation. Unlike most English misses he'd encountered, Emily did not eat like a bird, and her tastes, he'd noted, were distinctly adventurous.

Soon after the meal began, Emily complimented the begum on her chef's efforts, and from there neatly turned the conversation to the comments it was considered good taste to make over a hostess's table.

The topic carried them through the many courses until the begum's eunuch—Gareth had finally placed the oddness about the butlerlike individual—placed sweetmeats and jellied fruits on the table, poured thimblefuls of thick, rich coffee, then, leaving the ornate coffeepot on the table, bowed low and, at a word from the begum, withdrew.

Immediately the begum turned to Gareth, an anticipatory gleam lighting her eyes. "And now, Major, if you please, you will teach me all about dalliance. I have heard that the pastime is much indulged in at all the European courts."

She leaned closer. Gareth had to fight not to lean back.

Her eyes locked on his, her voice once more lowering to a decadently sultry purr, the begum declared, "You will instruct me in how it is done." Her gaze fell to his lips. The tip of her tongue appeared and slid slowly, languorously, over her lower lip. "You will demonstrate *every* little detail."

She already had a good grasp of the basics. Gareth stopped the thought from converting into speech, but how was he to refuse without offending the begum—without landing him, and even more Emily, in hot Tunisian water?

Exceedingly hot given he couldn't afford to risk asking any British official for help.

Eyes locked on the begum as she shifted still nearer, he wracked his brains for some way out. He didn't dare look at Emily, look away from the danger.

The begum started to stretch upward, to tip her face invitingly to his.

He wanted to leap to his feet and walk away, but didn't. Couldn't. The offense would be too great. Desperately battling his instincts, he felt as if he'd been turned to stone.

"No!" The outraged injunction burst from Emily's lips.

She'd been watching the begum in a sort of stupor, unable to credit that the woman would actually try to kiss Gareth in front of her—his majoress. Once the spell had been broken, she had no difficulty in continuing, "No, no, *no!"*

Reaching out, she caught the begum's arm and bodily hauled the woman upright—away from Gareth and his lips.

At least his lips had been edging back, away from the begum's, but what the devil was he think

The words were a challenge, one Emily knew well enough

to meet head-on. "Yes, but as in all things, as a foreigner you've missed the subtleties, the nuances." She drew breath, shot a sharp glance at Gareth hoping he'd have the sense to remain silent, then locked her gaze once more with the begum's. "*Not* all married ladies indulge with gentlemen not their husbands, and *not* all married gentlemen indulge with ladies not their wives. Only a percentage, in some circles a *very small* percentage, of married people seek . . . er, entertainment with others not their spouses."

The begum's expression darkened, tending moody. She glanced at Gareth. "This is true?"

Before he could answer, Emily stated, "Yes, it's true." The instant the begum looked back at her, she continued, "And in your case, when attending a European court as the bey's wife, you will need to maintain the strictest level of decorum, if on no other count than self-defense."

Confusion, and a touch of concern, flared in the begum's eyes.

Aha! Emily thought, and plowed on, "You will need to be on guard against any would-be seducers, for the only European gentlemen, married or not, who would approach the wife of a visiting potentate with a view to dalliance would have only one thing on *their* minds—either to discredit your husband by creating a scandal—you know how men are—or to learn more about your husband's business through you." Frowning, she tilted her head. "Or perhaps to blackmail you."

She refocused on the begum. "Well, that's more than one thing, but you can see the danger."

Abruptly realizing her approach had been less than complimentary, she hurriedly added, "It would be totally different if you were there *un*officially, not linked to your husband but just as yourself." Pausing to draw breath, she added sincerely, "You are a very lovely woman, after all, and I'm sure you would find many gentlemen willing to dally with you, but" —she shook her head— "not this time. Not while you are traveling as the bey's wife."

The begum's expression had grown increasingly despondent as Emily's lecture had progressed. The silence lengthened as she stared at Emily, then she glanced at Gareth. "You—"

"Neither the major nor I dally with others." Emily made the statement definite, definitive—it was true enough over recent times. She didn't look at Gareth, but caught the begum's eyes as she turned back to her. "I should perhaps add that in European cultures it is customary for the gentleman to make the first approach."

"But . . ." The begum looked thoroughly disgusted. "What use is that? One might be waiting forever."

"Indeed." Emily managed not to glare at Gareth as she said it. "However, now we've told you—warned you—about dalliance in our societies, I believe it's getting late, and we should thank you for your hospitality and return to our guesthouse." She shifted to unwind her legs from their cramped position.

The begum made a distinctly unladylike sound. "So," she grumped, "although I will walk in your ballrooms and drawing rooms, I will still be as cloistered as I am here at home." She looked up as Emily managed to get to her feet. The begum narrowed her eyes, then pointed at Emily. "Aha! Now I understand the reason for your gowns—why you dress so, all covered up, when you go into your society. Why outside your home, you dress like a nun, rather than a wife."

Emily bit back the information that they dressed in the

The begum frowned, then met Emily's eyes as she faced her once more. "So I will need to get my seamstresses to make up gowns like this, or my husband will be displeased and made ashamed when we reach the European courts?"

Emily hesitated, misliking the calculating gleam in the begum's dark eyes, but with no alternative, she nodded.

The begum smiled. "In that case, Majoress Hamilton, you will be doing me a great service if you will exchange gowns with me. We are much of a height and size—as a great favor to me, you will swap gowns, will you not?"

Emily tried not to look at the diaphanous creation the begum was draped in. Alongside the calculation, there was something else in the begum's eyes—a need to take something from this meeting. Something positive she could show others . . . Emily had heard that the begum lived in the harem, that she was the first wife, true, but just the first among many . . .

Emily nodded. "Yes, of course."

Jaw clenched, teeth gritted, Gareth followed Emily through the gate into the courtyard of their guesthouse. With a brusque nod, he farewelled the captain, pushed the gate shut, and latched it.

Striding after Emily as she crossed to the salon door, he picked out Mooktu in the shadows, raised a hand in acknowledgment, but didn't slow. Not knowing how long they would be at the palace, the others had divided the watches for tonight between them. He didn't need to concern himself with that tonight—besides, thanks to Emily, they now had the begum, traditionally the city's ruler in her husband's absence, firmly on their side.

Emily's cloak fluttered as she gathered it about her and climbed the shallow steps into the salon. Embroidered silk ankle cuffs and tassels peeked from beneath the cloak, and an ankle chain glinted in the moonlight, before she released the cloak and the gloom within swallowed her.

Every muscle locked tight, Gareth grimly followed. He'd never been so grateful for a lady's cloak in all his life. While Emily and the begum had retired to swap clothes, foreseeing the result and the danger therein, he'd hunted up the eunuch and asked for the cloak, left at the too-distant entrance, to be fetched.

Luckily the eunuch had returned with the cloak before Emily had reappeared. When she'd finally followed the begum, rendered reasonably presentable by Emily's gown, into the room, he'd sucked in a breath, held it, and tried not to react. At all.

A superhuman feat, one he hadn't achieved.

But Emily's blushes had abruptly focused him on something other than his own pain. He'd shaken out the cloak and held it up. She'd all but dashed across the room, anklets tinkling, to take refuge beneath the soft woolen folds.

Once covered, her chin had risen; her confidence had returned. She'd taken her leave of the begum with genuine smiles and courtesy all around.

The subject of gowns apparently united all women.

Still holding the cloak about her, Emily started up the guesthouse stairs. She glanced back as he stepped onto the lowest tread, smiled fleetingly in the moonlight. "That ended a great deal better than I thought it would."

No thanks to him. Gareth's jaw tightened. A chaos of roiling emotions condensed into a hot knot inside him, then rose slowly, inexorably, up his throat. "I'll buy you another gown."

His tone was angry, irritated—frustrated.

Stepping into the upper corridor, Emily glanced back. "Don't be nonsensical." S̶

. . . was it *disapproval?* radiating from him as he halted before her. Eyes narrowing, she tipped up her chin. "I did what was necessary to get us out of there without causing ructions—ructions we can't afford."

A muscle worked at the side of his jaw. "If you'd just left it to me—"

"If I'd left it to you that woman would have—" Realizing her voice was rising commensurate with her temper, she uttered a muted sound of frustration, flung open her door, grabbed his jacket front in one fist and jerked, then towed him into the privacy of her room.

She couldn't have moved him if he hadn't obliged, but presumably he was as keen as she to continue their discussion. The walls and door were sturdy enough to permit them to indulge in the "discussion" bubbling through her. How *dare* he not appreciate her saving him from a fate worse than who-knew-what at the hands, and various other parts, of the begum?

Releasing him, she swung to face him, all but nose to nose in the bright moonlight pouring through the open shutters. Her temper was well flown; belligerence had taken hold.

He'd turned to send the door swinging shut. As he turned back to her, she stretched up on her toes and locked her eyes on his. "Listen, you—I got us out of there tonight without losing anything vital—more, while keeping the begum's favor. What fault can you possibly find in that?"

His eyes, dark and narrowed, locked on hers. "It's *my* job to keep *you* safe."

"By whose decree?"

"*Mine*. It's the way things are—everyone knows that."

He was serious, she could see it in his face, but she wasn't about to back down. She wanted to forge a lifelong partnership with him, and she intended to start as she meant to go on. Folding her arms, catching her cloak in them to hold it in place, she kept her eyes on his. "Regardless of any and all accepted practice, the only way we're going to survive this— your mission and this unexpected joint journey—is to work together and protect *each other*. Tonight I was better placed to deal with the begum than you, so I did, and we walked away unscathed." Eyes narrowing, she gruffly stated, "You should be grateful."

Her tone gave Gareth pause. There was a hint of upset, of being upset because he wasn't applauding her actions, her quick thinking in rescuing them. He let his mind skate back, reliving the moments . . . his too-intense reactions flared anew and crashed through him again. His face hardened to stone. "Regardless—don't ever do that again."

"Do what?"

"Put yourself between me and danger." When she frowned, not understanding, he gritted his teeth and ground out, "When we first walked into the begum's presence, you stepped between her and me. Later, you kept deflecting her attention from me to you."

"I was protecting you!"

"I know. But—again—it's my job to protect you."

"*Again*, *I* wasn't under threat. *You were!*"

His jaw was going to crack. "Be that as it may—"

"*Arrgh!*" She flung up her hands. Her cloak slid from her shoulders. "You ungrateful man!"

With a soft thump, her cloak hit the floor.

She stood in the moonlight shafting through the open window, clad in gauze so fine he could see every curve lovingly outlined by the moonlight.

Abruptly she stepped close, face tilted to his, glaring at him from mere inches away. "Or did you *want* to lie with her?"

When the begum had worn the outfit, he hadn't had a

201

problem. After the first glance, he'd felt voyeuristic and uncomfortable, and had had no difficulty averting his eyes.

But Emily in gossamer silk, Emily's body . . .

"The only woman I want to share a bed with—"

He stopped, shocked. He'd said that aloud.

And even he could hear the lust thickening his voice.

His gaze remained locked on the pale, subtle curves of her breasts.

The silence stretched.

He had to think, but couldn't. Lust had suborned his brain.

"Yes?" A soft, expectant—hopeful—prompt.

He dragged in a tight breath, looked up, met her eyes— saw in the mossy hazel understanding and . . .

Enough blatant encouragement to knock his defenses flat.

He swore, and reached for her, hauled her to him.

Bent his head, crushed her lips beneath his—and kissed her with all the pent-up fury, frustration, and sheer need inside him.

She grabbed his head and kissed him back, equally fierily, equally hungrily.

The clash of emotions made his head spin. Transmuted anger and frustration to potent passion and powerful, spiraling desire in one short heartbeat.

Made him achingly hard, every muscle turned to steel.

Releasing her arms, he set his hands deliberately to her silk-clad body, and felt his pulse leap.

He closed his hands about her waist, and sensed her heart thud.

He'd been furious not just because she'd put herself in danger, but because he would have been helpless to protect her had things gone badly. Yet he'd had to let her handle it—he hadn't known how to, so he'd had to sit and keep silent, and let her risk . . .

Angling his head, he sank into her mouth, ravaged, plundered.

The countering pressure of her lips, the evocative taste of

her, the hunger in the passion that rose to meet his, reassured him as nothing else could.

She'd pulled it off, and they were safe. Alive.

And both of them now wanted, each of them needed . . .

The other.

The rational remnant of his brain quibbled that this was a typical reaction to triumphing over danger. He shouldn't take advantage—

He shut out that chiding voice. He didn't understand her motives, but he couldn't, wasn't strong enough to, deny her. Or himself. To hold back from what they both so openly, and blatantly desperately, wanted.

Needed.

Had to have.

He flexed his fingers, felt silk shift, sliding against skin equally smooth. Beneath his palms, the material had heated. He let his hands slide, glide over her back, felt the gossamer silk shift over silken skin in evocative, provocative temptation.

Spreading his hands over the long supple planes, he pulled her to him. Stepped into her as he did.

Gathered her—all warm womanly curves encased in featherlight silk—against him, locking her to him.

And she came.

Eagerly, wantonly, Emily pushed her arms up, stretched up on her toes the better to meet his lips, the better to return the increasingly fiery kiss. Winding her arms about his neck, with an abandon born of absolute

Even as, high on her toes, leaning into him she yielded her

mouth and knowingly taunted him to take, she desperately wanted.

More.

All.

Now.

Here in this room, bathed in moonlight, she wanted him with a certainty that blazed through her veins.

An absolute longing, one she'd never felt before, one far too vibrant, too acute to be questioned.

Her need simply was, just as she was his.

Just as he was hers.

Nothing else mattered. Nothing else held the power to break the compulsion—one she wholeheartedly embraced.

His hands slid, palms burning, over the sensitive skin of her back, the silk a tantalizing, senses-teasing barrier. It whispered of sultry nights, promised heated delights as it shifted over her skin, caressing not just where his hands pressed, but elsewhere, further, sending prickling awareness washing over her.

Sending heat sinking into her. He angled his head and plundered her mouth anew, reclaiming her attention, his tongue sliding heavily over and along hers as, with a blatancy she found impossibly arousing, he feasted.

Hot, heavy, his hands traced her hips, slid down, around, gripped.

He lifted her against him, molded her hips to his. The insubstantial silk did nothing to mute the thrilling male hardness of him, the solid rod of his erection that pressed through his breeches to impress itself against the taut softness of her belly.

With reined deliberation, he shifted against her, an evocative, provocative thrusting that made her fingers curl.

Heat streaked through her, an eruption of sweet warmth that spread beneath her skin, then slid sinuously down to pool low.

To swell. And throb.

On a gasp she broke from the kiss, desperate to breathe,

and caught a glimpse of his face, of the dark fire in his eyes.

Her hands had found his hair, her fingers tangling in the soft locks. Forcing her heavy, passion-weighted lids wider, she stared, oddly aware of her lips hot and swollen, slicked from their kiss, of her harried breathing, of the tightness of her chest.

Of the giddiness of her senses, the yearning in her blood.

Of the need that beat an irresistible tattoo in her veins.

Her eyes searched his, and she saw in the dark depths the heat ease back a notch. Saw rationality and a stubborn, bone-deep honor fight to rise above the heated compulsion, to transcend it and reclaim him.

Yet she stood on the brink. Teetering. So aware . . .

Of the heat that rose beneath every inch of her skin. That made itself known in the throb of her lips, and even more insistently in the throb of the soft flesh between her thighs.

For the first time she knew, felt, fully experienced the tell-tale greedy fire that flooded her and made her yearn. That made her body soften, melt. Made it long for a completion she'd never known with a violence that made her ache.

She caught and held his gaze. "Don't. Stop." Her tone would have done the begum proud—command, demand, wrapped in sultry, lustful, open greed.

The heat in his eyes flared anew. His chest swelled as he fought—the damned man fought!—to contain it. To suppress it.

She didn't need to think, to look, to wonder. Desire and

passion, lust and need—all were there in the heated compulsion that all but crackled between them, around them.

"I want this."

He still held her against him. Deliberately, boldly, she pressed closer still.

Felt him react, helpless to resist.

Felt the fire between them surge.

Stretching up, she lifted her face and breathed against his lips, "I want you." Eyes flicking up, at close quarters she held his gaze. "I need you inside me."

That and only that would quench the fire they'd lit. With achingly sharp clarity she knew that, and only that, would ease the escalating ache, would feed her hunger and satisfy her craving.

That *that* was what she needed to realize her dreams.

And *that* was what he—stubborn man—needed, too.

His hands hadn't eased their grip. The arms locked about her hadn't loosened.

She could sense the battle raging within him. He was still fighting—but he wasn't winning.

Inwardly smiling, she drew her hands from his hair, framed his face, held it steady as she stretched the last inch, and kissed him.

Voraciously, hungrily, demandingly.

She poured everything, every ounce of temptation, of enticement, of promise, into that kiss.

She held nothing back. She wanted him to stop thinking, desperately wanted him to cease being noble and take her to her bed.

She wanted him. Wanted this.

All. Now. Here.

Gareth heard her message loud and clear. He knew what he was doing, but he wasn't at all sure she did. Yet what could he do?

Resistance was futile, breaking from her impossible. His arms, his hands, his body, simply would not let her go. Not now, not after she'd made her wishes so abundantly plain.

I want you. I need you inside me.

206

What man could refuse such a plea?

Certainly not him. Not given it was her.

He wasn't even sure when he made up his mind—when exactly he surrendered.

Only knew that he had to be where she wanted, that he needed to be sunk deep within her as much as she needed him there.

That need, at least, was singularly clear, as genuine as the clawing demon that was eating him from inside out.

So he broke from the kiss that had become a ravenous, incandescent exchange, swept her up in his arms, and strode to the bed.

Her eyes glittered in the moonlight, her lips parting in a fleeting, satisfied smile as he laid her down.

Resisting the urge to simply follow her down, cover her, rip the flimsy silk away and sheath himself in her, resisting the driving urgency that already pounded through him, he forced himself to straighten and step back from her grasping hands. Standing, he peeled off his coat.

She watched, smiled—another of her soft, secretive, smug smiles of feminine triumph—then sat up, reaching behind her for the buttons of the barely there silk blouse that shimmered over her skin.

"No."

Surprised by his guttural decree, she glanced up.

"Leave it on—I want to peel it from you." Stripping off his cravat, he gestured with his chin. "Lie back and let me

Her heart was thudding, steady and sure. There was no chance of her cooling, not with his eyes on her.

Not with him swiftly stripping, garment by garment revealing more of the fascinating musculature of his chest and abdomen. Tossing aside his shirt, belt already gone, he unbuttoned the flap of his breeches as he turned and sat on the edge of the bed to remove his boots, giving her the chance to study his back, the long, defined muscles bracketing his spine, the wide heaviness of his shoulders.

Mouth watering, unable to stop herself, she shifted, reached out and touched. He jerked, flung her a dark look, but said nothing. Let her stroke, let her test the incredible resilience of his skin and the steely muscles beneath.

Let her be seduced anew by his heat. He was burning.

One boot hit the floor. Seconds later its mate joined it.

She drew back her hand. Breath bated, mouth abruptly drying, she waited for him to stand and turn.

He didn't. He rose up, slid his trousers past his hips and sat again to pull them free of his long legs.

She barely had time to register the maneuver before his trousers hit the floor and he turned, and was on her.

Sunk in the bed alongside, propped on one arm, he loomed over her.

She knew why he'd done it. He was now too close for her to see anything beyond the wide expanse of his chest. Naked and delectable though that was, she'd had further expectations.

Eyes narrowing, she opened her mouth to inform him she had three married sisters—

He kissed her. Filled her mouth with the potent taste of him, with power, passion, and promise.

Swept her away—effortlessly—on a tide of rising need, driven by an escalating, clawing sense of urgency.

His hand closed, hard, over one silk-clad breast. Possessively weighed, caressed. His thumb found her nipple and circled, stroked, teased . . . until she gasped through the kiss, body arching, pressing her flesh more firmly into his demanding hand.

That seemed all the encouragement he needed.

His hand roved her body, heavy, male, flagrantly demanding and commanding, drawing responses from her she'd never known she'd had it in her to give.

She'd thought she'd been heated before.

Now she burned.

Then he broke from the kiss, slid down and bent his head, licked, laved. Silk clung to her breast, to her tightly furled nipple. He drew back enough to see, then bent his head once more—and drew the turgid bud into his mouth.

And suckled.

She shrieked, fought to mute the sound. Fought to ride the wave of sensation he sent crashing through her. He continued to feast, until she was breathless, until she shifted and moaned.

Then his hand slid between her thighs and one blunt fingertip stroked her through the sodden silk covering her there.

She sobbed, clutched his head, holding him to her as she tilted her hips, wordlessly begging.

The blunt fingertip found her entrance and pressed in, just a little, the wet silk an excruciatingly frustrating barrier preventing real touch, deeper penetration.

She wanted . . . she knew more than enough to know exactly what she wanted.

Freeing one hand from the tangle of his dark hair, she reached down . . . and found him. Hotter than flesh should be, velvet over steel. Her fingertips reached just far enough

with him so she landed atop him in a hurry of silk. One large hand palmed her head and he dragged it down, dragged her down into a kiss so rapaciously possessive it literally curled her toes.

His other hand was busy. She only realized when the night air coolly caressed her naked back, then the gauzy blouse parted at the back. His hands helped it slide down her shoulders. She lifted one hand and forearm, then the other, stripped the garment off and flung it away, uncaring of where it landed.

Caring much more about being skin to skin with him, her breasts, full and achingly swollen, brushing, then pressing against the heavy muscles of his chest, her tight nipples tantalizingly abraded by the crisp black hair that adorned it.

She'd barely absorbed that sensation when she felt the tug as the silk harem pants slid down and over her hips.

Expectation leapt; anticipation skittered through her veins.

Nerves tensed, alive to every touch. Waiting as he drew the silk steadily lower, so it no longer screened her belly from his. She held her breath as he shifted, lifting her as he drew the garment down her thighs.

Her mind racing ahead in giddy delight, she remembered the ankle cuffs.

Just as he rolled again, pinning her beneath him.

Hands clutching his arms, she gasped at the sensation of being surrounded, trapped, by hot, hard male, then he kissed her—a forceful, demanding, conquerorlike claiming that left her reeling.

Gareth seized the moment to pull back from her and deal with the cuffs at her ankles, then strip the flimsy harem pants away.

He gave himself only one brief instant to drink in the sight of her lying rumpled and aroused, her rich brown hair disarranged and flung across the pillows, her lids at half mast, her lips swollen and sheening, her body lush and ripe—and all his.

Then he stretched over her and let his body down on hers.

Thrilled to the sensation of firm curves, supple skin, feminine softness cushioning him, the demon within all but slavering with delight.

Small hands braced on his chest. He found her eyes with his as she pressed, wasn't entirely surprised when she protested, albeit weakly, "I want to see you."

"Not now." The reply was a categorical growl. He didn't think he could stand the torment—not without reacting. Not while maintaining the control necessary to go slowly. He'd stake his life she was a virgin, so slowly was mandatory. Not that he'd had any experience in that precise arena—under his code virgins were not fair game—but so he'd always heard.

Despite her state, her jaw started to firm.

"Later." Inspired, he added, "Next time." *Perhaps.*

He didn't wait to see if she agreed, but bent his head and kissed her again.

The heat between them hadn't waned in the least—now it leapt to life, flames roaring, then escalating rapidly as hands touched and found nothing but hot dewed skin, as he shifted over her, nudging her thighs apart, as she parted them willingly and he settled between.

As she wriggled, accommodating him, then tipping her hips . . .

He sank into her, had pressed in the first inch even before he'd meant to.

And then there was no holding back.

She was tight. Tight enough to make him shudder. To back

deep, to the hilt.

And stop. Holding himself steady, every sense locked on her.

Beneath him, held trapped in the kiss, she'd made not a sound, but she'd frozen.

An instinctive reaction against a sharp pain. He waited; lips on hers, he prayed he hadn't hurt her too badly, that she—

He broke off the thought as she eased beneath him. As gradually, bit by bit, the pain-induced tension fell from her.

Beneath it, supplanting it, he sensed something in her that for all his experience he'd never previously encountered. It took him a moment to find its name.

Fascination.

She was utterly enthralled. Not just with his body, but with the sensation of their joining, of him being sunk so deeply within her.

He kissed her gently, and moved, drawing back slowly, then thrusting in again, and sensed her excitement, that fascination, flare.

Instinct, and the dance, took over.

Emily gave herself up to it, up to him, to the swirling exhilaration of their joining, wholly and completely embracing the act. Her mind couldn't contain her joy, her delight, the inexpressible relief that as last she was here, with him, and it was all so much better than she'd ever imagined, than her sisters had ever been able to describe.

She reveled, and urged him on. Did all and everything she could to meet him, match him, and learn what pleased him, to grasp every chance to share the abundant pleasure he was lavishing on her, and return it.

Loving was a sharing—she knew that to her bones. She threw herself into it, searching for ways to use her body to pleasure him just as he was using his to pleasure her.

And if they wrestled, she suspected he enjoyed it as much as she did. Their lips remained fused, but in the brief moments they parted she delighted in the ragged sounds of their breathing, in the urgency that so patently gripped him, and her, and made them strive, body to body, heart to thudding heart.

And then they would dive back—into the kiss, into the flames, into the rising indescribable heat. Even if this was her first time, she was eager to make it count, to welcome the glory, make it hers and search for more . . .

Until it sizzled in her veins, streaking through her, until it whipped the flames racing over her skin to a conflagration. One that sank deep, then coalesced, that drew in and tightened, inexorably, unrelentingly focusing . . .

He groaned through the kiss and thrust hard and deep, and an explosion of sensation rocked her. Shattered her, shards of pleasure so sharp they glittered flying down every nerve, every vein.

Until she flew, free of the earth, wholly taken by the glory.

For two heartbeats, Gareth savored her release, teeth gritted held desperately on, but the ripples of her sheath, tight and powerful, milked him, and drew him irresistibly on.

Release swept him, deeper than any he'd ever known.

Surrendering, letting his shuddering body have its way, he let go, and followed her into ecstasy.

Bliss. Emily decided there was no other word to describe the sensation.

Lying on her back in her rumpled bed, Gareth a hot heavy weight slumped on his stomach alongside her, she stared at

He'd slumped upon her at the end, but had roused enough to move off her rather than crush her into the mattress. Not that she'd minded; she'd rather liked the feel of his body all but boneless on top of hers.

Perhaps because she'd been responsible for reducing it to such a state.

Moving slowly, he propped himself on his elbows, then he turned his head and looked at her, a long assessing gaze. His hair was delightfully tousled, his features still rather slack, lacking their usual focused determination.

She felt her lips start to curve, let herself smile as sunnily as she felt. "That was rather wonderful."

He looked at her for a moment, then uttered a sound between a grunt and a humph, and shifted onto one elbow the better to look down at her. His expression had sharpened into his customary commanding mein. "We'll get married when we reach England, of course."

She held his gaze, not the least surprised by the decree. She'd expected something of the sort—no formal proposal, no down on one knee. Certainly no swearing of undying, enduring love.

But if she'd gained one thing from the night, it was absolute and unequivocal confirmation that he was, beyond all doubt, her "one," the one gentleman above all others she should marry.

Her response to his decree was, therefore, already decided. However . . . looking deep into his dark eyes, giving thanks for the strong moonlight that allowed her to do so, she realized that, courtesy of the begum and her seductive outfit, she and he had leapt ahead several steps.

She knew he was her "one," but did he know she was his?

That was a critical question, one she couldn't go forward to the altar without answering. Without knowing exactly why he wanted to marry her.

He was a man for whom honor was a real and tangible entity. That he would seek to use honor as a screen for marrying her was predictable, but she wasn't about to allow him to hide behind it. If he loved her as she loved him, as she hoped and prayed he did, then he should, and would, have the courage to own to it.

If he truly loved her.

For her, nothing else would do.

Eyes on his, she smiled, light and sweet. "Perhaps."

Lips still curved, she closed her eyes, reached out and patted his chest. "We need to sleep."

It was too warm for the sheet. She settled in the bed, let her limbs go lax.

Gareth stared at her, then, as she no longer could see, allowed his inner frown to materialize. *Perhaps?* What the devil did that mean?

To his mind, the matter was simple. He wanted to marry her—he'd known that since he'd first laid eyes on her in the officers' bar in Bombay—and now she'd given herself to him—all but seduced him—that, to his mind, settled that.

Frown darkening, he turned onto his back, and stared up at the ceiling. She'd been a virgin, she'd wanted him, and had got what she'd wanted. Marriage was the natural end of that tale.

Why *perhaps*?

His mind circled a thought he really didn't like, prodding the latent potential sore spot. Had she really wanted Mac-Farlane, but, when fate denied that, decided to try him as her second choice? Her second best? Was that why she wasn't sure?

He remembered. Wondered. Finally asked, "Why did you

Opening her eyes, she turned her head to look at him. He wiped the frown from his face before she saw it.

215

Her expression told him she was still floating in the aftermath.

She studied his face for a moment, then, lips still curved, waved again. "Does this always make one so . . . . lethargic? Sleepy, but not quite the same? I feel as if I haven't a bone to my name."

He felt a spurt of satisfaction that was almost pride. "Yes—that's how it should feel."

And given she did feel that way, there was no point pressing her for the right response to his decision on their future now. They had a journey to complete, and he knew how to persuade.

Raising his arm, he shifted closer, reaching across to lift her and slide his arm under her shoulders, turning her to him so she settled against his side, her head on his shoulder. "This is how it's supposed to be." He may as well seize the chance to establish the procedures he intended to adopt from now on.

Especially as, at the moment, she seemed entirely amenable. She wriggled and settled, then relaxed.

He felt the tension that had returned to him leach away.

He looked down at her head, then dropped a kiss on her hair. "Go to sleep."

He felt more than heard her soft humph, but she complied. He listened to her breathing slow.

Head back, he closed his eyes and inwardly smiled. They were going to be together for several more weeks. And, he vowed—a quiet vow in the fading moonlight—that by the end of their adventure she would be his. He wouldn't be letting her go.

Not ever.

Twelve

19th November, 1822
Early morning
Still in my bed, but now alone

Dear Diary,

    WELL! It happened. Finally. And yes, I can enthusiastically report that lying with a man—the right man—is every bit as wonderful as I'd imagined. Indeed, my imagination was sadly lacking in several pertinent respects, but no matter—the reality was better than my dreams.

    Of course, there was—as my sisters have indeed

any altar, I am determined to gain some assurance that he knows he loves me, some acknowledgment that

*in the same way he is mine, then I am his, that the
emotion that binds us is mutual, and not all on my
side alone.*

*I am hopeful that that is indeed the case, however,
his declaration of last night stemmed from honor, at
least he couched it in those terms, and thus it tells me
nothing of what he feels.*

*He will need to do better than that—especially
now that I have made my own declaration so plain. I
have given myself to him, and actions, as we all know,
speak much louder than mere words.*

*So that is where we stand. I am now his regardless
and forever, but before I allow him to put his ring on
my finger—my ultimate goal—I require his love to be
declared. Simply stated aloud will do.*

*As you know, dear Diary, I am bound and de-
termined to achieve my ultimate goal. I go forward
in hope.*

*Indeed, with a spring in my step, for I am sure I
am halfway there.*

                                                    E.

By noon that day, they were on Captain Dacosta's
xebec and crossing from the Lake of Tunis into
the Mediterranean on their way—at last—to
Marseilles.

Gareth strode the deck, feeling more confident than he had
for some weeks. He was pleased he'd made the effort, and
wasted the days, looking for Dacosta, the captain Laboule
had recommended. Like Laboule, Dacosta had been happy
to meet his requirements; neither the captain nor his small
crew would draw back from a fight.

With luck, there wouldn't be one, given they'd sighted no
cultists since Alexandria. Although at the time he'd been
sure the attack on him and Mooktu on their first day in Tunis

218

had been the work of the cult, he was no longer so sure. All had been uncommonly quiet subsequently, which was very unlike the cult.

Pausing by the prow railing, he scanned the horizon. There were ships out there—this was the Mediterranean—but none seemed to be taking any inordinate interest in them. More, the horizon itself was clear. The weather was fine and looked set to remain so for the immediate future.

His lips curved as he realized the same could be said of atmospheric conditions on his personal front. Emily was in a sunny mood, and while only he knew the reason for the quite notable smile that now inhabited her face, he suspected some of the others, at least, had guessed. Her maid for one; Dorcas had leveled a very strait look at him when he'd assisted her onto the gangplank.

He wasn't entirely certain whether he was glad or not that this was a typical xebec, on this voyage fully loaded with amphoras of fine cooking oil, and consequently space was at a premium. There were no private nooks anywhere, nowhere he and Emily could repair to for a private interlude.

On balance, he suspected that was just as well. He would use the time to Marseilles to work out his approach—his plan to get her agreement to their wedding, to being his wife, without any further discussion of his motives or feelings. The latter would prove difficult regardless; he had no firm idea what his feelings for her truly were, but he knew the outcome—that he needed her as his wife—and that was enough.

know more.

* * *

The lone cutlist sent to watch in Tunis carefully packed his bag. He had carried out his orders, and while he hadn't been able to capture the major, he had performed the most vital and imperative task laid upon him.

Once he'd sighted the major's party, he'd ensured word had gone out on the very next tide.

He hoped his master would be pleased.

Closing his bag, he looked around the small room, then, bag in hand, turned and walked out of the door.

19th November, 1822
Evening
Once more in a shared cabin on a xebec

Dear Diary,

> *We left Tunis today on a fair wind, which I have been informed by Captain Dacosta is likely to remain with us all the way to Marseilles. Dacosta is much like Laboule, and thus like Gareth, too, which brings me to my point.*
>
> *Men of action, like Gareth, our xebec captains, Berber chieftains, and the like, appear to share certain similarities of character, especially in a personal sense. I have been mulling over the wisdom the older Berber women—who have spent a lifetime observing such men—deigned to share. In taking guidance on the matter of Gareth Hamilton, I could do far worse.*
>
> *My conclusions are that while he clearly feels something for me, and indeed, all the signs point to that something being love, it is important—in fact, critical—for our future happiness that he acknowledges that fact, and accepts that love—mutual and enduring—is the true basis of our marriage from the start.*

So how do I bring that about?
As ever resolute.

E.

The attack came with the dawn.

Emily woke with a start. Her hammock swung wildly as she sat up. Shouts reached her from the deck above, followed by the unmistakable clang of swords.

Feet thundered past—the men belowdecks racing for the companionway ladders.

A heavy thump fell on their door, then it swung open to reveal Gareth in breeches and shirt, a pistol in one hand, sword at his hip.

He looked at her. "Stay here."

His gaze flicked to Dorcas and Arnia, extending the command to them, then he whirled and was gone, racing to join the fight.

Emily looked at Arnia, then Dorcas, then tumbled out of the hammock. There was only just light enough to see, a pearly wash spreading from the far horizon sliding tentative fingers through the small porthole.

Moments later, fully dressed, the three of them gathered at the foot of the stern ladder. They had no intention of staying out of the fight, of not helping their menfolk, but neither were they foolish.

In matters such as this, Arnia took the lead. Head up, she

had glanced around the ship's galley, but hadn't seen anything she wanted to use. Despite Bister's training, she didn't think she would be able to wield a knife—just the thought of sticking a blade into someone made her squeamish—but she'd noticed the pole the sailors used for tweaking the sails and ropes, similar to the pole she'd used in their previous shipboard fight. As before, the pole was stowed along the side of the stern housing; she would grab it the instant she gained the deck.

She was an Englishwoman; fighting with staffs was much more her style.

Arnia had been listening intently. Abruptly, she nodded. "Now."

She started up the ladder. Dorcas followed, with Emily close behind.

They reached the deck to discover not just chaos, but pandemonium. Schooners were sometimes fighting ships, and so better accommodated hand-to-hand combat. Most xebecs were solely merchant vessels. Their low railings and narrow walkways made their decks highly unsuitable for fighting.

And it was definitely cultists they were fighting.

Emily saw the black silk scarves she'd grown to fear wound about far too many heads. Arnia and Dorcas saw backs to attack and moved away. Stepping fully onto the deck, Emily ducked and bent to retrieve her weapon of choice.

She'd grasped the smooth wooden pole, and was dragging it to her when some instinct made her glance around.

A cultist had spotted her. Grinning widely, he came strutting forward, bloody sword in one hand, the other reaching for her.

He wasn't smiling an instant later when the end of her pole rammed into his groin.

She leapt up as he fell to his knees, kicked his sword out of his hand, then lifted her pole high and brought it crashing down over his head.

He slumped—unconscious, not dead.

She could manage unconscious without a qualm.

Two more cultists went down under her swinging pole, but she had to wait for her moment and get enough space to wield it . . . and, good God, there were dozens of them. The melee of bodies literally clogged the deck.

Then she saw why. Another ship much like their xebec had drawn close—close enough to send more cultists scrambling over the side onto their deck whenever the gray waves pushed the ships close.

One glance along the deck told the story. Their band, aided by the captain and his crew, were fighting valiantly, and to that point had held their own. But there was no chance they could hold out forever, not against the tide of cultists waiting to jump across and join the fray.

Fear gripped her. Eyes wide, she scanned the deck. Through the faint veil of morning sea mist, she located all of their party, all still on their feet, still doggedly fighting, but two sailors were already down. As she watched, another fell.

Casualties. And there were going to be a lot more. Unless. . . .

A sudden upheaval of the bodies to her left had her hefting her staff and swinging that way.

But it was Gareth who erupted out of the pack. He'd been fighting a little way along the deck.

His eyes met hers. There was cold fury in his, but before he reached her a cultist pressed in. With a snarl, Gareth swung to deal with the attacker, sword swinging fluidly, effortlessly.

She edged back to give him room, her mind darting,

little bottles. He uses lots of rags. Put the rags in the bottles, light them, and . . ." She looked up at the sails of their ship, taut in the breeze—the fair wind was still blowing—then looked at the other ship. The cultists' ship. It, too, was under sail. "If their sails burn—"

She didn't need to finish. Gareth grabbed her arm and pushed her toward the stern ladder. "Come on!"

He had to help her slide between desperately fighting men. Suddenly, he reached over and past a set of shoulders, tagging someone in a scrum beyond.

An instant later, Bister popped through. "What?"

"Come with us." Gareth pushed past Emily to clear the area around the stern hatch. As soon as she could, Emily darted behind him and went down. At a nod from him, Bister ducked down behind her.

Gareth dallied to deal with the two cultists who had seen them go below. A slash on his upper arm and two scrapes later, he whirled and went down the ladder.

He found Emily and Bister working frantically, readying their little incendiaries. Emily had found a basket. She thrust the last of the pottery bottles wicked with rags into it, looked at him. "Tinder?"

He reached into his pocket and drew out his tinderbox.

Bister did the same. "But . . ." His young batman eyed the bottles." We'll need to be on deck before we light them."

"Indeed." Gareth reached for the basket—a sudden ruckus in the corridor had him seizing his sword instead and swinging to face the door.

But it was Watson who appeared. He was bleeding from a gash on his face. "What's to do?"

Gareth lowered his sword, lifted the basket. "How's your aim?"

He explained as, with Bister in the lead, they hurried back to the stern ladder. Setting the basket at the ladder's foot, Gareth handed two bottles to Watson, another two to Bister, then took two himself, tucking them into his breeches' pockets. "I'll go up first and clear an area—you follow, get those lit, and aim for their sails. Mooktu and Mullins are up there somewhere. We'll give you cover and I'll get my two

224

away when I can. But we'll almost certainly need more than those"—he nodded at the bottles they held—"to get their sails fully alight. So once you throw the first two, come and get more."

He turned to Emily. "You stay here, *down here*, and hand up the rest of the bottles as we come for them." He reinforced the order with a commanding stare—it had always worked on soldiers.

It suddenly struck him that he wanted to kiss her—desperately wanted to taste her lips for just a fleeting instant. He knew how badly the odds above were stacked against them.

Gripping his sword, he turned, and pushed past Bister. "Come on!" Without a backward glance, he led the way up and out.

Back into the cacophony of a battle that was definitely not going their way. This attack was infinitely better planned than any of the previous incidents; whoever had organized this knew his business.

His reemergence in the restricted space around the stern hatch temporarily swung the odds in that corner their way.

He found Mooktu, and with a word and a glance had him shoulder to shoulder, then Mullins saw, and although not knowing why, came to join them in clearing the area around the hatch and holding all comers back.

Gareth noticed Arnia at Mooktu's elbow, and Dorcas behind Mullins. Both women looked dishevled, but neither had wounds, and both had knives. He knew Arnia could use

teen sail.

The oil soaked in, then flared, and the sail caught.

As he'd expected, the sailors rushed to douse the flames, but Watson lobbed his bottles in quick succession, and fires bloomed on the rear lanteen.

With shouts and curses, the sailors on the other ship rushed to fill buckets. But before the flames were fully doused, Bister hit the middle sail again, and the very top of the rear lanteen.

The other ship started to lose speed and fall back—bringing their front lanteen into Bister's firing range. Watson concentrated on keeping the fires going on the middle and rear sails.

One of the advantages that until then the cultists had had was that they could remain intent and focused, uncaring of what else was happening on the xebec. But with their own ship in difficulties, that changed. Distracted, they glanced across the waves, only to see their ship drifting further back and away.

The tide of the battle, until then with the cultists, swung the other way. Dacosta and his crew sensed it. They were quick to capitalize, pushing hard to lower the number of cultists they had on board.

Some cultists decided the waves were safer.

And then, quite abruptly, the fighting on the xebec's deck reached the mopping-up stage. Bister popped up at Gareth's elbow as he stepped back from the waning fray.

"We're out of incendiaries"—Bister nodded at the other ship—"but looks like we had enough. Watson even managed to hit their sail locker, so they won't be coming after us anytime soon."

"Not unless they run out their oars." Dacosta pushed through the others to join them in the stern. He looked at the ship sliding away in their wake, then up at his own sails, and shook his head. "No, not even then." He glanced at Gareth. "These cultists—how likely are they to be competent oarsmen?"

"Not likely at all." Gareth glanced at Emily as she joined them. She appeared unharmed. She grasped his arm as if for support and comfort, and something inside him calmed.

Dacosta had brought his spyglass. He trained it on the other ship. "His crew will need to get those burning sails down and ditched before they can think about the oars, and if the cultists aren't able, there's not enough crew to make much of a show." He glanced back, signaled to his first mate. "We'll keep all sail on—in these conditions, it can't hurt."

Gareth caught Emily's eye. "That was an inspired idea to use the oil."

Dacosta glanced at her, brows rising. "That was your notion, mam'zelle?"

Emily smiled weakly. "We had to do so something, so . . ." She suppressed the impulse to lean heavily against Gareth. Fighting was horribly draining . . . truth be told, it was simply horrible all around. She tried not to look as the crew checked bodies, then heaved the dead overboard. Those cultists who were able had already jumped.

But the xebec was safe again, and so were they.

Dacosta acknowledged that with a low bow. "It seems we all owe you a debt, mam'zelle. For me and my crew—and my brother who owns this ship—I thank you."

Emily inclined her head, and kept hold of Gareth's arm. She'd noticed his cuts. None were still bleeding, but she was conscious of a definite desire to take his hand, lead him belowdecks, and wash and tend them. She wondered if perhaps she might manage it later.

Dacosta had his spyglass to his eye again. "If you can explain to me one thing, Major. Why is it the captain there"—

Dacosta nodded. "All xebec carry guns, but only small ones, and not many. But at such close quarters, he couldn't

227

have missed, and because of the oil, we would go" —he made a gesture— "*poof.*"

A rueful smile touching his lips, Gareth met her gaze briefly, then faced Dacosta. "It's that thing I'm carrying that they want. For once, it protected us. If they'd blown up the ship, even if they'd just sunk it, they would lose what they've been sent to fetch—and their master wouldn't like that."

Dacosta nodded. "I see. This master of theirs, this Black Cobra. I take it he doesn't forgive well?"

Gareth shook his head. "Not well. In fact, from what I've heard, he doesn't forgive at all."

The Black Cobra's lack of forgiveness, more specifically the vindictiveness visited upon any of the cult who failed, ranked high among the thoughts crowding Uncle's mind.

From the safety of the deck of a small but swift fishing sloop bobbing on the waves at some distance from the action, through a spyglass Uncle watched the engagement unfold, and cursed.

This time, he'd taken no chances. This time, he'd planned, and sent a force all had agreed would be more than enough to overrun the major's xebec.

But no. Once again, his enemy had triumphed. Once again his quarry had escaped.

He ground his teeth, and quickly counted the black-scarf-encircled heads on the deck of the now becalmed vessel.

Of the large force he'd committed, less than a third were returning.

Since leaving India, he'd lost a lot of men. The leader wouldn't be pleased.

A chill touched his nape, slid slowly down his spine.

He shivered, then shook off the sensation, the sense of helplessness.

He would turn the situation around. He would redeem himself by capturing both the major and his woman, and treating them to the epitome of Black Cobra vengeance.

He would avenge his son, and triumph in his master's name.

Lowering the spyglass, he squinted over the water, quietly intoned, "Glory to the Black Cobra."

He invested the words with the reverence of a prayer. He believed, in his heart, that it was.

As if in answer, the morning sun rose, sending a wash of pink and gold spreading across the sea.

Uncle turned and walked to where his lieutenant silently waited. "Tell the captain to make all speed for Marseilles." He glanced across the waves at the stern of the fleeing xebec. "Our pursuit is not over yet."

20th November, 1822
Early evening
My hammock in our tiny cabin

Dear Diary,

We are still feeling the effects of the action yesterday morning. Although we won through with our lives and with the ship intact, as I had feared, there were casualties. Captain Dacosta lost two of his crew, and two others are too injured to work. Gareth and our people are helping as best they can—Dacosta has kept on all sail, even through the night, keeping us flying over the waves to Marseilles. He wants to make the most of the fair conditions while they last. I think ex-

it was necessary or we would have died, so it seems futile to repine too much upon the moment.

229

Englishwomen abroad are supposed to be resilient.

And, indeed, I am trying to be. I have just returned from keeping vigil by Jimmy's hammock, and am writing now because at last I can report he is awake, and in reasonable possession of his senses. While the rest of our party ended the incident on our feet, albeit with injuries many of which required tending, Jimmy was, at first, nowhere to be found.

We searched in mounting horror, fearing he'd been flung overboard, but Bister finally found him under some cultists. Jimmy had a bad knife wound and had lost a lot of blood, but Gareth assured us the wound wasn't life-threatening, and indeed it turned out Jimmy had been knocked unconscious. But he did not stir until this morning, when Arnia and Dorcas managed to get some broth down his throat. He then lapsed back into unconsciousness, and we again feared, head injuries being so difficult to predict.

But he is fully awake now, and Bister is teasing him, so while he may take some days to regain his strength, he will pull through, I hope without lasting damage. I am hugely relieved, for I would have felt considerable responsibility had he died. Jimmy is in my train—one of my people—and our involvement in Gareth's mission and the attendant danger stems from my wish to follow him. It was my decision that brought us here. If Jimmy—or any of the others—had died, I would have felt it keenly.

I cannot imagine how much of such weighty responsibility already rests on Gareth's broad shoulders. He has been a field commander for years, and in active service for more than a decade. I am starting to appreciate how much he, and others like him, do in our country's cause, and how much they silently bear on their conscience for ever after. It cannot be a light burden, yet they never speak of it.

I cannot help wonder how heavily the weight of MacFarlane's death rests on Gareth and the other three I met that long-ago day at the officers' mess. Bad enough the death of a subordinate, but the death of a friend. . .

I believe it must be honor that helps them bear the load.

Once again, I am feeling the restrictions of this xebec keenly. All yesterday, and even now, I feel the need to go to Gareth, to see him, touch him, reassure myself that he is all right. I know he is, and I recognize the impulse as stemming from our recent brush with death, yet still it persists.

I did manage to commandeer a corner of the deck and tend his wounds—three slashes, none too deep, thank heaven, and a host of scratches that were already half healed. Yet what I wouldn't give for a private room, preferably with a bed—even a narrow one would do. As it is, there is nowhere I might even kiss him—and I am perfectly certain, honor-bound as he is, he will never kiss me in public.

It seems the rest of this leg of our journey will, of necessity, be devoted to preparing ourselves for the next.

Gareth beside her, and watched the port of Marseilles materialize out of the low-lying sea mist.

It was going to be a clear day. By the time the xebec had negotiated the harbor entrance and angled into a mooring on the incredibly busy wharves of what was, after all, the busiest port on the Mediterranean, the sun had risen and burned off the mist, and they could see everything with crystal-clear clarity—which meant anyone watching would be able to see them.

Luckily, the level of the sea was significantly lower than the wooden wharves, so once amid the congestion of ships, unless a watcher was looking down from the wharf directly above, those on the xebec weren't visible.

That, to Gareth's mind, was the only point in their favor. Wolverstone's orders had directed him to pass through Marseilles. While he understood why, and if he'd had only his own people with him, would have accepted the need without hesitation, now Emily and her people had joined his, the stakes had risen.

Specifically, what he now had at risk, now stood to lose, was significantly greater than he'd assumed would be the case.

Still, needs must when the devil drives.

The xebec bumped against the wharf. He glanced around the deck as the sailors swarmed up to lash the ship to the capstans above. Their party was already assembled, ready to climb the wooden ladder and depart the docks as quickly as they could. The others were standing by their bags. After some discussion, they'd all reverted to their customary clothes, European or Indian; there was no longer any advantage in their Arab disguises. For himself, he'd once again packed away his uniform and donned civilian attire.

Beside him, in her dark cloak worn over a blue carriage gown, Emily looked fetching and feminine. She murmured, "So as far as possible, you and I should do the talking."

She'd spoken in fluent French. After his years of fighting on the Continent, he, too spoke idiomatic French. Reluctantly, he nodded. "But wherever possible, play the great lady and let Watson speak for you." Watson was the only other of their party who spoke French well enough to pass. "Mullins has enough to get by with carriage drivers, stable boys, and the like, but unless there's a real need, we—you, Watson, and I—should shield the others from having to speak. If we can pass for French provincials on our way home, we're more likely to slip through the cult's net."

There would be a net, one spread over the entire city. Marseilles was the port he and any of the other three heading home by routes other than the Cape were most likely to come through. The one point in their favor was that Marseilles was large.

And bustling.

After exchanging last farewells with Dacosta and his crew, their party climbed up to the crowded wharf. They merged with the throng of other passengers disembarking or embarking on the dozens of vessels of all types and nations lining the many wharves.

Without overt hurry, with Emily on Gareth's arm, they headed along their wharf, making for the nearest way out of the dock area. They all kept their eyes peeled.

It was Jimmy who, head still bandaged, first spotted the enemy. He came up to report to Gareth, "There's one of them over by that blue warehouse up ahead, but he doesn't look like he's seen us."

Gareth looked, saw the cultist, and nodded. "Good." He glanced back at the others. "Turn right at the end of this section."

So he doesn't know that we're expected, let alone that we're here, or what our party looks like?"

233

"No. But that will change, probably by later today."

Gareth held them to the same brisk but unhurried pace—that of a household departing the docks, intent on getting on with their business—as they turned right, wheeling away from the cultist lurking in the shadows of the blue warehouse's open door. "We have to assume that by later this afternoon, they'll be hunting us specifically. We have to find cover—a very good bolt-hole—before then."

"So we shouldn't go anywhere near the consulate."

"No." The opening of a narrow street lay ahead. He led them to it as if that had been their goal from the first. Turning up the cobbled street, feeling the shadows close around them, the danger of the open docks falling behind, he said, "A small hostelry in some poorer area away from the docks, not too close to, but with good access to, the main coaching inns and the markets—at least for now, that's what we need."

Watson located just such a place. A small family-run enterprise tucked away down a street off a tiny local square, the inn was built of old stone and brick, its front door giving off the cobbled street. The street housed a haphazard collection of shops—a bakery, an apothecary, two small taverns, a patisserie, among others—all set between residential buildings of various sorts.

The spot was far enough away from the docks and the central part of the town to be almost wholly French, but this was Marseilles, so Mooktu's turban and Arnia's colorful shawls attracted no special attention.

It was mid-morning when Emily followed Watson into the inn's front room. While Watson went forward to meet the host and arrange for refreshments, Emily glanced around assessingly. Everything—literally every item her glance lit upon—was neat and clean, spic-and-span.

Indeed, much cleaner than any place she'd stayed in since leaving England. The innkeeper, or more likely his wife, was clearly houseproud. As she slid onto one of the bench seats along the wall, Emily realized how accustomed she'd grown to making do with much less in the way of accommodation.

Gareth came to join her. The others hung back, sidling toward other tables further back—instinctively reinstating the division between master and servants—but Gareth saw and beckoned them to join him and her about the large front table.

He settled beside her, between her and the door, eyes checking their position. He glanced up as Mullins approached. "You can take point." With his head Gareth indicated the seat closest to the window to the street. "I doubt we need to set a watch just yet, but if anyone should look in, you're least likely to be recognized."

Mullins nodded and sat. The others settled around the table.

"We still need to think of things like that, don't we?" Watson asked. "We're not out of the woods yet."

"Far from it." Gareth hesitated, then said, "Indeed, if anything we're in greater danger now, and as a group will be until we reach England. Once there, colleagues will be waiting. I imagine some of you will be able to stay in a safe house while I ferry the scroll holder to its final destination."

Her gaze on his face, Emily inwardly snorted. He'd better not be thinking of leaving her behind, tucked away in safety, while he faced danger alone.

The innkeeper bustled out from the kitchen with trays bearing coffee, a pot of hot chocolate, and sumptuous pastries. They all waited while he served. Her mouth watering, Emily beamed and, with Gareth, thanked him.

He paused. All the others were listening intently. "We have two options at this point, and we need to choose which one to take." He glanced around. "I could make the decision—as I generally do—but in this case, we all need to decide together, because whatever comes of that decision will be something we all have to face. We're all in this together."

No one argued. He went on, "We could flee the town now—hire the first two carriages we find and head north at a run before the cultists here in France even know we've landed. That's our first option and it has a certain attraction. However, if we do that, we won't have time to find coachmen willing and able to help us, to fight on our side if need be, nor will we be able to acquire any of the supplies we will need for the journey—we'd need to rely on stoppping in smaller towns and being able to find what we need there." He paused, then added, "All of us with pistols are low on powder and shot, and now we're back in Europe, we have to assume any men the cultists hire will use firearms, so from here on, we're much more likely to need our own."

Stirring his coffee, Watson nodded. "In addition to that, from here, there's really only one route—one halfway fast and direct route—we can take to the Channel ports. If we're in danger, then we can't afford to dally, yet once on that road, we'll be easy to track, easy to find."

Grimly, Gareth nodded. "Precisely. Either way, whether we flee now, or seize the cover of being in a town as crowded with people of all races as Marseilles to first make proper preparations, once we're on the road north, the cult will quickly pick up our trail."

They discussed it—how much they could foresee, what preparations they might make before leaving Marseilles that would help them evade subsequent capture and speed their journey north. Mooktu pointed out that, while they would be easier to track once on the road, in the French countryside the cultists themselves would be much more visible.

When the coffee and cakes were gone and the discussion wound down, Gareth called a vote. To his relief, the decision was unanimous. They would remain in Marseilles until they were ready to make a dash for the Channel coast.

Thirteen

25th November, 1822
Evening
A comfortable room in a tiny inn in Marseilles

Dear Diary,

So we are settled in Marseilles for the nonce, and while I wondered what possibilities staying in one place—one that isn't rocking and affords a suitable degree of privacy—might hold, the cultists have already intruded on our calm.

Bister took Jimmy out for a walk—we are all agreed he needs exercise and fresh air to improve—

descriptions in hand, the cultists—and indeed there seem quite a number—will organize a methodical search. Our out-of-the-way location will protect us for a day or so, but not forever. And it has already become apparent that finding and hiring the right sort of carriages and drivers, and reprovisioning those items we must have for our journey, will not be accomplished in a single day.

I am, as you will understand, finding all this a trifle frustrating. I am irritatingly aware that I have been unable to consolidate the significant gain I made in Tunis. Knowing Gareth, the longer I give him to think about things, the more likely he will erect another wall between us—leaving me to once again scrabble to pull it down.

I have already stated my dislike of blood and battles, but when it comes to these aggravating cultists, if I were to come upon one while holding a loaded pistol in my hand, I doubt I would hesitate to remove him from my path.

My latest personal mantra is: A pox on all cultists.

E.

The next morning, garbed as any young Frenchwoman with her cloak over her shoulders, Emily walked the short distance to the town market.

Gareth strode by her side, his expression impassive, his eyes constantly scanning. He didn't trust anyone else with her safety, an irritating development, but one he wasn't in any mood to resist.

If he wasn't by her side, he'd be distracted, unable to make sound decisions, so there wasn't any point fighting the now insistent compulsion.

Dorcas followed behind them, a basket over her arm, Mullins by her side. Recalling what he'd noticed on the xebec's deck during the battle, Gareth suspected there was a bud-

238

ding romance there. Regardless, he was glad of Mullins's company, and Bister was ambling around them, sometimes ahead, sometimes behind in his usual role of scout.

They had no difficulty finding the market—they followed the noise and the smells. Some were savory, others less so, but once they reached the square and merged into the loud, constantly shifting crowd, all individual aromas melted into the rich potpourri of the market.

Although they didn't need food in the general sense, they'd agreed that once on the road they wouldn't stop for lunch, but would eat on the run as it were. After circling the stalls selling fresh fruit, Emily bought a sack of crisp apples, a selection of other fruits and vegetables that would keep, and handfuls of various nuts in their shells.

While Dorcas tucked the packages into her basket, Emily turned to him. "Can you see where the stalls selling cured meats and cheeses are?"

Raising his head, he looked over the crowd, saw those stalls along a distant wall. He also saw two cultists strolling down the aisle toward them. The pair were still some way ahead, but they weren't shopping.

He'd taken Emily's arm before he'd thought. Bending close, he spoke quietly as he turned her. "Cultists ahead— we'll backtrack, then circle around. The stalls you want are along the far wall."

She met his eyes, nodded, then calmly gathered Dorcas and Mullins as they passed. In good order they retreated out

"Just as well for us, I suppose."

Gareth returned a noncommittal grunt. If the cultists left

off their insignia, given the number of foreigners from every land under the sun to be found in Marseilles, he and the others would be in very big trouble. Not for the first time, he gave thanks for the cultists' arrogance.

They spent another half hour in the crowded market, every minute on high alert. By the time they quit the main square, loaded with the hams, blocks of hard cheese, and the fruits and vegetables, and headed via a series of narrow streets back to their inn, Emily felt exhausted, emotionally wrung out.

She felt like a piano wire that had been strung too tight for too long—she wanted nothing more than to snap and sag.

To find relief . . . release.

Much like another sort of tension, and the blissful release she'd discovered it could lead to.

She slanted a glance at Gareth, striding close beside her. Although he was looking ahead, alert and focused, she was sure that if she took one step in the wrong direction, away from him, his entire attention would snap back to her. If she walked into a room he was in, he glanced at her immediately. Every time she left him, she felt his gaze on her back until she'd passed out of his sight.

If she was in his presence, even if he wasn't looking at her, he knew exactly where she was.

The knowledge buoyed her, and comforted, too. If she had to walk through ever-present danger, having a possessive predator at her side was no bad thing.

But there was a counterside to that. Said ever-present danger was a very big hurdle in her path. While he remained focused on the enemy, and even more on protecting her, the chances of him initiating any intimate interlude were, she estimated, effectively nil.

Being intimate was a time when his guard was down. He wouldn't suggest it.

He'd warned that the danger—and therefore the tension—was only going to escalate, at least until they reached England, and probably beyond that. If they were to share any more interludes between now and the end of his mission, she would have to instigate them.

But should she?

She glanced at him as they turned into the street in which their inn stood. She detected no lessening in the battle-ready tension that held him, no easing of his all-but-constant surveillance of their surroundings.

Should she distract him—not now, but tonight?

Or should she acquiesce to what she knew would be his choice, and wait until they reached England and his mission was complete before again addressing their putative relationship?

If she waited, social mores would come to his aid. Once at home, it would be difficult for her to refuse his suit, even to delay, if he pressed. She was fairly certain he would. As matters stood, their marriage was no longer in question—it was the nature of said marriage they had yet to resolve.

She glanced at him again—and caught him watching her, rather speculatively, but he immediately looked away.

Was he thinking, imagining, considering, as she was?

She couldn't imagine the prospect of another interlude hadn't occurred to him, yet regardless of the prompting of his instincts, she would wager her life he wouldn't come to her bed. Not unless . . .

Unless she issued an invitation he couldn't—wasn't strong enough to—resist.

The notion tantalized her adventurous side.

Stifling a humph, she went inside.

241

26th November, 1822
Early evening
My room in the inn at Marseilles

Dear Diary,

Yesterday afternoon I announced my intention of taking the air, so of course Gareth came with me. I had intended to use the opportunity to address, in speech, our future, but the instant we set foot outside, the potential danger was thick in the air and his tension so palpable that it affected me. And so, far from resolving anything, I cut short our excursion, considering it dishonorable to put him so on edge, and myself as well, all for nothing.

Clearly, the direct approach is not going to work, not while he feels compelled to look everywhere at once, rather than at me.

Last night, in fairness to him, I lay in my bed and forced myself to fully evaluate the pros and cons of reestablishing an intimate connection at this time, one that will continue throughout the rest of this fraught and dangerous journey, and subsequently on into our married life. I rather rapidly reached the undeniable conclusion that if I don't, I am unlikely ever to learn what degree of feeling he truly possesses for me. Once in England, he will retreat behind that wall of polite civility that is the hallmark of an English gentleman, and I will never be able to winkle the truth out of him—he is made of such stern stuff, I swear he is near as stubborn as I, so that route simply will not do.

If I am ever to learn what he truly feels for me, I must act, and indeed, this journey is my best chance to learn all. My best weapon is propinquity, for while we race north through France, we will necessarily be in each other's pockets, and he will not, not for a minute, be able to overlook me.

I therefore resolved to act, however much brazenness that might entail. Faint heart never won all she wanted, and I am determined to have all—everything I dreamed might be once I found my "one." I have waited too long to make do with half measures—a marriage based on love yet with that love unacknowledged.

Sadly, having reached this point of calm decision, I fell asleep.

So tonight will be the night, dear Diary—wish me luck!

Whatever it takes, I will not be gainsaid.

E.

By dinnertime that evening, Gareth was desperate. In more ways than one, but he sternly forced himself to focus on his mission—on the undeniable imperative that he organize safe passage onward.

He knew what he needed—two fast carriages, with two drivers who understood, appreciated, and accepted the likelihood of attack. He refused to put men's lives at risk without their knowledge and consent. He'd prefer them enthusiastic.

the town. It would be a few days yet before the searchers reached their neighborhood.

243

He'd been silent through their meal. He'd felt Emily's gaze on his face a number of times, but hadn't met it. Finally, he set down his knife and fork, pushed his plate away, leaned back in his chair—and raised his eyes to hers.

She looked at him for a moment, then asked, "What's wrong?"

"No carriages." He explained the problem, and the increasing urgency.

Her gaze grew distant, then she said, "You asked at the major coaching inns. What about some of the smaller ones?"

He frowned, but before he could reply she leaned closer, laying one hand atop his where his rested on the table. He quashed an impulse to turn that hand and close it about her slim fingers.

"No." Her gaze slid past him, lingered for an instant, then returned to his face. "I was thinking, for instance, of this inn. It doesn't have carriages for hire—well, nothing bigger than a gig—but it's family run. And families have cousins, and uncles, and know other connections in the same business."

She again looked past him. He realized she was looking at the innkeeper further down the room.

"Why not ask our host?" She looked back and met his eyes. "We've been here two days, and they've been very good—interested in a nice way, not pushy, and Arnia and Dorcas get on well with the innwife. She helped with a tisane for Jimmy's headache." Enthusiasm infused her expression. "It won't hurt to ask."

Looking into her face, he tried to remember caution. "We'll have to take them into our confidence—what if, once we do, they think it too dangerous for us to remain here?"

"They won't turn us out—not if we explain properly." It was she who squeezed his fingers. "Come on—let's try."

He hesitated for a moment more, then returned the pressure of her fingers, reluctantly released her hand, and rose.

They'd dined relatively late, and the other diners—locals

for the most part—had already left. Only three men remained, sharing a jug of wine. The innkeeper was amenable to joining Gareth and Emily at a small table in one corner. At Emily's suggestion, he summoned his wife to join them. She came, curiosity in her eyes.

Gareth commenced by explaining he and most of their party were English, which came as no surprise, yet with Napoleon's defeat only seven years past there were formalities to observe. Luckily, most Frenchmen, especially those in trade, had reverted to treating the English with their customary, occasionally arrogant, tolerance. Nevertheless, Gareth omitted to mention his part in the earlier war, saying only that he'd been serving in India until recently, and was presently on a mission coinciding with his return to England.

In the sparsest of terms, he outlined their journey, and explained the existence and the intent of the cultists.

Eyes wide, the innwife asked about the cult. Leaning forward, Emily replied. Before Gareth could reassert control, she'd taken over relating their tale.

Her descriptions were more colorful, her answers more direct, and rather more sensational than his. He wasn't at all comfortable with her tack, let alone her openness, but one glance at the innkeeper's and innwife's faces and he shut his lips, and let Emily hold the stage.

And it was a performance. She seemed to know just what to say, and how to respond to the innkeeper's many questions. It wasn't just what she said, but how she said it; her

doubt as to where his duty lay.

Gareth had considered Emily's notion that the innkeeper's family connections would be sufficient to get them what they needed a long shot, but she'd been right. Spurred by their story—indeed, clearly thrilled to have been trusted and asked—the innkeeper summoned his sons and dispatched them hither and yon.

An hour later, numerous uncles and cousins had gathered, and the noise in the now otherwise empty front room had escalated as people exclaimed and shouted suggestions. Gareth had never seen the like before, but within a surprisingly short time, two fast traveling carriages had been organized, along with two experienced drivers who were very willing to offer their services in defeating the so-alien cult.

He shook hands with the two grizzled war veterans who had volunteered to take the reins and drive them to the north coast with all possible speed. "Thank you." They'd discussed and settled on their payment. "There'll be a bonus at the end, too."

"Heh!" one said, making a very gallic gesture. "The money is one thing, but to be part of an action against a worthy enemy again—that is a better incentive."

The other nodded emphatically. "But yes. Life has grown boring, you understand. A little excitement—this is what we seek."

With the good wishes and enthusiastic support of the innkeeper's family, their departure was organized for the day after the next.

"So you will have only tomorrow to get ready," the innwife yelled. She flung out her arms in an all-encompassing gesture. "No matter—we will help."

The gathering turned into something of a family occasion. Gareth took his lead from Emily, and they remained for some time, chatting with those who had come at the innkeeper's summons to so readily offer them aid.

He was still somewhat stunned that they had, but they were sincere in wanting to assist him and their group against the cultists, and he was equally sincere in his gratefulness.

Eventually Emily bade the company good night and re-tired. Shortly afterward, he did the same, climbing the stairs to his room. The din from downstairs faded as he closed the door. Crossing to the small side table, he lit the lamp upon it, then quietly, still pondering the garrulous warmth of those downstairs, he undressed.

He'd doused the lamp and was lying on his back, stretched naked beneath the covers, arms crossed behind his head, staring up at the dim ceiling, when the handle of his door turned.

He came instantly alert, but in the same instant, somehow, he knew.

Sure enough, the door opened and Emily, clad in white nightgown and cloak, whisked through, whirling to shut the door quietly behind her before turning to peer at the bed.

The room was cloaked in shadows, but she saw him, and relaxed.

Even more alert, and distinctly intrigued, he watched as she clearly debated, then elected to walk to the side of the bed further from the door.

Muscles all but imperceptibly tightening, he waited, un-moving and silent, to see what she would do, say.

She halted when she was close enough to meet his eyes. She narrowed hers fractionally in warning. "Don't say a word."

He wondered why she'd thought he would argue.

Letting her cloak fall, she reached for the covers, and slipped into the bed. He shifted to give her room. His greater

She dragged in a breath. "Now . . ." She lifted her head, looked into his face, one small hand rising to frame his jaw.

Then she levered up on one arm, rising above him. She looked down into his eyes. "Now this."

And she kissed him.

He kissed her back, took a long moment to savor the sweetness she so flagrantly gifted him with. Sensing she wished it, he let her keep the reins. For now.

She leaned into him, all soft, warm curves and slender, feminine lengths. Lying on his back beneath her, something within him purred. Closing his hands about her waist, he lifted and shifted her more fully upon him, settling her so her taut belly lay over his abdomen, the haven between her thighs just above the head of his engorged erection—both promise and torment, temptation and salvation. He vaguely recalled he'd decided to forgo her and this for the present, while they were traveling, but he could no longer remember any pressing reason why.

No convincing reason why he should decline the heaven she was so blatantly offering—and she'd come to him, after all.

She was already his—that was beyond question—so there was no reason he shouldn't indulge.

So he did.

Increasingly ravenously.

It gradually dawned that while she'd initiated the exchange, and had chosen the position, she didn't know quite how to proceed.

He showed her. Urged her up so she was on her knees straddling him, reached up, stretched up, and helped her draw her nightgown off over her head.

She flung the garment to the floor. She was already heated, already breathless and panting, already aching for him to fill her. The look she flung at him—eyes blazing fire in the night—said it all.

Before she could reach for him, and make matters that much more complicated, he hauled in a breath, locked his hands about her waist, positioned her, then nudged past her slick swollen folds and eased into her.

Eyes closing, her expression one of fraught bliss, she took over and sank down. Down.

Wriggled at the last, and then, wonder of wonders, she'd enclosed him all.

He sucked in a tight breath, closed his eyes in sheer lust as experimentally, she tightened about him.

Then she settled to ride him.

By the time he'd recalled her reportedly wild and expert ride down from Poona, she'd reduced him to a state of ravening urgency almost impossible to deny.

But he wanted more.

Eyes closed tight, her entire concentration locked on where they joined, Emily felt the heat, the stoking friction, well, swell and rise, taunting and beckoning, tightening inexorably . . . then she felt him shift beneath her.

She cracked open her eyes as, releasing her hips, he locked both hands about her breasts.

And played until she was gasping.

Then he rose up, leaned forward, took one tightly furled nipple into his mouth—and suckled.

She only just managed to mute her shriek, but that didn't deter him. He feasted—there was no other word for it. With lips, tongue, teeth and greedy mouth, he caressed, then blatantly possessed.

Eyes closing, she continued to rise up and slide down, increasingly intently, wanting, reaching, so tight she thought she would shatter, so hot she could feel the flames licking over her, sliding beneath her skin.

He released one breast, slid his hand down, tracing the

and incandescant pleasure erupted and lanced through her, streaking and sparking down every nerve before melting and merging into molten streams that flowed down every vein to pool in her throbbing womb.

He held her as she savored, as if he savored, too.

Then he turned. Taking her with him, he rolled, and pinned her beneath him.

A smile on her lips, she wound her arms about his neck, then arched beneath him, head falling back on a gasp as he thrust deeply and heavily into her.

To her immense surprise he withdrew from her, pulling back onto his knees.

Before she could react beyond opening her eyes, he grasped her knees and pulled them wide.

He looked down at her, at her most private place. Even though the shadows lay heavily upon them, she blushed, but she didn't try to close her knees, didn't try to inhibit his view.

The blood still pounding in her veins, she waited to see what he wanted, what he would do.

He bent his head and set his lips to her there, and she very nearly screamed.

Pleasure—different, sharper, headier—streaked through her. He pressed deeper, lapping, then probed with his tongue and in desperation she whispered his name—but what she wanted she couldn't have said. His tongue circled, then probed. She caught her breath, and clutched at his head, but her fingers, tangling in his hair, had no strength.

His exploration, his flagrant tasting of her, sent her senses soaring.

She was his—she knew it, and clearly he did, too, at least on this level.

That was undeniable as he feasted as thoroughly as he had earlier, his hot mouth a brand searing her, his experience trapping her senses, making them and her whole body—her nerves, her skin, her heart, every curve—his.

His to plunder, to savor as he wished.

Head helplessly threshing, she could barely breathe when she whispered his name, an outright plea—she couldn't take much more of the soul-wringing pleasure.

He heard, thank God. With one long, last lap, he lifted his head, gazed at her for a moment, then unhurriedly surged over her. Fitting his erection to her entrance, he thrust in, slow and relentless, deep and sure, impressing on her every inch of his length, then he sank home, reached down and raised one of her knees, hooked that leg over his hip. Poised on his elbows above her, he looked down at her face through the darkness, his expression a mask of intent, his features locked in the grip of a passion so intense she could feel its heated wings beating against her skin. Then he withdrew, and thrust home.

Again and again, harder and harder, deeper and deeper, until she sobbed his name, then, arched beneath him, fingers locked about his upper arms, nails sinking into his skin, she felt herself literally come apart.

Gareth swooped and covered her lips with his, drank her cry, her scream of pure pleasure.

Felt everything that was male within him exult.

Felt the primitive possessive being within him purr with a satisfaction that sank bone deep as he held still for an instant and savored the evocative ripples of her release, felt her sheath contract and grip.

Felt anticipation and blind need claw . . .

He surrendered and took, gorged, and filled his senses.

Eyes closed, he lost himself in her.

27th November. 1822

and see if the lure sank deeply enough.
The day went in making our final preparations.

*Thanks to the Juneaux, our hosts, all is as sound
and complete as might be, and everything lies in readi-
ness for us to depart tomorrow morning on our race
to Boulogne. That is the port Gareth's instructions
stipulate he should use. I must admit that while I will
be happy to see it, and indeed, to look upon England's
shores once more, I view this last leg as a succession of
opportunities—chances to prompt Gareth into recognizing and declaring his love.*

Preferably of the enduring variety.

Preferably before we see the green fields of England.

*I wait on tenterhooks to see if my ploy of last night
will yield the desired outcome—the first step in my
campaign.*

As ever, I am hopeful.

E.

His day had been a distracting round of last minute checks
and solutions. Nevertheless, as he climbed the stairs that
night, Gareth felt quietly sure that they'd done all they
could—that, indeed, courtesy of the Juneaux and Emily's
recruiting of them, their party was better placed to succeed
in their mad dash north to the Channel than he'd dared hope
they would be.

Reaching the upper corridor, he was conscious of a certain
tension, familiar, almost reassuring—the tension that came
on the night before a battle, when the certainty of being fully
prepared warred with the inevitability of having to wait until
morning to act.

He was too experienced to let it trouble him. Indeed, he
embraced it.

But the other tension sliding through him, coiling beneath
the first, was something else entirely.

That tension was wholly due to her—to Emily, and her
appearance last night in his room. More, her performance,

252

their activities, in his bed. He would have preferred it to be otherwise, but he couldn't deny it—couldn't pretend that he didn't feel expectation rise as he neared his door.

That anticipation didn't leap as he closed his hand about the knob.

Already half erect, his heart already thudding that telltale touch faster, he opened the door and went in. His gaze went directly to the bed.

It was empty.

In the dimness, his eyes scanned again, just to make sure, but he hadn't missed any alluring body.

She hadn't come.

Closing the door, he stood and stared at the bed.

One part of his brain had already skittered off into recriminations—last night he'd done something she didn't like, or he'd failed to do something she'd expected. Or—

The more rational part of his mind shut out the tirade of unhelpful suggestions. The part of him that was the experienced commander recalled and coolly evaluated.

Why hadn't she come? That was the question he needed to answer.

It took some moments before he thought back far enough to recall the particular deliberation with which she'd entered his room last night. And then to connect that with the assessing glances she'd thrown his way throughout the day, and especially that evening.

Last night, she hadn't come to his room on a whim—she'd

All of it true, but his need of her was something he would far prefer to hide, especially from her.

While on the xebec, there'd been no question of his joining her at night, and here . . . it had seemed wiser to keep his distance. For him to keep their future, and her, at a distance, at least until they reached England, whereupon he would have all manner of accepted practices behind which to hide.

To conceal just how deeply his feelings for her ran.

He didn't even know how those feelings had come to be—what they were due to, or when they'd afflicted him and sunk to his marrow—but they were there now, an obvious vulnerability, at least to him.

If he kept his distance, he could cling to the fiction that he was marrying her because they were generally compatible, and he'd weakened and seduced her, ergo marrying her was the necessary outcome, one with which he was comfortable.

He shouldn't go to her room, shouldn't reveal even that degree of need for her.

He could excuse not going on safety grounds—safer for them all if he wasn't distracted by having her beside him, let alone beneath him.

Then again, one very definite, insistent part of him was quick to point out that her safety would be even better assured if she spent the nights in his arms, and he would be far less distracted by thoughts of whether she was safe or not; if she were lying beside him, he would instantly know.

Given they'd be staying at inns such as this from now on. . .

He grimaced as his excuse evaporated.

To go, or not to go?

He shouldn't. He wouldn't . . .

Perhaps if he waited, she'd grow impatient and come to him?

Half an hour ticked by, and she didn't appear.

And he discovered her patience was greater than his.

With a muttered curse, he stalked to the door.

Her room was further away from the stairs and around a corner. He opened the door without knocking and went in, shut the door carefully, then walked to the bed.

She was lying there, wide awake, propped up on the pillows so she could more easily watch him approach. She'd tucked the covers up over her breasts, but her shoulders were promisingly bare.

As he halted by the bed, she met his eyes, her own wide, but nowhere near innocent. Even as he watched, her lips curved lightly in a smug, cat-who'd-managed-to-tip-over-the-cream smile.

He narrowed his eyes, pointed a finger at her nose. "I know what you're up to, and I'm not playing your game."

Emily felt distinctly wanton as she looked into his dark eyes. Brazen, she arched her brows. "You're here, aren't you?"

"My being here doesn't mean what you think it does."

"Oh?" She widened her eyes; beyond her control, her smile deepened. "What does it mean then?"

He studied her for an instant, then shrugged out of his coat. Growled, "We can talk about it later."

Dropping the coat on a chair, he reached for his cravat.

Smiling even more smugly, feeling anticipation well and spread in a rich warm glow throughout her body, she sank deeper into the pillows and waited.

For her lover—her would-be husband—to join her.

He didn't disappoint.

Some considerable time later, slumped, utterly wrung out and deeply sated in the depths of the bed, Emily finally managed to reassemble her wits, and discovered she was still smiling.

Her plan had worked.

ecstasy called forth entirely by his wicked hands and even wickeder lips and tongue.

And what had come after that had curled her toes. She still couldn't fully straighten them. Little tremors of delight still coursed through her, fading echoes of her second shattering climax.

She was lying on her stomach. Cracking open her lids, she studied him, slumped, as exhausted as she, beside her. He'd said they would talk later, but she suspected her sisters were right. Afterward, gentlemen didn't talk—they fell asleep.

Not that she was complaining, not in this instance. Closing her eyes, she let satiation and an even deeper satisfaction wrap about her. Her plan had worked, he'd come to her bed—he hadn't been able to stay away. Actions always spoke louder than words, especially with gentlemen.

His actions had spoken loudly enough for now.

Through the fringe of his lashes, Gareth watched her slide into slumber, and gave thanks. He'd been a fool to suggest they talk later—later meant now, and now . . . words of any sort about this and them were entirely too dangerous.

Entirely too unwise.

The possessiveness inside him lay quiet, serene, sated into oblivion; she'd given herself to him without reserve and that side of him had gorged. Lids closing, he felt satiation of a depth and weight he'd never before known drag him down. With an almost sinful sense of sinking, he surrendered. Later he would gather her into his arms, later he would settle her beside him.

Later, when she wouldn't wake up and through the darkness look at him with eyes that saw too much.

In that last gasp of consciousness, his mind circled, free. She already knew more than he would wish, but he couldn't turn back the clock. But as long as he didn't admit to more, didn't state what he felt for her aloud in words and make it real, he could cope.

He could cope with this. Perhaps she was right. Perhaps his sharing her bed every night would satisfy what he was starting to sense was her need. A need to know what he felt, to touch him and have him touch her, and so know . . .

It went something like that, he knew. So perhaps she was right, and his sharing her bed would satisfy her.

God knew, it satisfied him.

28th November, 1822
Early morning
Still abed, scribbling madly

Dear Diary,

> *My fingers are crossed, metapohorically at least.*
> *Matters appear to be progressing as I wish—my cam-*
> *paign to encourage Gareth to recognize and declare his*
> *feelings for me is under way, and with luck I have laid*
> *the groundwork for a continuing engagement. After*
> *last night, I am hopeful that he will be sufficiently*
> *motivated to join me in my bed at our various halts*
> *through France, and with luck, beyond.*
>
> *It is no doubt quite wanton to be plotting like this,*
> *but needs must. I am committed to hearing his true*
> *feelings declared, and with every day that passes, I am*
> *more convinced than ever that in order for us to form*
> *the true partnership I have always believed marriage*
> *should be, then hearing his love acknowledged and de-*
> *clared is a necessity, for both of us.*

E.

The small yard behind the inn was a frenzy of activity. Gareth ran his eye over the loaded coaches, watched as Mooktu and Bister handed up pistols, powder, and shot to Mullins, who stowed it with the rifles he'd cleaned beneath first one, then the other, driver's seat.

They were as ready as they would ever be.

Around him, the cobbled yard was awash with Juneaux, young and old, come to wave their two men on their way, and to wish the English and Indian party the garrulous clan had taken under their collective wing God speed.

He went to extract Emily from a knot of Juneaux. Many were female, and looked at him with bright, assessing eyes. He had little doubt what thoughts were passing through their heads, especially when one old lady whispered loudly that they made a so-handsome couple.

He pretended not to hear.

Emily was smiling happily. She looked up as he neared, and her smile changed. Quite how he couldn't have said, but it softened, became more personal, then she made space for him beside her.

He filled it, but only to smile generally at the others and remind her, "We must make a start."

Or they would be there all day.

Emily heard the unvoiced phrase, and had to agree. But then his hand brushed the back of her waist and she had to work to suppress a delicious little shiver—something the women around her didn't miss.

They beamed encouragingly.

She had to beam back, had to inwardly acknowledge how very good it felt to be the one Gareth—he of the broad shoulders and so-handsome brown-haired good looks—had come to fetch.

His hand touched again, a subtle prod. Squelching her reaction, she turned to the innwife and commenced her farewells.

Exclamations, good wishes, and effusive thanks were shared all around, then with his hand at the back of her

258

waist, Gareth steered her inexorably to the carriages. Finally reaching the door of the first, she turned and waved one last time to the assembled throng, then she took the hand he offered, felt his fingers close strong and warm about hers, and felt that little thrill of delight—of feminine possessiveness—streak through her again. Drawing in a calming breath, she allowed him to help her into the sleek carriage.

Gareth turned to the crowd, and with a genuine but faintly strained smile, bowed and, in more formal words, thanked them. Then he turned to the carriage and climbed up, pulled up the steps and shut the door.

Bister and the coachman were already on the box waiting. Dorcas sat opposite Emily. Gareth claimed the seat beside her as a whip snapped showily, the horses leaned into the traces, and their carriage lurched, then rumbled through the mews and out onto the side street.

Cheers and farewells echoed, then faded as the houses closed around them. He glanced back as they rounded a corner, confirming that the second carriage, carrying Arnia and Mooktu, Watson and Mullins, with Jimmy currently up with the driver, was following close behind.

"I assume we'll need to go slowly through the town."

He glanced at Emily, and saw she was peering out of the other window. "Yes—and it might be better to stay back from the windows."

"Oh." She drew back immediately. "The cultists are out there somewhere, aren't they?"

Emily and Dorcas played spot the monument as the two carriages preserved a decorous pace through the busy morning streets. Letting their disconcertingly normal exclamations and chatter wash over him, Gareth allowed himself to do something he hadn't until that point—he thought of the other three, wondered where they were, how they were faring.

All four had been through thick and thin together, ridden side by side into battles uncounted. Even though the last years as commanders had seen them spend more of their time in the saddle apart, it hadn't lessened their connection—that link that had been forged in the heat of battles in the Peninsula more than a decade before.

By choice, none of them knew what route any of the other three was taking home. He didn't even know who was carrying the vital original of the document they had to deliver to the Duke of Wolverstone to ensure the end of the Black Cobra's reign—he only knew it wasn't him. His was a decoy's mission, the parchment in his scroll holder, identical to the other three, no more than a copy.

But the Black Cobra and the cultists didn't know that. Given what was at stake, he had fully expected the Cobra to chase him regardless. In that, he hadn't been disappointed, which was all to the good.

Yet on this last leg before England, his orders from the man who had for years been known only as Dalziel were specific. He and his party were to do all they could to draw as many of the enemy as possible, and to reduce their numbers as much as fate permitted.

He'd interpreted those orders as indicating that whoever was carrying the vital original would also pass through the Continent on their way to England. Whichever of his three friends was running that most dangerous of gauntlets, their safety in part depended on him—on how effectively he carried out his mission.

He'd set out from India with Bister, Mooktu, and Arnia, all of whom—even Arnia—could take care of themselves in a fight. With just those three in his train, he'd been free to engage the enemy whenever and wherever he could.

But now he had Emily, Dorcas, Jimmy, Mullins, and Watson as well. Mullins could hold his own, but the other four, no matter their resourcefulness, weren't safe in a fight. All four needed protection, Emily most of all.

Especially Emily, especially now . . . now she'd come to mean so much to him.

So much more than he'd imagined was possible, than he'd known could possibly be.

As the horses trudged on, he gazed, unseeing, out of the window at the passing streetscapes, and wondered how he was going to carry out his orders while keeping her, and the others who were important to her—all now in his care—safe.

They'd passed through the town center and were ambling through the northern suburbs, already on the highway that would take them to Lyon and beyond, when he became aware of Emily's gaze on his face.

The feminine commentary had ceased. One glance revealed that Dorcas was already nodding, her eyes closed.

Turning his head, he met Emily's bright gaze.

Tilting her head, she smiled. "I was wondering . . . you told me you're an only child, but do you have cousins, other family?"

They were to marry, so she needed to know. He shook his head. "No. There's just me, now. My parents were only children, too. They married later in life, so were older when I was born. My father was a vicar, but he was one of

Happiness lit her face as she said, "I was born at Eldridge Hall, my parents' house—it's just outside Thornby, in

261

Northamptonshire. That's home—for me, and all my brothers and sisters. At least it was until they married—there's only me and Rufus still left in the nest, as it were, but the others visit often."

"You're one of eight, as I recall. I take it you have lots of cousins, too?" That, he realized, explained her ease with the Juneaux, her facility in interacting with them—something he'd lacked. Not that he'd known he'd lacked, not until he'd seen her engage with the large family in a way he would never have thought to do . . . probably couldn't have done even if he'd wished. He simply didn't know how, didn't know the ways.

"Yes, there's quite a clan—a horde of uncles, aunts, and cousins on both sides."

He didn't need to ask how she got on with her family—the answer was there in her affectionate smile, in the light that glowed in her eyes.

He'd never shared that sort of connection with anyone, not when he was a child, not later . . . until he'd joined the Guards and, from the first, had fallen in with Del, Rafe, and Logan.

"I don't have any siblings"—he met her eyes—"but you might say I have brothers-in-arms."

She looked into his eyes, studied them. "Those three in the officers' mess?"

He nodded. She didn't ask, didn't press, but as they rolled on up the highway and the northern outskirts of Marseilles fell behind, he told her how he'd met the other three—told her tales of their exploits and adventures. When she laughed, he asked about her brothers and sisters, and she reciprocated, opening his eyes to a love he'd never known. The closest thing to it was the camaraderie, the connection, he shared with the other three, yet even that fell short of the warmth, depth, and breadth of togetherness Emily described, that she'd experienced and embraced within her family.

The more she told him, the more he yearned for something he'd never known. When he married her . . .

The thought circled in his brain as he and she fell silent, and the carriage rumbled steadily on.

"He is like a cobra himself." The eldest of the three cultists sent to watch the highway leading north out of Marseilles hawked and spat on the rocky ground. "I would not be angering Uncle for anything today. He was in such a mood after the others from the docks came yesterday to report that they hadn't seen the major or his party."

The three were perched among rocks and boulders on a shoulder overlooking the highway.

The youngest grinned slyly. "Those men were lucky. I heard Akbar say that Uncle has lost so many men already that he won't discipline any—he needs every able-bodied man he has, at least for now."

"Ah—that explains it." The third man nodded. "I have never known Uncle to be so lenient before. Usually, one mistake, and—" He drew his finger across his throat. "The cult does not tolerate failure."

"This is true." The eldest nudged the youngest with the toe of his boot. "You will be wise to remember that if—as seems likely—the major manages to take this road north before the others can catch him in the town. If that happens, Uncle will gather most of us and head north in pursuit—and I know for a fact that the Black Cobra has placed many, many of us along this channel up there. If the major goes that way, Uncle will follow, and then he'll have plenty of men—and

The youngest bounced with excitement, then lowered the spyglass and held it out. "That is them—I am sure of it.

Look at the men beside the drivers. The first is the major's batman, yes?"

The eldest had taken the spyglass. After a moment, he nodded. He handed the glass on to the third man, then turned to the youngest. "You stay here until they pass, then follow, but not close. Stay off the road and do not let them see you. We" —he collected his comrade with a glance— "will go and take the good news to Uncle. When he and the rest of us catch up with you, Uncle will commend you as you rightly deserve."

Meanwhile the elder two, who had been staring at the sky for hours, would reap the glory of Uncle's approbation, but the youngest cultist knew that that was the way of the world, so he nodded. "I will follow them, and wait for Uncle and the others to join me."

Without further ado, the elder two scrambled back over the rocks to where they'd left their stolen mounts.

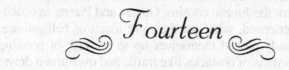

Fourteen

30th November, 1822
Mid-morning
In our carriage on the road to Lyon

Dear Diary,

    I am rushing to scribble this while Gareth is out of the carriage getting fresh horses put to. The last two days—and even more the last two nights—have been well worth my earlier efforts. My campaign has been assisted by the smallness of the village inns we've stopped at. As I invariably have the largest and most comfortable chamber to myself, and Arnia

E.

265

*T*hat evening they arrived in Lyon. They'd made excellent time, and Gareth thanked the twist of fate that had sent them the Juneau cousins, Gustav and Pierre, as coachmen. Experienced, with just the right touch of belligerence, they'd already proved themselves up to the task of pressing ahead regardless of obstacles like traffic and overturned drays.

They'd barreled through, and they'd reached their first major town without seeing hide nor hair of any cultist.

That, Gareth felt certain, would change all too soon.

With Emily, smiling sweetly, beside him, he walked into the town's largest hotel. It was a predominantly timber structure. He would have preferred stone, but the further they'd come north, the weather had turned damp and cold, and smaller establishments came with other hazards, namely easy access to the upper floors.

One glance confirmed that this hotel provided reasonable security. He continued to the counter at the rear of the foyer, Emily on his arm.

There were plenty of rooms to be had. He could easily request adjoining chambers for him and Emily, but didn't. Their party was already cognizant of the fact that they were sharing a bed, and every Frenchman or -woman who laid eyes on them instantly assumed they were already wed.

Neither Emily nor he made any attempt to correct that mistaken assumption, so there hardly seemed any point in hiring separate rooms.

Even if he did, he'd spend the night in her bed.

Quite aside from the fraught questions of whether he could gather strength enough to resist her lure, and even if he did, whether she would acquiesce and allow him to keep his distance, there was the undeniable fact that he wouldn't sleep, certainly not well, not unless she was within arm's reach.

With the rooms organized, he glanced at Emily. She caught his eye, smiled the smile of encouraging approval she often bent on him, then she turned to the clerk and set about ordering their dinner.

* * *

He and Emily dined in comfort in the inn's gilded dining room. In such an establishment, they were forced to observe the division between classes, so the other members of their party were dining in the bar. He and she joined them there afterward.

They chatted only briefly. He conferred with the other men, setting the watches for the night, a habit they'd reinstated after leaving the relative safety of the Juneaux' inn.

Shortly after, they all retired. After one last glance around the foyer and reception rooms, noting the shutters that had been closed against the night and the heavy locks on the main doors, Gareth followed Emily up the stairs.

Instinct was pricking, battlefield premonition coming to the fore.

He glanced at Mooktu, on first watch, sitting in the bay window at the end of their corridor. "Stay alert."

The big Pashtun nodded gravely. He, too, scented danger in the wind.

Hoping they would both be proved wrong, Gareth followed Emily into their room and quietly shut the door.

The attack—a typical cultist attack—came in the darkest watch of the night. Gareth himself, standing at the window of their room, Emily asleep in the big bed behind him, caught a glimpse of movement in the street below, hard up against the hotel's side, then saw the first flicker of flame.

He was downstairs, banging on the manager's door, Mooktu beside him, before the fire could take hold.

less efficiency—all under the terrified stare of the night clerk who had been left behind the desk.

Later, however, when, this being Lyon and not some outpost of an uncivilized land, the authorities arrived in the form of a disgruntled upholder of the local law, the clerk readily confirmed that the cultists had come in with daggers drawn—that they'd been intent on doing murder and the members of Gareth's party deserved a medal for protecting him and the many inn guests now gathered about exclaiming.

As said guests, taking in the dead cultists' outlandish apparel, vociferously agreed with the clerk, the chief gendarme huffed, and ordered the bodies to be carted away.

Gareth paused beside the innkeeper. His eyes on the activity in the crowded foyer, he murmured, "Don't worry. We're leaving at first light."

The innkeeper glanced sideways.

Gareth met his eyes.

The innkeeper nodded. "*Bon.* I will give orders for the kitchen to have breakfast ready early."

Hiding a cynical smile, Gareth inclined his head. "*Merci.*"

He passed through the crowd, receiving thanks from some, informing those of their party of the early start. That done, he found Emily. Her cloak thrown over a nightgown, she was talking and exclaiming with a French madame in a stylish wrap and with papers twisted in her bright red hair. Taking Emily's arm, he excused them, and turned her inexorably to the stairs.

When she glanced his way, brows rising, he said, "We're leaving at dawn."

Her lips formed an "oh," and she continued on.

On reaching her room, they went in. Closing the door, he watched as, slinging her cloak over a stool, she paused by the bed and looked at him.

A pregnant instant passed, then he released the doorknob and walked slowly toward her. "It might be an idea to take off that gown."

From the dark shadows beneath the trees in the park opposite the hotel, Uncle watched the bodies of the six best assassins he'd brought with him carted away.

He watched without reaction. There was no point gnashing his teeth. In this country, houses were sturdier; they didn't burn easily, especially not with such dampness in the air.

And the major, clearly, had been prepared, on guard.

The conclusion was obvious. Uncle needed a new plan, a better approach.

His old bones ached with the cold, but that was the least of his pain. Although he was following the Black Cobra's orders, his pursuit of the major was now driven by emotions that ran much deeper than his quest for honors.

He wanted to, was determined to, cause the upstart major the same pain, the same anguish, the major had dealt him. An eye for an eye, and a life for a life—but whose life?

The woman's?

Through the open inn doors, he'd glimpsed Miss Ensworth, who the Black Cobra wanted punished for her role in giving rise to the major's mission. He'd watched, and seen her turn and smile at the major as he'd joined her. An instant later, the major had taken her arm and led her out of sight.

Was she the major's woman now?

Thinking of how much his leader would like the female's hide, literally, Uncle smiled. That would make a fitting present—for his leader, and himself.

Akbar loomed at his shoulder. "We should leave."

Eyes still on the hotel, Uncle nodded. "Indeed. I have much to think upon."

pected but quite delightful consequences—we dragged ourselves out of bed at the crack of dawn, and were soon on the road. Under Gareth's exhortations, the Juneaux went at a cracking pace, putting distance between us and Lyon, also making us a difficult target to attack along the way.

As planned, we are making no prolonged or predictable halts, but using our stored victuals for lunches and snacks. All in all, we are bearing up well, but . . . why can't these blessed cultists simply go away?

The men's battle-ready tension, which had eased somewhat, has returned in full measure. In Gareth's case, I would say in greater strength. Who would have imagined the fiend, centered in India, would have such long arms? Regardless, as it should by now be obvious that his troops are not going to succeed, one would think he might desist and slink away.

Sadly, I doubt any of us expect that—which is only adding to the escalating tension. At least, thus far, conditions have not deteriorated to the point where Gareth feels compelled to forgo my bed.

Indeed, if anything, I sense the opposite, which is all to my good.

On reflection, as long as they keep their distance and do nothing to harm anyone, I believe I can tolerate the cult's continuing presence.

E.

They rolled into Dijon the next day. The sun was waning, sliding down the sky to disappear behind the fancy tiled roofs as they tacked through the cobbled streets, pressing deeper into the town.

Once again, they sought refuge at the best hotel. All senses constantly alert, they dined, then, pickets organized, retired.

Nothing had happened over the two days since they'd

270

departed Lyon. All of them felt as if they were incessantly looking over their shoulders.

As he closed the door of the large chamber he and Emily would share, Gareth suspected there was not one of their party who, somewhere in their psyche, couldn't feel the Black Cobra coiling, preparing to strike again.

Outside a barn in the woods around Dijon, Uncle stood before a fire and surreptitiously warmed his hands. It didn't do to show weakness, but the chill of these northern nights struck to his bones.

Gathered around the fire, the remaining members of the group he'd led from Marseilles—more than fifteen, more than enough—shifted and cast uncertain glances his way.

Finally, Akbar looked up and asked the question in all their minds. "When do we strike? If we go in force, and take them on the road—"

"No." Uncle did not raise his voice. He spoke quietly, so they had to listen hard to hear his wisdom. "Fate has shown us that that is not the way. Have we not tried and tried, only to come away with our noses bloodied? No—we need a new plan, a better tactic." He paused to make sure they would bow to his dictate. When no one protested, not even Akbar, he went on, "They are forever on guard, so we will use that to our advantage. We will wear them down with their own anticipation. We will make them wait, and wait, and wait . . . and then, when they are worn out with waiting and shut their

stated his decision. "We will keep following them—and we will choose our time."

6th December, 1822
Evening
Yet another room in a small village inn

Dear Diary,

Tomorrow we will reach Amiens. With every mile
further north, the weather has grown increasingly
wintry, with gloomy gray skies and an icy wind. We
have had to dig deeper into our bags. I am now wearing gowns I have not worn since leaving England.

My campaign continues, and while Gareth has
yet to declare his undying and enduring love, I am
pleased to report a greater degree of closeness between
us, driven no doubt by our shared nights, but also by
the emotions stirred by the fiend's latest tactics.

We have been watchful, of course, but other than
sighting the odd cultist from a distance, we had no
contact—not until we were leaving Saint Dizier. That
skirmish—so openly halfhearted on their part—has
solidified our suspicions that the relative quietness we
are experiencing is due to the fiend being distracted
with planning something far worse.

Something that lies ahead of us, between us and
England.

Far from reassuring us, our too-easy success outside
Saint Dizier has only made us more edgy, drawing us more
tightly together and making us more determined than ever to
defeat these villains and gain the shores of England.

Seeing England is a goal we now all cling to.

As for my other goal, I wish I had my sisters to
consult. How, precisely, does one wring a declaration
from a reticent man?

E.

272

The following day, they reached Amiens as the light faded from the sky. It was cold and tending crisp as Gareth returned from bespeaking rooms to oversee the unloading of the carriages. Everyone lent a hand, the faster to get out of the biting wind. After spending years in India, even his blood seemed too thin.

Once all the bags were in, the Juneau cousins led the horses off to the stable, and Gareth followed the others into the warmth.

Later, he and Emily dined together. He'd grown accustomed to the quiet time alone with her, a time during which he could air his thoughts, and she would share hers.

Pouring rich custard over his pudding, he murmured, "I'm starting to think we're being herded."

She opened her eyes at him as she took in a portion of trifle, then lowered her spoon. "That doesn't sound good. Herded into what? Do you think they're planning an ambush?"

He thought, then shook his head. "I can't see how they could. That's the beauty of Wolverstone's route. We could be heading to any of the Channel ports. Even after we head to Abbeville tomorrow, there are still five major ports, in varying directions, that we might make for."

"So they won't be able to stage an ambush because they won't know which road we'll be taking until we're on it?"

He nodded. "Precisely."

Dessert finished, Emily laid down her spoon and studied him. "So why 'herded'? What bone are you gnawing at?"

ing Wolverstone's plan will keep the cult's forces strung out—reaching Boulogne shouldn't be too hard. But the

273

weather's worsening. I'm no expert on Channel crossings, but I spoke with Watson. Apparently, if the winds come up badly, as they're threatening to do, the ports can be closed for days."

"So getting into Boulogne might be simple, but getting out . . . ?"

"We might be held up there for days."

Days during which the Black Cobra could come at them, again and again, in force.

Gareth didn't say the words—he didn't need to. He could see understanding in her eyes.

Eyes he'd grown accustomed to drowning in every night when she welcomed him into her arms, into her body. Eyes he delighted in watching every morning when in the soft light of dawn she came awake as he slid into her.

Those eyes saw him; they locked on him every time he entered a room she was in.

Now those same eyes studied his face. His expression was stark and grim, but he couldn't find it in him to laugh and lighten the mood.

Those eyes, and she, had to him grown immensely, almost unbelievably, important. He didn't understand how that had happened, only that it had.

He couldn't lose her. His future—something he'd had not the faintest idea about when he'd stood at the railings in Aden harbor—was now crystal clear in his mind. And she stood at the heart of it. Without her. . .

And, somehow, she knew. Knew she meant much more to him than a lady he felt honor bound to wed.

Yet she hadn't pushed, hadn't pressed for any declaration, as other ladies might have. She'd simply been there, been herself . . . and let him fall in love with her. No. Let him fall *more deeply* in love with her.

He looked into her eyes, and saw her watching, waiting, and he knew for what, but with infinite patience, infinite understanding, and compassion.

Lifting one hand, he held it out, palm up. Waited until she

placed her fingers in his. Closing his hand, feeling her delicate digits within his clasp, he said, "If my theory is correct, then we're more or less safe until we reach Boulogne."

Her lips curved in comprehension. Needing no further encouragement, he rose, drew her to her feet, and they went to find the others, to arrange the night watches before retiring to their room, to their bed, and the inexpressible comfort of each other's arms.

In a deserted woodcutter's cottage to the north of Amiens, Uncle paced the dirty floor. "There is no question about it." He glanced around at his assembled troops, letting his confidence show. "It matters not which port they flee to, once they reach it, they will be trapped." He waved the missive he'd received minutes before. "Our brothers already gathered on the coast have confirmed a great storm is blowing in. Let our prey run like mice for the coast—once they reach it, they will not be able to go further, to cross the water as they must." His eyes gleamed with malevolent anticipation. "They will have to stop. And wait."

Facing them all, he raised his arms. "The weather gods, my sons, have arranged for us the perfect opportunity to capture and torture the major and his lady—to the delight and the glory of the Black Cobra!"

Eyes shining, fists rising, the men echoed his words. *To the delight and the glory of the Black Cobra!*

"This time we will plan—and this time we will triumph."

> *8th December, 1822*
> *Early morning*
> *Our room at Amiens*
>
> *Dear Diary,*
>
> *I am huddled under the covers waiting for Dorcas
> to appear. It is still dark and, worse, sleeting outside.
> Gareth has already dressed and gone down. Today
> we set off on the penultimate leg of our mad dash for
> the coast—to Abbeville. From there, one more day
> of racing will see us at Boulogne, and the Channel.
> Although the expectation of being almost there is in-
> tense, I have taken Gareth's warning to heart and, am
> preparing myself for the frustration of having to wait
> some days for a crossing.*
>
> *As long as he shares my bed every night, holding
> me safe in his arms as I sleep, and allowing me to
> do the same in return, I will face all hurdles with the
> stoicism proper to an English lady.*
>
> *E.*

They departed from Amiens amid flurries of snow. Their
tension had already been high, yet Gareth could feel that
tension racking higher with every mile.

Yet, as he'd predicted, nothing occurred during the day-
long journey. The Juneau coachmen continued to perform
with outstanding skill, whipping their horses along. Bleak
winter fields stretching endlessly under a louring gray sky
flashed incessantly past.

Despite their relative speed, they didn't reach Abbeville
until evening. Their routine was well established. In less
than half an hour, they were all inside and warm, the others
sitting down to dinner in their hotel's bar while he and Emily
dined in reserved splendor in the great dining room.

Outside the wind howled, and hail rattled against the windows.

All of them retired early to their beds. Gareth, as he usually did, took the early-morning watch, between two and four o'clock. That way, he could fall asleep with Emily in his arms, and wake with her beside him, too.

She was already snuggled beneath the thick down coverlet when he reached their room, a fair-sized chamber at the end of one corridor. The fire had been built high, then banked for the night. With all the curtains drawn, the room seemed cozy.

It wasn't warm.

He stripped quickly, and joined her between the sheets, leaving the candle on the bedside table burning.

He shivered as the cold sheets touched his skin. Relaxed again when Emily wriggled and settled, all warm, silken, and blatantly female, against him. Gathering her close, he turned to face her. "I can't remember England being this cold."

"It isn't often." Draping her arms over his shoulders, she slid her hands into his hair, fingers riffling as beneath the covers she fitted herself to him, her curves cradling his heavier bones and harder frame. "But after India, this is doubtless a shock to your system."

His system was heating up quite nicely.

He looked into her eyes. For a long moment he drank in the assurance in the mossy hazel, the quiet confidence, the

faction, and the ultimate satiation would be theirs, that ecstasy was assured no matter what route they took to reach it.

277

No matter how long, how tortuous, and drawn out that route might be.

This time, they took a longer road. He kept the pace slow, deliberate, intent.

Focused.

Emily surrendered to the insistent drumbeat, the measured tattoo driving each heavy caress. Wonder bloomed as, from beneath the fringe of her lashes, she watched his face as he paid homage to her breasts. Glancing up, he saw her watching, briefly met her eyes, then, still moving so slowly her nerves tightened, taut with anticipation, he lowered his head, and possessed.

Thoroughly, with a devotion to detail that ripped her wits away, that sent her senses spinning.

Every little touch seared like a brand. Fingers, mouth, lips, teeth, and tongue, he used them all in concert, playing, orchestrating, until her body sang, until passion and desire rose up in sweet symphony and buoyed her on their tide.

And swept her away into the heated moment, flooded her veins, flushed her skin.

She was eager and aching, filled with fiery longing when he finally parted her thighs, settled heavily between, and filled her.

Head back, she caught her breath, then sighed. Reached with her whole body, with her arms, her legs, her all, reached for him and wrapped him in her welcome.

Held him there as, head bowed, his ragged breath a song by her ear, he moved on her and in her, the long planes of his back flexing powerfully as he thrust repeatedly, giving them both what they wanted.

What they needed.

Even as his body strove for release, strove to pleasure hers and claim the ultimate prize, some part of Gareth's mind watched and wondered—was filled with wonder, with a form of silent awe.

Things had changed since they'd left Marseilles, since at her insistence they'd begun sharing a bed every night.

278

Every night, the pleasure, the assurance, the wonder, grew. Intensified. Became measurably stronger, infinitely more addictive.

The simple act that before had always seemed so straightforward, so momentary and unaffecting, was now so much more. This . . . was heady, intoxicating. As he thrust deeper into her heated body and felt her clutch, felt her clamp and hold him, felt her arms tight about him, her legs clasping his flanks, her body cradling his . . . it felt as if she were feeding a part of his soul he hadn't even known existed, let alone was hungry.

Yet he was hungry for this—not just the physical pleasure and the aftermath of bliss, but the connection, the togetherness, the blessed release of having someone that close, of having someone . . . who was his.

The reins slithered from his grasp. As they both, he and she, spiraled out of control, as the demands of their striving bodies overwhelmed their minds and took control of their senses, he raised his head, found her lips and kissed her—claimed her, honored her, thanked her.

And let go.

Gave himself to her and took her in return.

And no longer knew where one ended and the other began.

The storm took them, wracked them, shattered their senses, left their bodies boneless, floating on passion's sea.

Left them melded, fused, joined at the heart.

Welded at the soul.

as they bustled in the stable yard, rushing in organized chaos through the flickering shadows cast by the inn's flares.

They were away before even a glimmer lightened the eastern horizon. Heading north at a cracking pace, they remained alert, on guard, yet Gareth felt certain they would meet with no resistance.

Sure enough, they reached Boulogne-sur-Mer without incident or delay. Courtesy of their early start, it was mid-afternoon when they rattled into the streets of the bustling town. This time, however, they did not stop in the town center.

As they passed the town hall and headed on down a hill, Emily looked inquiringly at Gareth.

"We need an inn close to the docks." He leaned forward and looked out of the window. "The Juneaux say they know the area around there."

The further they went, the more traffic there was. The carriages slowed to a crawl as they negotiated the streets around the marketplace, then continued along a fair-sized street until they reached yet another square. The Juneau cousins halted the carriages along one side.

The instant he opened the carriage door, then stepped down to the cobbles, the sights, sounds, and smells of the sea assaulted Gareth's senses. It hadn't been particularly windy above, but here the wind gusted, salty and tangy, damp with sea spray, slapping his face and tugging his hair.

Emily paused in the carriage doorway, looking out. "That's the Channel out there, isn't it?"

Gareth nodded. Beyond the quays and the harbor basin Napoleon had excavated in prepartion for the invasion of England that he never launched, out beyond the protective arms of the breakwaters and their lighthouses, lay a seething mass of water, waves churning a bilious gray green beneath a leaden sky.

A few gulls bravely wheeled below slate-colored clouds scudding before the wind. Behind them hung the denser, darker roiling mass of an oncoming storm.

That louring, threatening mass assured Gareth that his worst fears had come true; they'd be trapped for days. Looking at the cauldron the Channel had become, he confirmed that not a single ship had ventured out.

One glance at Emily's face as she stepped down to the ground told him he didn't need to explain the situation to her.

He turned as Gustav Juneau clambered down from his perch to join them.

"There is an auberge we know—this way." Gustav pointed with his whip to a narrow street leading away from the square. "It is close to the quay, and the people who run it know us." He glanced at Gareth. "But come and see."

Gathering Watson, and with Emily on his arm, leaving the others with Pierre Juneau to watch over the carriages, Gareth walked beside Gustav deeper into the dockside quarter.

The auberge Gustav led them to proved perfect for their needs, not least because its guestrooms were all presently empty. Gareth immediately negotiated to hire the whole of the upper floor. In addition, the auberge was within easy reach of the docks, with a direct route to the main quay, and, situated as it was, its common room was always full of sailors.

The owner and his wife, the Perrots, were delighted to accommodate them. "This weather!" Monsieur Perrot gesticulated. "It is very bad for business."

"True," Gareth said, "but before you welcome us, there's something you should know."

At his insistence, the Perrots sat down with him, Emily,

our company —he gestured to the crowded room—"will be happy to assist in foiling this villain."

Madame Perrot nodded, a martial light in her eye. "He and his heathens will not be able to set this inn alight—it is built of good sound stone."

Another of its many attributes. Despite his ongoing concern, Gareth knew a moment's relief. He couldn't have wished for a better billet, especially given they would, it seemed, be spending several days there.

Emily and Madame went upstairs to survey the rooms. Gustav, after a word with Perrot, stumped out to look at the stables. Gareth and Perrot reached agreement on the charge. Gareth paid half then and there, the other half to be paid on the morning of their departure. As to when that might be . . .

Appealed to, Perrot pursed his lips, shook his head. "Three days? It may be more. If you go down to the quay later this afternoon, I can tell you who to ask."

Smothering his frustration, Gareth inclined his head. "Thank you." He looked across the common room as Emily returned down the stairs. "We'll go and fetch the rest of our party."

They used the rest of the afternoon to settle in. At Gareth's suggestion and Emily's insistence, Pierre and Gustav would remain with them for the night, then start back on their long journey home in the morning.

After checking with Perrot, apparently a connection of a connection of the Juneaux, after lunch, Pierre and Gustav headed for the warehouses to see if there was any merchant with goods he wanted to send south.

Shortly after, armed with detailed directions, Gareth set out with Mooktu, Bister, and Jimmy to consult with the local weatherman, an old sailor whom the locals relied on to read the skies, the winds, and the waves.

When they reached the main quay, Jimmy's eyes grew wide. "I don't think I've ever seen so many fishing boats, not all at once. Not even at Marseilles."

"I've heard this is the biggest fishing port in France," Gareth said.

Mooktu nodded toward the neatly sculpted basin in which the fleet bobbed, as protected as they might be from the raging wind. "That is well thought out—a safe harbor."

"Indeed." Gareth hoped that would prove true for their party, too.

They found the old sailor.

What he told them left them grim.

"Four days!" Bister trudged alongside Gareth as they returned to the auberge.

There was nothing to say. The old man, his hearing all but gone yet his sight as sharp as ever, had stated categorically that the weather would worsen before it got better, that although the worst of the sleet would be gone by tomorrow, the wind would blow from the wrong quarter for the next three days.

On the fourth day, the weather would turn fair. They would, the old sailor had assured them, be able to set sail then—but not before.

As they neared the auberge, Mooktu studied it, stated, "It is as well that we have such solidly built walls behind which to wait."

There was nothing to say to that either. Every one of them understood that for the next three days they would essentially be trapped. Fixed in one place. The cultists would soon know where they were. And then . . . they could expect the might of the Black Cobra to be unleashed against them.

He was starting to understand why the French and English had over the centuries so often warred; the French, it seemed, were as enamored of a "good fight"—meaning one where they could indulge in the name of justice—as any Englishman.

The Perrots were unquestionably eager to meet the challenge.

"I will speak with our friends this very evening," Perrot declared. "They are trapped by this weather, too, and will be glad of the chance for action."

Unsure just what help might be coming his way, Gareth nevertheless gratefully inclined his head. "We will be happy to have whatever assistance your patrons might offer."

The news spread. Gradually at first, then with increasing momentum. Every hale and hearty soul who crossed the Perrots' threshold that night was regaled with the story. The version Gareth overheard when he fronted the bar to replenish their ale mugs was richly embroidered, dramatically, even passionately delivered, yet was essentially nothing more than the truth communicated in fine, histrionic French.

When he returned to their corner table, he found Emily shifted to the side, chatting animatedly to two older women.

Watson had drifted further down the room, and had been captured by a group of swarthy sailors who, Gareth suspected, were interrogating him as to the enemy's colors.

Gareth set down the refilled mugs before Mooktu and Mullins, and was about to resume his seat when Jimmy appeared by his elbow.

"If you please, Major Hamilton, there's some men over there who'd like a word."

Raising his head, Gareth looked in the direction Jimmy indicated, and saw a group of four, all clearly mariners, seated about a table at the back of the room. One, a captain by his cap, saw him looking, and raised his mug in a salute.

Gareth looked at Jimmy. "Where's Bister?"

Jimmy nodded down the room. "He's over by the door. His lot speak English well enough to get by."

Gareth nodded. "Why don't you go and help him?"

Jimmy eagerly headed off. Picking up his mug, with a murmured word to Mooktu and Mullins, Gareth headed deeper into the room.

Later, he was glad he had. The group of four were all captains, and all volunteeered those of their crews they could spare to help defend the inn against the "heathens." More important, however, one—the captain who'd saluted him—commanded one of the larger trawlers.

"Once the weather clears, if you wish it, I will take you to Dover. My brother-in-law has wine barrels to deliver there, so I will be going there in any case. My ship is large enough to take your group—there are nine of you, yes?"

Gareth nodded. "I must warn you that, although the cult has little experience of fighting at sea, it's possible they may attempt to attack any ship with us on board."

"*Pfft!*" The captain made a gesture signifying what he thought of the cult's chances.

"They might," Gareth persisted, "hire mercenaries—other Frenchmen who are more competent on the waves—to attack your vessel."

The captain grinned. "No Frenchman—not for miles around—would attempt to come against Jean-Claude Lavalle."

Gareth glanced at the others. They, too, were grinning. One slung an arm around Lavalle's shoulders. "Sadly, he is right," the other captain said. "You are not of your navy, but

tain mellowness induced by the readily offered camaraderie and the Perrots' fine ale butted against the heightened tension, the tightly strung sense of being on full alert that, despite the conviviality of the evening, hadn't waned in the least.

Although the Perrots' strapping sons had offered to stand guard overnight, Gareth had gently declined, pointing out that the men of his party would more readily recognize any cultist, and had been drilled in how to react. So, as usual, Mooktu was presently on guard in the upstairs corridor, seated by the head of the stairs, from where he could see the entire common room, all the way to the front door. Gareth exchanged a smile and nod with him as he went past. Mooktu would be relieved by Bister, who would in turn be relieved by Gareth, and Mullins would stand the early-morning watch. Watson, meanwhile, had a small room by the rear stairs, and was by all accounts a very light sleeper.

The sight of Mooktu refocused Gareth on the challenge he would face the next day. Entering the inn's main bedchamber, he absentmindedly closed the door, mentally juggling his options for managing the ragtag army he had, courtesy of that evening, apparently acquired.

"What is it?"

The query snapped him back to the here and now. To Emily, propped on one arm, one sweetly turned shoulder showing bare above the covers, her expression a medley of interest and demand.

Even as he strolled to the bed, his gaze caught by the way the candlelight flowed over the perfect silk of her exposed shoulder, he realized she expected to be told, that she expected him to share. To include her and, if she volunteered one, to listen to her opinion.

For a man like him—one who'd commanded troops for a decade—to discuss such matters with a female, let alone seek her opinion . . .

Halting by the bed, he smiled, leaned down, and kissed her.

Long, deep, lingeringly.

Eventually he pulled back, sat on the edge of the bed to take off his boots.

And told her all.

Propped against the pillows, she listened with her customary concentration. It was a heady realization that, when he spoke with her, even of mundane matters, he could be assured of having her complete attention—that he commanded it.

He'd never wanted any other woman's attention, but he savored hers.

He left her chewing on his problem for tomorrow—what to do with the various seamen, young and old, who'd formed the notion of haunting the inn in the hopes of engaging with any cultists—heathens—who happened to drop by.

Standing, he shrugged out of his coat. "They're going to get under the Perrots' feet, and although I'm happy to supply them with ale, they won't be any use to us drunk."

She frowned. After a moment, she said, "They're all sailors, aren't they?" When, free of his shirt, he nodded, she drew in a breath, hauled her gaze up to his face, stared for a moment, then blinked, and said, "They won't be used to drilling. Or shooting muskets. Or . . . any of the things your troop sergeants would normally school your men in."

Hands at his waistband, he raised his brows, considering.

"You have Mooktu and Bister, and Mullins, too—they could help you . . ." Her words faded as he tossed his breeches on a chair, then reached for the covers.

Emily shifted, swallowed, whispered as she reached for him. "But that's tomorrow."

the pleasure.

Hands traced, fingers wandered, palms shaped.

Excitement sparked. Need bloomed, burgeoned, and grew.

The fire that ignited, the flames that leapt, then roared, were familiar and welcome.

She opened her arms and embraced them, and him, took him into her body, let him fill her, and her heart, let the beat escalate and passion pour through him and her, and sweep them on.

Until desire gripped, and she clung, and he held her and thrust over and over until they both shuddered and she cried his name.

Ecstasy rushed in like a wave, and washed them to that distant shore where bliss spread, golden and molten, through them, over them, enfolded them.

No matter the challenges, no matter what was to come, this they had—this was already theirs.

Satiation dragged her down and she sank into slumber, at peace in the here and now.

No matter the danger, no matter the risk, he would yet be hers, and she forever would be his.

Fifteen

10th December, 1822
Morning
Our room in the Perrot auberge in Boulogne

Dear Diary,

I have reached two conclusions. One is that I have indeed fallen deeply and irrevocably in love with Gareth Hamilton, and despite my sisters' recommendations, I am finding the experience distinctly discomfiting. All this talk of the cultists staging a serious and sustained—and by implication potentially lethal—attack is exceedingly wearing on the nerves.

I have never felt such consuming concern, such worry for another, as I now do for him. I have en-

deavored to hide it, and will continue to do so—no gentleman likes a fearful female who clings—but the struggle becomes greater with every day.

I had no idea love would be like this. I have always prided myself on being practical and pragmatic, and while outwardly I hope I remain so, inwardly . . . how far I have fallen.

Which brings me to my second conclusion. Gareth must love me.

Why am I so certain? Because I recognize the angst in his eyes whenever I am in any way exposed to potential danger—the same angst I feel when he is in like circumstances. It is the same thing, driven by the same emotion. Nothing could be clearer.

He must love me, but is unwilling to state it, even to me, even in private. Given the sort of man he is, a warrior to the core, I can perhaps understand his stance, but it simply will not do.

Given my conclusions, before I go forward to the altar, I am determined to hear him say the word "love."

E.

he next morning, in the mizzling drizzle that had replaced the night's sleeting rain, they gathered in the stable yard to farewell Gustav and Pierre Juneau.

Despite their relatively short association, the hugs and farewells were affectionate and heartfelt, the admonitions to take care deeply sincere.

Gareth handed over a pouch with the rest of their fee, together with a sizeable tip. He clapped Pierre on the shoulder. "We wouldn't have fared half so well without you."

"Indeed." Emily beamed at Gustav. "We'd still be on our way here if we'd been in the hands of anyone else. We are deeply in your debt."

Both Juneaux made dismissive sounds, shook hands, then climbed up to their carriages.

Beside the first carriage, suddenly sober, Gareth looked up at Gustav. "Be on guard—at least until you're well south. I doubt there'll be many cultists left along the road, but until you're out of this area, have a care. That we're not with you won't matter—the cult is renowned for its vindictiveness."

Gustav tapped his coachman's hat. He glanced back at Pierre, who nodded that he'd heard, then Gustav looked down at Gareth. "We'll remember—meanwhile, take care of yourselves." His gaze rose to touch the others who had come to stand behind Gareth. "All of you—fare thee well, and when you get to England, make sure you rid us all of these *vipères*."

Assurances rang out, then Gustav clicked his reins, and the two coaches lumbered out of the yard.

Emily sighed. She slid her arm in Gareth's and let him turn her toward the auberge's door. "I'll miss them, but letting them go is a sign. We've come to the end of our travels through lands not our own—once we cross the Channel, we'll be home."

Gareth wished he could let her continue to imagine they were close to being safe and free, but . . . "There'll be cultists waiting for us in Dover."

She frowned. "But surely not as many as here?"

"I don't know how many, but they will be there. The Black Cobra is Ferrar. While England is home for us, it's home for

stretched along the coast this side of the town of Calais.

There were four couriers heading to England, this much

Uncle knew, but only the major had come this way. What news had reached him placed one of the other three far to the east, and the other two had traveled by sea around the Cape and had yet to make landfall.

His orders were to capture the major and, above all, retrieve the scroll holder he carried. There had been no opportunity to search the party's bags, but regardless, Uncle wanted the major. Nothing else would do—nothing else would avenge his son.

"It is as I foretold." Uncle smiled benevolently on his tools, his weapons. "Our pigeons are trapped, their wings clipped by the storm. They have taken refuge in the town and are huddling there, waiting to be *plucked*." Slowly he paced before his men, meeting their eyes, letting them recognize the brilliance of his planning. "While the winds blow hard, the sea is impassable. There is nothing they can do—no way they can escape us. Now we must devote ourselves to dealing with these upstarts as our leader would decree—as the glory of the Black Cobra demands!"

A rousing cheer went up. He waved, and it faded.

Before he could continue, Akbar, until then standing in the shadows to one side, stepped forward. "What about the coachmen? They helped our pigeons flee us—their families gave our enemies succor." A rumbling rose from the assembled men. Akbar kept his gaze on Uncle's face. "We should show the coachmen the vengeance of the Cobra, and make them pay his price."

There were nods and murmurings as the men turned eager faces to Uncle, clearly anticipating being unleashed.

Uncle smiled benignly. Magnanimously, he waved the coachmen aside. "We have better—more important—things to do than concern ourselves with lowly coachmen who have no further part to play. The Black Cobra demands service of the highest caliber, and it is critical not to be led astray by any quest for personal glory."

Uncle turned his smile directly on Akbar. Let his ambitious second dwell on that.

292

Unsurprisingly, his words had refocused the men's attention back on him. Raising a hand in benediction, he gave them their orders. "You must spread out and scour the land around the town. We must find the perfect place in which to hold and discipline the major and his woman."

Somewhat to Gareth's surprise, the rest of that day passed swiftly. With every hour, their news spread further, and more and more townsfolk, especially the men, found reason to drop by the Perrots' auberge. Some came to report seeing cultists lurking in the town and down by the docks over the past week, but by all accounts the "heathens" had since slipped away.

Two gendarmes dropped by to listen to their tale, retold with gusto by one of the Perrots' sons. The gendarmes nodded, wished them luck, and left. Heathen cultists and English, Gareth surmised, fell outside their remit.

Throughout the morning, brawny young men came to the inn to offer their services in repelling the heathen hordes. As Gareth had plenty of coin to supply ale, and he, Bister, Mooktu, and Mullins had plenty of tales to tell, it was easy enough to keep their new recruits amused.

A few brought rusty muskets. After a quick examination, knowing the cult would never resort to firearms and that by recruiting the locals themselves, there was little to no chance the cult could, this time, hire locals against them, Gareth decided that firearms in general weren't worth the risk.

but use the most basic moves. Once we see what they're like, we'll split them into groups."

The others—all ex-army—nodded, and followed him out into the yard.

They put their recruits through their paces, much to the amusement of the crowd that gathered to watch and exclaim.

In short order, the activity turned into an event, with performers and an appreciative audience, many of whom were female. Initially the murmurs, giggles, and sly glances irritated Gareth, but then, passing before a knot of girls, he heard, "I must rush home and tell Hilda about this."

After that, he watched the crowd more closely, and saw that girls were constantly coming and going. They couldn't stay for long because they were expected home—but once at home, they would talk.

He couldn't ask for a more certain way of spreading the news about the cultists. Once he realized that, he forgot about the crowd, and concentrated on drilling his inexperienced but enthusiastic troops.

The day ended with a flurry of ice and no cultists anywhere. Seated with the others in the common room, while they finished their dinner and Bister, Jimmy and Mullins entertained the table with tales of the new recruits and their varied skills, Gareth let the talk wash over him, and mentally ran through his preparations again.

The scroll holder—the item the cultists most wanted—was as safe as it could be. On the intial stages of their journey, Arnia had carried it, but in Alexandria, once he'd taken Watson's measure, he'd spoken with him. Watson was steady, loyal and dependable, with a deep streak of integrity. He was also the oldest of their group, the least likely to be involved in physical heroics. From Alexandria on, Watson had carried the scroll holder—exactly where, even Gareth didn't know.

If anything adverse were to happen to their party, Watson would take whatever survivors there were and make for England. He had money and letters of introduction and instructions from Gareth—and he had the scroll holder. No matter what, the scroll holder would reach England.

Gareth had also given Arnia money and letters of introduction. If the cult succeeded in breaking up their party, she would take Dorcas and head for England. Together, the women would manage, and the cult would ignore two women of lower caste.

The rest of them were potential targets. The cult would come for him and Emily, then, when they didn't find the scroll holder, would go for Mooktu, Bister, and Mullins. They might even consider Jimmy.

He was deep into trying to think like a cult commander, when Emily's hand closed about his wrist and pulled him back to the present. Raising his eyes, he met hers.

She studied his face, her own expression serious. After a moment of searching his eyes, she murmured, "They'll be plotting and planning, too, won't they? Gathering their forces and organizing?"

The others, hearing her question, fell silent and waited for his reply. He glanced around the table, then returned his gaze to Emily's face and nodded. "Even though Ferrar isn't here—at least I think it highly unlikely he will be—there'll be a commander of sorts in charge."

He looked at the others, let his gaze rest on Bister and Jimmy. "In whatever's coming, we shouldn't imagine we'll be facing any poorly disciplined group. The commander will almost certainly have brought assassins and some of

in, have them join the group here." Mullins made it a statement.

Gareth hesitated, then said, "I don't know what route the other three couriers are taking, but unless one of the others is near—and I don't think that's likely—then yes, I imagine that when the fight comes, we'll be facing a goodly number, not just ten or even twenty."

Dorcas shivered and gathered her shawl closer.

Gareth seized the moment to marshal his words, then quietly went on, "We need to remember my orders." In deference to all they'd been through together, he used the royal "we." "I'm supposed to do all I can to engage and remove as many cultists as possible, especially here—and while I don't know enough to appreciate why, we can trust absolutely that Wolverstone's orders are sound."

He met Bister's eyes. "Which is why our ragtag recruits are a godsend. We need to do all we can to whip them into reasonable shape, to prepare them to engage and defeat the cultists."

"One idea that occurs to me," Mooktu said, "is that the cultists fight with blades only, all close quarters, hand-to-hand. Yet many of our recruits are sailors and farm workers—many have abilities with implements that strike from a greater distance."

Mullins was nodding. "Like staffs, pitchforks, and the like—and slingshots, too." He looked at Gareth. "Perhaps we should encourage them to work with those."

"From what I saw, not many have any experience with swords." Gareth considered, then nodded. "Tomorrow we'll see what skills they do have, and work with those."

Once again he glanced around the table. "Of one thing we can be absolutely sure. The Black Cobra will have given orders that we are to be stopped. Here, in Boulogne. So the cult will come for us, and they'll come in force. For the cultists and their commander here, this will be their last stand."

Huddled in his cloak, Uncle slowly turned, surveying the large chamber in the light of the lanterns two of his followers held high. Then he smiled. "This will do nicely."

Looking at the young cultist who had come running to tell him of the tumbledown mansion hidden amid overgrown gardens not far from the town, Uncle raised his hand in blessing. "You have done well, my son."

He looked inquiringly as other cultists filed into the room. One bowed. "We have searched, Excellency, but there is no one here. It is abandoned."

"And big enough and sound enough for our headquarters?"

"It seems very appropriate, Uncle."

"Excellent. Make arrangements to move all our baggage here, and summon all our fighters. This will henceforth be our headquarters."

The men bowed.

Swift footsteps in the corridor outside had them all looking to the door.

Akbar appeared. He paused, taking in the ornate chamber—a drawing room, Uncle thought it would be called—then strode in. Pulling off his gloves, he met Uncle's gaze, then bowed curtly.

"The men watching the inn report that the major has commenced drilling locals in the yard."

Uncle frowned. "These are soldiers—militia?"

"No. Sailors, farmers—young men mostly, only a few older."

Uncle's expression turned contemptuous. "Lower orders." He waved dismissively. "They are no threat to us. It is not in

Uncle turned to the others. "Go and collect all that we

need to make this place into suitable quarters. You must also find for me all the implements I will require to properly punish the major's woman and, later, the major himself." A slow smile of vindictive anticipation spread across Uncle's face. Quietly, he crooned, "Do you know what I need?"

The cultists bowed low. The one in charge replied, "Yes, Uncle. We will fetch all the tools necessary."

"Good." Smile still in place, Uncle turned away.

Akbar waited for an instant, then curtly bowed to Uncle's back, turned on his heel and left the room.

In the corridor outside, his own second was waiting. As he strode down the corridor, the man fell in at his shoulder. "Well—what did he say? Are we to act to discourage these locals from joining with the major?"

His expression stony, Akbar shook his head. "No." After a moment, he added, "Old men and their delusions. They will bring us down yet."

The night passed without incident, and the day following continued quiet.

Too quiet for Gareth's liking.

The rain and hail had ceased, but the wind still blew at storm force. Luckily, the inn yard was protected by the surrounding buildings. Throughout the morning and into the afternoon, he, Mooktu, Mullins, and Bister worked with their volunteers, improvising both for weapons and techniques, and drilling them to instill basic levels of command.

By late afternoon, however, many were asking when the fight would be. When no definite answer was forthcoming, it became progressively more difficult to hold their troops' attention.

By evening, when he wandered through the common room, Gareth overheard too many comments on "the mad ideas of the English" to doubt that the excitement generated by the promised fight against the "heathens" was dissipating.

Resuming his seat beside Emily at their table, he caught his fellow trainers' eyes. "Whoever's commanding the cult this time is using his brains. There's been no sighting of a cultist since we arrived. The locals are starting to believe they don't really exist—that they've moved on, or were from the first a figment of our imaginations."

Mullins nodded glumly. "I'll wager that tomorrow we'll have less than half our numbers today."

Bister grimaced. "Nothing much we can do until the axe falls, is there?"

Gareth shook his head. "All we can do is hope that, when the attack comes, we'll have a reasonable enough force to hold off the first wave, so the doubters have time to come running."

Watson suggested they find a nearby bell, or something similar they could use as a summons.

While the others discussed that, Gareth leaned closer to Emily. Laying a hand over one of hers, he caught her eye when she looked his way. "You mustn't forget that from the first—in Aden—the cult had you in their sights. They must know of your role in getting the letter to us—you are a target as much as I am."

She raised her brows. "But I'm not the one carrying the scroll holder. If this is their last chance of stopping it from reaching England, then they'll be focused on that, not"— she waved her other hand—"side issues."

He held her gaze. "They won't see you as a side issue. Taking hostages is a common ploy for them." He hesitated, then went on, "And I suspect they know that I'll give any-

the realization of how much Emily meant to him—the insidious knowledge of how very vulnerable he was over her.

Fear for himself was something he'd learned to live with. Fear for her . . . was something else again.

In the kitchen of the deserted chateau, where his combined troops had gathered for the evening meal, at the head of the main table, Uncle rose to his feet. He waited for all heads to turn his way, for silence to fall. Then he raised his arms and smiled. "My sons—the time has come. Tomorrow will be our day."

Eagerness glowed on all the faces. Anticipation had reached fever pitch. Uncle could almost taste it.

"Tomorrow, we will triumph—we will act decisively to draw the major and his people into our net. We will draw them here, to this place—into a trap." He glanced at Akbar, seated to his left. "You, Akbar, will take five others and set a watch on the lane leading here, close to the town. When the major and his followers pass, you will send word to us here."

Akbar, of course, understood that he was being deliberately distanced from the action—from all chance of glory. He held Uncle's gaze—Uncle could see in his dark eyes the battle between the impulse to protest and the knowledge that this was a trial of his obedience. Caution won. Impassively, Akbar bowed his head. "As you wish, Uncle."

Uncle smiled. He turned to the rest of his troops. "Listen well, and I will tell you how we will capture our pigeons."

> *12th December, 1822*
> *Morning*
> *My room at the Perrots' auberge*
>
> *Dear Diary,*
>
> *I do not know how it is that quietness and calmness and nothing happening can feel so threatening. But so it is. There is a sense of some great disaster*

hanging over us, just waiting to crash down on our heads.

But if the locals are right, we have only this last day to weather. The captain who agreed to take us to Dover spoke with Gareth last night, and confirmed he expects to be able to put out of the harbor tomorrow. If so, we will be away, and no matter that there may be cultists waiting in England, just being home will buoy us all.

Meanwhile I will spend the day as I have the last two, seeking ways to support Gareth's efforts. Even if it transpires that we do not need our ragtag army, putting all possible defenses in place just in case is unquestionably wise. The right decision for an experienced commander, and Gareth is nothing if not that. Even if all I do is provide encouragement, that is nevertheless a contribution.

I cannot recall feeling so personally committed to someone else's goal as I do with Gareth's mission. It is as if his goal is somehow now mine—as if my love for him demands I embrace every aspect of his life, even this. While ferrying MacFarlane's letter to Bombay gave me an interest in seeing justice done, my commitment to seeing the scroll holder to the right hands in England is now predominantly driven by a need to

ors and farmhands armed with pitchforks and rakes.

> *If any attack comes here in Boulogne, Gareth will meet it face-to-face.*
>
> *Love, I am learning, can result in fear. I have far more reason to fear for him than he has to fear for me.*
>
> *E.*

The day started calmly, yet Gareth couldn't shrug off a sense of impending doom.

He was less than impressed when Mullins's prediction of how many of their ragtag troops would report for duty proved correct. Only a dozen with nothing better to do slouched into the common room, and from their easygoing expressions, they were there for the entertainment rather than with any expectation of seeing action.

As the skies had cleared, Bister and Mooktu took most of the group—ten youthful lads plus Jimmy—into the large yard at the side of the inn, and tested their defenses when attacked with long knives. Each lad had a pitchfork, shovel, or staff. Gareth meanwhile trained the two who had some skill with their swords.

After setting them sparring, he stood and watched, calling out comments and corrections, stepping in every now and then to demonstrate a thrust or parry.

He was watching critically when Emily appeared by his side.

She glanced over the yard. "Not many today. " She met his eyes as he briefly glanced her way. "Perhaps nothing will happen. They might have decided to make a stand in Dover."

"It's possible." He grimaced. "But unlikely. Have Dorcas and Arnia returned?"

"Yes. They said the priest would be happy to ring the bell should there be any need. Apparently, that's the recognized signal if there's any emergency in this part of town."

Gareth nodded vaguely, then stepped forward to correct a wobbly thrust.

When he stepped back, Emily murmured, "I'll leave you to your training."

Eyes locked on the would-be swordsmen, Gareth nodded.

Smiling, Emily stepped back. She stood for a moment observing the group Mooktu and Bister were working with, then spent another moment studying the onlookers—mostly old men and young girls—lining the pavement along the street side of the yard. There were far fewer than the first day, but clearly, people knew their party was still at the auberge.

Rather than push through the line of old men to reach the front door, she turned and headed down the side of the auberge for the back door to the common room. Located just around the corner, it gave onto the rear stable yard.

The cobblestones were old; she had to watch her feet. She picked her way around the corner, idly wondering what the weather in England would be like—and almost walked into a man.

With an "Oh!" she looked up.

Caught her breath on a gasp as not one but two men gripped her arms hard, one on either side.

The man on her left—black-haired, dark-eyed, nut-brown skin—leered as he pressed close—and pressed the tip of a knife into her side. "No sound."

She didn't move, didn't even blink. She could feel the cold bite of the knife—with just a touch it had sliced through her gown. The slightest push and it would cut into her.

live. Pray none of your friends notice—if they do, we will have to kill them."

303

She had no choice. Even if she swooned they would simply drag her along. But once they reached the street, someone would see, would notice . . .

Her hopes died as they rounded the far corner of the auberge and she saw a dogcart waiting. They half lifted, half pushed her onto the front bench. The man with the knife followed and sat beside her. The third man took the reins and climbed up to sit on her other side, while the other man climbed on behind.

Wedged between the cultists, the horrendously sharp knife still pressed threateningly to her side, she had to sit silently and be driven out of the lane, into the square, and away.

Gareth was thinking of calling a halt for luncheon when Dorcas came into the side yard. She looked around. A frown formed on her face.

When her gaze returned to him, he raised his brows.

She walked across to him. "Have you seen Miss Emily?"

"Not recently. She was out here about an hour ago, but went inside again."

Dorcas shook her head, looking toward the street. "We can't find her. No one's seen her, not since . . . well, it must be since she spoke with you."

A chill coursed through his veins, but Gareth told himself not to leap to conclusions. "If she's not in her room . . . is there anywhere else she might go to fill in time?"

"Not that I can think of. And . . . well, I don't want to cause a fuss that might be unnecessary." Dorcas met his eyes. "There haven't been any sightings of cultists for days—no one's come into the common room to say otherwise."

"We haven't seen or heard of anyone lurking around, either."

"So there's no reason to suppose anything dreadful has occurred." Dorcas looked across the yard, then drew in a breath and rushed on, "But to go off somewhere without telling you, or me, especially now, when we're all so on edge . . . that's very unlike Miss Emily. Still, perhaps—"

"No." Grim, Gareth caught her eyes as she looked at him. "You're right. She wouldn't vanish of her own accord. Which means—" He cut off the thought, instead said, "We search. Find whoever you can, and search thoroughly upstairs. I'll get Bister and our recruits to check outside, while Mooktu and I will talk to the Perrots and search the ground floor. We'll meet in the common room as soon as we're done."

Eyes wide, Dorcas nodded and hurried back to the auberge.

Grim-faced, Gareth turned to the men in the yard.

The search didn't take long. Ten minutes later, Gareth strode into the common room to find Dorcas already there, the normally stoic maid wringing her hands, a worried Arnia standing beside her.

"She is not upstairs," Arnia said.

Gareth turned as Perrot, who had gone himself to check his basement while his sons checked the stables and outbuildings, joined them.

The auberge keeper spread his hands. "There is no sign."

"All our carriages and horses are still here," one of the sons added.

Mooktu arrived from the kitchens and storerooms. Grimly, he shook his head.

Watson and Mullins rose from the table where they'd been waiting.

The front door crashed open and Bister barreled in, Jimmy

the cart were well wrapped up. Hoods drawn an' all, so no one saw their faces." Bister looked at Dorcas. "They said she was wearing a pink gown and had a purple shawl. Brown hair up."

Dorcas paled. "It was a lavender gown."

Bister nodded. "Like they said—pink." He looked at Gareth. "It was her."

Tight lipped, Gareth nodded. "Any advance on 'south'?"

"Bister and I ran to the end of the street," Jimmy put in. "There were lads at the corner, lounging about—they remembered and showed us the road the cart took. It's not a main road—seems it goes south along the coast a ways."

An angry rumble had been growing from the locals. Shock was quickly giving way to outrage. Now someone called out, "That's the Virgejoie road."

Gareth glanced at Perrot.

The auberge owner clarified, "It is the road that leads to one of the old aristo-family homes—a chateau."

"Who lives there now?"

Perrot spread his hands. "No one. It has been deserted since the family fled during the Terror."

"What condition is the chateau in—is it liveable?"

Numerous local men pulled faces, tilted their heads, then one vouchsafed, "The outbuildings and barn are derelict, but the main house still has walls, shutters and doors, and most of its roof."

"Fireplaces, too," another put in. "One could shelter there even in this weather. Gypsies sometimes do."

Gareth exchanged a glance with Mooktu as the exclamations and rumblings rose anew. "That's where they'll be."

Mooktu nodded. "They've taken her so you will come for her—they will wait until you do."

He meant "wait before they do anything drastic"; the cult was well known for forcing men to watch as they tortured their loved ones. His heart like lead, Gareth nodded—tried to push his reactions, his emotions down enough to think.

He had to think or he'd lose her.

He wasn't going to lose her.

Perrot tugged his sleeve. "You have to let us help." The

306

auberge owner gestured to the crowd thronging the common room as the locals who'd come in for lunch were joined by a steady stream of others, alerted by yet others who'd gone out to spread the news. "This cult—they have played us for fools. They have attacked and carried off the lady while she was here, under my roof, and we scoffed and thought you were safe." Like an aging bantam, Perrot stuck out his chest. "You must let us expunge this stain on our honor by letting us help you get her back."

Many locals, young and old, cheered and clamored in Perrot's support.

Gareth glanced at Mooktu, Bister, and Mullins, waiting, ready for action, to one side, then he raised his hands and waved to quiet the crowd. Into the ensuing silence he said, "Everyone who wishes to assist—we'll gladly accept your help. *But*" —he spoke strongly over the swelling cheers, silencing them once more— "we must do nothing that puts Miss Ensworth's life at risk. *So*." He paused, felt the familiar yoke of command settle on his shoulders, combined with a sharply threatening imperative. His mind raced. After a moment, he knew. "Here's what we have to do."

He sent Bister, Mooktu, and Mullins to circle past the cult's pickets. "They'll have more than one or two along the road into the estate, close enough to town to have time to race back and warn those at the chateau of our approach. Take positions between them and the chateau, as close to the chateau as possible without being seen from the building,

Turning back to the gathering rabble—older locals as well as an increasing number of sailors and others who had days before formed part of their impromptu militia—Gareth waved at the door. "Let's take this outside. Form up, and I'll tell you exactly what we must do."

Must do. Exactly. He needed these men, but if he didn't control them, neither Emily nor he would see England again.

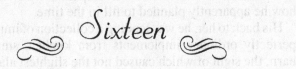

Sixteen

*T*ied securely to a once-elegant chair in the middle
of a dusty half-derelict drawing room, Emily stared
wide-eyed at the old Indian man her captors had delivered her to. Garbed in traditional Indian dress of dun-
colored trousers and tunic, with a colorful woven vest, hat,
and a shawl in deference to the cold, he appeared almost
kindly, until one looked into his eyes and saw the fanatical
light gleaming in the darkness.

She wasn't sure he was entirely sane.

He was, however, indisputably in charge. The three who
had brought her there, the knife pricking her side all the way,
had bowed and scraped and looked thrilled to receive just a
word in reward.

Killing Gareth and the others—she knew he, and all the
rest, too, would come after her.

That, it seemed, was the old man's plan.

What horrified her, held her stupefied with terror, was how he apparently planned to fill in the time.

His back to her, he was tending a collection of implements, perfectly ordinary implements from kitchen, smithy, and barn, the sight of which caused not the slightest alarm—not until they lay heating on a bed of red-hot coals in a brazier set before a crumbling hearth.

If that weren't bad enough, to one side a once-superb gaming table displayed an array of knives. Not ordinary, run-of-the-mill knives. Many she'd seen only rarely, on docks, at the fishmonger's or the butcher's. Filleting knives. Flaying knives.

Her blood had run cold long ago. She looked at the knives and felt sick.

She didn't know what to do. With her feet tied and her arms lashed at elbow and wrist to the chair arms with old curtain cords, she was helpless to move, but she wasn't going to simply sit and be burned and cut.

It took effort to force her mind to work—to think of what might distract this man—Uncle—from his grizzly entertainment, at least long enough for Gareth to reach her.

She couldn't think beyond that point. She didn't need to. Once Gareth reached her, nothing would stop them. Together they would win through.

But what could she do to gain time?

Was there any way she could make it easier for him to find her, so he could reach her more quickly?

She recalled the chateau as she'd seen it from the drive. Most of the windows were shuttered, except for this room. Because of the fumes from the smoking fire in the hearth and the brazier, they'd opened the shutters and set the windows ajar. As with all the front rooms on the ground floor, those windows opened to a paved terrace that ran the length of the house.

Talking seemed her best option.

She cleared her throat. "Excuse me, sir?"

He glanced around, arrested, as if surprised she could talk.

Her expression innocent, she raised her brows. "Would you mind telling me what's going on?"

He frowned, straightened, a pair of hot pincers in one hand. "I" —he set his other fist, closed, to his chest— "am a representative of the great and mighty Black Cobra. You are here on my master's orders, and soon you will die a most painful death—to the great glory of the Black Cobra!"

She fought to ignore the vision his words conjured, to ignore the heated pincers he held. She forced a confused frown. "You'll pardon me if I seem a trifle obtuse, but . . . I've never met this Black Cobra person. Why would my death mean anything to him?"

Uncle blinked at her. "But . . ." Then he drew himself up. "You were instrumental in delivering the letter a Captain MacFarlane stole in Poona to a Colonel Delborough in Bombay."

She opened her eyes wide. "That letter? Was it important? I had no idea. I thought it was a personal message from the captain to his commanding officer." She did her best to look intrigued. "What's in it?"

Uncle hesitated, then said, "I do not know."

She frowned harder. "You mean you'll kill me—and presumably many others—and you don't even know why?"

He bridled; his dark eyes lit. "It is my master's orders."

"So he gives orders and you obey—even though you don't

hasn't said anything to me about it."

"He has it—or a copy. This is why I have been sent."

"To find the copy?"

"Yes."

"Was that you all along—back in Aden and on the Red Sea?"

He answered, and she knew she was safe for just a little while—as long as relating their journey and the cult's many actions would take. Like many such men, Uncle was vain enough to want to claim any and all victories he could. She was careful to preserve a suitably innocent mein, encouraging him to impress her with tales of his guile and standing.

He spoke in ringing tones, declaiming and making grand statements.

She asked her questions as loudly as she could.

All the while she listened, strained to hear any activity outside.

Any sign that rescue had arrived.

Inwardly, she prayed.

If the cultists in the chateau saw Gareth's impromptu army marching up the drive, the first thing they would do was slit Emily's throat.

Gareth knew that for an absolute fact. He was consequently unbending in imposing absolute authority over his ragtag forces.

He'd collected those who knew the chateau's grounds, and kept them with him at the head of the ranks as they marched in good order out of the town. He halted them all at the bottom of the chateau's long drive, and impressed on everyone the need for absolute silence from then on.

With quite remarkable stealth, they crept further up the drive. Those familiar with the place told him how far they could go without being seen from the chateau windows, or even from the roof.

Seated on a flat rock by the drive's edge, Mullins was waiting at that very spot. He stood and saluted Gareth. "We caught two of the blighters hurrying back to warn their friends."

Mullins whistled—a bird call. An instant later, Bister appeared from one side, then Mooktu came out of the bushes on the opposite side of the drive.

Gareth nodded. Now came the trickiest part of his plan. He'd spent the march to the chateau juggling options, seeing if any fitted the situation better, but . . . he glanced at the five "lieutenants" he'd appointed, each leading a group of men. "Here's what we'll do." He assigned each of the five groups their positions—two groups to circle the chateau and attack from the rear, another two to cover the sides and the front, the last to spread out and block any attack from cultists who might still be closer to town and inclined to fall on them from behind. "But before anyone makes so much as a sound, I and my men will go in, and find and rescue Miss Ensworth."

"One set of windows in the front are unshuttered," Bister reported. "Otherwise, all activity's at the rear."

Gareth nodded, and returned his attention to the assembled men. "Three of us will go in and liberate Miss Ensworth." Knowing the cult's ways, he felt certain she would still be alive. He prayed she was also unharmed. "Once we have her safe, Bister will signal to Mullins here." Gareth tipped his head to the grizzled veteran. "Mullins will then give the signal to attack. Once you receive *that* signal, you can overrun the place. You do not need to hold back—I assure you they won't. They will fight to the death, because that's their way. Don't expect them to fight by our rules—they have

Bister turned and went, sliding through the shadows beneath the old trees, leading them up and over the slight ridge

313

that hid the dip where their army was gathered from the chateau beyond.

The building was a typical rectangular structure in stone. What had once been a wide *parterre* was overgrown and choked with weeds. Bister led them to the left corner of the building. A raised, paved terrace ran all along the front. With the windows mostly shuttered, they could approach and climb up with little risk of being seen.

Gaining the terrace, Gareth caught Bister's shoulder, leaned close to whisper, "No guards?"

Bister shook his head. "Seems they're relying on the pickets. We found six strung out, but only two reported back."

Gareth nodded. He studied the open terrace for a moment, listening . . . a faint murmur of voices reached him. Someone was in the room with the open windows. The faint tang of smoke teased his nose.

Drawing the primed pistol from his belt, he cocked it, then, holding the weapon ready in one hand, he walked silently, step by step, along the chateau wall toward those open windows.

There was rubble on the terrace. He was careful to avoid it. He didn't need to check to see if Mooktu and Bister did the same, or even if they were following. They'd fought together for so long, in situations like this they acted as one.

Halting two feet from the slightly open window, more accurately a French door, for which he gave thanks, he listened again. Getting into the room would be easy, but he needed to know if Emily was there, and how many men there were.

An older male voice reached him, the cadences distinctly Indian. "So we knew the major and his party would be trapped on the coast . . . and so, here you are."

A pause ensued, filled with burgeoning malevolence. The hair on Gareth's nape rose. Was it Emily the unknown man was talking to?

The voice went on, now cloyingly crooning, "And soon—very soon—the major will arrive, and *then* you will learn why you are here."

"You think to use me—to torture me—to make him give you the letter?"

Emily, and her voice was strong.

"Why, yes, dear lady. Don't you think that will work?"

Gareth signaled to Mooktu and Bister, then, pistol raised, stepped across the French door, kicked it wide, and went through.

Emily, at first glance unharmed, was tied to a chair. An older, black-bearded man—the cult commander Gareth had seen in Aden—was standing, stunned, beside a brazier before the hearth.

Gareth scanned the room, pistol tracking as he searched for guards, and found none. Halting between Emily and the old man, he lowered the pistol. Behind him, Bister and Mooktu worked to cut through the cords binding Emily.

Slack-jawed, the old man glanced from him to the window. "Where are my men?"

Emily abruptly stood, massaging her wrists, stamping her feet free of the cords. The old man looked back at them, at Gareth. Realization washed over his face.

He did something none of them had imagined he would— he *shrieked*. Not a scream, but a sound of pure rage, one that pierced the walls and echoed down corridors.

Gareth jerked up his pistol and fired.

But the man had lunged at the weapons in the brazier; the shot struck him in the shoulder and spun him away. He stumbled back and abruptly sat down before the hearth.

more or less in the center of the room. She sensed her men trying to back, being forced back as they strove to prevent any cultist getting behind them. She grabbed the chair to which she'd been tied, went to shove it aside, saw a cultist trying to come around Bister—she heaved and sent the chair crashing into the cultist, knocking him back.

Bister shifted postion to cover that angle. Both Gareth and Mooktu stepped back.

Emily couldn't see much past their shoulders, but she'd fought cultists with these three before—this fighting was different.

These cultists were stronger, better trained. She remembered Gareth saying the leader would most likely have some of the cult's feared assassins with him. Mooktu and Gareth shifted. She managed to peek between them, and realized matters were even worse. More cultists were pouring through the door.

She glanced around wildly, searching for some weapon.

But there was nothing. Nothing. . . .

Except for an old, mildewed curtain.

Two steps took her to it. The windows were tall. She grabbed the curtain with both hands and yanked. The material parted from its anchors and fell, covering her in dust and musty, disintegrating silk, but the cotton lining, although thin, was intact.

Intact enough. She flung out the curtain, then, arms stretched to her sides, swiftly gathered the fabric in both hands as she hurried up behind Gareth. As she prayed. . . .

She halted immediately behind him. "Gareth—*duck*!"

She waited only to see him start to move, then with all her might she flung the curtain up and out.

Mooktu leaned away to let the material whip past him. The curtain fell on the three assassins facing Gareth and Mooktu, trapping their blades, enveloping them in its folds.

Three seconds later, there were three less cultists.

Four more pushed in, but were hampered by the tangle of bodies.

Behind the four, another cultist leapt into the air and flung a dagger—at Emily. She yelped and ducked—felt the blade sheer through her sleeve and graze her upper arm, but only shallowly. "I'm all right, I'm all right!"

Gareth halted his instinctive turning to her. Teeth gritted, he met the cultists before him with renewed ferocity.

Never had he fought with such unfettered recklessness. Never had fear and fury so controlled him.

He slashed, countered, and inwardly swore. Bister had risked his life to give the signal. Where the hell were his troops?

Almost on the thought, he sensed the change—the turning of the tide. Cultists to the rear of the pack pulled back, listened, then rushed for the door.

Grim determination gripped him. With Mooktu at his shoulder, Bister close on his left, he redoubled his efforts, beating back the assassins.

He and Mooktu simultaneously felled the pair before them, then looked up, and realized all the others were at the door, rushing out. The last in line was the old man, moving surprisingly swiftly.

In the doorway he turned, features contorted, dark eyes blazing.

He raised a hand and threw a knife. Not at Gareth. Past him.

Gareth flung himself back and to the side, connecting with Emily and taking her to the floor.

He felt the impact of the knife. A second passed, one of sheer horror and desperation, before pain bloomed and he

[illegible] and Bister. What are you waiting for? Go after him!"

Mooktu and Bister were only too ready to rush after the assassins.

"No!" Gareth's firm order had them halting on their way to the door. His left arm held tight against him, he propped himself up on his right. "We don't know if there are any others lurking. We need to remain here, and let the others finish it. Let them do what they came to do, what they've trained to do. What they need to do to salvage the honor of their town." He paused to breathe in through the pain. Managed to keep his voice steady to say, "We'll wait here until they're done."

Mooktu and Bister understood. They turned and came back.

Emily glared at him, then, lips tight, looked up at Mooktu. "In that case, you can help me get this out."

By the time the sounds of battle finally died away, Gareth was sitting on a wobbly chair Bister had found in another room, the wound in his upper arm tightly bound. Mooktu had jerked out the dagger—a long, fine krislike blade that, luckily, hadn't struck anything vital. His arm still worked.

Before he'd allowed anyone to tend to him, he'd insisted on looking at Emily's wound. Impatient, she'd jigged while he'd widened the tear in her sleeve, but the skin beneath it, although scratched, wasn't broken.

Of course, *his* wound had bled. Emily had cursed and, using strips torn from her petticoat's flounce, had bound it tightly. "We need to get that cleaned as soon as possible." Standing beside the chair, she'd scowled down at him. "As we're doing nothing here, can't we leave?"

He'd looked up at her, smiled, took her hand, and kissed it. "Thank you. But not yet."

She'd humphed, but had left her hand in his.

They were still like that, she standing beside him, her hand in his, when the door opened wide and Mullins strode in. The grin on his face told them all they needed to know, but he snapped off a salute, and reported as the others—

the Perrots, father and sons, the various seamen, farmhands, and most of their ragtag group—crowded in behind him.

Many were sporting injuries, some more than minor, but all looked thoroughly delighted. Victorious.

The gist of Mullins's report was that, as expected, most of the cultists had fought to the death. There were only three survivors—two young men who were clearly very low on the cult tree, and the old man.

"They called him Uncle," Emily said. "He was their leader."

Perrot asked, "Should we bring him in?"

Gareth thought, then rose to his feet. "No. Better we interrogate him in town."

At his suggestion, Perrot and the other elders organized a detail to bury the dead, and another to escort the three prisoners to town. That done, and with the more critically wounded sent ahead, the rest of them trailed back down the drive and onto the road.

With Emily beside him, her arm twined with his, her hand beneath his on his sleeve, her fingers gripping, Gareth discovered that no matter how he tried, he couldn't stop smiling.

Around them, excited tales of cultists defeated and dispatched, of acts of derring-do, circled, but in that moment only one fact had any purchase in his mind.

She was with him. Alive, well, and unharmed.

And he was still alive to rejoice over that.

As he'd expected, the younger two were little more than terrified boys. They knew nothing, so had nothing to tell. At

Perrot's suggestion, they were escorted away to be handed over to the gendarmes for attacking various locals.

The cult commander, Uncle, was an entirely different subject. Gareth elected to sit back and let Mooktu question him.

Defeated, the wound in his shoulder roughly bound, Uncle was cowed, confused, and clearly unable to believe he and his men hadn't triumphed, yet malevolence rolled off him, and something that struck the gathered listeners as the distillation of pure evil ran beneath his answers.

Mooktu led him to describe his mission, and all that he'd done in following Gareth's party. Uncle readily related what he saw as his clevernesses, yet revealed nothing they didn't already know, or hadn't already surmised. With every word out of his mouth, Uncle drew the noose tighter; he didn't seem to understand that his listeners didn't share his opinion of his greatness, much less his belief in his right to do whatever he chose in the Black Cobra's name.

Often the crowd shifted uneasily, exchanging glances.

Convinced that Uncle had no information of any value to them, Gareth turned his mind to what to do with the man.

When Mooktu reached the end of his questions, Gareth turned to the crowd. "Did this man attack anyone here?"

As he'd expected, the answer was no.

He looked at Perrot. "Uncle attacked me, and he ordered the kidnapping of Miss Ensworth and threatened her life, and, as you've heard, he's ordered much worse while pursuing us. However, with luck, my party will cross the Channel tomorrow." He looked inquiringly at Captain Lavalle, who had offered days before to take them.

Lavalle nodded. "The wind has turned. Tomorrow we can sail."

Gareth looked back at Perrot. "So we can't hand this man to the gendarmes, for there will be no one here to press charges against him."

A dark murmur passed around the room. Before dissatisfaction could bloom, Gareth stated, "*However*, once we sail for England" —he looked at Uncle— "his mission will have failed. And his master, and the cult, have a long-standing practice of punishing failure with death."

Gareth didn't need to ask Uncle for confirmation— awakening terror etched his face, there for all to see. "I suggest," Gareth said, "that the best way of dealing with this fiend is to hold him here, in the basement of the inn, until tomorrow. Then when my party is safely away, on our way to England, release him, and drive him out of town." Gareth glanced around the crowd. "There are cultists still roaming the countryside. They'll find him—and mete out the same punishment he would have dealt to any other of his kind who failed."

Looking again at Uncle, he continued, "There's no need for us—any of us—to sully our hands dealing with this sort of man."

Murmurs rose up, some calling for blood, yet there were enough wise heads among the crowd to ensure agreement. Realizing what they planned, what would happen . . . Uncle seemed to crumple before their eyes.

When Perrot, having consulted with his neighbors, turned back, slapped the table, and declared, "We will do it—just as you say," Uncle cowered.

Gareth noted it. With a nod to Perrot, he straightened, was about to rise when, quick as a striking snake, Uncle shot out his hand and clutched Gareth's wrist.

Gareth's skin crawled. He froze.

"Please . . ." Uncle whined.

deserve nothing less—but *please* . . . tell me—where is my son? Where is his body?"

Gareth frowned. "Your son?"

"He led the party who came against you with the Berbers in the desert."

Gareth glanced at Mooktu, Bister, and the others. "Any ideas?"

Mullins looked at Uncle. "He was the leader of that lot— the cultists with the other group of Berbers?"

Uncle nodded. "Please tell me—where lies his body?"

Mullins snorted. "God only knows." He looked at Gareth. "I think he was taken with the rest of them."

"Taken?" Uncle looked from one to the other. "He lives?"

Gareth looked at the hope in the man's eyes. "Did you send him to lead that raid?"

"It was his chance to gain glory—it is the way of the cult."

"In that case, you and your cult have delivered your son into slavery. He'd promised the Berbers they could have us to sell—the Berbers took him and his men instead."

Uncle's face blanked. After a moment, he whispered, "My son . . . is a slave?" To him, it was unthinkable.

"No." Slowly Uncle shook his head. "No, no, *no-ooh*!" Wrapping his arms around himself, he started to rock, softly keening.

The others stood, Perrot with them. "We will take him down and lock him up."

Lavalle came forward. "The tide will be favorable tomorrow morning at ten."

Gareth sighed, glanced at Emily beside him. "This isn't over yet." He looked at Uncle, being led off to the basement by the Perrots' strapping sons. "There are cultists still out there. He knows there are." Turning, he arched a brow at Bister, who grimly nodded. "And we know there are. There were some we didn't pick up keeping watch along the road." Gareth met the captain's eyes. "We'll need to make arrangements to ensure we get safely aboard."

The captain grinned and clapped him on the back. "You

have given us much excitement in a time of boredom. Come, sit, and we will drink to your health—all of your healths. And then we will make our plans."

Hours later, mellowed by good cognac and the sweet taste of triumph, however temporary, Gareth followed Emily up the stairs to their chamber.

Their plans for tomorrow organized, the others had retired some time ago. The common room had largely emptied, the stories all told.

Tomorrow they would leave. The unknown, most unpredictable, unquestionably most dangerous part of their journey was behind them, weathered and survived. Tomorrow they would start a new leg, hopefully with less threatening challenges.

Tonight, however, was a time for . . .

Thankfulness. Gratefulness. Rejoicing.

Emily heard him shut the door, shut out the world. She paused by the bed, waited for him to draw near, then turned directly into his arms.

He smiled. His hands fastening about her waist, he bent his head to kiss her—

She placed her fingers over his lips. "No, wait. There's something I have to say."

He studied her eyes, arched his brows.

Her palms on his chest, she held his gaze. "Thank you for rescuing me."

indomitable Englishwoman and I've traveled the world, but you being hurt is something I can't bear." From close quarters, she stared into his eyes, one, then the other, then categorically stated, "I love you—do you understand that? I *love* you—so you mustn't get hurt. Not anymore."

She held his gaze for an instant more, then pushed her hands up over his shoulders, wound her arms about his neck, stretched the last inch and pressed her lips to his. "But thank you." She kissed him.

"Thank you." Another kiss.

"Thank you." She whispered the last thank you over his lips, then met them in a kiss that this time didn't end, but lengthened, strengthened, deepened as he took over, took charge, took her mouth, and she gave.

Surrendered.

Murmured, when his lips left hers to skate down the arching column of her throat, "Don't you dare laugh."

"I'm not." His breath feathered over the sensitive skin where shoulder met neck. "I'm . . . cowed."

She laughed, a short burst of disbelief that ended in a hiss as his hands closed about her breasts. After that, conversation was on neither of their agendas. Only one thing was.

One need, one want.

One passion, one desire.

One overwhelming craving.

Gareth had expected that—the age-old need to crown death's defeat with a celebration of life, of the pinnacle of living.

Loving.

Loving her—and having her love him. The knowledge invested his every touch, made every caress she gifted him with one of precious delight.

Clothes drifted to the floor. Incoherent murmurs rose and fell as they uncovered, discovered, and feasted. As they fell on the bed and skin met skin, and passion rose and desire sparked, arced and drew them in.

Into the familiar whirlpool of sensation, into the hungry, greedy joy.

Into the delight, the pleasure, the giving.

That night they loved.

Loved in a way they hadn't before, at a deeper, more con-certed, more attuned level, one where the sharing was richer, more vibrant, more vivid, and every moment resonated with a more powerful meaning.

Alive, wondrously so, naked they wrestled, taking, giving, wanting, yearning, gasping, and surrendering.

She took him in and rode him, wild and abandoned, her pearly skin kissed by the silvery moonlight, her breasts full and peaked as she rose and slid down, concentration etching her features as she pleasured him, pleasured him.

Loved him, loved him . . .

On a groan, he rose up and tipped her, rolled with her, sinking again into her welcoming warmth as her arms closed about him and he returned the pleasure.

The loving.

The love.

Until their bodies were filled, full and cresting, until pas-sion was spent and desire razed and their blood pounded and their senses imploded and ecstacy rushed in, seized them, took them, shattered them.

Wracked them.

Bound them together with silken strands and slowly low-ered them back to earth, back to the rumpled sheets, and the haven of each other's arms.

They lay there, tangled, unable to move, unwilling to part, even just an inch. Hearts thundering, skin damp, breathing

Where he needed her to be from now on.

One arm bent behind his head, he stared at the ceiling, the

other arm holding her close. After a moment of comfortable silence, he ventured, "So . . . does that mean: Yes, you'll marry me?"

He felt her lips curve against his chest. "Perhaps. My answer is still perhaps."

He didn't want to ask, but . . . "Why perhaps?"

"Because . . . I want something more."

He didn't ask what more she wanted—he knew. *I love you*. He hadn't given her the same, or even equivalent words. He'd answered her truly—he'd felt cowed. Awed by her confidence in uttering them—those infinitely powerful three little words. He'd heard women were like that—strong in such things, confident in their feelings.

Men—especially men like him . . .

Even now he had to quell a shudder at the thought of letting those words pass his lips. It was bad enough that he knew they were real. That his inner self, his heart—it seemed his very soul—had already accepted that reality.

Yet all he'd ever need to make him shy from saying those words was to remember how he'd felt earlier that day. When he'd heard she'd been taken, he'd felt . . . eviscerated. As if someone had reached into his chest and stolen his heart—literally. He'd felt empty there, hollow, as if he'd lost something so vital he'd never know warmth or happiness again.

The feeling had been profound, absolute, unshakable.

If anything could make him wary of love—of admitting it out aloud—it was that. He'd barely been able to function as he'd needed to, to take command as he'd had to, to get her back.

He'd been a soldier all his adult life. Never before had he felt vulnerable. Today, instead of the habitual invincibility essential to all good commanders, that sense of being protected by impenetrable armor even though one knew that wasn't true, he'd felt . . . as if someone had carved a hole in his armor directly over his heart.

That vulnerable feeling hadn't left him, not until he'd had her in his arms, not until he'd known that all danger to her had passed.

Even then . . .

She'd fallen asleep. He listened to the rhythm of her breathing, marveled at how soothing he found it. How reassuring the soft sound was, how he recognized it, knew it, at some level he couldn't explain.

He was on the cusp of sleep himself when a stray truth wafted through his mind.

Today, she had been first and foremost in his thoughts—he hadn't thought of the scroll holder and its safety. Hadn't really thought of his mission per se.

For days—weeks—she'd been highest in his mind. She, her safety, and even more, her happiness.

He was a man of duty—he lived by that code, and always had.

Yet he put her above his duty—to his comrades, to his country, to his king. And he always would.

And that, he thought, as sleep dragged him down, said it all.

"We must strike tomorrow—we will get no other chance." Akbar sat amid the ruins of the kitchen of the old mansion and looked at his second, then at the other two cultists who had been watching the road and had escaped with them.

"What about Uncle?" one of the pair asked. "Surely we should free him?"

"It was Uncle who led us to our terrible defeat." Akbar flung out his arms. "How many comrades have we lost—has *he* lost—in this campaign?"

Akbar nodded. "We must stop the major and retrieve the scroll holder he carries, whatever the cost."

The other two nodded. "You are right. So how will we do this?"

They discussed, and discussed, until the truth became clear.

"We cannot do both," his second stated. "We can stop the major, or get the scroll holder, but with only four of us . . . we cannot do both."

Akbar hated to choose, but . . . he nodded. "If we kill the major and his woman, the Black Cobra will be pleased, and those waiting in England will have a better chance of retrieving the scroll holder."

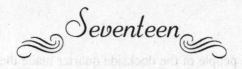

Seventeen

13th December, 1822
Morning
Our room in the Perrots' auberge

Dear Diary,

I am almost there. I can almost taste the ultimate victory—the joy I will feel when Gareth finally, finally, tells me he loves me. In words. Out loud.

He told me the truth last night, not in words, but in actions. Actions that spoke far too loudly for me to mistake his message.

So yes, he is now and forever my "one," and yes,

It's really quite exciting, this new life unfolding before me.

E.

he people of the dockside quarter made their departure into an event. News had spread, and by nine-thirty that morning, when Gareth's party needed to leave the auberge and board their ship, the narrow streets were lined with well-wishers, all smiling and clapping and cheering them on.

The sheer numbers of locals ensured no cultist would be likely to get close.

Gareth sent the baggage, then the others in twos and threes ahead. Their route lay straight down the street opposite the auberge, which led to the main quay, then to the left a short way, and out along one of the lesser wharves. Captain Lavalle's ship was berthed midway along.

The skies were gray, but neither sleet, snow, rain, nor gales threatened. The streets were damp, if not dry, and the breeze was blowing offshore.

At the last, after much touching of cheeks, slapping of backs and shaking of hands, he and Emily took their leave of the Perrots, and emerged from the inn.

Smiling, nodding to those in the crowd they recognized, they walked briskly down the street, onto the quay, and out along the wharf.

They were within a hundred feet of Lavalle's ship, had paused to farewell a group of sailors, and were just moving on, when Gareth heard a telltale *shi-ing*.

He grabbed Emily, pushed her back and down, covering her body with his—but not before that first arrow sliced across her forearm. The next arrow thudded into the wharf beside her.

Two more found their mark in his back, but too weakly to do more than pierce his skin.

Pandemonium erupted all along the wharf. More arrows

rained down, one slicing across his arm, but the archers had misjudged their range; the force behind the arrows was enough to wound, but only by sheer luck could they kill. Realizing that, some sailors seized craypot lids and other makeshift shields, and formed a protective wall between Gareth and Emily and their ship. Other sailors swarmed aboard the two ships from whose crow's nests the archers were shooting.

Hauling Emily to her feet, Gareth rushed her to the gang-plank and up it. Gaining the deck, he looked around and saw one cultist-archer dive from one crow's nest into the harbor, while the other had been subdued and was being manhandled down the mast.

Captain Lavalle came striding up. The gangplank was already aboard. "We're away. You'll be glad to see the last of these attackers—"

Steel clanged on steel. Lavalle whirled. Looking past him, Gareth saw two cultists in the bow, wet and dripping, swords viciously slashing at sailors armed only with knives.

He thrust Emily at Arnia and Mooktu. "Tend her wound."

With an oath, Lavalle ran for the action. Drawing his sword, Gareth followed, grimly pleased to have a release for the emotions roiling within him, evoked by having Emily hurt, especially while he'd been standing beside her.

He'd been helpless to protect her more than he had, but he wasn't helpless now, and one of the cultists paid. Lavalle dispatched the other.

the wound, he could see a thin line of blood on the edge of her slashed sleeve.

"That's just a scratch." Jaw firming ominously, she tugged harder. "Come on. Don't argue."

He consented to let her drag him along. "Mine is just a scratch, too."

"Mine is a real scratch—it hardly bled at all."

He halted. "That's worse than mine. You—"

She turned on him, rising up on her toes to, quietly, shriek in his face, "You have two arrows in your shoulder! Don't talk to me about scratches—you weren't supposed to get hurt again, remember?"

He'd forgotten about the arrows. Reaching over his shoulder, he found them, yanked them free of the thick weave of his coat, then brought them around to show her the arrowheads. "See—hardly any blood. They barely broke the skin."

She studied them, humphed. "Perhaps. Regardless, you will come below now and let me tend your wounds."

Looking into her face, registering her tone—determined and one level away from shrill—he nodded, and when she turned and led the way, meekly followed her to the stern companionway.

Half an hour later, Gareth checked with Lavalle, then, seeing Emily standing at the stern watching Boulogne sink below the horizon, went to join her.

She didn't say anything, didn't look his way, just lifted her face to the breeze, then sighed. "They were nice people—the Perrots and all the others—even if they were French."

He smiled. "True." After a moment, smile fading, he murmured, "However, I doubt I'll be rushing to return, not in the foreseeable future."

"Hmm."

A long moment passed, then he quietly said, "I've had enough of traveling." He glanced at her. "How about you?"

She turned her head, looked into his eyes. Then she smiled. "Me, too." She looked over the water. "I've had enough of adventure, of being in danger. Especially now that I've found what I was searching for."

332

They both thought of what that was. Of what it would lead to.

The seas grew choppier and he shifted to stand behind her, wrapping his arms about her, shielding her from the worst of the snapping breeze as they watched Boulogne disappear and their past fall behind them, sliding away in the wake of the ship, and consciously let their minds look ahead. To the lives they would lead, and the future they would share.

13th December, 1822
Afternoon
Aboard Lavalle's ship bobbing in the Channel

Dear Diary,

> *He still hasn't said he loves me, but I would be foolish indeed to doubt it. Even more than his actions, his motivations, his reasons, his reactions, all of which have remained unwavering for some weeks, speak of his true feelings.*
>
> *I can no longer doubt him on that score, so my question now is how much more—what else—should I seek from him in order that our marriage is based from the first on the very best foundation possible?*
>
> *Once again, I feel in dire need of my sisters' advice.*

ing stories of home and hopes for the future.
For him . . . the future was not yet.

Emily, thank heaven, understood. Sliding her arm in his, she leaned against his shoulder. "We'll be dodging cultists again shortly, won't we?"

He nodded. "This is my first sight of England in seven years and . . ." When she said nothing, just waited, he dragged in a breath and said, "I can't help thinking how lucky I am, cultists and all. MacFarlane won't see home again—and I don't know where the others are, if they'll make it home, too."

Her hand slid into his, and she gripped. "You know what they're like, those three friends of yours. I saw them, remember? They're as determined as you. They'll fight, and win through. They always have, haven't they?"

His lips quirked. He inclined his head.

Eyes on the still distant land, he forced his mind to the immediate future. "The Black Cobra is going to know we're here soon after we land. Once he does, he'll come at us with even greater—even more deadly—force. He'll do everything he can to stop us—to stop the letter I'm carrying getting into Wolverstone's hands." He paused, then went on, "Even after that, we—none of us in our party—will be safe. Not until the Black Cobra himself is brought down."

Her fingers tightened on his. "We will win. We'll see this through, and after that . . ."

Perhaps. His jaw firmed. "When this is all over, we'll talk about . . . what's next."

About their marriage. He now knew beyond question that he would do whatever he needed to to ensure she said yes. To ensure she remained his—his lover, his wife, and more.

Coming home with her by his side was both a joy and a burden. That he had found her, the only woman he'd ever considered marrying, that she was with him, and one way or another would remain, was all he could ever have dreamed of by way of joyous homecomings. Yet the potential danger she would face setting foot on English soil by his side muted that joy, placed a heavy weight on his shoulders and set a vise about his heart.

Returning the pressure of her fingers, shifting his to close his hand around hers, he silently vowed that no matter the threat, he would keep her safe. If he wanted a future, he'd have to—without her, he wouldn't have one.

They stepped off the gangplank and onto the docks, shrouded in gray drizzle with night rapidly closing in. With heavy coats and thick cloaks wrapped about them, they followed their baggage, loaded on a small cart, out of the harbor and into the town.

Bister appeared at Gareth's shoulder. "Cultist on the far corner to the left. He's seen us."

Gareth glanced through the damp veil and saw a shocked brown face staring in their direction. "They didn't expect us to get through their blockade, which means there'll be no huge welcome waiting for us around the corner."

Bister shivered artistically. "Just as well. We need to get out of this wet before the cold gets into our bones."

They'd all forgotten England's dampness.

Wolverstone had stipulated they put up at the Waterman's Inn in Castle Street. They reached it without incident. Giving his name at the counter, Gareth discovered that rooms had already been arranged—the entire first floor of one of the inn's wings.

"Arranged by a gen'leman who's waiting in the tap, sir." The innkeeper nodded to a doorway to the right. "Him or his friend's been in every day for a week, now. Would you like me to fetch him, or . . . ?"

through the open doorway.

There was a goodly crowd dotted about small tables and

booths, couples and friends sharing a drink at the end of a winter's day. A cheery fire burned in the hearth. Pausing on the threshold, Gareth scanned those present. His gaze halted on a brown-haired man seated in a booth along the side wall, trying to read a news-sheet in the light shed by a wall sconce.

Even as he looked, the man glanced their way—an idle glance that immediately grew more focused, more intent.

Lips curving, Gareth steered Emily toward the booth.

As they neared, the man stood, slowly uncoiling to his six-foot-plus height. Brown brows remained level over shrewd hazel eyes. "Major Hamilton."

It was a statement, uttered with the same assurance Gareth felt in approaching the man. Like recognized like. This man had been in the Guards, too, and there wasn't any other in the tap who could possibly have been one of Dalziel's ex-operatives.

Gareth smiled and held out his hand. "Gareth. Wolverstone didn't convey any names."

"He never does." Their new guard shook hands. He had a ready smile, one he shared equally between Gareth and Emily. "I'm Jack Warnefleet, here to make sure you remain hale and whole throughout the rest of your journey."

Gareth introduced Emily. Jack shook hands, then waved them into the booth. While they settled he asked, and went to fetch drinks—mulled wine for Emily, ale for Gareth and him.

When he returned with their glasses and passed them around, Gareth sipped, smiled. He glanced at Emily, then looked across the table. "Speaking of our onward journey . . ."

"Indeed, but first, is all to your liking here? How many do you have with you?"

Gareth told him.

Jack nodded. "We've bespoken enough rooms. Before we look forward, tell me how you've fared." Jack's gaze included Emily.

And Gareth recalled no one knew she was with him. "I'm unsure how much you know of the beginning of this venture, but Miss Ensworth was instrumental in ferrying the vital letter from MacFarlane to us in Bombay."

Jack looked at Emily with growing respect. "I was told some lady had." He smiled charmingly. "It's an even greater pleasure to meet you, Miss Ensworth."

"As it transpired, Emily left Bombay at the same time I did, and our paths crossed at Aden—luckily, as it happened, for cultists were stalking her, too. From there . . ." Gareth condensed their travels to the minimum, including only the operational information.

Jack's expression grew satisfied as he absorbed the details of their recent encounters at Boulogne. "As usual, I don't know what Royce—Wolverstone—is planning, but I suspect he'll view the number you've managed to draw and elimi-nate around Boulogne as something of a victory. You're one of the decoys, so drawing the enemy and reducing numbers was precisely what you were supposed to do."

"Have you heard anything of the other couriers?" Gareth asked.

"Delborough's here—he came in two days ago through Southampton. I gather his route will be via London and then on into Cambridge, to Somersham Place. I haven't heard anything yet about the other two."

"So what's our onward route?"

Jack grinned. "Your first stop is Mallingham Manor.

Good. In that case, I'll take the news of your arrival back to the manor, and we'll send off a messenger hotfoot to Royce. Then, tomorrow morning, Trentham and I will join you for breakfast here, and we'll make our plans." He glanced at Emily, then back at Gareth. "If you think you'll be ready to go on?"

Gareth nodded decisively, from the corner of his eye saw Emily do the same. "We will be."

"Excellent." Jack stood, and they did, too. They shook hands again, then he saluted them. "Until tomorrow."

He strode out, leaving the tap by the street door. With Emily on his arm, Gareth headed for their room.

Uncle trudged along a road—he didn't even know where it led. Darkness had fallen; he needed to find shelter of some kind to see out the freezing night.

The villagers of Boulogne had chased him out of their town. He was still stunned that they had dared to lay hands on his august person. He'd gone to the chateau expecting to find men, weapons, and the coin cache hidden there. But the chateau had been deserted. Someone had found the coins and taken them.

Mindlessly, he'd turned south. He refused to let himself think of his son. The major had lied—he must have. His jailers had told him some cultists had attacked the major's party on the docks, but again had been defeated. The attackers had been killed. Was there no one left?

On the thought, a shadow separated from the trees just ahead. Uncle reached for a knife, but he no longer had one. Then he recognized the man beneath the cloak. Uncle brightened. "Akbar!"

Uncle made his legs go faster, already making plans. "How many others have we?"

Akbar didn't move, didn't reply, not until Uncle halted before him and peered into his face.

"None," Akbar said.

"*All* gone?" Uncle couldn't credit such failure. Facing forward, he narrowed his eyes. "We will have to cross the Channel and join—"

"No."

He blinked, focused on Akbar's face again. "What do you mean, no?"

Akbar's eyes, flat and cold, held his. "I mean . . ."

Uncle felt steel slice through skin, through flesh, slide between his ribs . . .

Akbar's lips curled cruelly. "I've been waiting for you, old man, just so I could tell you that this" —he thrust the knife in to the hilt— "is the last deed I will do in the Black Cobra's name."

Jerking the blade out, Akbar stepped back, watched as Uncle crumpled to the ground. "To the glory and delight of the Black Cobra."

For Gareth and Emily, the evening passed with myriad adjustments, small points of recognition and relaxation as they slipped once more into English ways. Custom once again forced them to dine apart from the others, in a private parlor. Reacquainting themselves with English fare was an adjustment they found amusing.

Later, with the watches set and everyone irrepressibly relieved to be once more within a society in which they felt at home, they retired.

Much later, in the small hours of the morning, Gareth slid from beneath the covers, silently dressed, and went to take his turn on watch.

Half an hour had passed, and he was sitting on the land-

"I went to India to find a different sort of gentleman." She spoke softly, her words just above a whisper, her gaze on the darkness of the hall below. "I'm twenty-four. I'd been looking for a husband, as young ladies of my station are expected to do, for years, but I'd never found a single man capable of capturing my attention—a man I thought of after he'd passed out of my sight."

He didn't move, didn't interrupt.

"I was labeled picky—rightly so. But my family understood, so when my uncle was sent to India, my parents suggested I visit, so that I might meet a wider range of men. Perhaps a style of gentleman I hadn't met before." She tipped her head toward their room. "I was just thinking, recalling, what my vision was on my way out to Bombay. What I thought of as my goal—what I was searching for. I had it all clear in my mind—I was looking for a gentleman with whom I could share a life. Not my life, not his life, but a life that would be ours. That we, together, would create for us both."

She paused, then went on, "Once I remembered, I realized nothing has changed. That's still what I want." She turned her head and met his eyes. "That's what I want with you."

The darkness made her eyes impossible to read, yet still he held her gaze. And sensed, within him, words lining up, waiting to be said—a response he hadn't thought of, hadn't censored, that just came. Just was. "My home . . . well, I don't have one, none I can claim. My family wasn't like yours—I have no fond memories, no experience of having brothers and sisters, all that comes of a large brood. I was alone. Until recently, until you, I always have been. When I resigned and turned my sights once more on England, I couldn't see beyond the end of my mission. I could see no future—had a blank space in my mind where a vision of my future should have been. No framework, no ideas—not even a skeleton of a concept. Until recently, until you, my future was a blank slate."

And now?

Her gaze hadn't wavered, steady on his face. She didn't say the words, but they both heard them.

He drew breath, and plunged in. "Where would you prefer to live? Near your family home, or in town?" Before she could ask, he added, "I don't care where I live." *As long as it's with you.*

She nodded slowly, as if she'd heard the words he hadn't said. "Not in town. Near my parents' house, but not too close. In the surrounding shires, close enough to easily visit."

He nodded. "Village or country town?"

Her lips curved. "Village. But with a town with a market square nearby."

"Manor house or mansion?"

Emily opened her eyes wide. "I have a choice?"

He held her gaze; she felt trapped in his dark eyes. "You can choose anything, or everything. Whatever your heart desires. This is our future—we get to choose, and as my slate is blank . . ."

She'd stopped breathing, had to drag in a tight breath. "Manor house, then, with the sort of rambling, rolling gardens children love to run in."

"Children?"

She nodded. "Lots."

That stopped him. For a long moment he stared at her through the dark, then he nodded. "All right."

He didn't say more, ask more, just gathered her close, and rested his chin on her head.

They sat quietly for a while, listening to the inn slumbering around them. Then he murmured, "That's a start. You've

14th December, 1822
Morning
Our chamber at the Waterman's Inn, Dover

Dear Diary,

> *If Gareth had asked me to marry him last night,*
> *I would have said yes, regardless. Quite clearly, his*
> *vision of the future is mine—literally. What more*
> *could any woman ask?*
>
> *I know that he loves me—he's shown me he does*
> *more times than I can count, and continues to do*
> *so—and while I still would like to hear the words, a*
> *declaration of his heart, I am no longer so certain that*
> *matters. At least, not as much as it did.*
>
> *When I consider what, to me, is most vitally im-*
> *portant in marriage, then knowing I am his, and he is*
> *mine, must top any list.*
>
> *And that, dear Diary, I already know, to the*
> *bottom of my soul.*
>
> *Whatever happens in the days to come, Gareth Ham-*
> *ilton, my "one," will not be slipping through my fingers.*
>
> *E.*

"Royce wants us to draw and eliminate as many cultists as possible, but primarily in a specific area." Tristan Wemyss, Earl of Trentham, met Gareth's gaze over the breakfast dishes. "Specifically the swath between Chelmsford and his residence at Elveden, north of Bury St. Edmonds."

Gareth nodded. "So we're to act as hares to our fox—in this case, the cult."

"And" —Jack held up a finger— "possibly the Black Cobra himself. Ferrar knows the area—his father has a house in Norfolk."

Jack had returned that morning as promised, Tristan in tow. After the introductions, they'd sat down to a large and varied breakfast. The men were doing the inn's cook proud.

Emily glanced from Jack, to Tristan, to Gareth, and inwardly shook her head. Aside from the obvious physical similarities consequent on all being ex-Guardsmen, all three shared a distinctly robust attitude toward the cult, as if they couldn't wait to engage.

"Sadly," Tristan continued, "Royce doesn't want us to come north just yet. In the interim, he wants us to make you disappear, make you invisible to the cult."

Gareth raised his brows. "How?"

"We're to transfer you and your entire party to Mallingham Manor." Jack smiled predatorially. "Without the cult tracking you there."

Gareth grimaced. "While they're not always well trained as fighters, they are distressingly good at tracking and locating."

Tristan smiled, a gesture very like Jack's. He tipped his head at his friend. "So are we. And once we locate, we eliminate."

Gareth's brows rose. "I see." He popped the last of his gravy-soaked bread into his mouth, chewed, swallowed, then nodded. "All right. So how are we going to do that?"

14th December, 1822
Early evening
Our chamber at the inn in Dover

First and foremost, we are clearly no longer alone in our battle against the fiend and his forces. Both

343

Trentham and Warnefleet are undeniably able men, very much like Gareth. The addition of two such warriors to our party makes us, I judge, well-nigh invincible. Which is an enormous relief.

Even more heartening, I have learned from Trentham that there are ladies at his manor—not just his wife and Jack's wife, but many others, too—his great-aunts and various cousins and dependents. From all I could glean, for the first time since leaving Aunt Selma in Poona, I will have ladies of my ilk with whom to converse—and from whom I might gain further insight into living with, and being married to, males of Gareth's ilk. That will be a boon I will be glad to seize. One should never close one's ears to advice from the experienced.

More, I am conscious of a buoying of my spirits, a greater certainty that Gareth's mission, complicated by being that of a decoy, will indeed end successfully enough to satisfy him, which will allow him to, once it is over, turn his back on the recent past and focus with all his heart on shaping our joint future. I know his feelings over MacFarlane's death run deep, and a successful outcome to this mission is essential to permit him to lay those feelings to rest—to leave that last part of his past behind him.

I have just heaved another relieved and happy sigh. After being trepidatious and tense for more days than I can count, in looking forward to tomorrow, it is amazing to feel only eager and intrigued interest.

My only quibble in all this is a nebulous niggle that somehow, in some way, Gareth is yet uncertain. Not of me, or our future, but of something between us. I cannot put my finger on what it is, but I will.

But now I must hurry and dress!

E.

Their move to Mallingham Manor was accomplished in three stages through a morning that was gloomy and gray, cold, but not raining. At ten o'clock, Mullins, Dorcas, and Watson set off in the inn's gig as if to visit some house in the countryside to the west. Twenty minutes later, Mooktu, Arnia, and Jimmy set out in a cart laden with all the bags and trunks, and headed north. Half an hour later, Gareth, Emily, and Bister departed in another gig, and took to the London Road.

The cultists in Dover, already scrambling to reorganize in light of their unexpected arrival, had to scramble again, but two cultists succeeded in trailing the first gig, another followed the cart, and one settled to shadow the gig Gareth was driving.

Tristan and Jack watched, noted, then acted. Those handling the reins—Mullins, Mooktu, and Gareth—had instructions not to drive too fast, but to eventually head north and west into Surrey. Ultimately, after halting for lunch along the way, all would climb a certain hill not far from the Manor.

Mounted on good horses, Tristan and Jack removed the cultists, then raced across country to that hill. In mid-afternoon, when Mullins tooled his gig up the long, open rise, Jack and Tristan were in position, watching from the hilltop, from where they could see spread before them all the surrounding land.

When an hour later Gareth finally drew rein on the crest

Gareth nodded, met Jack's eyes. "How many?"

"I got two." Jack glanced at Tristan. "He got two more.

345

Enough to whet our appetites, but I don't think there are more, so we'll be on your heels."

Gareth nodded, flicked the reins, and sent the gig rolling on.

True to Jack's word, they'd only just reached the stable yard behind the manor—only just stepped down into a circus of grooms, footmen, and a bevy of ladies, most old, two not so old, all talking and exclaiming—when Tristan and Jack rode up.

While they dismounted and handed their horses to the grooms, one of the younger ladies, a confident matron with dark hair, swept up to Gareth and Emily. "Welcome—I'm Leonora, Tristan's wife." Smiling delightedly, she shook hands with Gareth, then squeezed Emily's fingers. "We're very glad to see you, not least because those two" —she tipped her head to Jack and Tristan— "have been on tenterhooks for the last week, awaiting your arrival."

"Indeed." The second matron, taller and rather stately with dark mahogany hair and an openly commanding manner, joined them and offered her hand. "I'm Clarice, Jack's wife. I gather you've had adventures untold—you must come in and tell us all about them."

Those words proved prophetic. Before Emily could do more than give her name and touch fingers, she and Gareth were swept up by a wave of older ladies, led by Tristan's great-aunts, Lady Hermione Wemyss and Lady Hortense Wemyss, carried into the big house and deposited in a large, long family parlor that was clearly the older ladies' domain.

"I'm afraid" —Leonora angled her head close to Emily's as they settled side by side on one of the many chaises— "that it's best—easiest, certainly—to humor them. They mean well. If any of their questions disturb you, just look to me or Clarice, and we'll rescue you." She glanced at Gareth and smiled. "You, too, Major—feel free to call on us for aid."

Gareth met her eye, inclined his head. "Please call me Gareth."

Once all the ladies had subsided, he sat in the armchair next to the chaise. Emily looked around. "Jack and Tristan?"

"Have escaped." Clarice smiled from an armchair opposite.

"We don't need them." Lady Hortense dismissed her great-nephew and his friend with an arrogant wave. Her eyes, old but bright, fixed on Emily and Gareth. "It's you two we want to know about—and we're a great deal too old to waste time being delicate. So, how did you come to be in India in the first place?"

The old ladies were dogged, determined, and quite shockingly direct, but there was no doubt of their sincere interest, or of their shrewdness. There were fourteen in all, an Ethelreda, a Millie, and a Flora among them. All had questions, and with so many minds focused on the task, each and every little detail was winkled from them, and examined and commented upon.

Which should have put them out, put their backs up, but instead the kindness and understanding the old ladies exuded made their interrogation feel more like a confession and absolution.

Almost an exorcism.

Emily found herself responding to their inquisition with increasing freedom. She suspected Gareth, too, revealed more than he'd expected to—possibly more than he was comfortable with in response to their encouraging probing. Certainly, when after half an hour Jack and Tristan looked in, using the [illegible] drawn, the fire built up, and eventually the questions died.

"Well," Hermione declared, "you and your major have certainly lived through thick and thin, up hill and dale. So when will we be hearing wedding bells?"

"Aunt!" Leonora attempted to frown down her outrageous relative-by-marriage.

Who pooh-poohed and waved her objection aside. "Plain as a pikestaff which way they're headed—and see?" She waved at Emily. "She's not denying it, is she?" Hermione leaned closer and peered. "Indeed, she's not even blushing."

Emily realized she wasn't. In fact, she couldn't help but smile. She glanced at Leonora. "It's quite all right." She looked back at Hermione and the other old ladies, all eagerly waiting. "We haven't yet set a date. We're still discussing all the little things I expect people do."

"Good gel!" Hortense nodded approvingly. "Get the basics agreed to before you set your hand in his."

A loud *bo-oo-oo-ong* rolled through the house.

"Time to dress for dinner," Leonora announced.

The old ladies sat up, gathering their trailing shawls and handkerchiefs, grasping the heads of their numerous canes and pulling themselves out of their chairs.

Leonora rose beside Emily. "Just in time," she murmured, "or they would be giving you advice on how to manage your wedding night."

Clarice chuckled as she joined them. "I'm rather curious as to what they might say."

So was Emily.

The three of them followed the older ladies up the stairs, lending a hand when needed. When they reached the first floor, and their elders had stumped off to their rooms, Clarice following, distantly supervising, Leonora conducted Emily to a lovely room overlooking the park to one side of the manor. Dorcas was already there, laying out one of Emily's few evening gowns, and—bliss—a bath stood by the fireplace, steam wreathing above its sides.

Leonora glanced at Emily's rapt expression and laughed. "Take your time—we won't be starting dinner without you."

She met Emily's eyes. "And if there's anything you need, anything at all, please ask."

Emily heard the subtle message, saw confirmation in Leonora's very blue eyes of the sincerity and universality of her words, and felt a connection she'd never felt with any but her sisters stir. "Thank you." She smiled, and stated equally sincerely, "I will."

Leonora's smile blazed. She squeezed her hand. "Good. Now I'll leave you to it."

Dinner with the fourteen old ladies and the other two couples proved a warm and relaxing affair. Emily could feel her tension—so consistent and persistent over the last weeks that she'd forgotten it was there—evaporating.

Despite being less used to such rousing—not to say ribald—female-dominated discussions, or the warmth and clear support that flowed so freely through the room, Gareth, too, found himself lowering his guard—he had to remind himself the cultists were still in the country, that they had to assume their pursuers might still find them.

When he realized that the ladies didn't intend to leave the three gentlemen to the port and brandy, instead joining them in partaking of those liquers, he grasped a moment to quietly mention to Tristan the need to set watches through the night.

Lady Hermione, seated between them, overheard. "Oh, you don't need to trouble yourself—or your people—with that. We would be happy to stand the watch."

and we'll have Henrietta and Clitheroe to back us up, and raise the alarm if need be."

Gareth's gaze slid to Clitheroe, the aging butler.

Clitheroe bowed to Lady Hortense. "As you say, my lady."

"Henrietta," Jack called down the table, "is Leonora's wolfhound. She's already been introduced to your people, but you haven't yet met her."

"She has the run of the house at night," Leonora put in. "She's very protective."

"Not to put too fine a point on it," Tristan said, "she'll savage anyone who tries to break in."

Later, after the company had adjourned to the drawing room, Henrietta was called in and introduced to Gareth and Emily. At that point, Gareth dropped all objection to the older ladies' arrangements. When he sat, Henrietta's shaggy head, and her highly impressive jaws, were level with his head.

Later, when he climbed the stairs with Tristan and Jack, having ensured the ground floor was secure and that Ethelreda, Edith, and Flora, taking first watch, were happily ensconced by the fire in the central hall—with Henrietta a shaggy rug at their feet—Gareth admitted, "It's been so long since I've felt our party is not under threat . . . it takes a little getting used to."

Jack humphed. "It took over a year before I stopped checking everyone in every room I entered—such is the legacy of having been a spy."

Tristan nodded. "At least a year. Some part of you thinks you have to still be watching. It takes time for that to fade."

"Especially with ladies about." Jack grinned. With a jaunty salute, he headed down one corridor.

Parting from Tristan with a smile, Gareth went through the gallery and on to his room. Emily's room was the next one along and, very helpfully, there was a connecting door.

Ten minutes later, wearing only his robe, he tried the door, discovered it unlocked, and padded through to find her already abed, but not asleep. She'd left the windows uncurtained; shadows dappled the room and moonbeams danced as the wind stirred bare branches outside.

Laying aside his robe, he slipped between the covers, heard the giggle she stifled as, as usual, the bed dipped and she rolled toward him. He caught her, drew her close, settled her within his arms. "What were you thinking about?" *Lying here in the dark.*

She nestled her head on his shoulder. "This house—the household, all the old ladies. It's so very English, and so comfortable. Now I'm home again, it's as if I have to relearn—remind myself—what it is I most like, what I most value about things here, in this land."

"Oh?"

There was enough wariness in the syllable to make Emily struggle up on one elbow to look into his face. "I was thinking about houses and households, and combinations of people. About families and atmosphere and comfort."

"I see." Through the dimness he tried to study her eyes. "So you're not revising what it is you like about gentlemen?"

"No." She smiled. "Although . . ." Lowering her lips until they almost met his, she murmured, "Perhaps I should revisit all the things about you that I like—just to make sure they're still up to the mark now we're here."

His chest quaked beneath her as he laughed. Still smiling, she kissed him.

And set about compiling a thorough inventory, one that fully satisfied her, and him.

"It could have been worse. We might not know Hamilton's exact whereabouts, but we do know he's gone to ground in this area, and, as Alex pointed out, it's likely the couriers are making for somewhere in Norfolk. Our watchers on the roads between here and there will pick up Hamilton and his party as soon as they move. We've more than enough men to leave a sizable group ready to close in behind them the instant they cross the Thames."

Daniel watched Roderick frown into his glass, and waited.

The three of them—he, Roderick and Alex—all scions of the noble house of Shrewton, all children of the current earl, had found one another some years ago. Their shared paternity led them to like, value, lust after the same things— primarily money and power. Power over others, power that could be wielded as cruelly as they wished, as their whims dictated.

When Roderick had taken a position in Bombay, Daniel and Alex had followed him, and the three of them had found the opportunities the subcontinent presented very much to their taste.

They'd created the Black Cobra cult, and had lived in luxurious and vicious splendor.

Until a stray letter, written in the Black Cobra's name and signed with the Black Cobra's distinctive mark, and by unlucky circumstance sealed by Roderick with the family seal ring that reposed immovably on his little finger, had fallen into the hands of a group of officers sent to identify and expose the Black Cobra.

Those four officers and their friends now knew Roderick was the Black Cobra. What they didn't know—what no one outside the cult's inner circles knew—was that Roderick was only one of three. But to preserve the power the Black Cobra had amassed, Daniel and Alex needed Roderick.

Unfortunately, they'd heard of the letter and the threat it might pose too late to stop the four officers leaving Bombay for England. To successfully arraign Roderick, favorite son of the Earl of Shrewton, canny aristocratic politician and indispensable ally of Prinny himself, nothing less than the original letter with its telltale seal would do.

One of the four officers was carrying the threat. The other three were decoys. But which was which, and who in England had accepted the challenge of receiving the letter and taking it before the courts and the Lords, was what the Black Cobra didn't know.

So they'd set cultists and assassins on the four officers' trails, and come home to England, scrambling to assemble a formidable force of fanatical followers. Fate had smiled, the winds had blown fair, and they'd managed to get ahead of the four officers, and now they and their forces lay in wait to pick each off, one after the other as they arrived in England, until the threat of exposure was no more.

Colonel Derek Delborough, the senior of the four officers, had landed in Southampton four days ago. An immediate assassination attempt had, by ill luck, been foiled, and the colonel had reached London. He hadn't, however, passed on his letter, but still had it—copy or original—in his possession. They'd managed to install a thief within the colonel's party. By hook or by crook, the colonel's letter would soon be theirs.

With the colonel's letter, at least, all but taken care of, Daniel and Roderick had ridden for Dover as soon as the news that Hamilton had landed had reached them. Their original plan had been to stop Hamilton from crossing the Channel, but clearly the senior man in charge of his pursuit had failed.

But by the time Daniel and Roderick had reached Dover,

staring at the brandy. "If we sit and wait for Hamilton to show his face, we might be sitting here for days. That might be what they want—us to focus on him, and miss the other two as they come in."

"Very likely." Daniel drained his own glass. "We have enough men down here, stationed all along the roads, to be certain that we'll hear as soon as Hamilton breaks cover and heads north—or anywhere else, for that matter. If we leave now, we can ride through the night and catch up with Alex. See whether Creighton has found us a new base in Bury."

That morning, through Larkins, Roderick's gentlemen's gentleman and right-hand man, they'd learned that Delborough was heading into Cambridgeshire, close to the Norfolk houses where many of the most wealthy and powerful spent Christmas. Alex, the shrewdest tactician of the three of them, had decreed they should move their base from Shrewton House in London to somewhere better placed to intercept the couriers.

Creighton, Daniel's man, had suggested hunting for a place in Bury St. Edmunds. Alex had agreed. While Roderick and Daniel had ridden south to deal with Hamilton, Creighton had gone to Bury, and Alex had stayed in London to organize their move.

Roderick drained his glass. "I need to check on Larkins, too—I want to be there when his little thief hands over Delborough's letter." Roderick caught Daniel's eye. "Given we've heard nothing of the other two yet, then Delborough is where the action is."

Rising, Daniel went to the window. Drawing aside the curtain, he looked out. "There's snow coming. If we stay here, tomorrow we might not be able to leave—and Alex's messengers might not be able to reach us."

Chair scraping, Roderick stood. "Time to go."

Dropping the curtain, Daniel nodded. "Hamilton won't risk traveling through a snowstorm. That gives us time to go north, deal with Delborough first, then be in position when Hamilton heads north. Let him come to us, onto a field where we'll have more men to deal with him. That will leave us in prime position to deal with Monteith and Carstairs, too, when they arrive." He met Roderick's gaze, nodded. "Let's go."

Five minutes later, they were on the road, riding hard for London.

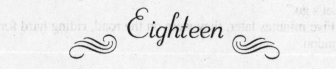

Eighteen

16th December, 1822
Morning
My bedchamber at Mallingham Manor

Dear Diary,

*Fate has been kind. Today is shaping up to be
a perfect opportunity to examine the ins and outs of
what might well be the perfect sort of marriage for
Gareth and me.*

*It took mere minutes of conversation with Leonora
and Clarice to realize that they have similar views
of life, and gentlemen, as I do. And from what I observed last night, their marriages, at least on the surface, appear to hold all the elements, and offer all the
comforts, that I would wish of mine. Consequently, I
plan to devote today to learning all I can from them.*

*Apropos of my aim, it has snowed heavily. We
could not continue on, even had that been our plan,
and we will all be spending today indoors.*

In my case, subtly inquiring.

E.

*B*y late afternoon, when she, Leonora, and Clarice slipped into the smaller parlor and, laughing, collapsed on the sofas, Emily had learned all she wished and more.

"Your children are delightful." Lifting her head, she beamed at Clarice and Leonora. "Even the tiny ones are perfect."

Leonora smiled fondly. "You'll get no argument from us, but we're biased, of course. Still, I'm glad they behaved."

Clarice waved a languid hand. "All you needed to enchant them was to speak of monkeys. Caleb and Robert are already planning how to persuade Jack to let them have one." She frowned. "I must remember to mention to my other half that *I* have no wish to have a monkey in our house."

"No, indeed!" Leonora agreed. "But then I already have three." She glanced at Emily. "Have you and Gareth spoken of children—of how many you might like?"

Emily nodded. "I said *lots*—I come from a big family." Then she frowned. "However, Gareth doesn't. He was very much an only child."

"That means little," Leonora said. "Tristan was an only child, too, but his attitude is that we should have as many as possible—I think to fill the void as the old ladies pass on. He'd be lost if any of his houses were quiet."

Clarice was nodding. "I have three brothers, and I did wonder how Jack would manage with the unaccustomed noise, but he seems to thrive on it—apparently, if it's *his* offspring making it, it's music to his ears."

ried life—specifically the sort of married life she wanted. With the help of the other two, she'd defined her holy grail—

the vital elements that, if they were present between her and Gareth, would guarantee the type of future she wanted.

Gentlemen, as her hours with Leonora and Clarice had confirmed, could not be expected to achieve this shining goal alone, by themselves. They needed help in emotional matters, guidance. She would need to steer and prod and nudge, but she was sure that Gareth would, indeed, want the same style of marriage she had set her heart upon.

Entering her room, she found Dorcas laying out her other evening gown. While she dressed, they chatted of household matters. When she sat on the dressing stool and Dorcas brushed, then started pinning up her hair, they fell silent, and her mind returned to its principal preoccupation.

Perhaps that was what she sensed Gareth was still uncertain over—the specific style of marriage she wanted. Especially for a man like him, a warrior who had spent so many years out of society, he would be feeling his way. Given his background, he would have far less experience of marriages of any sort than she.

They would need to sit and talk—but when?

They might have another day here, in relative safety, yet his mission still hung over his head—and hers, too. She retained a personal interest in seeing poor MacFarlane avenged. And once they set out again . . . the last thing she would want was to distract Gareth, or herself, with thoughts of something so deeply absorbing as marriage.

That issue deserved, indeed demanded, their full and undivided attention.

So . . . not yet. She would use the time to better define her ideas and visions, and find the best words with which to describe all she now longed for, all she believed they could have.

"There." Dorcas tapped the top of her topknot and stepped back. "You look just as you ought." She met Emily's gaze in the mirror. "But I warn you, if we stay here much longer, you're going to run out of evening gowns."

* * *

Later that night, as she climbed into her bed, Emily envisioned the reaction if she appeared clad in the begum of Tunis's version of an evening gown.

The thought made her smile; even now she could barely believe she'd had the courage to don the scandalous outfit.

When Gareth arrived to join her, he found her in a pensive mood. "Penny for your thoughts," he said as he climbed into the bed beside her.

She let herself roll into his arms, an action she delighted in every night—mostly because he caught her so readily, settling her against him as if she belonged there. "I was just thinking . . . while on our travels I did things I would never imagine doing—would never have the courage to do here, in England." Wriggling around, leaning an elbow on his chest and rising up, she regarded him through the shadows. "Have I lost my courage, now I'm home?"

His smile was slow and infinitely warming. "No—never. Your courage is a part of you—you can't lose it. And adjusting to social reality, knowing and understanding what you can and can't do without risking ostracism—that's a strength, not a weakness."

After a moment, she smiled back. "I hadn't thought of it like that."

Gareth looked into her eyes, too cloaked in the night's shadows for him to read. This pensive mood was new to him, but only intrigued him all the more—yet another aspect of

and Clarice's, like Tristan's and Leonora's. He had no real idea of the modern institution, but what he'd seen of their relationships . . . that would suit him, too; he doubted it would be easy, but the benefits would be great.

More, he could *see* himself with Emily in a relationship like that, but he didn't know—truly had no clue—how to make it happen, what such a union was based on. What agreements were necessary to underlie the whole.

"I . . ." What? What could he say? I want what Jack and Clarice have?

They weren't Jack and Clarice.

And he wasn't sure she loved him enough. He seemed to be rushing forward, tripping over his feet in his haste to secure her, to discover the "more" he could entice her with in lieu of those three little words, but he needed to go slowly, surely, step by step.

Sliding his hand into the silken fall of her hair, he drew her down.

Arm braced on his chest, she held back. "What were you going to say?"

He shook his head. "Later." Once he'd worked it out, once he'd found the words.

She opened her mouth, but before she could probe further, he kissed her.

Caught her and waltzed her into the passion, into the fires that rose so readily, into the latent whirlpool of their desires.

Here, on this plane, all was straightforward, all within his ken. Here, he knew just what made her gasp, what made her moan—what she liked.

What she wanted.

He set himself to give her that—and more. Committed himself to the task of showing her what he'd yet to find the words to convey.

Palming her head, holding her steady above him, he took his time savoring her mouth, languidly reclaiming the sweet hollows, the succulent softness she'd so readily yielded. He stroked his tongue alongside hers and felt her bones melt. Felt desire rise.

He took his time. Running his hands over her shoulders, down the supple feminine planes of her back screened by her fine nightgown, sculpting her body as it rested over his, her breasts, her waist, her hips, her taut thighs, her rounded derriere, relearning her curves, her valleys and contours, reclaiming them, too, making them his.

The first step of many.

She grew restless, wordlessly demanding. He rolled, taking her with him and settling her beneath him in the billows of the bed. His lips held hers, held her awareness; he fed and supped with lips and tongue while between them his fingers slipped buttons undone.

Until he could push aside her nightgown's bodice enough to bare her breasts. Enough to close his hands about the firm peaks, and caress. Possess. He kneaded until she arched, until beneath his lips she moaned and surrendered.

The first of many such moments.

He drew back from the kiss, through the shadows surveyed the bounty that filled his hands, then he bent his head and set his mouth to the furled peaks, and feasted. Her hands fisted in his hair, clutched as her body arched, as, breathless, she accepted and asked for more.

Begged, her body subtly surging beneath his, primitively taunting, urging him on.

Still he took his time, thoroughly laving the swollen mounds before divesting her of her nightgown inch by slow inch, and claiming each inch of skin revealed by touch, by

wielded them.

Drove her, consistent and insistent, scaling the familiar

peak via a long, tortuous and novel path, while he assessed, weighed, worshipped.

Under his hands she felt precious. Every drift of his fingers over her skin screamed with primal possessiveness, while every brush of his lips, every subtle caress, was laden with reverence.

She felt like a goddess as he stripped her bare, as he drew back, parted her thighs, bent his head and kissed her there—as he used lips, tongue, teeth and his hot, demanding mouth to drive her wild. To, steady and sure, push her ever higher, until she gripped his hair, body bowing as a silent scream ripped from her throat and a cataclysmic climax shattered her.

He lapped, fed, continued to taste her until she eased back to the bed.

Then his hard palms smoothed over her fevered skin— a primitive claiming and a promise of more—as in the night he rose above her, pressed her thighs even wider, and the broad head of his erection found her entrance and he pressed in.

Slowly, deeply, completely.

The feel of him there, solid and hard, hot velvet over steel stretching her sheath, swamped her mind. She knew nothing beyond the fact that he filled her, that he banished the hot, aching, restless emptiness within her, that he completed her and fulfilled her and he was hers as she was his.

He withdrew and thrust in again, deeper still, demanding.

Hands sliding blind, splayed, over and around his chest, arms locking, she embraced him, rose to his rhythm, to the driving beat, meeting him and matching him in the compulsive dance, clinging as it whirled them high.

Worshipped him with her body as much as he worshipped her. Tipped her head back, found his lips with hers, and kissed him.

Engaged him in a duel as heated as the communion of their straining bodies. Nerves flayed by the indescribable friction of tautly encased, hair-dusted muscle, heated and hard, moving constantly, repetitively, over her satin skin, abrading the excruciatingly sensitized peaks of her breasts, by the rhythmic thrusting of his body into hers, the way he rocked her, by the echoes that found expression through the flagrant mating of their mouths, she joined with him and climbed, nails sinking, scoring as they reached the peak and her nerves snapped, unraveled.

He thrust in one last time, hard, deep, and she came apart.

And fell. Plummeted from the peak. Fractured and broke.

Disintegrated as ecstasy swept in, as it claimed her, filled her, buoyed her.

Joy followed, sweeping inexorably in as, over the pounding of her heart, she heard his ragged groan. As he went rigid in her arms, holding deep within her as his seed flooded her womb.

As at the last, muscle by muscle yielding to the inevitable, he collapsed, crushing her beneath him.

A smile curved her lips as she hugged him close, as satiation slid in and claimed them both.

17th December, 1822
Early evening
My bedchamber at Mallingham Manor

Dear Diary,

... I can hold back from it. Indeed, when we come together, it is increas-

ingly in mutual fascination and devotion. Together, we accept, embrace, and worship. On that front, at least, our way forward is clear.

I did not write this morning as, on the wider question of our marriage, I was still formulating my thoughts. And with the snows, although melting, still confining us to the house, in this place of relative safety where danger and its distractions are held at bay, I have indeed been able to make progress—at last.

Speaking with the old ladies—they truly are dears—and through further observing Leonora and Tristan, and Jack and Clarice, I have defined and confirmed what the principal elements necessary to underpin a successful marriage between Gareth and myself are.

Trust. Partnership. An appreciation and acceptance of each other's strengths, and a willingness to allow for the other's weaknesses. A sharing freely given and readily accepted in all areas of our lives, allowing the other to share the burdens, to help meet the challenges, and share fully in the triumphs.

Those are the elements I need to explain to Gareth, to make him see and understand how vital they are, and how wonderful our marriage and our future will be if we can work together to embrace them.

I do not imagine that will be simple and easy, but then nothing worthwhile ever is.

So now, dear Diary, I am clearheaded and resolved, and waiting—here is the waiting—on only one thing. The end of Gareth's mission. The end of the Black Cobra. In my view, that cannot come soon enough.

My resolution and clearheadedness have given birth to a certain eagerness. I feel I am standing on the cusp, not just of great happiness, but of an exciting

journey that will fill the rest of my life—but I cannot
take the first step until that wretched Black Cobra is
caught and put down.

We are hoping to hear from Wolverstone soon.
Pray that it is so.

E.

A messenger from Wolverstone rode in late that evening.

The greatcoated rider handed his packet to Tristan in the front hall. "Would have been here earlier, m'lords, but the drifts are still thick through Suffolk. Howsoever, I was to tell you that as per those orders" —he nodded at the packet— "you shouldn't have any trouble getting through, seeing as you'll be in carriages and there's no more snow coming down."

"Thank you." Tristan handed the man over to Clitheroe, then followed the others back into the drawing room, where they'd been sitting and chatting by the roaring fire.

They resumed their seats and waited expectantly as Tristan opened the packet. Frowning, he pulled out two folded sheets, then handed one to Leonora. "From Minerva." He glanced at Gareth and Emily. "Royce's duchess."

Opening the second missive, Tristan scanned the lines within, then glanced up with an anticipatory smile. "Tomorrow we're to travel via Gravesend to Chelmsford, seeing what cultists we can draw along the way, especially north of the Thames. After spending the night in

options, the ladies contributing as much as the gentlemen, the missive to Leonora having contained an invitation from Minerva for Leonora and Clarice to visit Elveden with their families. Jack and Tristan exchanged a glance, but didn't argue, clearly deeming Elveden to be safe enough, especially as they would soon be there.

In the end, it was decided that Leonora and Clarice would travel with their children in their own carriages, with their customary retinue of coachmen, grooms, and guards, taking Dorcas, Arnia, Watson and Jimmy with them. They would go via London directly up the Great North Road, then across via Cambridge and Newmarket to Elveden.

Gareth and Emily would go in another carriage, with Mullins driving and Bister and Mooktu as guards. They would follow Wolverstone's stipulated route, shadowed by Jack and Tristan on horseback.

"The better to eliminate any cultists we find," as Jack put it.

The two family carriages would leave three hours after Gareth and Emily's, but as their route lay along major highways, it was likely the families would reach Elveden first.

With a glance at the clock, then at Clarice and Emily, Leonora rose. "It's late, and we'll need to leave as early as possible." She looked at the men. "We'll leave you to organize the carriages, coachmen and horses while we organize the people."

The men nodded, and returned to their planning.

Rising with Clarice, Emily followed Leonora into the hall. Leonora rang for Clitheroe.

Emily had the simplest task. She explained to Watson what had been arranged, knowing she could rely on him to alert the others and have everyone ready in good time in the morning. Leaving Leonora deep in discussion with her housekeeper, and Clarice issuing instructions to her senior nursemaid, Emily climbed the stairs and headed for her room.

By the time she reached it, excitement had taken hold. Entering, she found herself smiling.

One last push from Mallingham Manor to Elveden, and their journey would be over. Two more days, and she and

Gareth could turn their attention to their future—their marriage—to planning both.

She was in her nightgown, but, too excited to sit let alone lie still, she was pacing before the fire with a shawl about her shoulders, imagining, when the door opened and Gareth came in. She halted, eagerness lighting her face.

Closing the door, he met her eyes, read her expression, and smiled. But as he closed the distance between them, he sobered. Halting before her, he looked into her eyes. "Two more days." He hesitated, then, to her surprise, he reached for her hands, enclosing them in his.

As his eyes searched her face, she remained silent. Wondering.

Eventually he drew a curiously tight breath. "I wasn't going to say anything, not until this was all over. But . . . I can't let us go on, into the next two days, without saying at least this much. Downstairs just now, we made plans, all straightforward and direct—we do this, go by this road, and we reach Elveden and it's over." His eyes held hers. "But it won't be that easy. We know the Black Cobra will be marshaling his forces between us and Elveden, that he'll have his best troops—his elite—waiting to intercept us. He will be, should be, desperate to seize the scroll holder. That's what we're counting on—that he'll be desperate enough to commit his forces so we can reduce them, and that at some point he'll make a mistake that will paint him even more definitively as the Black Cobra than the letter one of us is

touch. Not properly. I want to—I intend to—but I might yet be killed, or badly injured, and if I was,

I wouldn't want you tied to me." She frowned, opened her mouth, but he spoke over her. "I wouldn't want you to stay by me if I didn't have a life to offer you. *But . . .*"

This was the difficult part, and at least she'd remained silent and was listening as intently as he could wish. Keeping his gaze locked with hers, he drew strength and steadiness from her moss-green eyes. "I want to marry you, and I want a marriage like Jack and Clarice's, like Tristan and Leonora's. I don't know if that's possible—if I can do what's needed to have that sort of marriage—but I think I can, and I want to try. With you. Because I want us to have that, even though I can't describe what 'that' is."

Understanding shone in her eyes, her expression transformed to one of glowing happiness. The hard knot of trepidation in his chest eased.

She stepped closer. Freeing one hand from his, she laid her palm along his jaw. "I can describe it. I've spent the last days thinking of nothing else—looking and studying to learn what made marriages like Jack and Clarice's, Tristan and Leonora's, what they are—what makes them work. I know what we need to do—that we need to trust each other, value each other, and share everything in our lives—and yes, I want that, too."

She smiled, and in that shimmering moment he could see her heart in her eyes. "There is nothing I want more in life than to have a marriage like that, with you."

His heart cartwheeled, but he raised his hand and placed a finger across her lips. "Don't say anything more."

Eyes widening, she tilted her head, looked her question.

"It's an old . . . I suppose you'd call it a superstition. A soldier's superstition, yet there's logic behind it. In going into battle, any battle, you try to ensure that you, personally, have the least possible to lose. It's tempting fate to go into an engagement knowing you have something worth more than life itself at stake. More, it's dangerous, because going on the offensive inevitably clashes with defensive instincts—and you'll be caught, torn, at the worst possible moment.

Facing an enemy knowing you have something of immense and staggering worth to lose gives you a weakness that the enemy doesn't have. It's a distraction, a handicap.

"And *that* is why I want you to know what I want with you, but I *don't* want us to speak of it—to make any declarations or decisions now." He searched her eyes. "Do you understand?"

Her smile only grew more confident. She moved into him, molding her body to his. His hands slid around her, his arms instinctively closing about her. She raised her other hand to join the first, framing his face. "I understand—no declarations, no details, no mutual decrees. But you need to understand something, too—we're already there. Words are necessary, but actions speak louder, and our actions have been declaring our truth for weeks, even if we haven't been paying attention. What we need to have the marriage we both want—trusting, valuing, sharing all aspects of our lives, a partnership on all levels—we've been working on that, are well on our way to achieving that, and if we continue to grant each other those things, we *will* win through to the end. To the end we both want. We have to have faith in us—in what we are and can be together. And if we do, nothing—not even the Black Cobra—can deny us."

Emily smiled into his eyes, her confidence, her faith, her unfettered joy all openly on show. "Together we're stronger. Together we'll weather this—whatever comes in the next two days—and *then*—"

profound, so powerful, she couldn't contain them—had to allow both expression.

Had to, was compelled to, reward him. This man—her man, her one and only "one"—was no more blind than she. Thank heaven. To have had to prod and nudge and work to make him see what would be best . . . she'd been prepared to do it, but to her soul she appreciated his courage in facing and embracing their truth.

This was what they were. What, for them both, their marriage needed to be. Breaking from the kiss on a laughing gasp, she steered him back toward the bed, along the way helped him out of his coat, out of his waistcoat while he dealt with his cravat. His legs hit the end of the mattress and he halted. Mouth watering, she opened his shirt, pushed the halves wide. Savored with hands and eyes while he muttered and reached around her to undo his cuffs.

Then she slid her hands down, palms to his warm, resilient skin, skating over muscles that tensed beneath her touch, to the waistband of his trousers. Two quick flicks and the buttons there were free. But before she could open the placket and reach within, he uttered a breathless laugh. "Shoes first."

His voice sounded strained.

Eyes dark with desire, he stepped aside and toed off his shoes, stepped out of them, and reached for her. She flung her shawl aside as she went into his arms, needing his heat, rejoicing as it enveloped her.

She lifted her face, wordlessly offered her mouth. He bent his head and took, claimed, filled. She responded, letting the familiar sensations—the welling desire, the burgeoning taste of passion, rising urgency and hungry need—fascinate and absorb them.

While she plotted, planned.

He'd let her explore before, but the pleasure she experienced when he worshipped her with his mouth made her wonder if this wasn't the time for turn and turnabout. For her to pleasure him.

She thought it would work, but knew of only one way to know for certain. Without breaking from their kiss, from the increasingly heated exchange, she slid her hands down, around, and sent his trousers sliding down his legs to the floor.

He was busy with the buttons closing the front of her nightgown. She only did them up so she would have the small pleasure of having him undo them, the hunger in his touch fueling her own, racking their desire one notch tighter.

While he was engaged, she reached between them, found the rigid rod of his erection, closed her hand boldly and stroked. Sensed the sudden hitch in his breathing, the momentary deflection of his attention.

But then he swung it back to her with renewed intent, renewed urgency.

Even greater hunger.

He wrenched the halves of the nightgown's bodice wide, baring her breasts, but instead of bending his head to feast, he slid an arm around her upper thighs, lifted her off her feet.

She blinked, and was on her back in the middle of the bed, with him leaning over her, his hot gaze on her breasts, one heavy thigh pinning her legs.

One hard hand closed over one of her breasts, took possession. Her lids fell; she moaned with sheer pleasure as he worked her swollen flesh, tortured the tight bud . . .

In less than a minute, she would lose all chance to take charge.

Her hands had come to rest on his shoulders. She slid them

still on her breasts, and distract her again, she swooped down and kissed him—voraciously, hungrily, greedily. She poured every ounce of heated passion she could summon into the rapacious kiss—and succeeded in dragging his attention to it, succeeded in snaring his awareness and holding it there, deep in the kiss. Succeeded in sliding one hand down his chest, down his side and in, and closing that hand possessively around his erection.

He stilled, and she pulled back from the kiss.

"Just wait," she murmured, sliding lower in the bed as her fingers caressed, stroked, promised.

While her hand played, she dipped her head and placed kisses—hot damp kisses—across his collarbone. Then she searched the mat of crinkly dark hair and found the flat disc of his nipple, kissed, licked, then nipped.

He shifted beneath her. One hand rose, sliding beneath the fall of her hair to glide over her nape, then lightly grip her skull.

His breathing quickened as she shifted lower still, trailing kisses with abandon, the fingers of one hand lightly razing her path while her other hand remained wholly devoted to pleasuring his turgid member.

When she shifted lower yet, and her kisses reached his navel, Gareth sucked in a breath and couldn't release it. Couldn't breathe.

From wanting. From hoping.

Anticipation dug her claws deep, locked him in place—held him helplessly immobile for her.

Expectation was a rising tide within him, urgent and greedy. Needy.

It had been a very long time since any woman had pandered to him as she was—as she was promising to do. But what held him in thrall, hers to tease and please as she wished—however and for however long she wished—was the simple fact that this was she—Emily, the woman he wanted as his wife—that it was *she* who was intent on pleasuring him.

Wonder and so much more held him ensnared. Held him captive as she slid lower yet and her lips finally—finally!—grazed the aching head of his erection.

Instinctively his hand tightened on her skull, fingers clenching in the silk of her hair as he fought to remain still, to keep his hips from jerking upward in greedy eagerness.

Head back, he stared unseeing at the ceiling, wondering just what she would do—willing her, hoping, praying . . . then he felt the wet stroke of her tongue sliding slowly, sinuously upward from the base of his shaft to the sensitive head.

His lids fell. He locked his jaw. But then with the tip of her tongue she traced the excruciatingly sensitive rim, and his lungs seized.

Her breath, soft and sultry, washed over his damp flesh. Every nerve, every particle of awareness he possessed was locked on her, on what next she would do.

The sensation of her soft lips and luscious mouth sliding over him, taking him in, drawing him deep into that slick heat ripped a groan from him.

Which was all the encouragement she needed. She set to work with the devotion, the abandon, that characterized everything she did. She might have been a novice, yet in short order she reduced him to a state of clamoring need. Both hands sunk in her hair, his breathing increasingly ragged, his heart pounding, blood surging, he clung to sanity—to some semblance of control—while she sent wave after wave of pleasure crashing through him.

While she shredded his reins and stripped away all pretense and left raw need and primal passion blazing through him.

held the power to drive him wild.

And wilder. He groaned again as, experimenting, exercising

her newfound power, she curled her tongue about his length and slowly stroked upward, then took him in again and settled to suck, something he seemed to especially enjoy.

How far could she take him? She put her heart and soul into finding out.

Only to have him gutturally declare, "Enough!"

He eased a finger between her lips, withdrawing from her mouth and then grasping her shoulders, lifting her and rising in one smooth movement. She expected him to tumble her onto the bed and follow her down. Instead, he set her back on her knees; coming up on his, he seized the folds of her nightgown and lifted it off, over her head.

She drew her arms from the long sleeves. Her hair tumbled over her face; she brushed back the long strands so she could see.

The bed rocked around her. She nearly tipped over, but a steely arm around her waist caught her, held her up—she saw her nightgown drifting to the floor beyond the bed, and nothing else—and realized he'd come up on his knees behind her.

His arm about her waist held her steady as he shifted nearer, closer, until, head rising, spine straightening, she could feel his heat like a flame from her shoulders all the way down her back, all the way down the backs of her thighs.

His head dipped; his lips cruised her ear. "You can be my *houri* any day, any night."

There was a promise in his words that sent a shiver of expectation dancing down her spine. His warm breath washed over the side of her throat. His lips followed. Eyes closing, she felt the familiar heat rise.

Felt the insistent prodding of his erection, hot as a brand, against her bottom as he pressed near. One hard hand clamped over her hip. His arm about her eased, shifted, that hand drifting lower to splay over her belly. Then he raised his head, murmured close by her ear, "And like any good master, I'll enjoy my slave."

Her breath hitched. One of her hands had come to rest on

374

the arm he'd wound around her. Her grip tightened, nails sinking in as he held her against him and the hand over her belly slid lower, fingers seeking.

Finding. Stroking. Probing.

Pressing in and possessing.

Until she was arching against him, sobbing and panting, wanting so much more.

Holding her hips against his, he pressed her shoulders down until on a gasp she braced herself on her arms.

And he slid into her from behind.

Her eyes opened wide, unseeing, her senses trapped, wholly focused on where they joined, on the feeling of fullness as his shaft stretched her sheath, as he thrust in and filled her to the hilt.

She heard a shuddering gasp, followed by a low moan as he slowly withdrew. But then he thrust in again and she nearly sobbed.

The friction was acute, the sensations of him filling her, taking her, claiming and possessing her, all so much more primitively, passionately real . . . her reality spun away into a furnace of primal heat, her wits suborned by the overwhelming need to mate, by a tattoo pounding through her blood, driving her—and him.

His hips thrusting steadily, repetitively, Gareth leaned forward and filled his hands with her breasts. Kneaded, found the tight peaks and squeezed.

Her head threshed alongside his. She was so close, almost

wash through him, hips bucking hard against her bottom as he spilled his seed deep within her.

She collapsed and took him with her. He sprawled over her, unable to move, his heart thundering, his mind an utter blank, his senses purring.

His more primitive self slumped, sated to its toes, satisfied beyond imagining.

With an effort, he disengaged and slumped on his side beside her. She turned her head his way. Moss-green eyes glinted beneath her lashes.

Then she smiled. "I rather think I like being your *houri*."

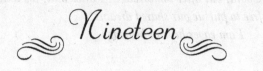

Nineteen

19th December, 1822
Very early morning
My bedchamber at Mallingham Manor

Dear Diary,

I am huddling under the covers scribbling madly
before Dorcas arrives with my washing water. Gareth
has just left—and what a night, and a morning, we
made of it. But the essential news I have to impart is
that we are in accord—utterly and completely!—over
our future life.

He saw the possibilities, too, and wants that type

to secure everything we want our joint life to be.

*All that stands in our way is that wretched Black
Cobra, but after tomorrow . . . after that, we will be
free to pursue our shared dreams.*

I am eager beyond bearing.

E.

hey left at first light, as the dark skies turned a paler
gray and a chill east wind whipped snow from the
lingering drifts bordering the roads.

Inside the carriage, tucked beneath traveling rugs and
with two warm bricks beneath her boots, Emily watched the
winter landscape slip past, watching for any hint of cultists.
Gareth, seated beside her, his hand wrapped around hers,
looked out the other way. They were all on edge, on the one
hand ready to repel any attack, but on the other believing
that while they might be followed, the cultists were unlikely
to engage until they crossed the Thames.

"Aside from all else," Tristan had pointed out as they were
preparing to start out, "the forests north of the river provide
much better cover, and places ideal for an ambush."

He and Jack were on horseback, somewhere out in the
wintry chill.

They'd been traveling for hours and, according to signposts,
Gravesend was close, when Emily leaned nearer the window
and peered out. "I haven't seen Jack or Tristan at all."

"You won't. I suspect they're old hands at this sort of thing.
They want to spot any cultists trailing us, but don't want to
be seen themselves. You might catch a glimpse when they
pass us at Gravesend."

As arranged, they halted the coach at the Lord Nelson, a
large coaching inn, and went inside to take refreshments.
They wasted a tense half hour over a teapot and scones, allowing Tristan and Jack to go ahead to the jetty north of the
town.

When, once more in the carriage, they reached the jetty,
Jack and Tristan were nowhere to be seen, but a ferryman

was waiting with his ferry to take them across to Tilbury, on the north bank. He confirmed that the gentleman who bespoke his services and his companion had already crossed on another barge.

The crossing was short, but difficult, the flat-topped ferry rocking perilously, but the ferryman and his crew took the choppy, rushing river in their stride. They reached the Tilbury jetty, not far from the richly decorated watergate of Tilbury Fort, without incident.

With the coach once more on dry land, Gareth helped Emily back inside, then, shutting the door, went to help Mooktu calm the restive horses. Mullins was already on the box, checking the pistols stowed under the seat while he held the reins.

Bister had gone scouting ahead. He came pelting back as Mooktu climbed up to his position beside Mullins. Gareth paused by the carriage door.

Snapping a salute, Bister went past, grabbing the straps at the back of the carriage and swiftly climbing to the roof. "Spotted three of 'em—there might be more. They're watching from a rise outside the town—lots of forest behind them."

Brows rising, Gareth opened the carriage door and climbed in.

Given that news, they dallied over luncheon in Tilbury's main inn, giving Tristan and Jack plenty of time to ease their appetites and, mounted once more, get into position behind

spot for an ambush—just as we crested that rise."

"They might not want to be seen by others." Emily gestured to a carriage going the other way.

"True. The further north we go, empty stretches of road will become more frequent. Maybe that's why they haven't yet attacked."

However, as they traveled unhurriedly through the afternoon, often along stretches where the forest closed in on both sides of the road and other conveyances grew few and far between, still no attack eventuated. At one point, Bister, riding on the roof with their bags, hung down the side of the coach to report that although they were definitely being followed, he'd seen no indication of the cultists moving to flank them or get ahead to a position where they might ambush the coach.

Gareth frowned. "That must mean something."

"Perhaps when Jack and Tristan join us, they'll know more." Emily leaned forward, looking ahead to where roofs could be glimpsed across open fields. "I think that's Chelmsford ahead."

It was. They rattled into the town, rolling up the High Street past the large church to the inn Wolverstone had instructed them to stay at overnight. Once again, they were expected. From the flurry of activity that enveloped them the instant Gareth made himself known, it seemed likely Wolverstone himself had made the arrangements.

Once he saw the rooms assigned to their party—a set of four chambers on the first floor comprising all the rooms in that wing and overlooking both the front and the rear of the inn—Gareth felt even more sure the duke had taken a hand. Before the light faded, he, Mooktu and Bister prowled outside, noting hiding places, checking for windows and doors through which attackers might gain access.

The inn was built of stone, with a sound slate roof, and was remarkably secure—another comfort. Although Gareth wanted nothing more than to engage with the cultists and reduce their number, satisfying that part of his decoy's mission, he was unable to forget he had Emily with him. Mission or not, he wouldn't willingly wish her in danger.

After settling into the room she and Gareth would share, Emily went downstairs and found Mullins waiting in the private parlor set aside for their party. Gareth appeared before she could inquire as to his whereabouts. A tea tray arrived on his heels, then Mooktu and Bister joined them, and they settled to wait for Jack and Tristan.

It was full dark, nearly dinnertime, before the door opened and Jack walked in. He smiled rather wearily in greeting, and nodded when Gareth raised the bottle of wine he'd broached.

While Gareth poured him a glass, Jack drew out a chair at the table, fell into it, and groaned. "It's been years since I've spent an entire day in the saddle."

Tristan came in, blowing on his hands. "It's not just the hours in the saddle, it's that damned wind."

He, too, accepted a glass of wine. Gareth waited until both were seated and had taken a revivifying swallow, then asked, "So where the devil are the cultists?"

"Out there." Jack pointed south. "And yes, they're definitely there, and in surprisingly high numbers."

"To start at the beginning," Tristan said, "one picked up the carriage not far from Mallingham, then two more fell in once you hit the main roads. Those three followed all the way to Gravesend, then one went ahead, crossing to Tilbury. He didn't return. We don't think the other two crossed the Thames, but turned back after you'd got on the ferry."

Gareth nodded. "Probably returning to keep watch on the coast."

Tristan nodded. "They have eight—nine if their messenger returns. The coach has three outside, one inside. You'd think the odds would appeal."

"They must have orders to follow and send word forward, but not to engage—meaning not yet." Jack smiled wolfishly. "I do believe this is getting interesting."

Emily frowned. "Interesting how?"

Gareth replied, "Because it seems we're being herded again. As long as we move forward, those behind will hang back and simply follow—because there's some force ahead of us that's bigger, and more certain of capturing us."

"It appears the Black Cobra isn't taking any chances," Jack said. "Odds are he's planning a trap for the coach to drive into somewhere along the road tomorrow, a trap you won't be able to escape. Or so he thinks."

"Indeed." Tristan's eyes gleamed. "And would anyone care to wager that's exactly what Royce designed his scheme to achieve? The news that the Black Cobra is lurking between us and him—in Essex or Suffolk—is going to make him very happy."

Jack waved his glass. "No bet. That's precisely what he would have set out to achieve." He met Gareth's eyes. "You and yours chose exceedingly well in appointing Wolverstone your guardian angel."

"He's certainly a stickler for detail." Gareth outlined his observations from their earlier reconnaissance. "In a defensive sense, this place is ideal."

A tap on the door heralded the innkeeper with their dinner. Mooktu, Bister, and Mullins went out to the tap for theirs.

Once those in the parlor had finished their meal and the innkeeper had cleared the table, Gareth went out and invited the other three back.

They'd just settled when the innkeeper looked in. "Messenger for Lord Warnefleet."

Jack beckoned and the innkeeper drew back to allow a middle-aged groom to enter. The man bowed, then drew a sealed missive from his pocket and presented it to Jack. Jack broke the seal and opened the sheet, scanned it.

The groom cleared his throat. "I'm to inquire, my lords, as to your situation here."

Tristan replied in a few succinct phrases conveying their observations and their belief that they were being herded into an ambush ahead.

The groom repeated the salient points. Tristan nodded his approval.

Jack handed Wolverstone's missive to Gareth, then looked at the groom. "You can also report that we'll do as your master requests, and make a copy of the letter in question."

The groom bowed. "If there's nothing else, my lords, I'll be on my way."

Tristan dismissed him. The groom turned and left.

Emily had been reading the duke's letter over Gareth's shoulder. "I'll fetch paper and ink, and make a clean copy." Rising, she glanced at Jack. "Why does he want it?"

"Details," Jack replied. "Given Delborough's sacrificed his copy and gained something from it, then we might decide to sacrifice ours in the same way, which leaves Royce with nothing to study. He'll want to confirm that there's no other clue hidden in the wording. A code, even—it's the sort of thing he would think of and know better than anyone to look for."

"Which he can't do" —Tristan accepted the duke's communique from Gareth— "unless he has the letter, a good copy at least, in front of him."

Nodding her understanding, Emily left.

"I'm just glad Delborough's through and safe, and that

about the watches? We'll need to remain vigilant."

Emily returned, bearing a ladies' traveling writing desk

with an ornate mother-of-pearl lid. She set it down on the table, opened it, and drew the lamp near. "The letter?"

Gareth drew the scroll holder from inside his coat, and under the fascinated gazes of all there, undid the complicated locking mechanism. Opening the holder, he drew out the sheet it contained, and handed it to Emily.

Smoothing the single sheet, she sat, dipped her nib, and started to transcribe.

"May I see that?" Jack nodded at the scroll holder.

Gareth smiled and handed it over.

While the others played, opening and closing the holder, and Tristan and Jack asked questions about such oriental devices, Emily kept her head down and her mind on her task.

She'd seized the chance to contribute something to Gareth's mission—to do something, however minor, that would materially assist in bringing down the Black Cobra. Hers and Gareth's impending happiness had made her sorrow over MacFarlane's death more acute; she now had a better appreciation of all he'd had taken from him—by the Black Cobra.

Whatever she could do to bring the fiend to justice, she would do.

By the time she'd duplicated the Black Cobra's mark as best she could, and had blotted off her copy, the men had decided the order of the watches. She handed his copy back to Gareth. He rolled it and slid it into the holder, then closed the holder and tucked it inside his coat. Now she knew where it rested, she could see the bulge, but it wasn't that obvious; its presence was less obvious still when he carried it in his greatcoat pocket.

With the time for their departure on the morrow agreed upon, they all rose and retired. Mullins took the first watch. They left him sitting in a chair at the end of their corridor, looking back toward the stairs.

The first alarm came at midnight. Bister was suddenly knocking on their door. Gareth reached it first. Emily grabbed her cloak and slung it over her nightgown as she rushed to join him.

He glanced at her. "Someone's trying to break into the parlor downstairs. Bister and I will go down—wait here."

"Not on your life." She grabbed the doorknob. "You two go ahead, I'll follow."

Gareth hesitated, but in truth he'd rather she wasn't far from him. The cult might mount a two-pronged attack, one downstairs, the other above. Curtly, he nodded. "Just stay back."

He pretended not to see her roll her eyes.

Jack, Tristan, Mullins, and Mooktu were already in the corridor. Jack held a finger across his lips, then mimed that he and Tristan would go down the back stairs and circle outside. Mooktu and Mullins would remain by the bedchambers in case of an unexpected incursion there.

Gareth nodded, and they silently parted.

Bister followed Gareth down the stairs. Emily followed on Bister's heels, treading close by the wall so the stairs wouldn't creak. Halfway down, Bister found her hand in the dark and pressed the handle of a knife into her palm. Emily gripped, nodded in thanks when he glanced back.

She clutched the knife and felt a trifle less vulnerable, but her primary concern was Gareth, slipping through the darkness of the inn's ground floor to the parlor door. She and Bister obeyed Gareth's signal and hung back. He cracked the door open a fraction, listened, then slowly opened it wider.

Then he disappeared into the blackness beyond.

Bister just beat her to the door. She followed him in, and through the gloom saw Gareth, a large dense shadow, wait-

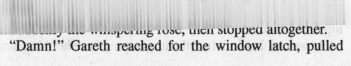

denly the whispering rose, then stopped altogether.

"Damn!" Gareth reached for the window latch, pulled

the window open, unfastened the shutters, and pushed them wide.

In the faint moonlight, across the inn yard they saw two shocked faces turned their way—then the cultists took to their heels and fled.

Seconds later, Jack and Tristan appeared before the window, looking toward the trees through which the cultists had vanished. "What happened?" Tristan asked.

"They gave up." Disgust rang in Gareth's voice.

The others grunted. Hands on hips, they stared at the forest, then shook their heads, waved, and trudged back around the inn.

Gareth leaned out, caught the shutters, resecured them, then closed the window. Bister took back his knife before Gareth turned and waved Emily and Bister up the stairs.

They climbed back to bed rather less quietly than they'd come down.

Emily woke some hours later. Uncertain what had drawn her from her dreams, she lay still—then abruptly sat bolt upright.

The movement woke Gareth. He looked at her. "What is it?"

She drew in a deep breath, let it out in a rush. "Smoke— and yes, I'm sure."

Gareth was already rolling from the bed.

Scrambling into her cloak, Emily joined him at the door, but then frowned and turned back. "It isn't so noticeable over here."

Her side of the bed was nearer the window.

Gareth had gone into the corridor. Mooktu was on watch, sitting closer to the stairs the better to hear any sounds from below. But neither he nor Gareth could smell any smoke in the corridor or the stairwell.

The inn roof was slate—no danger there. Puzzled, Gareth returned to their room—to find Emily at the window, working the latch free.

He was on her in a heartbeat, grasping her shoulders and

pulling her away from the glass. "Be careful! Your night-gown's white—they'll be able to see you."

"Yes, but—"

"I know." The scent of smoke was more definite near the window. "Let me."

Releasing her, he closed his coat to his throat, then stepped to the window, tugged the latch free and eased the pane open.

A gust of wind blew the acrid smell of woodsmoke into the room.

He pushed the window wider, using the glass pane as a shield of sorts, until he could look down and along the inn. He could see smoke trailing from somewhere toward the rear. Following it back . . . through the deep gloom he could just make out three figures in heavy frieze standing staring at a pile of wood stacked against the inn wall.

They'd tried to set the wood alight, tried to train the flames back onto the wooden shutters, but it was December in England; the wood was damp. They'd managed to light a tiny blaze at the base of the stack. One crouched and blew—just as a rain squall struck, sweeping down, pelting the men and quenching the nascent fire, creating yet more smoke.

Coughing, hands waving, the three men stepped back. They muttered amongst themselves, then turned and walked away into the trees.

From above, Gareth watched them go.

"What's going on?" Emily hissed.

in Bury St. Edmunds, Daniel looked at Roderick, waited for his response.

He and Alex had just received a nasty shock. It appeared the letter Roderick had brought them there to intercept held a far greater threat than any of them had realized. Roderick—the idiot—had absentmindedly included Daniel's and Alex's real names. While no one else reading the letter would recognize the connection, if the letter—even a copy—found its way into the Earl of Shrewton's hands, their father would certainly recognize his bastards. Roderick was his favorite legitimate son. As Alex had pointed out moments earlier, if push came to shove over the Black Cobra, the earl would unhesitatingly offer up his bastards as sacrificial lambs to save Roderick—nothing was more certain.

But Roderick couldn't function as the Black Cobra without Daniel and Alex. And he knew it.

Eyes narrowed to ice-blue shards, his face like stone, Roderick curtly nodded. "All right. I will."

"How?" Eyes of an even more wintry, unforgiving ice blue, Alex took up a position before the fireplace. "Tell us how, brother mine."

Roderick glanced at the copy of the letter Delborough had been carrying, which Roderick had been forced to kill his own man, Larkins, to secure. "Hamilton's at Chelmsford. I sent eight men to follow and harry their party, to keep them in sight. Tomorrow, I'll take a force of our elite, and join the eight. We'll have overwhelming numbers—there's only four men counting Hamilton, and he has the woman to protect as well. We'll stop him, seize him and the woman, and bring them here."

Roderick shot a venomous look at Alex. "I'll have to leave them to your tender mercies—I've just got word Monteith's in the country. And he, too, is heading this way, but from the direction of Bath, with two guards, as Delborough had, and a pirate captain in train. I'll have to go west to keep him out of Cambridgeshire."

"This is rapidly degenerating into the worst possible scenario," Daniel said. "The four couriers are landing at widely distant ports. Our watchers on the coast are stretched thin.

Although we've already lost men, admittedly we have more, but knowing where to send them in time—"

"It's just as well," Alex said, tone dripping superiority, "that our four pigeons are making for a single roost, and that whoever this puppetmaster they're reporting to is, he's nearby." Alex cast a lethal look at Roderick. "Which is why I suggested we move up here. I'll hold the fort—man our inner rampart—here, with M'wallah and my guard, but you two will have to take command in the field."

Alex's gaze shifted to Daniel. Silently, almost imperceptibly, he nodded. Neither he nor Alex trusted Roderick any more than they trusted his—their—sire.

Unaware of the interplay, Roderick nodded curtly. "I'll take Hamilton tomorrow. We've already got a force quartered on the other side of Cambridge—enough to deal with Monteith." Roderick looked at Daniel. "You could—"

"No. Leave Monteith for the moment," Alex said. "He's not close enough to demand immediate action—we can wait for better details of his position before making our plans. As you say, we already have men in the area. Have we heard anything of Carstairs?"

"Not since he left Budapest." Roderick ran a hand through his hair. "He's still somewhere on the Continent, and hasn't yet reached the coast."

"As far as we know," Alex dryly replied.

Daniel uncoiled his long legs and stood. "In that case, I'll assist with Hamilton."

seize Hamilton, meddling Miss Ensworth, and the letter."

Alex's features had eased to their customary elegant

serenity. "That sounds excellent." Alex met Roderick's eyes, lightly smiled. "I'll look forward to celebrating your success."

20th December, 1822
Still night
Our room at the inn in Chelmsford

Dear Diary,

This is it—our final day on the road. And I have never felt so torn in my life. I want so much to reach Elveden with Gareth and the others all safe and well, if I could just wish us there now . . . but that would mean we miss what will be our last and possibly best chance to engage with the enemy and reduce the cult's numbers, especially in this area, which is apparently the crux of Wolverstone's plan.

As Tristan and Jack, and even Gareth, clearly hold Wolverstone in high esteem, I have to believe his plan is both sound and worthwhile. That as the three of them believe it is important and incumbent on them to engage and eliminate cultists, then it truly is.

I have to believe—and in my heart I do believe— that striking a blow against the cult today will be worth whatever risk it entails.

Whatever eventuates, as an indomitable English-woman who has traveled widely and survived innu-merable attacks in recent weeks, I intend to play my part. I almost hope something happens so that I can, so that I can make a real contribution to avenging poor MacFarlane.

His face is with me still. His bravery will always be with me.

390

*I have absolutely no intention of letting Gareth die
at the hands of the Black Cobra.*

E.

While they breakfasted by lamplight, Gareth told the others
of the attempt to set fire to the inn. "Standard practice for
cultists, but to no purpose here."

Later, while Mooktu, Mullins, and Bister readied the carriage, Gareth showed Jack and Tristan the evidence of the
abortive attempt. They found three different spots where
fires had been lit.

"Determined beggars, aren't they?" Tristan spread the
ashy remains of one fire with his boot. "But perhaps they
achieved what they intended."

Gareth grunted. "That occurred to me. No one could have
imagined a fire would take hold long enough to do any real
damage. They just wanted to keep prodding us."

Jack gazed at the charred logs. "Anyone care to wager
we'll see action today?"

"No bet," Tristan returned. "Given this, today is the day."

A *hoy* brought them back to the front yard. For the benefit of
the cultists they were sure would be watching, Jack and Tristan
shook hands with Gareth, then mounted and, with cheery
waves, trotted off south through the town, as if parting ways.

In reality they would circle around and fall in behind the
band of cultists following the carriage, as they had the day

He climbed into the carriage, shut the door, and they were
off.

They rolled sedately out of the town, heading north on the road to Sudbury and Bury St. Edmunds. Once they'd left the last cottages behind, Mullins flicked the reins and the horses lengthened their stride.

His hand locked around one of Emily's, Gareth watched the winter-brown fields flash past—and waited.

He was still waiting—they all were—when the carriage rolled into the village of Sudbury. He recognized the tactic, one cult commanders often employed—make the target wait and wait and wait until, inevitably, they relaxed, then pounce—but he still felt the effects. *When?* was the question occupying all their minds.

After rattling across a bridge over the River Stour, Mullins drove into the market square, paused to ask directions, then headed on a short way and turned into the yard of the Anchor Inn.

Climbing down to the cobbles, Gareth took one look at the ancient inn Wolverstone had directed them to, and felt expectation leap. The inn was so old it was a hodgepodge, a conglomeration of additions made over the centuries with wings here, there, and entrances everywhere—perfect if one wanted men to slip unobtrusively inside.

Leaving Mooktu, Bister, and Mullins to watch over the carriage and arrange for fresh horses, he ushered Emily through the front door.

The innkeeper popped up before them. "Major Hamilton?" When Gareth nodded, the man beamed. "Please—come this way. You're expected."

Both he and Emily eagerly followed the man down a narrow corridor. The innkeeper halted, tapped, then opened a wooden door that, from its solidity, dated from Elizabethan times, and bowed them in.

Emily led the way, wondering who was expecting them. The answer had her eyes growing wide.

The room was full of large gentlemen, and it wasn't a small parlor, but one of the inn's main reception rooms. A quick head count said ten; she was surrounded by ten men—ex-Guardsmen by the look of them—but it was the man at the center of the group, the one she found herself somehow facing, who captured and held her attention.

He was dark haired, but so were many of the others. He was by no means the tallest of the group, yet he was the most powerful.

Emily knew that without question.

His face was austere, the planes hard edged, but his mobile lips curved as she instinctively curtsied. "Wolverstone, Miss Ensworth—it's a pleasure to make your acquaintance." He took her hand and bowed over it. "I understand you played a key role in getting the Black Cobra's letter to Delborough here."

Emily glanced at the man beside the great Wolverstone, then beamed. "Colonel Delborough—I'm delighted to see you again."

"And I you, Miss Ensworth." Delborough bowed. As he straightened, his gaze went past Emily, and his face lit. "Gareth!"

Emily stepped aside, delighted indeed as she watched Gareth shake Delborough's hand and share a heartfelt embrace.

As he stepped back, Gareth asked, "Logan and Rafe?"

"Logan landed at Plymouth and is heading this way. He should reach us tomorrow. Rafe . . ." Delborough grimaced. "We haven't heard anything, but you know Rafe. He's just as

likely to turn up on Wol————————

————————————————————————

bered to introduce Emily. "Devil Cynster, Duke of St. Ives."

393

Emily found herself taken on a round of introductions, as Gareth eagerly renewed acquaintance with a host of Cynsters and an earl called Gyles, and Delborough introduced them both to two men Gareth didn't know, who proved to be ex-colleagues of Jack and Tristan, all ex-operatives of Dalziel—Royce by another name.

Her head was whirling by the time the door opened to admit the innkeeper with a small tribe of helpers laden with platters. And on their heels, Jack and Tristan strolled in, to a general and hearty welcome.

The innkeeper and his team withdrew, and their group—now numbering fourteen—settled about the table, Royce at the head, St. Ives at the foot. Royce sat Emily on his right. Somewhat to her relief, Gareth sat beside her. She'd heard enough from Jack, Tristan, and Gareth to expect Wolverstone to impress, but the reality exceeded her imagination by a significant degree.

They all passed the platters. Emily found herself pressed to try this and that, but then all attention focused on their plates. Silence descended for two minutes, then Gareth glanced at Delborough, seated opposite. "We heard that you sacrificed your letter—what happened?"

Delborough nodded, and took up the conversational reins, relating how the confusion arising from combining his party with that of a lady he'd unknowingly been elected to escort north had allowed the Black Cobra to insinuate a thief—a young and very much coerced Indian boy—into their combined households. While he, the lady, and their combined guards had defeated the Cobra's forces and won through to their destination of St. Ives's country home, the boy, Sangay, had stolen the scroll holder, but had then been trapped at St. Ives's house by the recent heavy snowfall.

"We could see from the snow that no one had entered or left the house, so we searched, and eventually found him. Once we convinced him we could keep him and his mother safe, he helped us to set a trap for the Black Cobra." Delborough snorted. "In, of all places, Ely Cathedral."

Delborough went on to describe how the trap had been sprung, but the Black Cobra, Ferrar, had presumably struck, killing his own man to escape unseen with the scroll holder.

"However, it contained only a decoy copy." Wolverstone looked at Gareth. "Which is why we're here—because he'll know that by now, and having tried for Delborough's and succeeded, he'll try for the holder you're carrying, too. Nothing is more certain."

Wolverstone let his gaze travel around the table. "Which is exactly what we want, because we need to reduce the cult's forces, especially in this area. My scheme is designed to have Ferrar racing back and forth across these counties, losing men at every turn. Delborough accounted for fourteen. I hope we can take out a similar number today, and Monteith and those with him, more again tomorrow."

Gareth murmured, "So Rafe . . . ?"

But Royce only smiled.

"You don't need to know what you don't need to know." Jack caught Gareth's eye. "That's the way it always goes."

"Indeed." Royce pushed aside his empty plate. "So let's see what we can accomplish today." He looked inquiringly at Tristan and Jack. "What's our situation?"

"They're here, and in force." Jack straightened in his chair. "We've been following a group of eight who've been tracking the carriage since Tilbury. Today they were joined by a larger force, another ten, just north of Braintree. That

potential . . . lieutenant, let us say. And he's English. If any chance offers, we need to catch him." He looked at Tristan and Jack. "So by Braintree they were eighteen against a carriage with four men. What happened? Braintree is what? Twelve or more miles from here?"

"About that," Jack said. "I wasn't close enough to hear the conversations, but my best guess is that the dark-haired one wanted to attack, but Ferrar refused and had the whole lot of them shadowing the carriage, more or less flanking it all the way to Sudbury."

"Once the carriage crossed the bridge into Sudbury, they peeled away and skirted the town." Tristan tipped his head to the north. "We left them waiting on a rise from where they can watch the Bury and the Lavenham roads."

Royce nodded. "They've guessed from Delborough's destination that the carriage will head north, but they don't know exactly to where. So they're in position to pick up the carriage when it leaves here." He glanced down the table. "Any guesses as to why they put off an attack?"

All eyes turned to Demon Cynster. "My guess is that Ferrar, having some familarity with the area, knows that the stretch from Sudbury to Bury, or Sudbury to Lavenham, is better for mounting an attack."

"Did someone bring a map?" Royce asked.

Vane Cynster had. He drew it from his pocket and unfolded the large map, which showed most of the Eastern Counties. Various hands helped smooth it out and anchor it in front of Royce and Gareth.

Demon leaned forward to point. "Here's Sudbury. This"—he pointed to a position just to the north—"is where Ferrar's waiting."

Royce studied the map. "If you were he, where would you choose to ambush the carriage?"

Without hesitation Demon placed a finger on the map. "Here—just a little way past the lane that leads to Glemsford and Clare. There's also a country lane that leads up to Bury, just a little way along that lane. In terms of position, that spot is close to perfect."

"Remember Ferrar and the cult tend to rely on overwhelming force." Del looked at Demon. "Can he attack with all his men from there?"

Demon nodded. "There's plenty of cover in stands of trees back from the road, but just there the usual hedges fall back and the road has wide, shallow ditches, open and clear, excellent for approaching a halted coach. All he'll need to do is send men across the road to halt the coach, and then it's trapped and at his mercy."

"So we let him do that, commit his force against the coach, then we fall on them from the rear and wipe them out." Devil Cynster smiled. "Easy."

There were sounds of eager agreement all around.

"Yes, but is that the best we can do?" Royce murmured.

All talk ceased.

Devil looked up the table at him. "What now, o ye of devious mind?"

There were grins all around, including from Royce, but then he sobered. "The truth, as many of you have guessed, is that this entire scheme is designed not just to get the original copy of the Black Cobra's letter into my hands, but if at all possible to provide further proof—more direct and damning proof—of Ferrar's guilt. Ideally, I'd like to catch him with a scroll holder literally in his hand—have more than one of us see him so there'll be multiple witnesses. If I have to accuse him with only the letter as proof, I will, but I'd far rather have something more—something less easy to destroy—as evidence."

on the map, just south of Sudbury.

"All right." Royce nodded. "So we have Ferrar here—the

first thing we need. We have the scroll holder—the thing we want in his hand. If we go forward into the attack he has planned, Ferrar won't show his face, he'll sit back and watch the action. When we triumph over his forces, he'll turn and ride away. Even if we've witnessed him sending the cultists to attack the carriage . . ." Royce shook his head. "That's far too easy to explain away. He'll deny all connection to the cult, and without the letter—even with the letter—it's possible he, or more likely his father, will prevail, and he'll go free. So doing the obvious—merrily going forward and letting them attack—will let us reduce cult numbers, but will not gain us the greater prize."

When Royce fell silent, Devil prompted, "The alternative being . . . ?"

Royce frowned. "We have to get the scroll holder into Ferrar's hands. If we can somehow convince the cultists to take it in some way that won't make them or Ferrar suspicious, they'll take it back to him—and then we'll have him." He looked at the scroll holder. "But how do we *innocently* give the damn thing up after Hamilton and his men have fought so hard to get it here?"

That undoubtedly was the question.

The men leaned forward, making suggestions, expressing opinions, evaluating options.

After a moment, Emily eased back her chair—easing herself out of the ensuing discussion. She had an idea, but she needed quiet to think it through, enough to hear her own thoughts.

Gareth glanced at her the instant she moved, smiled vaguely, and drew back her chair.

She thanked him and retreated to the window seat across the room. Sitting in the alcove, she looked out at the view beyond and methodically worked through her notion.

The men had reached the point of considering ways to lose the holder "accidentally," when she rose and headed back to the table.

The Cynster called Gabriel shook his head. "Accidentally

losing it won't work. The instant you try that, they'll know it's a decoy, and therefore of no worth—otherwise you'd never lose it, not after all this time—and also, ergo, that it's bait. And bait means a trap, so they might well turn tail altogether, and then we'll lose even the chance of reducing numbers."

Royce grimaced. "If we can't make the loss appear believable—"

"I could do it." Emily halted behind the chair she'd occupied.

All the men looked at her, then Gareth asked, "Do what?"

She looked at him. "I could leave the scroll holder in a hedge for the cultists to take in such a way that it would appear unthreatening, unsuspicious." She glanced at Jack and Tristan, then looked back at Gareth. "As if you, and Jack and Tristan, too, if they know about them, don't know I've left it."

It was Royce who asked, "How?"

Emily drew in a breath, reached out and picked up the scroll holder, then, still standing, lightly tapping it in her hand, she talked them, walked them, through her plan.

None of them liked it, of course, but . . . all had to admit that it was so unexpected, it just might work.

"And you'll all be there, within hailing range at least," she pointed out with exemplary patience. "Not that anything is likely to go wrong. There's no reason to imagine I'll be in

she arched her brows, he took her elbow and steered her across to the window seat.

He halted facing the window, his back to the room, with her beside him. His face felt like stone. "You can't do this." He kept his voice low, but even he could hear the tension in his tone. "It's too dangerous."

Head tilting, she regarded him for a moment, then quietly said, "Yes, there's an element of danger involved, but only because we can't predict everything. On balance . . . this is our best way forward, and you know it."

"I may know it, but that's not the point." He shifted restlessly. "You know what we discussed—our future. You know how much you mean to me—"

Emily cut him off with a hand on his arm, even though the words were music to her ears. "I know what we discussed. Trust. Partnership. Sharing in all things." She waited until he glanced her way, caught his gaze and held it. "I have to do this, Gareth, for myself as well as to help you and the others, and you have to let me do it. This time you have to support, not lead. You have to support me so I can do what only I can."

His jaw tightened. His eyes didn't leave hers.

"I told you—our life together has already began. We've already started a life partnership, and, in this, you have to honor it." She gripped his arm, unsurprised to feel the muscles beneath the fabric all steel. "Honor is the guiding principle you live by, and today, in this, honor dictates you let me knowingly take a calculated risk."

"I don't like being forced into . . . some kind of test."

She inclined her head. "No more do I. This situation isn't by my choice, but the Black Cobra and his machinations have brought us to this. All our travels, all the attacks, all the fighting and escapes—they'll mean little if we don't see it through to the end, and wring everything we can from the final hand we've been dealt."

His eyes searched hers; she sensed his resistance wavering.

Letting her lips curve in wry affection, she leaned closer. Eyes still locked with his, she murmured, "You're strong enough to do this, and so am I—and we'll never forgive ourselves if we don't try."

He held her gaze for an instant longer, then sighed. Lips still tight, he nodded. "All right."

They returned to the table to find the point for her excursion had been settled as just beyond the turnoff to Glemsford and Clare, just before the stretch Demon had described as perfect for an attack. "It's likely," Demon said, "that they'll be in a stand of trees just here, and so be able to see you clearly."

Emily looked at the map, then glanced at the clock on the mantelpiece. Then she looked at the faces around the table. "Time is passing, gentlemen—shall we get on?"

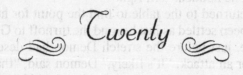

Twenty

hey drove on in silence. On hearing the plan, Bister and Mooktu had stared at Gareth as if he'd lost his mind, but Mullins—who knew her best—had nodded. "Worth a try," he'd said, then clambered up to his seat.

Emily wished the others had rather more faith in her histrionic abilities, but as the carriage rolled steadily north toward Bury St. Edmunds, she put their faint hearts firmly from her mind and concentrated on what she had to do.

The impression she had to convey, not with words, but in actions.

If she succeeded, she would make a major contribution to the success of Gareth's mission. She would be instrumental in bringing the fiend to justice—and for MacFarlane most of all, she was determined to do her best. To give her all.

She spied the signpost for the Glemsford turnoff just ahead. "Almost there. Stop the coach."

Gareth reached up; as the lane flashed by on their left, he rapped on the carriage roof. Immediately, the horses slowed.

When the carriage rocked to a halt, she glanced out, and mentally blessed Demon Cynster—the road just there was lined with high, thick hawthorn hedges, brown and leafless now, but still dense enough for her purpose. And a few steps back there was a stile.

She glanced at Gareth, squeezed his hand, felt his fingers return the pressure, then he reluctantly released her. "Wish me luck."

His eyes darkened. "Just come back soon, and put me out of my misery."

She had to fight to banish her smile as she swung the door open and climbed out onto the step, then clambered down to the road. Clutching her muff, into which the scroll holder had just fitted— thank goodness it was winter—she marched the few paces back down the road to the stile. Nearing it, she turned, looked, and made imperious "turn around" gestures at Mooktu and Bister, who as per their orders had turned to stare back at her.

Once they'd grudgingly complied, frowning, lips compressed, she strode to the stile and climbed over—as if intending to answer a call of nature.

But as soon as her feet hit the ground on the other side, and she was out of sight of the carriage, she let her demeanor change. Gone was all confidence. She bit her lip, glanced around furtively. Then she dragged in a breath, and scurried a little way along the hedge, further from the carriage.

Then she stopped. Halted, raised her head, then she let her shoulders slump again, and started pacing. Back and forth, one hand gesticulating—clearly arguing with herself. Desperately, as if at her wits' end and unsure which of two equally bad options to choose.

Again she halted. Closing her eyes, she drew a deep breath, then pulled the scroll holder from her muff and, without even glancing at it properly, raised it

waiting to hear her scream. His mind had thrown up all manner of horrible scenes. The cultists had

bows and let fly at her. A number rode up, sabers flashing . . .
he blanked out the resulting image, cursed. Yet when dealing with the Black Cobra, anything was possible.

He was literally quivering with the effort to remain still,
to not open the door and rush out to see where she was, when
he heard her footsteps returning.

The relief that swept him nearly brought him to his knees.

Then the door handle turned, tugged. Releasing it, he
pushed back on the seat.

The door swung open and she was there, staring at him,
a question in her eyes. He didn't know what was in his face,
but he managed to lift a hand and beckon her inside.

She climbed up onto the step, leaned back to order, "Drive
on!" then she ducked into the carriage, slammed the door
behind her, and fell onto the seat opposite.

The smile that wreathed her face was nothing short of
radiant.

The coach jerked, then rolled on, picking up speed.

He cleared his throat. "All right?"

She bounced upright and beamed at him. "I think I just
gave the performance of my life."

He devoured her with his gaze, but forced himself to wait
until the carriage rounded the next bend—having passed the
long stretch deemed perfect for an attack without even sighting a cultist—then he leaned forward, seized her about her
waist, lifted her into his arms, onto his lap, and kissed her to
within an inch of her life.

On a hill to the southwest of the scroll holder's new location,
Royce, Del, Devil, and all the others, saving only Jack and
Tristan, who were still in their roles of guards and shadowing
the carriage on the other side of the road, waited and watched.

Spyglasses trained on the spot, they'd viewed Emily's performance with critical detachment.

When the carriage door closed behind her and the carriage
rumbled on, eventually passing through the field of likely
attack and out of sight without challenge, Royce lowered his

spyglass. "If I didn't know better, I might just believe she'd lost her nerve entirely, and jettisoned what she sees as the cause of all their trouble."

"The Black Cobra has a penchant for breaking people, men and women—of using fear to terrorize until whoever it is does what he wants—so her ploy stands a better-than-might-be-expected chance of succeeding." Del kept his glass trained on the scroll holder in the hedge. "Ferrar is used to people giving him what he wants."

"There go Jack and Tristan." Lucifer Cynster pointed to where the two guards were fleetingly visible as they passed over a rise, heading north in the wake of the carriage.

"Wherever he is, Ferrar shouldn't have missed seeing them," Devil said.

"No, he shouldn't." Royce raised his glass again, focusing on the relevant section of hedge. "So as far as he knows, the scroll holder is just sitting there, waiting for him to send someone to fetch it. Even if he only half believes, I can't see him leaving it. The need to have it—to know if it's a copy or the original—will surely be too great for a man of his ilk to resist."

Del snorted. "He's never been denied anything in his life. He won't resist. All we need to do is wait."

In a dense stand of trees on a rise overlooking the stretch of road Roderick had decreed was the perfect place to attack the carriage, Roderick and Daniel stood with spyglasses to their eyes, staring at the scroll holder jammed in the hedge.

Daniel snorted, lowered his glass. "It's a trap, of course.

That damned woman rode like the devil to bring the letter down from Poona, then delivered it to Delborough. And then she attached herself to Hamilton, no doubt intending to avenge MacFarlane. So why would she suddenly give up—give the letter up—now?"

"Because she's reached the end of her tether." Roderick's tone was one of utmost reasonableness. "We've seen it often enough. We attack and attack and keep the attacks coming, and eventually it all just gets too much. They're nearly at the end of their journey, nearly through to safety. And it was she who left it behind. If it had been Hamilton or one of his men, I'd be much less likely to credit it—and the two guards have gone on, too." Lowering his spyglass, Roderick smiled at Daniel. "So if it is a trap, who's left to spring it?"

Daniel wasn't convinced. "What about those others who trapped Larkins in the cathedral?"

"They're from near Cambridge." Roderick waved to the northwest. "If they'd thundered down here, we would have seen them."

Daniel wasn't so sure, but as the minutes ticked by and the scroll holder just sat there, in the pale light of the winter afternoon, he knew leaving it there wasn't an option. "So what do you propose?"

"I'll send one of the men to pick it up while the rest of us watch from up here. If there's no sign of a trap, he'll bring the holder to me, I'll take whatever it contains, and ride for Bury." Roderick glanced at Daniel. "By the lane—not the road. If they're waiting ahead for me to come prancing by, the letter in my hand, they'll be disappointed."

That was Daniel's greatest fear. Roderick seemed to have covered the weakness, but . . . Daniel's thumbs were still pricking. "All right." Snapping his spyglass shut, Daniel moved to his horse's side, stuffed the glass in the saddlebag. "I'll ride ahead and tell Alex of your unexpected success—how you retrieved the letter without losing more men."

"Indeed," Roderick purred. "Alex *should* be impressed."

Daniel swung up to his saddle, gathered his reins.

Roderick looked up at him, held his gaze. "Incidentally, while you're discussing matters with Alex, you might mention that I would look favorably on an *appropriate* welcome. I said I'd get us out of this—and I am. Alex—and sadly, sometimes you, too, Daniel—would do well to remember who among us is Shrewton's legitimate son."

Daniel looked down into Roderick's cold eyes. His half brother was clearly not as oblivious to his and Alex's view of him as they'd thought. A point to discuss, indeed—if Roderick succeeded in retrieving all four letters, he'd be cock of the walk, king in the Black Cobra's domain. Which didn't auger well, not for Roderick.

But now Daniel merely nodded, his expression saying nothing of such complex thoughts. "Alex and I will be waiting in Bury." About to spur off, he paused to add, "Remember to come in the back way."

Roderick waved him off, his attention returning to the holder in the hedge. "Don't fret—I'll come via the ruins."

Daniel stared at him for a second, sensing again the shift in dynamic that had occurred since the three of them had stepped onto English soil. Then he turned his horse and made for the small lane that led north to Bury.

A cultist came out of a stand of trees to the north, from the position Demon had suggested any attack on the carriage along that most amenable stretch would come.

Unhurriedly, his eyes scanning the

"While most of the cultists we've stumbled on are foot soldiers, not well trained with arms, the men with Ferrar will be his closest guards—his elite. They're cavalry trained, good with sabers, but they fight like we do—you won't run into any surprises with them. The assassins are another matter—they fight with half swords and shorter knives. If you find yourself facing one of them, expect the unexpected. They fight to win whatever the cost."

"There's definitely other riders in the trees he came out from," Demon reported. "Exactly how many, I can't be sure, but a goodly number."

"We're looking for eighteen," Royce said. "Could there be that many hidden there?"

Demon nodded. "Easily."

Gervase was suddenly there. He'd gone down to the fields to get a different line of sight. "One of the gentlemen just left, riding hard up the lane over there." He pointed to the west of Ferrar's assumed position.

"That leads to Bury," Royce said.

"Here we go," Devil said. They all watched, sharing six spyglasses among them, as the cultist carried the holder openly back across the fields, and up the treed rise to his master.

"I can see Ferrar from over here," Lucifer called. The others all shifted, refocused.

Just in time to witness Ferrar receive the scroll holder from his man. In short order, he opened it. Those with the glasses quietly relayed what they saw.

"He's pulling the letter out, unrolling it." Royce smiled. "It's a decoy, so the instant he realizes . . ."

His voice trailed away. Those without glasses shifted restlessly.

"What's happening?" Gabriel Cynster asked.

"He's smiling. Delightedly." Devil handed his glass to Gabriel, looked at Royce. "If it's a decoy, why is he so thrilled to have it?"

Frowning, Royce lowered his glass, then gave it to Gervase. "If he's keen to retrieve the copies as well as the original, that suggests there's something else in the letter that's a threat to him, something in the words we've missed. Just as well Hamilton made another copy."

"It has to be that." Del handed his spyglass on. "Just look at his face."

Royce's eyes narrowed. "There's definitely something we're missing in this. Something more going on."

"He's leaving," Gabriel reported. "He's tossed aside the scroll holder and put the letter in his inside pocket. Now he's riding off up that lane to Bury." A second later he reported, "He's taking only eight cultists with him—the others are heading south."

"Probably returning to the north bank of the Thames," Del said.

They watched the eight cultists, totally assured, ride past their position.

"Let them go." Royce looked north, at the eight elite guards and assassins riding easily in Ferrar's wake. "We need to reduce their numbers in this area, not further south."

Devil glanced at his cousins, at Gyles. "There's six Cynsters, one Rawlings—seven. We volunteer."

"Do we need to take prisoners?" Lucifer asked.

"No—no use." Royce hesitated, then said, "I have oversight of the magistrates in the area, so I'm charging you seven, ex-Guardsmen and peers, with the task of removing those eight cultists. We know they've committed atrocities in India, and if we had the time to spare, we could catch them, try them, and hang them—but that will cost our country time and money. These men

Ferrar has gone ahead. We'll circle around and catch up with him, but given the distance between him and his men, I want you to remove them without alerting him."

Devil looked at the cultists heading north. They could still see Ferrar merrily riding ahead. "You do like to be difficult."

"The request shouldn't be outside your scope." Royce glanced at Demon. "You both know the country well—they don't, or they wouldn't be hanging so far back, not if they're his guards."

Demon glanced at Devil. "The bend before the windmill?"

Devil nodded. "I was thinking the same thing."

Less than a minute later, they were all mounted, streaming down the rise to circle to the west, to follow and overtake the band of cultists, and separate his guards from Ferrar.

Jack and Tristan caught up with the carriage a little way out of Bury St. Edmunds.

"Not a cultist in sight," Jack reported. "They must have taken the bait, which means they should be coming up the road behind us."

"I don't know about you" —with his glance, Tristan included Mullins, Mooktu, and Bister— "but after all this, I'd like to be in at the end."

"Me, too," Jack said. "So we vote to stop at an inn in Bury, get the carriage off the road, and watch Ferrar and his flunkies go past. Then we can join the others on their trail."

No one argued. They found the perfect inn in Westgate Street, and hired the front parlor, from which they could see back down the road up which they'd come, as well as see some distance left and right. Whichever route Ferrar took, he was likely to pass their position; they settled to wait.

Fifteen minutes later, Ferrar, alone, came jauntily riding along Westgate Street, smiling as he tacked this way and that through the late-afternoon traffic. He passed the inn window right to left. Emily seized Gareth's sleeve. "He didn't come the way we did."

Jack and Tristan crowded the window, peering at Ferrar's

back. "He must have taken that minor lane to Bury." Tristan stared the other way, in the direction from which Ferrar had come. "Where are the others?"

For a full minute, they looked back and forth, at Ferrar's back, then the other way, hoping to spot their comrades, who should have been on his trail.

"Damn!" Jack said. "He must have lost them."

He and Tristan were out of the door on the words. Gareth rushed after them; Emily rushed after him. Jack's and Tristan's horses were still saddled. They swung up to their backs and rode out of the inn yard.

Using his major's voice, Gareth commandeered a carriage horse. It had no saddle, but the long reins were still there. Grabbing the horse's mane, he swung up to its back.

"Gareth!"

He looked down into Emily's eyes.

"You can't leave me here!"

He could. But . . . teeth gritted, he beckoned her closer, bent, gripped and hoisted her up to the horse's back before him. "Hold on. But if we need to ride hard, I'll have to set you down."

"No, you won't." Locking her hands in the horse's mane, she stated, "I have it on excellent authority that I'm a devilish good rider."

Be that as it may . . . he guided the horse, a steady beast, into the traffic thronging Westgate Street. Bury was a market town; from what they'd seen, today was market day. Which was helpful . . .

. . . might have known." His gaze was resting on Emily.

Gareth shot him a look that stated very clearly: *Yes, he might.*

Emily ignored him. "We thought you'd lost him." She wriggled and tried to look back. "Where are the others?"

Wolverstone regarded her for a moment, then decided not to take issue with her first statement. "Delborough, Gervase, and Tony are behind me. The Cynsters and Chillingworth remained to engage the cultists. Sadly, only eight stayed to play."

Emily looked into his eyes, and got the impression she was treading very close to some edge. She looked ahead, nodded forward. "Jack and Tristan are closer. Do you have any idea where he might be going?"

"No." On the word, Ferrar turned into a commercial stable. Royce angled his horse across Gareth and Emily's, steering them to the curb. "We'll wait here and see what he's up to."

Up ahead, Jack and Tristan had similarly halted by the opposite curb. They were chatting as if they were neighbors.

Royce looked at Emily, then Gareth. "If Ferrar comes out, try to keep your heads down—we don't want him to recognize you. Although I have to admit he's been singularly unwatchful thus far."

Emily was too keyed up to even pretend to chat. Then Ferrar came striding out of the stable and crossed the street. He passed within yards of Tristan and Jack. They shifted to keep their faces from him, but he didn't even glance their way.

Looking at Royce, Emily saw that his head was up, that with a glance he was collecting his men.

Ferrar strode on, oblivious, heading away from the center of the town, then without breaking stride, he turned through a wide gateway set in the thick stone wall bordering the other side of the street.

Royce frowned. "The abbey ruins are through there."

As soon as Ferrar passed through the gateway and out of sight, they all hurried across the road, closing in on Tristan, who stood waiting in the gateway's shadows. Jack had already slipped through.

Delborough, Gervase, and Tony joined them as they halted by Tristan's side.

Jack reappeared. He looked faintly surprised. "He's . . . wandering. Aimlessly ambling as if he had not a care in the world—as if he's out for a stroll among the ruins, as, incidentally, quite a few others are." He glanced back through the gateway. "I had no idea ruins in winter twilight were so much in vogue."

Emily frowned at him. "You should read the *Ladies' Gazette*."

To a man, they stared at her, then Royce said, "Is he early for a meeting? Or . . . is he a student of ruins?"

"He stabled his horse, so his lair must be near," Delborough pointed out. "Within walking distance."

"Which covers the whole town." Royce walked through the gateway, rapidly scanned the area, then came back. "Here's how we'll handle this."

He directed Emily and Gareth to stroll through the gateway, then along the stone wall to where they could observe the grassy promenade that ran across the backs of the buildings built into the west side of the ruins—houses filling the arches of the old abbey, as well as the town's cathedral built out of the old abbey's main gate. "You'll be able to keep your distance, but still see if he goes into one of the houses, or even into the cathedral. From there he can reach the rest of the town." Royce looked at the others, his expression predatory. "He might have seen all of your faces, but he hasn't seen mine. I'll follow him directly—or as directly as I can without alerting him

the tower that had once housed the abbey's main gate and now afforded an unrivaled view of the abbey ruins far below—Alex stared down at Roderick—and the men who were fanning out ominously in his wake. "Just *look* how many followers he's managed to collect!"

Daniel stared in disbelief. "He doesn't even seem to know they're there."

Horror-struck, they watched from above, as Roderick paused, leaned back against a large fallen stone, reached into his coat, and drew out a rolled white paper.

"He's got it—copy or original, it matters not." With one last deadly look over the parapet, Alex whirled and strode for the stairs. "Come on!"

As they clattered as fast as they could down the dark stone stairs, Alex thought furiously.

When they reached the bottom and stepped out into the cathedral foyer, Alex seized Daniel's arm. After one quick glance around to make sure no one had seen them, with head lowered Alex steered them quickly out of the cathedral and along the narrow passage down the side, then leaned close and hissed, "Roderick's gone. Nothing we can do will save him. He has the letter, and those following him know it. Did you see the men hunting him? See how they moved—see their *faces*?"

When Daniel returned a puzzled look, Alex shook his arm. "*Aristocratic* faces—the faces of men of power, of the ton, who *will be listened to*."

They emerged onto the promenade at the back of the cathedral and swiftly crossed into the ruins. Alex's eyes scanned the deepening shadows, the fallen stones.

Alex's voice lowered even more. "They're going to catch Roderick, and this time, he won't be able to talk his way out of it—not even our sire will be able to explain why he's got that letter in his hand. Any second, and they'll have him." Halting, Alex looked into Daniel's dark eyes. "No one knows of *our* involvement. We can just walk away. But Roderick can't. Not this time."

Alex paused, then asked, tone colder than the descending wintry chill, "Do you think, once caught, he'll let you and me slip away?"

Lips tight, Daniel shook his head.

"Nor do I. And I'm not about to let all we've worked to create with the Black Cobra be wiped out by Roderick's insufferable belief in his own superiority." Turning, Alex led the way deeper into the ruins. "Come on. We have one chance—only one—to escape."

Daniel might have inquired as to how, but Alex had always thought faster than he. Much faster than Roderick. And there was Roderick ahead of them. He was ambling along, the letter—their vital missive—in one hand, tapping it nonchalantly on his other palm. He saw them, waved the letter.

Alex halted in the center of an archway, three steps above the broken floor Roderick was traversing. Daniel halted one step behind.

Roderick smiled, a smile of overweening superiority, and came on. As he neared, he said, "O ye of little faith. You have no idea how easy this was."

He looked down as he climbed the steps.

Alex stepped forward as Roderick reached the last step. He looked up.

Just as the bells summoning the faithful to evensong started carolling.

Just as, aided by Roderick's momentum, Alex slid a dagger past Roderick's ribs, directly into his heart.

Daniel's breath seized at the look of utter, astounded disbelief that washed over Roderick's face.

ng, Alex blew out a breath, grabbed Daniel's sleeve and hauled him around. Head close, Alex murmured, "We walk slowly, sedately. We're just another pair of worshippers heading to the cathedral for evening service."

Daniel glanced back, saw Roderick, ice-blue eyes wide, slump to the ground.

Roderick's eyes glazed—and the Earl of Shrewton's favorite son was gone.

The cathedral bells were peeling and the light was fading fast. Emily tugged Gareth's sleeve. "Come on—we need to get closer or he could slip past us in this gloom."

Gareth surrendered, and strolled with her along the promenade behind the buildings, searching the ruins, what they could see of them in the failing light.

Abruptly, Emily halted. "What's that?"

He followed her gaze diagonally into the ruins, and saw . . . dark material spread over pale stone steps. "It's a body."

They rushed down the avenue, but before they reached the spot, Royce materialized. He stepped past the slumped form, up through the archway beyond, then crouched.

Delborough, Tristan, Jack, Gervase, and Tony reached the archway as they did. Royce looked up, his face unreadable. "This just happened. Did any of you see anyone fleeing?"

They all shook their heads.

Royce's lips tightened. He rose. "Search!"

They did, until the light was gone, but found nothing. They returned to the body, all wondering, rethinking.

Hands on hips, Royce stood looking down at the body, now barely visible. He glanced at Delborough. "The dagger—it looks to be the same sort as the one used on Larkins."

Crouching, Del inspected the ivory handle, nodded as he rose. "It's a type the cult assassins use."

"The letter?" Jack asked.

"Gone." Royce glanced around at the circle of faces. "No one even vaguely suspicious?"

They all shook their heads. "There were couples leaving, and numerous worshippers heading for evening service,"

Tristan said, "but no one was rushing, hurrying, trying to get away. No one glancing around."

Royce grimaced. They all stared down at the body of Roderick Ferrar. "So," Royce said, accents clipped, "we have the man we were certain was the Black Cobra, but he's been eliminated. Leaving us with two very big questions: Who killed him? And why?"

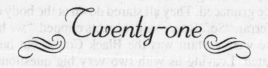
Twenty-one

20th December, 1822
Late afternoon
My room at Elveden Grange

Dear Diary,

I have come up to wash off the dust of travel before rejoining the others downstairs. What a day! We are at the end of our adventure, Gareth's mission is complete, but Ferrar has turned up dead and no one is clear what that means.

Yet even more excitingly, the exigencies of the day put Gareth's commitment to our partnership to the test—and the dear man came through with flying colors! He let me out of his sight, let me walk into potential danger to do what I alone could in leaving the scroll holder for Ferrar to take, even though, as was later made clear to me in emphatic fashion, the moment cost him dearly. Yet he did not leave me behind at the inn, either, but allowed me to remain by his side as we hunted Ferrar.

After today, I could not possibly doubt the strength of his commitment to our future—a future I cannot

418

wait to address! My heart feels like it's bubbling, so full of effervescent happiness am I.

But first we have to deal with the unexpected conclusion of Gareth's mission, and I must rush downstairs to play my part.

E.

o we're left with the questions of who killed Ferrar, and why." Standing before the hearth in the large drawing room of Elveden Grange, Royce glanced up as Emily returned. He'd just concluded relating the events of the day for the benefit of the assembled ladies—Deliah Duncannon, who had arrived with Delborough, Alicia, Tony's wife, Madeline, Gervase's wife, Leonora and Clarice, Kit, Jack Hendon's wife, Letitia, Christian Allardyce's marchioness, and his own duchess, Minerva, who had, he'd discovered, invited all the families of his ex-colleagues to join their family here for Christmas.

When he'd stared at her, dumbfounded, she'd smiled and patted his chest. "Your timetable runs too close to Christmas—the men can't be sure of getting home in time, and you all have young families."

He knew better than to argue. There were battles he could win, and ones he wouldn't. Such, he'd learned, was the nature of married life.

Those of his ex-colleagues already there and seated about the room had no doubt learned the same. Christian and Jack Hendon were there, ready to, in a few days, play the roles as-

signed them. The

part of a larger whole.

"I agree." Gareth frowned. "If the Black Cobra is not

Ferrar, then presumably the Black Cobra killed him, or ordered the killing—so that still means the Black Cobra is here, in England."

"Here in Suffolk, or close by," Tony said.

After a moment, Delborough shook his head. "Ferrar had to be very high in the cult's organization. He was vital to the cult's success through his role in the governor's office, and given his nature, I can't see him taking any subordinate position while knowing he was the lynchpin for the cult's fortunes." Delborough met Royce's eyes. "We saw Ferrar giving orders, and the elite guards, including the assassins, obeyed. I'd suggest that all we know favors the notion that the Black Cobra is a group—two, three, or more, we can't say—but Ferrar was one. Presumably the other Englishman we saw was another."

Royce nodded. "And that other Englishman, who appeared to be Ferrar's equal, might have been the one who killed Ferrar, or had him killed."

"If we accept that the Black Cobra is a multiheaded beast," Gyles Rawlings said, "then it's most likely the other members are known acquaintances of Ferrar."

Royce met Gyles's eyes, then nodded and glanced at the window, at the dark beyond. "It's nearly evening, but I believe it's time we paid the Earl of Shrewton a visit. If we leave now, we'll be at Wymondham before he sits down to dine."

They'd brought Ferrar's body to Elveden in a dray, ready to deliver to his father at Shrewton Hall.

"What about Larkins?" Devil asked. "Did Ferrar kill him, or was it someone else?"

"From what you told me," Royce said, "it was most likely Ferrar—it was someone Larkins trusted implicitly, so unlikely to be merely one of Ferrar's friends. However, now that Ferrar's dead, that's neither here nor there, but we'll certainly take Larkins's body with Ferrar's—it might help convince the earl that he needs to do whatever he can to assist us."

There were a number of volunteers eager to help convince

the earl, but Royce kept the group to four—Christian, the other most senior peer, and Delborough and Gareth, both of whom could with authority bear witness to Ferrar's deeds, and those of the Black Cobra, in India.

When Devil tried to insist that he, too, should go, Minerva narrowed her eyes at him. "You"—she waved an imperious finger indicating all the Cynsters and Gyles Chillingworth—"will ride back to Somersham Place immediately. None of you might be seriously incapacitated, but I can see cuts—great heavens! I can see *blood*—and your wives would never forgive me if I didn't send you home to be tended. *Now*."

Seven large men stared back at her. Minerva didn't budge, didn't bat an eyelash.

Nor did the ladies gathered around her, who, as the silence stretched, brought their gazes, too, to bear on the recalcitrant males . . . until they broke.

With one last dark look, Devil inclined his head. "Very well." He glanced at Royce, who'd been studying the ceiling. "We'll see you tomorrow, no doubt."

"I'll send word later tonight, once we've learned what we can from Shrewton and—I hope—heard from Monteith's party. They should be at Bedford tonight."

Devil raised a hand in salute, and led the others out.

Royce followed with Delborough, Gareth, and Christian, bound for Shrewton Hall.

The other members of the Bastion Club and Jack Hendon exchanged glances

start at the beginning—when did you go to India?—and more importantly, why?"

Emily looked from eager face to interested eyes, and saw no reason not to comply.

In a cold stone room off the laundry of Shrewton Hall, near Wymondham, the Earl of Shrewton stood staring down at the body of his favorite son.

Roderick Ferrar's body lay on its back on one of the room's benches. The earl's servants had laid Larkins's body on another bench nearby, yet the earl had given no sign of even noticing Larkins. From the moment he'd led them— Royce, Christian, Delborough, Gareth, and the earl's elder son, Viscount Kilworth—into the room, the earl's attention had fixed on his son's remains.

The shock on the earl's face was there for all to read.

Kilworth, too, was visibly shaken. "We didn't even know he was in the country."

"Who did this?" The earl swung to face Royce. "Who killed my son?"

"A friend of his known as the Black Cobra." Succinctly, Royce explained their interest in the Black Cobra cult and its leaders. "We were following your son because he'd fetched and was carrying a copy of a letter from the Black Cobra that the Black Cobra wants back. The original of that letter is signed with the Black Cobra's distinctive mark, and sealed with your family seal." Royce indicated the seal ring on Ferrar's finger.

Head lowering so they could no longer see his eyes, the earl said nothing.

Royce swung to the other body. "The day before, Larkins— your son's man—seized another copy of the letter, and he, too, was killed."

The earl made a dismissive gesture. "I want to know who killed my son."

"They were killed with identical daggers," Royce said, "of a type used by the Black Cobra cult's assassins. The Black Cobra killed your son, or ordered him to be killed. So we have a common goal in that both you and I want to know who the Black Cobra is."

Royce paused, then, including Kilworth with a glance, asked, "Do you know who the Black Cobra is?"

The earl snorted. "Of course not—I have no interest in any foreign mumbo jumbo."

"There's not much of that about the Black Cobra cult—they're solely interested in acquiring money and power, and are very willing to use terror and vile deeds to gain both." Royce kept his gaze fixed on the earl. "Do you or Kilworth know the names of any of Roderick's friends in Bombay? Has he mentioned anyone as associate or friend, who might be involved, or might know more?"

The earl stiffened and lifted his head. "I know nothing about any cult—it's ridiculous to even suggest my son was involved with such people."

"Your son's seal is on the letter," Royce coolly reminded him. "There's no doubt of his involvement at some level. The original of that letter, with Roderick's seal, will be delivered to me shortly, and given the interest at the highest levels that the depredations of the Black Cobra cult has engendered, that letter will, sooner or later, find its way into the public domain. Any assistance your family can provide in identifying the Black Cobra—the man who killed your son—will, naturally, mitigate any adverse implications."

Gareth glanced at Delborough, and Christian beside him, and saw they, too, were suppressing satisfied smiles. There was steel beneath Royce's smooth tones, leaving no doubt in anyone's mind what would happen if the family did not assist. Yet no threat had actually b

"He's in shock," Kilworth said, as if in exculpation, then

added, "Well, so am I." He ran a hand through his hair. "But Roderick was his favorite, you see." His tone made it clear that if it had been he lying dead on the bench, he doubted his father would be half as exercised. He gestured to the door. "Come. I'll see you to your horses."

As he walked beside Royce down the long corridors, Kilworth kept talking—he was the sort of man who did. The rest of them were happy to listen.

"We knew nothing, you see—last we heard he was off to India to make his fortune. He wasn't one for writing letters. Well, we had no idea he'd even come home." He glanced at Royce. "Did he just arrive?"

"He landed in Southampton on the sixth of this month," Delborough said.

"Oh." Kilworth's expressive face fell, then he grimaced. "As you can see, we aren't close—weren't. Roderick and me. But still . . . I'm surprised he didn't contact the old man."

"You're sure he didn't?" Christian asked.

"Yes, I'm sure." Kilworth saw their doubts, and smiled. "The servants never liked Roderick, but they like me, so they always tell me . . . things like that. None of us here knew Roderick was in England, of that I am completely sure."

They'd reached their horses, held by grooms in a side courtyard.

Kilworth halted, waited while they mounted, then he looked up at Royce. "I doubt you'll get anything from the old man, and the harder you push, the more he'll dig in his heels and bluster. But . . . I'll contact those of Roderick's friends I know of here, in England, and ask if any of them have heard what he was up to in India, and if he mentioned who were his closest friends there."

"Thank you." Royce inclined his head. "You'll find me at Elveden Grange until this is over."

Kilworth frowned. "It isn't over?"

Royce shook his head as he turned his horse. "Not by a very long chalk."

* * *

424

They returned to Elveden Grange to discover that the ladies had held dinner back for them. The instant they walked into the drawing room, Minerva rose and directed the whole company to the dining room. Over a relaxing meal they reported on the earl's recalcitrance, and the possibility that Kilworth might manage to learn more.

"The countess is long dead, and his sisters are older and have been married and living in their own households for years," Minerva said. "I doubt they would know anything."

"Roderick was his father's favorite for a very good reason—father and son were cut from the same cloth." Letitia sat back in her chair. "Whatever viciousness you detected in Ferrar, he learned at his father's knee. Kilworth, on the other hand, is a much more gentle, rather scholarly soul. He took after the countess, much to Shrewton's unveiled disgust. Shrewton tolerates him only because he is his heir."

"And now his only surviving son." Minerva rose. All the ladies followed suit.

Royce glanced at the men, saw his inclination mirrored in their faces. He pushed back his chair. "We'll join you in the drawing room. There's much still to be discussed."

While the men followed the ladies down the hall, Royce's butler approached him with a missive on a salver. Royce took it, opened it, and read the message within, then slid it into his pocket, and went on, following the other men into the drawing room.

Once they were settled in the comfortable chairs and chaises, Royce began, "When

original letter exposing his involvement has evaporated. He can no longer reveal who the real Black Cobra is. Yet you say Ferrar was thrilled to have retrieved a copy, suggesting there's more in the letter than we've yet discerned. Regardless, if after this evening the Black Cobra doesn't call off the cultists harrying Monteith, then we can be certain there's something else about the letter that threatens the real Black Cobra."

"Indeed." Royce nodded decisively, and looked at Emily. "Do you have your copy?"

She'd been carrying it in her pocket in anticipation of that request. Pulling it out, she unfolded the sheet, and handed it across.

Royce took it, read it aloud, then passed the sheet around.

Del regarded him. "You're more used to evaluating covert communications than anyone else here. So what do you think?"

Royce considered the sheet, by then doing the rounds of the ladies. "I can comprehend the purpose behind the second half of the letter, where the Black Cobra is making overt advances. But why bother with the first half—the social chit-chat?"

The copy had reached Minerva's hands. She studied it as she said, "Some might say it's simply camouflage for the rest, but . . ." Head rising, she looked at Royce. "Not you."

He smiled. "No, not me." Transferring his gaze to the others, he went on, "It's almost certainly the case that the first half has a purpose, but it's hidden."

Gareth frowned. "It's common for princelings—and Govind Holkar, to whom the letter is addressed, is an epitome of the type—to crave acceptance into the upper echelons of local English society. I"—he glanced at Del—"all of us interpreted the first half of the letter in that light. As a social inducement, if you like."

"That may be so," Christian said, retaking the letter, "but that suggests that this Govind Holkar would be specifically interested in knowing that at least one of these ten people named would be visiting Poona. Given he was negotiating with the Black Cobra, who we now know to be more than one person, what are the odds that at least one of these people is part of our multiheaded beast?"

"If the attacks on Monteith continue, then those odds increase." Royce looked at Del. "I take it Poona is a hill-station?"

"In effect," Del replied, "it's the monsoon capital for Bombay. All those English who can, including the governor and his staff, relocate there for the season. All the wives and families usually remain there throughout the monsoon period, although their menfolk often go back and forth. But Poona was once the Maratha capital, and many of their princelings, like Govind Holkar, live there much of the time. That's why, when we thought the Black Cobra was Ferrar alone, we took the first half of the letter to be . . . well, merely information the writer, Ferrar, knew Holkar would be pleased to know."

Gareth grimaced. "If we'd known those names might have greater significance, we could easily have learned more before we left."

"Spilt milk," Royce said. "Now we know, how can we learn more?"

Gareth looked at Emily. "Do you know any of those named?"

Christian handed her the letter. She took it, scanned the names she'd transcribed the day before. "I was only in India for six months, but then again, I was in the governor's house-hold." She paused, her eyes on the page, then she grimaced. "It's as I remembered. All these people are members of what is popularly known as the G

. . . . last, and she is a master of understatement."

"Which," Clarice said, brows high, "makes that section of the letter even more believable as a social bribe."

Royce took back the copy, folded it. "Regardless, we'll know the truth very soon—by tomorrow at the latest." He looked at the others. "I've received confirmation that Monteith reached Oxford yesterday. He should be at Bedford tonight. With luck, he and his escort will be joining us tomorrow."

"His escort?" Gareth inquired.

"Two more of my ex-operatives," Royce said. "Charles St. Austell, Earl of Lostwithiel, and Deverell, Viscount Paignton."

"Ah." Minerva rose and crossed to tug the bellpull. "That means Penny and her brood, and Phoebe and hers, will arrive tomorrow—I must organize their rooms."

Royce looked at her, but made no comment while she quickly spoke to the butler who'd appeared.

However, as the butler retreated and Minerva returned to sit alongside him, Royce continued, "Apparently, Monteith has a lady with him, too."

"A lady?" Del frowned. "Where did she come from?"

"Guernsey, apparently. For some reason, the major ended up there, and then . . ." Royce frowned. "I'm not clear about the details—St. Austell was his usual oblique self—but I gather she was instrumental in facilitating Monteith's journey to Plymouth, and consequently, he felt it necessary to keep her with him, safe from the cultists."

Gareth and Del exchanged glances. They knew all about keeping those who helped them out of the cultists' hands. Especially women.

"So," Royce continued, "if Monteith strikes no further opposition, we'll know that the exposure of Ferrar as part of the Black Cobra was the only thing about the letter that the Black Cobra feared. Conversely, if the cultists keep attacking, trying to seize the copy Monteith's carrying, then clearly there is indeed something in the words—and it would have to be the names—that the remaining parts of the Black Cobra have reason to fear us learning."

Emily blinked at him. "But we already have a copy of the letter—we already know the names."

Royce met her gaze and smiled. "True, but the Black Cobra doesn't know that. Indeed, why would we bother making an extra copy if it's the seal that to us is the key?" He held her gaze, his own growing distant, then he looked at the others. "But that raises a valid point. We already have the text of the letter, yet those names mean nothing to anyone here. From what Emily says, those names are unlikely to be recognized by many in England, not in terms of what those people have been getting up to in India."

He paused, then went on, "There has to be someone the Black Cobra fears us showing the letter to. Someone for whom those names, some of them at least, will mean something—enough to identify one or more as Ferrar's closest associates."

"Family would be the obvious candidates," Christian said, "but I don't think Shrewton was lying, much less Kilworth. They have no idea who Ferrar was consorting with in India."

"Perhaps it wasn't in India," Emily said. "Perhaps it was here, in England, before Ferrar left. If he was close to people here, and the same people turned up there—surely they would be his closest friends."

"Closest, and most likely to have worked with him to set up the Black Cobra cult." Gareth glanced at Del. "Because the cult's genesis occurred a little after Ferrar's arrival in Bombay, we were certain that h

Monteith tomorrow, but if the Cobra keeps striking, then

we should certainly put more effort into learning who were Roderick Ferrar's erstwhile friends."

An hour later, Emily preceded Gareth into the bedchamber she'd been given. He had his own room down the hall, much smaller, more a place to leave his bags than anything else.

No one in this household bothered with pretense.

All but dancing, she whirled, fetching up before the fireplace in which a lovely fire crackled and burned. Outside it was freezing, but inside . . . she'd never felt so relaxed, so triumphant, in her life.

Arms spread, she swung to smile at Gareth. He'd closed the door and had followed close behind her. "We're here!" Bringing her hands in, she locked them about his lapels and drew him close; smiling, he came. She beamed up at him. "I can barely believe it. After all those miles, all those attacks, all those horribly dangerous times—here we are, hale and whole." She met his eyes, let herself fall into the tawny hazel. "And we're together."

Hands closing about her waist, then sliding further to hold her in a loose embrace, he nodded. "We are. But I have a confession to make."

Taken aback, she searched his eyes but saw nothing beyond the warmth she'd grown so accustomed to shining back at her. Reassured, she made her tone encouraging. "What?"

"Yes, well, that's the thing." His lips curved, rueful yet still relaxed. "I was determined never to let the words cross my lips, had sworn I would never utter them, but after today, after sitting in that carriage, blind, out of sight of you, not knowing if you were in danger, if some terrible fate was threatening you . . ." His expression changed, all warmth falling away, leaving an emotion far more stark and powerful etched over the chiseled lines of his face.

Her heart thudded as, amazed, she recognized what that emotion was.

"I nearly broke. Nearly overthrew all caution, all sense, nearly flung open the carriage door and came after you."

Locked in his dark gaze, she released one lapel, placed that hand on his chest, over his heart. "But you didn't."

"No. I didn't. It was a close run thing—but I didn't." He nodded, lips firming, his eyes on hers. "So yes, Emily Ensworth, we're going to have a life partnership—we're going to have the trust, the sharing of all life's challenges. Before, when we spoke of this, I wasn't sure how far I could go—how much of what you wanted I could give you—but now I know. Today showed me. Not that you were up to the task—that I never doubted, not from the instant I met you in Bombay after you'd ridden in with the letter from James. I was so proud of you—I admired you, your strength and character, from then. I knew long before today that *you* could handle anything, including the challenge of sharing your life with me. But today I discovered that *I* was up to the task, too— that I could, if pushed, trust your strength and put my faith in your abilities as you, so often on our travels, put your faith in mine."

He drew a huge breath, his chest swelling beneath her hand. She didn't say a word, too enthralled, too eager to hear what next he would say.

Gareth looked into her shining eyes, the moss-green bright, shimmering with encouragement and a love he'd never thought to find. "Having you go into danger without me at your side is never going to be something I will willingly countenance, but today I learned that I could live through the vulnerabilty, so there's no longer any point in not saying

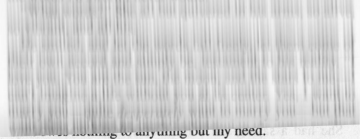

"I need you—I need your love. I need you to *be* my future.

431

We started, before, to paint in my blank slate, but I can't finish the picture of my future without you at its center."

She pressed closer, pushed her hands up over his shoulders, winding her arms about his neck. Sheer happiness bubbled in her voice as she said, "I was so *proud* of you today—when you let me do what I could do. I was never so much as vaguely attracted to MacFarlane, but women can have honor, too, and I wanted to—needed to—do something, something real, to help catch the Black Cobra. And now I have, I can leave it to you and all the other men here to catch the fiend, whoever he is, and bring him to justice.

"Now"—she stretched up on her toes, bringing her lips to within a whisker of his—"I can turn my attention—*all* my attention and energy—to us. To our partnership, our future—our marriage."

Her eyes all but glowed, shimmering with emotion as she stared into his. "You are my one—the one I've been waiting to find for so long, the one I went to India to seek, the one I love with all my heart. Now I've found you, I will never let you go."

He felt his lips curve. "Good."

He kissed her—or she kissed him. Between true partners, it didn't matter which it was. All that mattered was the heat that instantly sprang to life, that flared and curled comfortingly all around them.

That drew them in and seduced them.

Then flamed.

Clothes scattered, discarded with abandon.

They barely made it to the bed.

And then there was nothing beyond the flames and the passion, the desire and the need to be one.

Together.

Linked, twining, merging.

Giving and taking and striving for more.

Possessing, then surrendering.

She had a saying she was fond of, that actions always spoke louder than mere words. If he'd doubted the veracity of that claim, she would have convinced him that night.

She took him in with a joy that eclipsed all he'd ever known, embraced him and gave him more than he could fathom.

She was his all, his everything, then and evermore.

Emily could imagine no greater joy than when she shattered beneath him and, looking up through awestruck, lovestruck eyes, saw his face in that instant when he lost himself in her.

Saw all he'd until then tried to shield.

Saw vulnerability acknowledged, accepted, and held close.

Saw love and abject devotion in his eyes.

Finally saw him, all he was, clearly—her warrior with an unshielded heart.

They slumped together, arms tight, possessive even in aftermath, waiting for their thundering hearts to slow, waiting for reality to reclaim them.

When he finally eased from her arms, withdrew from her and slumped on his stomach beside her, she was already planning. "We'll wait here." Turning her head, she caught his eye. "I'm happy to wait here until the other two—Monteith and Carstairs—arrive. Until they're safe." Sliding around, down into the bed beside him, she raised a hand and traced one heavy shoulder. "You won't be able to concentrate on our future until then—and in truth, neither will I."

The one eye she could see held hers, then he humphed and turned his head fully b

, and her smile deepened. "I was just thinking: If only my family could see me now."

He looked at her in mock horror, then lifted his head and dropped it back into the pillow. "Thank God they can't."

"You do understand that he had to die, don't you?" In the drawing room of the house they'd made their headquarters in Bury St. Edmunds, Alex topped up Daniel's glass from the decanter of fine brandy Roderick had liberated from the locked sideboard.

How very apt, Daniel thought, as he took a healthy swallow. As usual, Alex was abstemious, but tonight he was also sipping from a glass.

"Poor Roderick." With a shake of the head, Alex replaced the decanter on the sideboard. "So . . . sadly ineffectual."

"Indeed." Daniel took another swallow. He was still a trifle shocked—not by Roderick's death itself—that had, he suspected, been coming for some time; it was his idiot half brother's lack of thought for consequences that had landed the three of them in this mire after all. Still, he hadn't seen it coming—hadn't seen Death in Alex's eyes until the dagger had slid home.

But Alex had been right. Roderick had had to die, then and there, in that moment. Thanks to Alex's quick thinking, the pair of them had got clean away.

Daniel raised his glass, locked eyes with Alex, now seated on the sofa nearby. "To Roderick—the idiot—who was convinced to the last that our sire would always save him. He was a fool, but he was our brother." He drank.

Alex sipped. "Half brother." Alex's lips curved. "Sadly, he missed the better half—the cleverer half."

Daniel tipped his glass in acknowledgment, but said nothing. He and Alex shared a father, but their mothers had been different, so the cleverer half Alex alluded to he had missed as well. He looked at his glass, and decided he'd better stop drinking.

"But Roderick no longer matters, my dear. We do." Alex's voice was low but clear, as always compelling. "And we need to take steps to ensure our necks remain free of the hangman's noose."

"Indubitably." Setting down his glass, Daniel met Alex's eyes. "As ever, I'm yours to command, but I suspect I'd better go and check on Monteith. We need his copy of the letter."

Alex nodded. "While you're doing that, I'll organize another move. Sadly, here, we're too close to where Roderick met his end. Our opponents might think to search. I'll have somewhere else organized—not too far away—by the time you get back with Monteith's letter."

"And then we'll need to get a welcome in place for Carstairs."

"Indeed." Alex's eyes glittered. "I'll start work on that tomorrow, too. Now we know he's coming down the Rhine, and at speed, then it's all but certain he'll pass through Rotterdam. I've already sent orders to all those on the other side of the Channel to ensure he runs into a very warm reception. But given that the other three have all come this way, what are the odds, do you think, that he's making for either Felixstowe or Harwich? They are, after all, the closest and most convenient ports to this part of the country."

"He'll be carrying the original, won't he?"

Alex nodded. "Just the fact he's coming in on the most direct route . . . our puppetmaster isn't trying to draw out cultists with him, but to give him the shortest and safest road, the best possible chance of reaching the puppetmaster. That's why he's the last, and also why Monteith is coming in from the opposite direction."

"So Carstairs won't be long."

"Where exactly are they?"

"In a deserted barn outside a village called Eynesbury. I left them with strict orders to keep watch for Monteith and make sure he doesn't reach Cambridge. They'll know where he's spending the night." Daniel smiled, envisioning carnage. "I believe I'll pay Major Monteith a midnight visit."

Alex understood what he was planning. "Very good. And who knows what possibilities tomorrow might bring? Take care, my dear—I'll see you later tomorrow, once you have Monteith's copy."

Daniel saluted. "Until then."

He turned away and strode for the door, and so didn't see the way Alex watched him.

Didn't feel the cold, piercing weight of those ice-blue eyes.

After he'd passed through the open doorway and disappeared, Alex sat staring at the vacant space.

Debating.

Several minutes ticked past.

Then Alex turned and looked toward the doorway at the far end of the room. "M'wallah!"

When the fanatical head of Alex's personal guard appeared, Alex coldly said, "Have someone saddle my horse, and lay out my riding breeches, jacket, and my heavy cloak. I expect to be out all night."

Turn the next page for an
excerpt from the next installment
in The Black Cobra Quartet
THE BRAZEN BRIDE

Coming soon from Piatkus

December 10, 1822
One o'clock in the morning
On the deck of the Heloise Leger
The English Channel

ell hath no greater fury than the storms that raked the English Channel in winter.

With elemental tempest raging about him, Major Logan Monteith leapt back from the slashing blade of a Black Cobra cult assassin. With his saber countering the second assassin's strike and using his dirk, clutched in his left fist to fend off the ...

As one, the assassins surged, beating him back toward the prow. Blades met, steel on steel ringing, sparks flaring, pinpricks of brightness in the engulfing dark. Abruptly, the deck canted—and all three combatants desperately fought for balance.

The ship—a Portuguese merchantman bound for Portsmouth that Logan had been forced to join five days before, when, on reaching Lisbon, he'd discovered the town crawling with cultists—was in trouble. Battered by pounding waves, buffeted and tossed on the storm-wracked sea, the ship wallowed and swung, no longer held into the wind. Whether the rudder had broken or the captain had abandoned the wheel, Logan couldn't tell. He couldn't spare the time to squint through the rain-drenched dark at the bridge.

Instinct and experience kept his eyes locked on the men facing him. There'd been a third, but Logan had accounted for him in the first rush. The body was gone, claimed by the ravening waves.

Logan struck, saber swinging, but was immediately forced to block and counter, then retreat yet another step into the narrowing prow. Further confining his movements, reducing his options. Didn't matter; two against one in the icy, pelting rain, with his grip on his dirk and saber cramping, leather-soled boots slipping and sliding—the assassins were barefoot, giving them even that advantage—he couldn't go on the offensive.

He wasn't going to survive.

As he met and deflected another vicious blow, he acknowledged that, yet even as he did, his innate stubbornness rose. He'd been a cavalry officer for more than a decade, fought in wars over half the globe, been through hell more than once, and survived.

He'd faced assassins before and lived.

Miracles happened.

He told himself that, even as, teeth gritted, he angled his saber up to block a slash at his head—and his feet went from under him, pitching him back against the railing.

The wooden scroll-holder strapped to his back slammed into his spine.

From the corner of his eye, he saw white teeth flash in a dark face—a feral grin as the second assassin swung and slashed. Logan hissed as the blade sliced down his left side, cutting through coat and shirt into muscle, grazing bone, before angling across his stomach to disembowel him. Instinct had him flattening against the railing; the blade cut, but not deep enough.

Not that that would save him.

Lightning cracked, a jagged tear of brilliant white splitting the black sky. In the instant's illumination, Logan saw the two assassins—dark eyes fanatically gleaming, triumph in their faces—gather themselves

A long forgotten prayer formed on his lips.

The assassins sprang.

Crack!

Impact—sudden, sharp, catastrophic—flung him and the assassins overboard. The plunge into turbulent depths, into the churning icy fury of the sea, separated them.

Tumbling in the watery dark, instinct took hold; righting himself, Logan struck upward. His dirk was still in his left fist; he'd released his saber, but it was tied to his belt by its lanyard—he felt the reassuring tap of the hilt on his upper thigh.

He was a strong swimmer; the assassins almost certainly weren't—it would be a wonder if they could swim at all. Dismissing them—he had more pressing concerns—he broke the surface and hauled in a huge breath. He shook his head, then peered through the water weighing down his lashes.

The storm was at its height, the seas mountainous. He couldn't see beyond the next towering wave.

The ship had been in open water in the middle of the Channel when the storm had hit, but he had no idea how far the tempest had tossed them, nor any clear idea of direction. No idea if land was close, or ...

He'd been losing blood when he'd hit the water. How long he would last in the cauldron of icy waves, how soon his already depleted strength would give out—

His hand struck something—wood, a plank. No, even better—a section of the ship's side. Desperate, Logan grabbed it, grimly hung on as the next wave tried to slap him away, then gritting his teeth, he hauled himself up and onto the makeshift raft.

The cold had numbed his flesh. Even so, the cut down his side sent burning pain lancing through his entire body.

For a long moment, he lay prone on the planks, gasping, then gathering his ebbing strength, steeling himself, he inched and edged further onto the planks, until he could lock his right hand over the ragged front edge. His feet still dangled in the water, but his body was supported to his knees; it was the best he could do.

The waves surged. His raft pitched but rode the swell.

Beneath the lashing roar of the storm, waves crashed. Cheek to the wet wood, he listened, concentrating, and confirmed; the waves were crashing against something near.

The ship was, he thought, wallowing in the unrelieved blackness to his right. Breaking up. Sinking. Given how he and the assassins had been flung, the impact must have been midship. Whipping up his failing strength, he lifted his head, searched, saw debris but no bodies—no other survivors—but only he and the assassins had been so far forward in the prow.

He didn't even have time to swear before the top of the mast thumped down across him and the world went black.

"Linnet! *Linnet*! Come quickly! Come *see*!"

Linnet Trevission looked up from the old flagstones of the path that ran from the stable to the kitchen door. She'd left the stable and was nearing the kitchen garden; directly ahead, the solid bulk of her home, Mon Coeur, sat snug and serene, anchored within the protective embrace of stands of elm and fir, bent and twisted into outlandish shapes by the incessant sea winds.

At present, however, in the aftermath of the storm that had swept over them last night, the winds were mild, coyly coquettish, the winter sun casting a honey glow over the house's pale stone.

"Linnet! *Linnet*!"

She smiled as Chester, one of her wards—a tousle-headed scamp of just seven—came pelting around the side of the house, heading for the back door. "Chester! I'm here."

The boy looked up, then veered onto the stable path.

"You have to come!" Skidding to a halt before her, he grabbed her hand and tugged. "There's been a wreck!" His face alight, excitement and more bubbling in his voice, he looked up into her eyes. "There are bodies! And Will says one of the men is *alive*! You have to come!"

Linnet's smile fell from her face. "Yes, of course." Swiping up her skirts—wishing she'd worn her

444

breeches instead—she strode quickly toward the back door, inwardly reviewing the necessary tasks—tasks she'd dealt with often before.

On the southwest tip of Guernsey, dealing with shipwrecks was an inescapable part of life.

Chester trotted at her side, his hand gripping hers—too tightly, but then his father had been lost at sea three years ago. As they neared the kitchen door, it opened to reveal Linnet's aunt, Muriel.

"Did I hear aright? A wreck?"

Linnet nodded. "Will sent Chester—there's at least one survivor. I'll go straightaway—can you find Edgar and the others? Tell them to bring the old gate and the pack of bandages and splints."

"Yes, of course. But where?"

Linnet looked at Chester. "Which cove?"

"West one."

Grimacing, Linnet met Muriel's eyes. Of course it would be that one—the rockiest and most dangerous. Especially for whoever had been washed up. "Broken bones, almost certainly."

Nodding briskly, Muriel waved her off. "Go. I'll have everything ready here when you get back."

tne edge of the low cliffs.

"Hold up!" Linnet called as they rounded the southern headland of the long northwestern side of the island and the west cove that opened up below them.

Chester halted at the top of the path—little more than a goat track—that led down to a strip of coarse sand. Beyond the sand lay rocks, exposed now that the tide was mostly out, a jumble of tumbled pieces from fist-sized to small boulders that formed the floor of the cove. The cove wasn't all that wide; two promontories of larger, jagged rocks enclosed it, marching out into the lashing gray waves.

Looking down, Linnet saw three bodies, two flung as if carelessly discarded on the rocks. Those two were dead—had to be, given the contortions of limbs, heads, and spines. The third she could only catch glimpses of; Will and Brandon—another two of her wards—were crouched over the man.

Aware of Chester's pleading look, Linnet nodded. "All right—let's go."

He was off like a hare. Linnet kilted her skirts, then followed, leaping down the familiar path with an abandon almost Chester's equal. As she descended, she scanned the cove again, noting the flotsam thrown up by the storm; to her educated eyes the evidence suggested that a good-sized merchantman had broken up on the razor-sharp rocks that lurked beneath the waves out to the southwest.

Reaching the sand, Chester bounded toward Will and Brandon. Suppressing the urge to follow, Linnet carefully made her way out onto the rocks and confirmed that the other two men were indeed dead, beyond her help. Two sailors by the look of them, both swarthy. Spanish?

Leaving them where they lay, she picked her way through the rocks back onto the sand, then walked to where the third body lay close to the cliff.

His back to her, Will looked up and around as she neared, his fifteen-year-old face unusually sober. "He was on this piece of siding, so we lifted it and carried him here."

Halting, she dropped a hand on Will's shoulder and answered the question he hadn't asked. "It was safe to move him if he was already on the planks."

Shifting her gaze from Will's face, she got her first look at their survivor. He was lying on his stomach on the section of planking, a wet tangle of black hair screening his face.

He was large. Big. Not a giant, but in any company he would rank as impressive. Broad shoulders, long heavy limbs. Running her gaze down his spine, she frowned at the bulge distorting his sodden coat. Bending, she reached out and touched it.

"It's a wooden cylinder in oilskins," Will said. "It's slung in a leather holder with a loop through his belt.

saw no evidence of breaks or wounds. He was wearing

447

breeches and a loose coat, the sort many sailors wore. His right arm was extended, the fingers of his large hand curled around the front edge of a plank. His other hand, however, lay level with his face, fingers locked in a death-grip around the hilt of a dagger.

That seemed a trifle odd for a shipwreck.

Conscious of her pulse thudding—the run to the cliffs shouldn't have made her heart beat so rapidly— she bent to look at the dagger. Not just a dagger, she realized—a dirk. The fine scrollwork on the blade was exquisite, the hilt larger than that of most knives, with a rounded stone set in the crosspiece. Reaching down, she pried long, hard, ice-cold fingers away from the hilt, then handed the dagger to Will. "Hold that for me."

The man hadn't stirred; not a single muscle had so much as tensed. Linnet drew back, aware of her instincts twitching, flickering in definite warning, yet for the life of her she couldn't make sense of the message.

The stranger was all but dead—indeed, she wasn't sure he wasn't—so how could he be dangerous?

From his position kneeling on the other side of the planking, Brandon said, "He's got a sword, too. On this side."

Linnet circled the man, looked where Brandon pointed, then crouched and unhooked the lanyard that attached the weapon to the man's belt. Drawing the blade carefully from under the man's leg, she straightened, studied it. "It's a saber—a cavalry sword." She'd seen enough of them during the war, but the war was long over, the cavalry largely disbanded. Perhaps this man had been a trooper and after the war had turned to sailing?

"We *think* he's alive," Brandon said, "but we can't find any pulse, and he's not breathing—well, not so you can tell."

Leaving the saber with Brandon, Linnet returned to Will's side, where the man's head lay turned.

"He must be alive because he's bleeding," Will said. "See?" He lifted the clothes along the man's side and a rent parted, exposing pale flesh and a long, nasty cut. A recent cut.

Crouching beside Will, Linnet looked and recognized a sword slash. That explained the dirk and saber. While Will held the clothes, she leaned closer, examining the wound, following it up—to the side of the man's breast. Thick muscle had been sliced through. Tracing the wound down, she sucked in a breath when she saw bone—a rib. But that was lower, where there wasn't so much muscle between taut skin and ribcage.

"He's bleeding," Will insisted. "See there?"

Linnet had noted the pale pinkish liquid seeping from the cut. She nodded, not yet ready to explain that

inward, angling down and across the man's belly. She

449

couldn't see further than the side of his waist, but a gut wound ... if he had one, he was almost certainly dead.

Lying as he was, the pressure of his body, combined with the effects of the icy sea, might have held the wound closed, inhibited the usual bleeding.

She glanced at Brandon's face, then at Will alongside her. Chester was hovering at her shoulder. "I need to check the wound across his stomach. I need you to help me ease this side of him up—enough for me to look."

The boys eagerly reached for the man's left shoulder, his side. Settling on her knees, Linnet placed Brandon's hands on the man's shoulder, positioned Will's hands beneath the left hip, and set Chester ready to help support the shoulder Brandon would lift. "All together, then." Linnet licked her lips, said a little prayer. She was too experienced in matters of life, death, and the sea to allow herself to become invested in a stranger's survival; she told herself it was for the boys' sake that she hoped this stranger lived. "Now."

The boys heaved, pushed, propped. As soon as they had the man angled up and steady, Linnet ducked down, close to the heavy body, peered beneath to trace and follow the wound—then exhaled the breath she hadn't realized she'd held. Easing back, she nodded. "Let him down."

"Will he be all right?" Chester asked.

She couldn't yet promise. "The wound is less deep over his belly—no real danger. He was lucky." A scenario was taking shape in her mind—a picture of how the man had received such a wound. It should have

450

been a killing, or at least incapacitating, slash. He'd escaped death by less than an inch, just before his ship had wrecked.

"But he's still not really breathing," Brandon said.

And she still wasn't sure if he was alive. Linnet checked for a pulse in the man's wrist, then in his strong throat. There was none she could detect, nor any discernible rise and fall of his chest—but all that could be due to being close to frozen. There was no help for it; shuffling nearer, with one hand she brushed back the fall of black hair hiding his face, bent close, focused—and stopped breathing.

He was heartbreakingly, breathtakingly beautiful. His face, all clean angular lines and sculpted planes, embodied the very essence of masculine beauty—there was not a soft note anywhere. Combined with the muscled hardness of his body, that face promised virility, passion and direct, unadorned, unadulterated sin.

Such a face did not belong to a man given to sweetness but to action, command, and demand.

Chiseled lips, firm and fine, sent a seductive shiver down her spine. The line of his jaw made her fingertips throb. He had winged black brows, a wide fore-

else.

Men like this—who looked like he did, who had bodies like his—led women into sin.

And into stupidity.

Dragging in a breath, she forced her eyes to stop drinking him in, forced her mind to stop mentally swooning. She hesitated, needing to get nearer—and too rattled to lightly risk it.

Maintaining her current, already too-close distance, she held her fingers beneath his nose. And felt nothing.

Turning her hand, she held the sensitive skin of her wrist close but could detect not the smallest waft of air.

Lips thinning, mentally muttering an imprecation against fallen angels, she leaned down, close, in—angled her cheek so that it was a whisker away from his lips …

And felt the merest brush of air, a breath, an exhalation.

She eased back, straightening on her knees, and stared at the man's face for an instant longer. Then she turned to the wound in his side, checked again. And yes, that was blood, not just seepage. "He's alive."

Chester whooped. The other two grinned.

She didn't. Getting back to her feet, she looked down at trouble. "We need to get him up to the house."

452

CAPTAIN JACK'S
WOMAN

Bored by society's rules and strictures, Kathryn 'Kit' Cranmer yearns for adventure – and finds it... In Britain's rugged eastern coast, dressed as a boy, at the head of a ragtag band of smugglers. But finds is another who rules the night: the notorious Captain Jack, ruthless leader of a rival gang... who stops Kit's breath with his handsome features and powerful physique.

When Captain Jack sees that though Kit's breath disguise, he tempts her with kisses that compel her to surrender her cherished independence. But has her lover's true heart than

THE LADY CHOSEN

Tristan Wemyss, Earl of Trentham, never expected he'd need to wed within a year or forfeit his inheritance. But he is not one to bow to the matchmaking mamas of the ton. No, he will marry a lady of his own choosing – the enchanting neighbour next door. Miss Leonora Carling has beauty, spirit and passion; unfortunately, matrimony is the last thing on her mind . . .

Once bitten, forever shy – never again will Leonora allow any man to capture her heart and break it. But Tristan is a seasoned campaigner who will not accept defeat, especially when a mysterious blackguard with dark designs on Leonora's home gives him the excuse to come to the lady's

A GENTLEMAN'S HONOUR

The season has yet to begin, and Anthony Blake, Viscount Torrington, is already a target for every matchmaking mama in London. But there is only one lady who sparks his interest . . .

Desperate and penniless, but determined, Alicia plans to make an excellent match for her ravishing younger sister. But one moonlit stroll may prove Alicia's undoing when it leads to an accusation of murder.

Every instinct Tony Blake possesses tells him that Alicia – the exquisite beauty he discovers standing over a dead body – is innocent of serious wrongdoing. His social prominence will certainly work in her favour. But it is more than honour that compels Tony to protect her – and he will do everything in his seductive power to make Alicia his.

978-0-7499-4028-7

A LADY OF HIS OWN

Impatient to find his bride-to-be yet appalled by the damsels of the ton, Charles St Austell seeks refuge in his castle and discovers Lady Penelope Selborne walking the deserted corridors at midnight. Years ago they'd consummated their youthful passion one unforgettable afternoon. While the ardent interlude still haunts Charles, Penny vowed never again to be seduced by the dashing Earl.

But resisting a stronger, battle-hardened Charles proves difficult, and when a traitorous intrigue threatens them both, Penny discovers that her first love is her fated champion and protector- and will not rest until he has made her his own . . .